I know
my
name

C.J. COOKE

I know my name

GRAND CENTRAL
PUBLISHING

NEW YORK   BOSTON

Copyright © 2017 by C.J. Cooke
Cover design by www.blacksheep-uk.com. Cover photography © Nigrechok, Deposit Photos.
Cover copyright © 2018 by Hachette Book Group, Inc.

Grand Central Publishing
Hachette Book Group
1290 Avenue of the Americas, New York, NY 10104
grandcentralpublishing.com
twitter.com/grandcentralpub

First published in 2017 in Great Britain by HarperCollins*Publishers*

First Grand Central Publishing edition: January 2018

Grand Central Publishing is a division of Hachette Book Group, Inc. The Grand Central Publishing name and logo is a trademark of Hachette Book Group, Inc.

The publisher is not responsible for websites (or their content) that are not owned by the publisher.

The Hachette Speakers Bureau provides a wide range of authors for speaking events. To find out more, go to www.hachettespeakersbureau.com or call (866) 376-6591.

LCCN: 2017948567

ISBNs: 978-1-5387-4444-4 (hardcover), 978-1-5387-4443-7 (ebook), 978-1-4789-7689-9 (audio download)

Printed in the United States of America

LSC-C

10 9 8 7 6 5 4 3 2 1

For Summer
Little lover of horses

The Girl on the Beach

March 17, 2015

Komméno Island, 8.4 Miles Northwest of Crete

I'm woken by the sounds of feet shuffling by my ears and voices knitting together in panic.

Is she dead? What should we do? Joe! You know CPR, don't you?

A weight presses down against my lips. The bitter smell of cigarettes rushes up to my nostrils. Hot breath inflates my cheeks. A push downward on my chest. Another. I jerk upright, vomiting what feels like gallons of disgusting salty liquid. Someone rubs my back and says, *Take it easy, sweetie. That's it.*

I twist to one side and lower my forehead to the ground, coughing, choking. My hair is wet, my clothes are soaking, and I'm shaking with cold. Someone helps me to my feet and pulls my right arm limply across a broad set of shoulders. A yellow splodge on the floor comes into focus: it's a life jacket. Mine? The man holding me upright lowers me gently into a chair. I hear their voices as they observe me, instructing each other on how to care for me.

Is that blood in her hair?

Joe, have a look. Has the bleeding stopped?

It looks quite deep, but I think it's stopped. I've got some antiseptic swabs upstairs.

My head starts to throb, a dull pain toward the right. A cup of coffee materializes on the table in front of me. The smell winds upward and sharpens my vision, bringing the people in the room into view. There's a man nearby, panting from effort. Another man with black square glasses. Two others, both women. One of them leans over me and says, *You OK, hun?* I nod, dumbly. She comes into focus. Kind eyes. *Well, Joe,* she says. *Looks like you saved her life.*

I don't recognize any of these people. I don't know where I am. Whitewashed stone walls and a pretty stone floor. A kitchen, I think. Copper pots and pans hang from ceiling hooks, an old-fashioned black range oven visible at my right. I feel as though all energy has been sucked out of me, but the woman who gave me coffee urges me to keep awake. *We need to check you over, sweetie.* There's an American lilt in her voice. I don't think I noticed that before. She says, *You've been unconscious for a while.*

The younger man with black glasses tells me he's going to check out my head. He steps behind me and all of a sudden I feel something cold and stinging on my scalp. I gasp in pain. Someone squeezes my hand and tells me he's cleaning the wound. He looks over a spot above my eyebrow and cleans it, too, though he tells me it's only a scratch.

The man who hoisted me into the chair sits opposite. Bald, heavyset. Mid to late forties. Cockney. He takes a cigarette from a packet, plops it into his mouth, and lights it.

You come from the main island?

Main island? I say, my voice a croak.

From there to here on her own? the younger man says. *There's no way she'd have managed in that storm.*

I think that's the point, Joe, the bald guy says. *She's lucky her boat didn't capsize before it hit the beach.*

The woman who served me coffee brings a chair and sits at my right.

I'm Sariah, she says. *Good to meet you.* Then, to the others in the room, *Well, she's awake now. Why don't we stop being rude and introduce ourselves?*

The guy with glasses gives a wave.

Joe.

George, says the bald man. *I'm the one who found you.*

Silence. Joe turns to the thin woman at his right, expectant. She seems nervous. *Hazel,* she says, her voice no more than an exhalation.

You got a name? George asks me.

My mind is blank. I look over the faces of the others, fitting their faces to these names, and yet my own won't come. I feel physically weak and battered, but I'm lucid and able to think clearly.

It's OK, sweetie, Sariah is saying, rubbing my shoulders. *You've had a rough time. Take it easy. It'll come.*

You holidaying on the main island? George asks again.

My head feels like someone is pounding it with a hammer. *I'm sorry... what is the main island?*

Crete, Sariah answers. *Whereabouts were you staying?*

5

You staying with family? A group of girlfriends? the guy with glasses asks. *Hey, she might have come from one of the other islands. Antikythera?*

I don't think so, offers the tiny woman with red curly hair—Hazel—in a low voice. *The currents between here and Antikythera are worse than traveling to Crete. And Antikythera is farther.*

I'm sorry, I say. *Did someone say I'm in Crete?*

See? George says.

No, no, I try to say, but Joe cuts me off.

She asked if she's in Crete, Joe answers. *This is Komméno, not Crete.*

Well, we'll need to let whoever you've left behind know that you're still in one piece, George says. *You got a number I can ring?*

He pulls a small black phone from a pocket and extends an antenna from the top. Crete. Was I staying there?

I can't remember, I say finally. *Sorry, I don't know.*

The kind woman, Sariah, is holding my hand. *We'll call the police on Crete the second we get a signal on the satellite phone. Don't worry, sweetie.*

The big guy—George—is still watching me, his eyes narrowed. *Where are you from, then?*

I'm light-headed and nauseous, but I think I should know this. It's ridiculous, but I can't even call it to mind. Why can't I remember it? I try to think of faces of my family, people I love—but there's a complete blankness in whatever part of my brain holds that information.

George is leaning on one hand, taking slow, thoughtful drags from a fresh cigarette, studying me. The others are halfway through cups of tea. I have no recollection of anyone putting cups out or boiling a kettle. Time lurches and stalls. I rise from my chair and almost fall over. My legs are jelly. Sariah moves to hold me up.

Easy now.

The large window at the other side of the kitchen frames a round moon in a purple sky, its glow bleaching fields and hills. A burst of light crackles across the ocean, lighting up the room. A few moments later thunder pounds the roof, rattling all the pots and pans. I am disoriented and weak. I begin to shake again, but this time it's from shock.

Sariah wraps an arm around me. *We're going to move you into the other room, OK? Deep breaths.*

But before we have a chance to move, I hear a deep voice say, *Maybe she's a refugee.*

Sariah hisses, *George!*

He gives a loud bellow of laughter. It makes me jump.

I'm joking, aren't I?

Pressure builds and builds in my head until I'm gasping for air and clawing at my throat. The two women lean forward and tell me to breathe, and I'm trying. They ask me to tell them what's wrong but I can't speak. Someone says, *We need to think about getting her to a hospital.*

March 17, 2015

George Street, Edinburgh

Lochlan: I'm having afternoon tea with a client at The Dome when my phone rings. It's an important meeting—Mr. Coyle is interested in setting up a venture capital fund to invest in some new technological companies—and so I pull it out of my pocket and hit "cancel."

"Sorry about that."

Mr. Coyle arches an eyebrow. "Your wife?"

It was, actually. Right before I hit "cancel" I saw her name appear on the screen.

"No, no. Anyway, what were we saying?"

"Google glass?"

I pour us both some red. "Ah, yes. This company's creating something similar, only better. It integrates seamlessly with new social media platforms and user trials have rated it at five stars. The first product is scheduled to retail for around five hundred pounds in September."

My phone rings again. This time Mr. Coyle gives a noise of irritation. "ELOÏSE" appears in white letters on the screen. I make to hit "cancel" again, but Mr. Coyle gives a shooing gesture with his hand and says, "Answer it. Tell her we're busy."

I stand up and walk to the nearest window.

"El, what is it? I'm in a meeting..."

"Lochlan? Is that you, dear?"

The woman at the other end of the line is not my wife. She continues talking, and it takes a few moments for me to place the voice.

"Mrs. Shahjalal?"

It's the Yorkshirewoman who lives opposite us.

"...and I thought I'd best check. So when I opened the door I was surprised to see—are you still there?"

From the corner of my eye I see Mr. Coyle hailing a waitress.

"Mrs. Shahjalal, is everything all right? Where's Eloïse?"

A long pause. "That's what I'm telling you, dear. I don't know."

"What do you mean, you don't know?"

"It's like I said: the man from the UPS van brought the parcel over to me and asked if I'd take it as nobody was in. And I thought that was strange, because I was sure I'd seen little Max's face at the window only a moment before. So I took the parcel, and then an hour or so later I saw Max again, and I thought I'd best go over and see if everything was all right. Max was able to stand on a chair and let me in."

I'm struggling to put this all together in my mind. Mr. Coyle is rising from his chair, putting on his jacket. I turn and

9

raise a hand to let him know I'll be just a second, but he grimaces.

"OK, so Max let you into our house. What happened when you went inside?"

"Well, Eloïse still isn't here. I've been here since three o'clock and the little one's mad for a feed. I found Eloïse's mobile phone on the coffee table and pressed a button, and luckily enough it dialed your number."

The rustling and mewling noises in the background grow louder, and I realize Mrs. Shahjalal must be holding Cressida, my daughter. She's twelve weeks old. Eloïse is still breastfeeding her.

"So...Eloïse isn't in the house. She's not there at all?" It's a stupid thing to say, but I can't quite fathom it. Where else would she be?

Mr. Coyle glowers from the table. He straightens his tie before turning to walk out, and I lower the phone and call after him.

"Mr. Coyle!"

He doesn't acknowledge me.

"I'll send the fact sheet by e-mail!"

Mrs. Shahjalal is still talking. "It's very odd, Lochlan. Max is dreadfully upset and doesn't seem to know where she's gone. I don't know what to do."

I walk back to the table and gather up my briefcase. The brass clock on the chimney breast reads quarter past four. I could catch the four thirty to London if I manage to get a taxi on time, but it's a four-and-a-half-hour train ride from here and then another cab ride from King's Cross to Twickenham. I'll not be home until after ten.

"I'm heading back right now," I tell Mrs. Shahjalal.

"Are you in the city, dear?"

"I'm in Edinburgh."

"Edinburgh? *Scotland?*"

Outside, the street is busy with traffic and people. I'm agitated, trying to think fast, and almost get knocked over by a double-decker bus driving close to the curb. I jump back, gasping at the narrow escape. A group of schoolkids on a school trip meander across the pavement in single file. I wave at a black taxi and manage to get him to stop.

"To Waverley, please."

I ask Mrs. Shahjalal if she can stay with Max and Cressida until I get back. To my relief she says she will, though I can barely hear her now over Cressida's screams.

"She needs to be fed, Mrs. Shahjalal."

"Well, I know that, dear, but my days of being able to nurse a baby are over."

"If you go into the fridge, there might be some breast milk in a plastic container on the top shelf. It'll be labeled. I think Eloïse keeps baby bottles in one of the cupboards near the toaster. Make sure you put the bottle into the sterilizer in the microwave for four minutes before you use it. Make sure there's water in the bottom."

"Sterilize the breast milk?"

I can hear Max in the background now, shouting, "Is that Daddy? Daddy, is that you?" I ask Mrs. Shahjalal to put him on.

"Max, Maxie boy?"

"Hi, Daddy. Can I have some chocolate, please?"

"I'll buy you as much chocolate as you can eat if you tell me where Mummy is."

"As much chocolate as I can eat? All of it?"

11

"Where is Mummy, Max?"

"Can I have a Kinder egg, please?"

"Did Mummy go out this morning? Did someone come to the house?"

"I think she went to the Natural History Museum, Daddy, 'cos she likes the dinosaurs there and the big one that's very long is called Dippy, he's called Dippy 'cos he's a diplodocus, Daddy."

I'm getting nowhere. I ask him to put me back on to Mrs. Shahjalal, who is still wondering how she is to sterilize the breast milk, and all the while Cressida is drilling holes in my head by screaming down the phone.

Finally, I'm on the train, posting on Facebook.

I don't usually do this but...anyone know where Eloïse is? She doesn't seem to be at home...

Night falls like a black sheath. The taxi pulls into Potter's Lane. We live in a charming Edwardian semi in the quiet suburb of Twickenham, close to all the nice parks and the part of the river inhabited by swans, frogs, and ducks, and close enough to London for Saturday-afternoon visits to the National History Museum and Kew Gardens. A few lights are on in the houses near us, but our neighbors are either retired or hardworking professionals, and so nights are placid round here.

I pay the driver and jump out onto the pavement. Eloïse's white Qashqai is parked in the driveway in front of my Mercedes, and my hearts leaps. I've been on and off the phone to Mrs. Shahjalal during the train ride from Edinburgh, checking in on the kids and trying to work out what the hell to do about the situation. Mrs. Shahjalal is very old and forgetful. More than once El has climbed through the window to open the front door because she locked her keys inside. In all likelihood this is a big mistake; I've lost a client while El's been upstairs having a shower or something. I ran out of battery on my phone some time ago and all the power points on the train were broken. Mrs. Shahjalal hasn't been able to contact me. But the Qashqai's here. Eloïse must have arrived back already.

I turn my key in the door and step inside to quietness and darkness.

"El?"

I head into the playroom and see the figure of old Mrs. Shahjalal sitting on the edge of the sofa, rocking the Moses basket where Cressida is lying, arms raised at right angles by her tiny head.

"Hi," I whisper. "Where is she?"

Mrs. Shahjalal shakes her head.

"But...she's here," I say. "Her car is outside. Where is she?"

"She isn't here."

"But—"

Mrs. Shahjalal raises a finger to her lips and looks down at Cressida in a manner that suggests it has taken a long time to settle her to sleep. Cressida gives a little shuddered breath, the kind she gives after a long paroxysm of wailing.

"Max is upstairs, in his bed," Mrs. Shahjalal says in a low voice.

"But what about El's car? The white one in the driveway?"

"It's been here all the time. She didn't take it."

I race upstairs and check the bedrooms, the bathrooms, the attic, then switch on all the lights downstairs and sift the rooms for my wife. When that proves fruitless I head out into the garden and stare into the darkness. In that moment a daunting impossibility yawns wide. I barely know Mrs. Shahjalal, save a few neighborly waves across the street, and now she's in my living room, gently rocking my daughter and telling me that my wife has vanished into thin air.

I take out my phone and begin to dial.

March 17, 2015

Komméno Island, Greece

Somehow I find myself in a rocking chair with a thick orange blanket around me, next to a crackling fire. My right sleeve is rolled up and someone's tied a belt tight around my bicep. The tall skinny bloke with glasses, Joe, is standing next to me with a cold instrument pressed to my wrist. The room smells funny—like seaweed. Or maybe that's me.

"Only a couple more seconds," he says.

"What are you doing?" I say, though it comes out as a strangled whine. The inside of my mouth feels like sandpaper.

"Checking your blood pressure."

There's a heated discussion going on among the others in the room and I sense it's about me. I still feel queasy and limp.

Eventually he removes the belt from my arm. "Hmmm.

Your blood pressure is a bit low for my liking. How about the tightness in your chest?"

I tell him that it seems OK but that I'm weak as dishwater. He reaches forward and gently presses his thumbs on my cheeks to inspect my eyes.

"You're in shock. Little wonder, given that you rowed across the Aegean in a full-blown storm. Let's get your feet raised up. And some more water."

The woman—Sariah—lifts my feet and supports them on a stack of cushions.

"How's your head?" she asks.

"Sore," I say weakly.

"You don't feel like you're going to pass out again?" Joe asks, and I give a small shake of my head. It's enough to make the pain ratchet up to an agony that leaves me breathless.

"It's after midnight, so getting you to a hospital has proved a little tricky," Sariah says, folding her arms. I notice she has a different accent than the others. American, or maybe Canadian. "There's no hospital or doctors anywhere here," she says. "George has contacted the police in Heraklion and Chania."

"Did anyone report me as missing?"

"I'm afraid not."

She must see how this unnerves me because she lowers on her haunches and rubs my hand, as though I'm a child. "Hey, don't worry," she says. "We'll call again first thing in the morning."

Nothing about this place feels familiar. It feels like I'm seeing everything here for the first time.

"Do I live here? Do I know any of you?" I ask her.

"We saved you," George says flatly. I can't see him, but sense his presence behind me.

"There was a storm," Joe adds, though something in his voice sounds uncertain, hesitant. "Big sandstorm coming across from Africa, no doubt. George and I went out to check that our boat hadn't come loose from its moorings. And then we saw you."

"Where was I?"

"On Bone Beach," Joe says.

"Bone Beach?"

"The small horseshoe beach with white rocks that look like bones. Down below the barn." He grins. "Crazy that you managed to survive all that. Someone up there must like you."

"You were in a boat," Sariah explains. "You don't remember if you were with anybody?"

I have a terrible feeling that I *should* know all of this, that I should know all about the boat and the beach and where I'm from. And I have no idea, absolutely no clue, why I don't know these things.

"Why did you come to Komméno, anyway?" George asks, moving to the light as he reaches for a pack of cigarettes. "I mean, it's not like there's anything here."

"What's 'Komméno'?" I say.

"It's the name of this place," Sariah says, a note of sadness in her voice, as if she's addressing someone very stupid, or ill. "Komméno Island."

I hesitate, hopeful that an answer to George's question will surface in me automatically and provide an explanation for all this.

But it doesn't.

March 18, 2015

Potter's Lane, Twickenham, London

Lochlan: It's after midnight. My wife is officially missing. I'm trying to get my head around this.

The facts are as follows: (1) I Facetimed Eloïse on Monday night shortly after seven while she was making pancakes in the kitchen and our two kids were playing happily in the family room, and (2) sometime between ten and one today, while our children were asleep in their beds upstairs, she disappeared from our home. Also, (3) there is no indication that anyone has been here, Max didn't see anyone come in, and (4) Eloïse's clothes, passport, credit cards, car, driving license, and mobile phone are still at home. She has therefore no way of making contact and no way of paying to get anywhere: not the tube, not a taxi, not a flight, and no way of paying for food or drink. Lastly, (5) no one seems to have any clue where she might have gone.

We have run out of expressed breast milk. I'm so out of sorts that Cressida shrieked for an eternity until it dawned on me that she was probably due another feed. An hour ago I phoned a taxi company and paid them fifty quid to go and buy some formula milk at a supermarket and bring it here. Cressida was a little confused at first, both by having to suck a plastic teat again and by the weird taste of formula, but finally she relented and drained it in one sitting.

Mrs. Shahjalal has gone home. She lives alone at number thirty-nine, across the road. She has offered to come again in the morning and help in any way she can. Right now, I'm mired in bewilderment and can't think straight.

On the train from Waverley I set about contacting Eloïse's friends to see if anyone had heard from her. Of course, they'd seen neither hide nor hair of her since yesterday or the day before. My Facebook post was met with weeping emojis and well-wishing; in other words, nothing of any use. With great reluctance, I texted Gerda, Eloïse's grandmother, to ask if El had gone to their place in Ledbury. It was a long shot, of course, given that the kids were still here, but I had quickly run out of possibilities.

I've searched the whole house four or five times in total. Wardrobes, the bathroom closet, that weird space under the stairs, even under the beds and in the loft, then running around in the back garden with a torch, checking all the bushes and the shed. I guess I thought she might have got stuck somewhere. I felt like I was going insane. All of this whilst Max was running around after me asking if we were playing a game and could he hide, too, and whilst Cressida realized she was being held by someone other than her mother and wanted half of London to know all about it.

Gerda rang back to say no, she hadn't seen El since last week, though she spoke to her on Sunday night. She started to ask questions and I stammered something about El not being home when I got back this afternoon. There was a long pause.

"What do you mean, El's not home? Where are you, Lochlan?"

"I'm back in London."

"And where are the babies?"

"They're here."

"Lochlan, are you saying Eloïse has left?"

"I'm saying she's not at home. Her car is still there, her keys and her mobile phone. Everything."

"Call the police."

"I've already done it."

I checked El's mobile phone, examining all her messages in case there was some unforeseen emergency she'd been called away for, but all I found was an eBay inquiry about a high chair, e-mails from Etsy, Boden, Sainsbury's, and Laura Ashley, as well as Outlook reminders about Max's parent-teacher meeting at nursery next Friday and Cressida's jabs at the health clinic.

At eleven o'clock Max came downstairs, bleary-eyed and wrapped in his *Gruffalo* robe, his blond hair longer than I remembered it being, dandelion-like with static.

"Hi, Daddy," he said, yawning.

"Hey, Maxie boy. How are you doing?"

He padded across the room and climbed up on my lap. I kissed his head, flooded with a sudden tenderness for him.

"Is Mummy back?"

How much it pained me to tell him that she wasn't.

He curled into me. "Did Mummy have to go to the shops? Did she forget that me and Cressida were in the house?"

"I don't think so, Max."

"Did she get lost coming home?"

I shook my head, and he started to grow upset.

"Want Mummy, Daddy. Where's Mummy?"

When I began to feel overwhelmed at my inability to console him—and by the thought that he might well wake Cressida—I told a fib.

"I think maybe she's gone to take her friend some flowers."

"Which friend?"

"Uh...the lady with the long black hair from playgroup."

He straightened. "Sarah?"

"Yes, Sarah."

"No, it can't be Sarah, 'cos Sarah got her hair yellowed."

"Niamh, then."

"Why is Mummy taking Niamh flowers? Is Niamh sad?"

"I think so."

"What kind of flowers?"

"I don't know, Maxie."

"Can you call Niamh on your mobile and tell her that we need Mummy to come back to us now, please?"

"Soon, darling, soon. Let's go back to bed."

In a fleeting moment of clear-mindedness I remembered the high-spec baby monitors that El had installed when Max was born—seriously, they're like surveillance cameras—and checked El's phone to see if any footage had been recorded. But no, the recording facility had been switched off ages ago. Of course it had.

I bribed Max to go to sleep without Mummy bathing him and reading him his favorite story by promising to take him to

Thomas Land. Even so, he insisted on staying downstairs with me and cried himself to sleep.

It's almost two in the morning when a police car pulls up outside and two uniformed police officers appear at the door, a man and a woman. I show the officers into the living room and attempt to console Cressida so that I can actually hear what they say. Her face is beetroot-red, tears rolling down her cheeks, and she punches the air with her fists. Max has fallen asleep on the sofa, holding the quilt Eloïse made for him up to his chin and murmuring occasionally.

"When did you last speak with your wife, Mr. Shelley?" the male officer asks as I rock Cressida back and forth.

"I already gave all this information on the phone," I say. I want answers, resolutions, for the police to wave their magic wands and materialize my wife.

"Sorry, but there's some information we've got to confirm. We'll ask a few additional questions before we begin enquiries."

"I've been in Edinburgh since Monday but I spoke to her around seven on Monday night via Facetime," I say with a sigh. "Sometimes I call during the day as well, but it's been really busy at work. I didn't get a chance."

"Where do you work?"

I shift Cressida into a different position, away from my ear. She's still tiny at three months so she fits along the length of my arm. I bounce her there and she lets out a huge belch. I say "Good girl!" but she starts to cry again.

"I work at a company called Smyth and Wyatt. Four days a week I'm based in Edinburgh, the rest of the time I'm at the London branch on Victoria Embankment."

The male officer jots this down as "*Smith & White South— a bank.*"

"It's not a bank, it's a corporate finance firm."

He scores out his note. "OK. Did you and your wife have any disagreements? Anything that might have made her leave?"

"Look, I've already explained this. My wife has not *left*. Cressida's only twelve weeks old. El's still breastfeeding."

I'm mad as hell, frustrated, but above all I'm anxious. I can't help but feel that El must be worried, wherever she is, because she's fought to breastfeed Cressida after some difficulties with Max and ensures she feeds on demand. This is hard to put across—*my wife hasn't left, you see, because she wants to breastfeed.* They ask about El's line of work, and I explain that she's a stay-at-home mother but still goes on TV to talk about her work.

"She set up a small charity some years ago for refugee children and it's become quite successful," I say. "She gets asked to do the occasional media event. I guess I'm worried that, maybe...I don't know. A lot of nutcases out there." I know I'm clutching at straws, but my mind is racing, my body buzzing with adrenaline. I keep glancing at the front door, waiting for her to walk in.

"Did she mention anything of that nature? Threatening letters, stalkers, that kind of thing?"

"No, nothing."

He gives me a moment in case something comes to mind, but it doesn't.

"Can you describe what she was wearing when you last saw her?"

"I think she was wearing gray yoga pants and a pajama top.

Like I said, it was seven o'clock at night. I should have called her this morning but I was running late..."

He writes this down, asking for more of a description. Does she have any tattoos or visible scars? No. Any jewelry? I tell him she would likely be wearing her wedding band and engagement ring. I've not found them anywhere in the house.

"Have you asked your neighbors if they saw anyone come into the house?"

I nod. "Mrs. Shahjalal from across the road was the one to find out she was missing."

More writing, slow, slow, slow, as if he's taking orders for a takeaway. "We'll follow up with Mrs. Shahjalal. What about your bank accounts? Any withdrawals? We might be able to trace her last steps if we have that information."

I've already checked our bank account on my mobile phone. We have a joint account and no money has come out today, with the exception of direct debits for the water bill and council tax. Of course, I've said all this. It was one of the first things I checked.

"Tell me a little about Eloïse," he asks. "Age? Height? Weight? Personality?"

Cressida begins to squawk so fiercely that the female police officer rises to her feet and holds her arms out.

"May I?" she says.

"Please," I say, handing Cressie to her. The female officer holds her cheek against Cressida's and speaks softly to her. Ten seconds later the screaming stops. It's only then that I realize that most of the noise is coming from inside my head.

"How old did you say she is?" the officer asks.

"Twelve weeks. Max turned four in January."

The officer smiles at Cressida, who gawps back. "I have a

little boy, he's ten months old. And he's huge. But you, you're dinky!"

"She was slightly premature," I say. It is a huge relief not to be screamed at. I sink down into the sofa beside Max and rub my temples. The male officer is looking at me expectantly.

"Eloïse is thirty-seven. She's about five foot six, fairly slim. Not sure what she weighs, exactly. Maybe ten stone. She just gave birth."

"Is that a recent photo?" he asks, glancing up at the new studio photograph mounted between two thick slabs of glass on the wall behind me.

Cost a fortune, that photo, but we all look so happy and I'm glad I deferred and had it taken. Eloïse is holding Cressida, who's a scrawny sparrowy thing at three weeks old, and although I know she felt self-conscious, begging me to kneel slightly to the right so my head would cover her swollen stomach, Eloïse looks amazing. Buttery blonde hair hanging loose by her shoulders, that lovely smile and perfect skin of hers, as though her veins contain LED lights—luminescent, that's the word. I know I married a looker, miles out of my league.

"Is Eloïse the sort of person who would just up and leave?" the male officer asks. "Has she done anything like that before?"

"No, no, no. Absolutely not."

The officer stares, blank-faced. "No problems with drugs, alcohol, anything like that?"

I shake my head. "Nothing like that. She stopped drinking when she became pregnant with our son. She maybe had the occasional glass of wine. She's...Look, I can't emphasize enough that Eloïse is the last person on earth who I would expect to go missing like this. She's quiet, reserved. You know, a home bird."

"So she wouldn't have, say, popped out to pick up a message? For five minutes or so?"

I can feel myself losing patience, almost on the verge of tears, which freaks me out. "*Our kids were here.* She wasn't expecting me back from Edinburgh until tomorrow night. There's no way she'd leave our children on their own. El won't even leave Cressida downstairs when she's taking a shower. We've a car seat in the bathroom and a baby rocker in the kitchen."

The police officer nods. "OK. When you came home were there any signs of someone having been here? Any signs of an intrusion?"

I shake my head. "Everything was locked up."

"What about the back door. It was locked?"

I think back. Was it?

My hesitation prompts him to glance around the room. "What about any other entrances to the house? Windows? Back doors?"

"We have had a problem with the back door, now that I think about it. The lock froze and it's not been closing properly. I meant to get it fixed, but…" I've been so busy. I close my eyes and sigh, speared with panic. How careless could I have been to leave the back door accessible?

He rises and walks to the back of the house. I follow. It's dark, however, and the view from the window isn't helpful.

"What's behind your garden?"

"A back alley, then the gardens of the street behind us. Larkspur Terrace."

He writes this down. "You keep any money in the house? Any valuables, expensive items?"

"We've a couple of hundred quid in a box in the kitchen. For emergencies."

"Is it still there?"

I nod. "So is all of El's jewelry."

"Are you sure?"

The doorbell cuts me short. I stride into the hallway to answer it and find Gerda and Magnus standing there, both angry and worried. I tell them that the police have arrived.

"She's still not returned?" Magnus barks. Magnus is Eloïse's grandfather, bullish, well-dressed, and immortal, like Clint Eastwood—the man's had I don't know how many triple bypass surgeries and cancer treatments and yet he only seems to grow more robust with age. Not quite as priggish as Gerda, a little more down-to-earth, but still not the sort of man I'm ever likely to get drunk with.

"Did you come from Herefordshire?" I ask. They have properties all over the place—Switzerland, Greece—and I had wondered whether El had gone to one of them. But they're all completely remote and impossible to get to. And besides, El would have no reason to go there.

Gerda ignores me, having swept into the living room and spotted Maxie asleep on the sofa. "The children aren't in bed? Isn't it rather late?"

The police officers make brief introductions in sober tones. Gerda sits down beside Max, pursing her lips as she tucks the blanket around him. Magnus walks around the room as if trying to identify something out of place.

"This is Gerda and Magnus Bachmann," I tell the officers, remembering how I would always add *fresh from the crypt* under my breath when I was referring to them. El would give me a slap on the arm, though she'd always laugh. "Gerda and

27

Magnus are Eloïse's grandparents. Naturally, they're very concerned."

I don't explain that they're the world's most interfering in-laws. Gerda flips open a gold mobile phone and dials a number with a manicured finger. "Eloïse, darling, it's Mamie. This is the twentieth time I've called you, and I won't be stopping until you reply. *Please* can you call one of us soon to let us know you're all right?"

Gerda's accent is elocution-English with clipped Swiss tones. It reminds me how El occasionally sounded foreign from the years she spent in Geneva as a teenager. She speaks French and German fluently, as well as conversational Italian, and has been teaching Max. I go to tell Gerda that Eloïse's mobile phone is sitting on the dining table next door, but right then it rings loudly. For a faint moment Gerda's eyes light up, as though she's found Eloïse, and then the penny drops.

The house feels deathly still, hollowed out. In a daze I pour Magnus a whiskey and make cups of tea for me and Gerda. Then the five of us sit in the living room, bewildered and lost for words. Despite how late it is my mobile phone continues to bleep with texts and Facebook messages, and although I check every one of them I find nothing that tells me where my wife may have gone.

"Have you spoken to her friends?" Gerda asks.

"Of *course* he'll have done that," Magnus snaps.

I give a weary sigh. "I've contacted the baby groups she sometimes goes to. I've spent all afternoon on the train phoning libraries, cafés, the swimming pool, our GP, the dentist... until my batteries died. Everyone I can think of."

Magnus sits down, then stands again. "That's good. Someone's bound to have come into contact with her."

I say, "I made a list of people who saw her yesterday, but no one saw her today. Except the kids."

"What did Max say? He must have seen something," Gerda says for the hundredth time.

"He said they made gingerbread men in the morning and then he had a nap. When he woke up he searched the house and garden but couldn't find her. That was when Mrs. Shahjalal came over."

I stand and begin to collect everyone's glasses and cups. "Well, I best be getting the children to their beds. I'll call you both in the morning, shall I?"

Gerda looks affronted.

"Oh, no. We'll be staying. I'm sure Eloïse will be back soon but until then the children will be needing us."

March 18, 2015

Komméno Island, Greece

I wake to find myself in bed in an attic room. Dust motes visible in the air, picked out by bright sunshine streaming through a porthole window. The ceiling is crisscrossed with ancient wooden beams and spiderwebs in the corners. Hewn stone walls and a cloying stench of dust and damp make the room feel like a cave.

I pull myself upright, gasping from the pain in my head and from a series of aches that announce themselves in my right shin and ankle, my upper back, all the muscles in my neck and forearms terribly strained. It feels like I got in the way of an elephant stampede. I reach around and touch the spot where my skull had been cut open. No fresh blood, but I can feel where the bleeding has matted my hair.

The events of last night turn over in my mind like stones.

The people I met, the ones that saved me from a boating accident on the beach. They were writers, weren't they? Here on a retreat? I try to summon my name to mind. It doesn't come, so I say it aloud. *My name is...* My mouth remains open as though the sound of my name will find its way inside of its own accord. I have the strongest sensation of having left something behind somewhere, and although I pace and try to will it to surface, it won't reveal itself.

Water. I need water. I move my legs to the edge of the bed and drop my feet to the floor. Cold. I'm wearing a T-shirt with a faded pineapple print on the front and baggy black swimming trunks.

I hobble like a foal toward the door, but when I turn the doorknob I find it is shut tight. I tug at it, one hand on top of the other, wrapping my fingers around the knob and twisting with all my strength. The knob turns and turns but the door won't budge. For a moment I really think I'm going to lose consciousness. With a hand pressed against the wall I let myself sink slowly down to the floor and rest my forehead against the door, taking long, trembling breaths. A large gray spider taps across the floor by my bare feet. I flinch, and in a second the spider is gone, darting into one of the dusty crags in the walls. I'm left with enough adrenaline to lift a fist against the heavy wood of the door, banging it once, twice, three times. I can hear a low murmur of voices somewhere in the house.

Eventually, the door pushes open, knocking into me. Someone swears and squeezes through the gap before helping me to my feet.

"The door was locked," I say, trying to explain.

"Locked?" Joe's voice. He inspects the door quickly and

says, "Not locked. Always jams, this door. Come on, let's get you something to eat."

After shouting downstairs for one of the others he slips a hand on the back of my head and the other firmly on the small of my back. Soon one of the women is there, too, and I recognize her as the kind one from last night, the woman who looked at me with such concern. Sariah. She helps Joe lift me to my feet and, very slowly, we all head down a winding stone staircase, one, two floors, Joe in front of me, Sariah behind, in case I fall.

The architecture of the house suggests it was once an old farmhouse, with remnants from its past hung on the wall as vintage ornaments—old breastplows, some fairly mean-looking pitchforks, and the wheel of a chaffcutter, as well as cow or goat bells. A room at the bottom of the stairs features a rocking chair—I remember sitting there last night, hunched over and trembling—and a beautiful inglenook fireplace that smelled of burned toast.

The kitchen looks different in daylight—long and brightly lit, with a large range oven, refrigerator, white granite worktops, and a wooden table in the middle surrounded by four wooden chairs. A little decrepit and dusty, but nowhere near as creepy as it seemed last night. The room has an earthy odor about it, as though it's been unused for a long time, though as I head toward the cooker it gives way to the rich smell of grilled tomatoes and fresh pita. Sariah says, "Let's get you something to eat," and makes for a pan on the hob.

Joe walks me slowly to a chair by the table, then makes for the sink. He's a good deal younger than I'd placed him last night. Maybe early twenties, a whiff of the undergrad about him. Long, pale, and thin, his black hair standing upright on his head in a gelled quiff, black square glasses shielding his eyes.

He hands me a glass of water, which I gulp down. Sariah fills a plate with the contents of a pan. Dressed in a red skirt and floaty kimono patterned with orange flowers, she looks magnificent: long dark fingers ringed with gold bands, heavy strands of colorful beads looping from her neck, ropes of black hair coiled on top of her head and tied with an orange scarf. She sets a plate of food in front of me—fried cherry tomatoes, olives, pita bread.

"Thank you," I say, and she grins.

"Mind if I take a little look at your head?" Joe asks.

I feel his hands gently touch the wound through my hair at the back of my head.

"How does it look?"

"Clean. Some bruising around the area. How's the neck?"

His fingers brush the sides of my neck gently and he tries to move my head from side to side.

"Stiff."

"I'll find some painkillers."

A kettle whistles to the boil on the hob. Sariah walks toward it and begins to make coffee, asking if I'd like milk. It all feels so strange and disorienting. I say yes to the milk but even that seems odd, the sound of my voice distant and distorted. I dart my eyes around the room, willing it to make sense, to become familiar. It doesn't.

The other woman—Hazel, I hear Joe call her—scuttles in from somewhere else, rubbing her hands and muttering about tea. She's short and thin, orange curls leaping on her head like springs, an oversized black woolen jumper pulled over a

C.J. Cooke

bottle-green skirt. She holds something in the crook of an arm. A notebook.

She stops in her tracks when she spots me, as though she hadn't expected me to be here. "Hello," she says warily, and she sits down, placing the notebook carefully on her lap. Her accent is English, like Joe and George.

"Hello."

"Are you going to stay with us?" she asks.

Sariah answers from the sink. "We're still working out how to get her to see a doctor."

Hazel glances from me to Sariah. "Joe's a doctor, isn't he?"

"I do first aid," Joe corrects from the other end of the room. "I found these," he says. "Paracetamol."

"Thanks." I press a couple of tablets out of the foil and take them with a swig of coffee.

I feel Hazel watching me, her small gray eyes absorbing every inch of me. "You were in quite a state last night," she says. "It was all very exciting. Do you remember what happened?"

I suspect she means if I remember what happened before I ended up in their kitchen. There's a smile on her face, as if the sorry state of me amuses her. It makes me wary.

"And you still don't remember how you ended up here?"

"I don't think so..."

"What about your name?"

I open my mouth, because this should be right there, right on the top of my tongue. But the space in my mind that should be bright with self-knowledge is blank, closed, emptied.

Hazel's eyes blaze with excitement at my hesitation. I see Sariah giving her a look of caution, and instantly she looks away, shamefaced.

"Don't sweat it," Sariah says. "You've had a rough night, a bump on the head. Give it a few hours. It'll all come back."

The sound of heavy footsteps grows louder at the back door. Moments later, George appears, glistening with sweat and exhaustion, his gray vest soaked through. Hazel fidgets in anticipation as he heads toward us.

"Did you find it?" Sariah asks.

George shakes his head, too worn out to speak. He's very overweight and so red in the face that I brace myself for the sight of him falling to the ground with a tremendous thud. He pulls a towel from the shelf above the sink and wipes sweat from his brow and face.

"You mean, the boat?" Hazel says in a shrill voice. "We've lost the boat?"

No answer. Hazel and Sariah watch George as he leans back in the chair and catches his breath. Both of them look worried. The mood in the room has plummeted.

"What boat?" I ask, and my voice is small and hesitant. It sounds odd to me, as though someone else is speaking.

"We rented a powerboat from Nikodemos so we can travel back and forth to Crete for supplies," Sariah says in a low voice.

"The only reason we found you was because Joe and I went out to check that the boat was moored properly during the storm," George pants, pulling off his wet boots, and then his socks. The sour smell of sweat hits me instantly. "And then we came across you. But the boat's gone."

"I thought Joe said it would likely be washed up on one of the beaches," Hazel says.

George tilts his head from side to side, emitting loud cracks from his neck. "I've checked everywhere, trust me. Boat's gone. Sunk, most likely."

"What will Nikodemos say about his boat sinking?" Hazel says. "He'll be cross, won't he? Very, very cross."

"What will Nikodemos *charge* for his boat sinking?" George corrects. "That's the question."

"We're covered by insurance, aren't we?" Sariah says, turning back to the hob to crack eggs into a pan. Her movements are rough, erratic.

George scratches a rough belt of stubble under his chin. "We'll need to work out another way to get supplies from the mainland. Not to mention delivering our guest back to wherever she came from."

I feel that this is my fault. I don't belong here. I shouldn't be here, and I feel helpless and awkward. George and Hazel acknowledge this with a quick glance in my direction, which only confirms that they feel I'm to blame. "I'm so sorry about your boat," I say.

"We'll work it out," Sariah mutters without turning, and I wonder if she's detected that I'm feeling pretty awful. Joe is at the back door, a bundle of peaches gathered in the hem of his black T-shirt. George opens his mouth and begins to tell him about the boat situation, but Sariah cuts in.

"Want some breakfast, Joe?"

Joe dumps his peaches on the worktop. He rubs his hands and glances at the pan on the hob. "Thanks."

"George, you want some?" Sariah asks.

"Okeydokey." He glances up at me. "Sariah's the cook in this operation, in case you hadn't noticed."

"And what am I in this operation?" Hazel pipes up from the table.

"The cleaner," Joe says through a mouthful of omelet. He looks at me. "Hazel likes to clean and tidy everything in sight.

She'll take a glass out of your hand before you've even finished drinking to wash it."

Hazel shrugs, clearly bristling. "Nothing wrong with being clean, is there? Next to godliness."

"Still, I'd hold on to your plate," Joe tells me. "She'll take it off you."

"And what about you?" I ask Joe. "What do you do?"

He tosses a cherry tomato in his mouth. "First-aider."

"She means, what do you do *here*, dum-dum," George says.

"Oh. Well, I tagged along, didn't I?" Joe says. "I'm the— provider of medical attention?"

"House first-aider," George interprets.

"George is the fixer," Hazel tells me.

"And what does that mean?" George asks.

"It means you fix things, George," Joe says. "Unless 'fixer' is Mongolian for 'grumpy old git.'"

"I'll fix *you* in a minute."

"See?" Joe says to me, arching a thick black eyebrow.

Sariah brings the last of the food, a plate of chopped figs and tomatoes. She removes her apron and slings it on a hook by the oven, then sits at the table beside me while George cups water on his face and armpits at the sink. Despite how terrible I feel, I'm incredibly relaxed in their company, as though I've known them for ages. It makes an otherwise alarming situation quite bearable.

"So, if you can't remember your name, how come you can remember how to talk?" Hazel asks.

"It doesn't work like that," Joe tells her. "It's called amnesia. It doesn't stop people's ability to function."

She purses her lips. "So, you can't remember if you've got any weird fetishes?"

"I don't think so," I tell her.

She looks thrilled, a sudden energy sweeping through her. "I want to study you for my new book. Do you mind if I ask you some questions?"

I go to say that I don't mind, but Joe interrupts.

"Look at you, such a busybody," he tells Hazel, throwing her a wry smile.

She shoos his comment away with a wave of her hand. Then, to me: "Do you know what you like to eat?"

"I guess I liked what I just ate."

But Hazel isn't satisfied. She tosses question after question at me: Who's the current President of the United States? What year it is? What's the name of my primary school? When was I most embarrassed? And so on. I'm still too foggy headed to answer most of these, though I'm relieved that I'm aware of what year it is. But not who I am.

"You could be *anybody*," Hazel says, at once exasperated and curious. "How do you have a sense of who you are if you don't remember anything?"

"Well, how do any of us have a true sense of who we are?" Joe interjects, making quotation marks with his fingers. "We're all of us many people in a single skin."

"I'm not," George says. "Cripes, you make it sound like we're all...what are those Russian dolls called?"

"They're called Russian dolls," Hazel says drily.

"Identity is performance," Joe says. "Ask any psychoanalyst and they'll tell you the same."

Hazel lifts an eyebrow. "Well, next time I bump into a psychoanalyst on this *uninhabited* island, I will!"

I'm shocked by this. " 'Uninhabited?' "

Joe nods.

"This whole island is uninhabited?"

"An uninhabited paradise," Sariah says dreamily. "Just this old farmhouse and a few Minoan ruins. And us."

I glance out the window and see a patch of dry earth rolling down to the ocean, nothing but blue all the way to the horizon. Hazel starts to tell me that the nearest island is Antikythera, which is eight miles away, but this sparks a debate with Joe about whether Crete is closer. I'm no longer listening. *Eight miles of ocean to the nearest town.* I'd assumed that there would be other people on the island, people we could speak to in order to provide answers to my situation, or who might help locate the missing boat. That I would be able to contact the authorities and find out where I came from.

"But—how do you get supplies?" I ask.

"There used to be a big hotel on the south side," Hazel tells me, as if in confidence. "There was a restaurant, a few shops, even a bowling alley. But they closed it down last year. The recession, you know. That's where we got our supplies before. Nikodemos—the man who owns the island—well, he loaned us a powerboat this time round..."

"...which seems to have sunk," adds George.

"There's no Internet here, either," Joe warns.

No Internet means I can't use social media or Google to search for reports of a woman of my description going missing from Crete.

"Nikodemos gave us a satellite phone," Sariah says, observing my unease. "And thank goodness. With the boat gone, we really *would* be stranded."

This, I do remember. The satellite phone that George pulled from his pocket last night. The phone they said they'd use to contact the police on the main island.

"Have the police been in touch?" I ask quickly.

"I called them again first thing," George says, and for a moment I feel relieved. But then he adds: "No one's filed a missing person's report. I asked them to correspond with some of the stations in the other islands and they said they would." He shrugs. "Sorry it's not better news."

"Maybe we could call the British Embassy?" I suggest. "Anyone looking for me is likely to leave a message there."

"Okeydokey."

He pulls the phone from the pocket of his jeans and extends the long antenna from the top. Then he rises sharply from the table, dialing a number and heading toward the window, apparently to get a better signal.

"I need to be connected to the British Embassy, please?" I hear him say.

My heart racing, I stand and make my way toward him, full of anticipation.

"Athens, you say?" He holds the phone away from his mouth and tells me, "There's no British Embassy on Crete. The closest is Athens."

When I ask how far Athens is, the answer is depressing: about sixteen hours from here by boat, which of course we don't appear to have.

George turns back to the phone. "Hello, yes? Yes, I wish to report a missing British citizen. At least, we think she's British." He glances at me, expectant, but I have no answer to give. I don't know whether I'm British or not. He turns back to the phone. "She's turned up here on Komméno and can't remember much about anything. Yes, Komméno. We're about eight miles northwest of Crete."

He gives a description of me and nods a lot, clicks his fingers for a piece of paper and a pen and jots something down. Then he says good-bye and hangs up.

"No one has contacted them about a missing British woman," he sighs. "Though of course it would help if we knew your name."

Sariah frowns. "They're based in Athens, though," she says. "Maybe we should try the police in Chania?"

George looks reluctant but dials a number. After a few moments he begins pacing the room, looking up at the ceiling. "No signal," he says. "I'll try outside." He goes out the back door but returns a few minutes later shaking his head, and I can't help but feel stricken. No one has reported a missing person. No one has reported me.

Despite all their efforts to make me feel at home, the news saps what small amount of my strength had returned. My head and neck begin to throb again, and—bizarrely—my breasts are sore and hot; they feel as though someone's injected molten lead into them. As Sariah begins to clear the table I pull my T-shirt forward subtly and peer down. My senses prove right: my breasts have swollen into two hard white globes, blue veins crisscrossing them like maps.

"Are you all right?" Sariah asks.

I let go of the neck of my T-shirt, embarrassed. "I'm not feeling so good. Would you mind if I had a lie-down?"

Sariah tells me of course it's fine, and Joe is already on his feet, offering to help me to my room.

"Are you sure you don't need me to check you over?" he says, helping me up the stairs. I tell him that I'm fine, but the pain across my chest is alarming and bizarre: a strange tightening sensation that wraps right around my back. It feels like someone has rammed hot pokers through my nipples.

By the time I get to the bed I'm in tears, unable to hide it any longer. I can't decide if I've torn some muscles in my chest or if I'm having a heart attack. Sariah is suddenly there by the bed, Joe on the other side, both of them asking me what's wrong, why am I crying.

I just want to sleep.

March 18, 2015

Potter's Lane, Twickenham

Lochlan: I don't sleep all night. Gerda and Magnus decamp to the spare bedroom and I carry Max up to his bed and settle Cressida in her cot after another bottle. Then I turn one of the armchairs around to face the window, overlooking the street, and pour myself a glass of gin.

For hours I lurch between incredulity and devastation. Amazing how you can almost convince yourself of conversations that didn't happen, of realities and explanations that promise to restore balance and bat away anguish. For a good half hour or so I almost manage to persuade myself that Eloïse told me she was going away for a conference and that I had simply forgotten. Desperation grows possibilities where none are usually found. I play out mental scenarios involving El falling down the stairs and banging her head, becoming disoriented and stumbling out into the street, a burglary gone wrong. Or maybe she became suicidal and couldn't do it in front of the children. Each possibility is as bonkers as the other.

The thing is, Eloïse is absolutely the last person you would worry about doing something out of the ordinary. She's the person who keeps us all together. If I lose my keys, a file, a document, Eloïse will intuit its exact location. She's like a sat-nav for lost objects. No, more than that: she's *steady*. I know, it sounds boring, but it's true. Countless times I've come home to find someone in the house being consoled, counseled, or cajoled by Eloïse. She's the sort of person people gravitate toward for reassurance.

Around five, the fear that accompanies thoughts of an abduction or burglary gone wrong makes me hold my head in my hands and force back tears. Finally, when exhaustion kicks in and my body shouts for sleep, I reach the absolute bottom of the well of self-questioning. She has left me. It's the only answer to this most complicated of riddles, the only piece that fits the puzzle. As punishment for all the times I've put work before her and the kids, for all the times I've not listened or exploded over something small, she has left me, and most likely for someone else. It is why her phone and credit cards are all here. She's been using another phone to talk to him. He has money. They'll come back for the kids.

My vigil propels me through the spectrum of emotions. Anger, self-pity, sorrow, paranoia, a surreal kind of acceptance. Around six I hear Cressida begin to wail. I get up and make up a bottle, then take it upstairs to Cressida. Gerda is already stooping over the cot, trying to quiet her. She mutters to her in German.

"It's OK, Gerda," I say wearily. "I've got what she wants."

Gerda turns and, without meeting my eye, takes the bottle from me. Then she lifts Cressida out of the cot and settles in the nursing chair to feed her.

"There, there," Gerda says. "Mamie's here. Take your milk, *meine Süße.*"

I lean against the cot woozily and watch Gerda as she feeds Cressida. I feel I ought to say something to her but don't quite know what. After a moment Gerda says, "Seems only five minutes since I was feeding Eloïse like this. Cressida is the image of her."

She looks up at me with narrowed eyes.

"I need you to be very honest with me, Lochlan. Has Eloïse left you?"

Even though I'm well used to my grandmother-in-law's thinly veiled contempt for me, her question—or rather, the sudden hardness of her tone—catches me off guard.

"I don't know," I mumble. "I've no idea where she is."

She purses her lips and beholds me with that arrangement of her features that I've come to understand is designed for me and no one else.

"You were one of the last people to see her, Lochlan. Did she seem..."

"What?"

"Well, I don't know. You're her husband. Have you been fighting again?"

"No," I say, and I feel a spike of anger toward Eloïse for divulging our problems to Gerda. I know Gerda's family, that she raised my wife, but I have had not unpleasant daydreams about Gerda kicking the bucket. And following swiftly on the heel of rage is the re-realization that El's missing. My wife is missing. Like people you see on posters, or on *Crimewatch*. And I have absolutely no answers, no map, by which to find her.

Gerda is pacing behind me, her arms folded.

"Surely she must have said *something*."

"Like?"

She gives a hard sigh. "Eloïse would hardly just leave the children behind."

"I know that."

She stops pacing.

"Unless..."

"Unless what?"

"Well, unless you gave her some *reason* to leave the children behind."

Her voice—nasal, clipped, withering—lands me back in the night El and I announced our engagement. Eloïse's mother is out of the picture, having dragged El around England for most of her formative years in pursuit of heroin. She died when El was twelve. At that point, Gerda and Magnus stepped in and raised Eloïse, giving her a fantastic education and a strict home life. I had only met Gerda once by the time I asked El to marry me, and clearly I had somehow made a very poor first impression.

We were in the dining room of their home in Geneva, El switching between French and German as she showed off her engagement ring to a roomful of family friends and distant relatives. I was in a corner, fiercely attempting to abate my social inadequacies with gin, when I spotted Gerda taking Eloïse by the elbow and leading her into the kitchen. I followed, but when I reached the door I heard Gerda speaking in a tone of voice that suggested I'd better not interrupt. I hid behind the door and leaned toward the sound. She was speaking in English, presumably so none of the other guests would understand. But I did.

Are you sure you know what you're doing, Eloïse?

What do you mean?

Well, you've only just met. Couldn't you wait a little longer?

Eloïse laughed. *We've been dating for a year...*

Your grandfather and I courted for three years before we even thought of marrying. It's a serious thing, you know. Very serious...

I know how serious it is, Mamie—

What does his father do?

I think his father is retired now. He used to work in the mines.

In the mines?

Does it matter?

A long sigh.

I'm sorry.

Sorry? For what, dear?

That you're not as happy for me as I thought you'd be.

I stepped back, thinking that the conversation was over. But then Eloïse said:

This is about my mother, isn't it?

Gerda straightened, affronted, and when she spoke her voice was louder.

Just...be careful, OK? I love you so, so much, meine Süße.

I love you too, Mamie.

Gerda comes back into focus, the bottle of milk almost finished and my daughter beginning to fall asleep in her arms. I clench my jaw, bracing for a row.

"There isn't someone else in the picture, is there?" Gerda says slowly, still not quite looking me in the eye.

"Someone else?"

She shrugs, as if this is an entirely reasonable thing to be asking me. "Another man. A lover."

I bristle. "I hope not."

"And she definitely left all her belongings behind. Her credits cards, passports..."

"Pass*ports*?" The word is barely out of my mouth when I realize what she means: El has two passports. Her British one and her Swiss one from long ago. Gerda eyes me expectantly, so I say, "Yes," though I haven't located the Swiss passport. I'd forgotten that one. It's bright red with a white cross on it, so shouldn't be too hard to find. I make a mental note to ransack the house for it immediately, though El's not used it in ages. I should think it's out of date.

Gerda's gaze skitters from mine. "You must have given her some reason to leave."

Her words are like shards, designed to wound, but I refuse to rise to it. It's precisely what she wants. Instead, I turn on my heel and walk out of the room.

Max is asleep in his pirate ship bed, surrounded by yellow Minions and clutching his quilt, thumb stuck firmly in his mouth. He'll be bursting with questions when he wakes up, and I have no idea what to tell him. I can hardly tell him that his mother is still away taking flowers to a friend.

I check the filing cabinet in the spare room in which El keeps things like birth certificates and baby books, but there is no sign of her Swiss passport. It's not in the drawer under our bed either. I can't think of anywhere else to look. I have a brisk shower, and my mind turns to my e-mails and text messages, as well as Eloïse's Facebook page and Twitter account. Both are full of queries, stickers, emojis: *El, are you OK?* Sad face. *DM me!* Shocked face. *Where are you? I heard something's up?* Gravely concerned face. *Hey, El, are we meeting up for lunch today?* A heart.

I have text messages from our friends asking if they can do anything, and I scroll through them all, willing one of them to say something to the effect that Eloïse has been found.

I check my voice mail for the millionth time but there's nothing from Eloïse. There is, however, an urgent message from my boss, Hugo, about an account—one of our biggest clients is furious about an admin error and is threatening to take his thirty million quid elsewhere. I send a quick e-mail to Hugo, asking for clarification, and his reply pings back. Basically, I need to resend a bunch of paperwork by special delivery to the Edinburgh branch, pray for a miracle, and Mr. Husain and his millions should stay put.

Gerda pads downstairs in a gray cashmere robe, a cigarette and a lighter in one manicured hand, heading for the back garden. She stops when she sees me and looks oddly penitent.

"Look, Lochlan. If Eloïse really *is* missing then we need to be devising a plan of action for her return."

I continue rifling through the cupboard by the stairs for my briefcase. "That's precisely why I've already spoken with the police."

"The police in this country will do nothing," she tuts. "We need to be proactive about this, Lochlan. We need to put a plan in—"

"I *am* being proactive."

She cuts me off: "—place to ensure that she's not gone any

longer than is necessary. Unless, of course, that's what you want?"

What I want is to slap her. And in the same moment as I feel that ugly, tantalizing impulse, I recall an argument with Eloïse that I ended by telling her she was just like Gerda. She asked me what the hell I meant, and I told her the truth: She had a tendency to twist my words and corner me with her own. Or she'd stonewall me. There's no winning with passive-aggressive fighters. You've got to ignore them, for all you want to gouge their eyes out.

"Will you be all right getting Max and Cressida their breakfast?" I say calmly. "Cressie's bottles have to be sterilized, and I think there are a couple of cartons of formula in the fridge. Max takes Weetabix and milk heated in the microwave for thirty seconds."

"You're leaving?" Gerda says, following me across the room. "Where on earth are you going?"

I grab my keys from the kitchen island. "Work, I'm afraid."

"*Work?*"

Gerda's got a face like a bad ham. Good. I stride toward the front door, jump into my car, and drive off as fast as I can.

Eloïse and I met eight years ago at a charity event in Mayfair to which I'd begrudgingly gone to wave the company flag. I'd already been to one too many of those sort of things, and although I've spent much of my life in London there's enough Weegie in me yet to find the whole canapés and air-kissing malarkey worse than sticking needles in my eyes. Not only that, but I'd been informed that my ex-girlfriend Lauren was going to be there and I desperately wanted an out.

But then this beautiful woman got up on the platform. She

was unassuming and sweet, a hand drawn across her waist to clasp the elbow of the other arm. She spoke quietly into the mic, introduced herself: Eloïse Bachmann. She was starting a crowdfunded project for refugee children who had wound up in the UK. The more she talked about the causes behind this project, the more she seemed to come alive. Her voice grew louder, her posture changed, and suddenly people were paying attention. When she finished, everyone applauded. Even in the bright spotlight I could see that she was overwhelmed.

It's not that Eloïse isn't beautiful—she's slim, blonde, and gorgeous—but back then, she wasn't my type. She's sensible and quietly confident, probably the smartest person I know. Back then I tended to be drawn to theatrical, insecure women who embarrassed me in the company of friends; the type that tended to slash my tires after an argument. My relationships were like social experiments. I'd become cynical about love, saying it didn't exist, that I didn't even want it, when really I was a blithering idiot with an addiction to sociopaths. And then I found myself two feet away from the girl who had captivated a roomful of millionaires with her earnest passion, and I felt like I'd come home.

She took persuading. None of my old tactics worked. Eloïse wasn't into fruit baskets or restaurants with dress codes. Neither am I, but I'd been moving in certain circles for so long that I'd assumed these things would woo her. In desperation I cornered a colleague who was friendly with Eloïse and asked her what I should do. "Take her to Skybright," she said simply. I had no idea what Skybright was. Turned out to be a café run by volunteers, where people could pay what they wanted for the food, enabling the homeless to eat there. I invited Eloïse and she accepted. Three months later, I proposed.

51

She very sweetly said no. A month later, I tried again, on both knees. I knew that I had never, ever felt about another human being what I felt for her, and I wasn't giving up. Luckily, this time she said yes.

We had two weddings—a real one, attended by the two of us, the priest, and a couple of friends in one of Magnus's properties, and one for our families back in England a couple of weeks later. We spent the next few years backpacking and sailing around the world. El's a fantastic sailor. Magnus taught her—it was the thing that kept them close, much closer than El and Gerda. We lived in a little beach hut in Goa for months, waking up to the sunrise and swimming in the warm ocean before breakfast. Making love under the stars. We traveled down the Amazon, spotting anacondas and tribes washing in the river. We hiked along the Great Wall of China, then made our way to Australia, where we spent a month sailing around the Whitsunday Islands. I thought I'd struggle, coming home from all of that, but I was so much more in love with Eloïse after that time spent together that I'd have been happy anywhere, doing anything.

I must stress that I adore my children. I really do. I know that I'm a lucky man. But.

The life that we'd lived before Max came along drew to a screeching halt the morning he came into the world. Our spontaneous weekend breaks in New York or Venice: gone. A full night's sleep: gone. Mental faculties: vamoosed. Whereas El and I had spent the previous four years of our relationship in a state of contented, loved-up bliss, now we only ever seemed to see each other at our worst. I learned that there was actually a spectrum of exhaustion, and I always seemed to have fallen off the far end. We started having fights about things like housework and money. We had more fights during Max's first year than we'd had in our entire relationship.

I remember about six months into parenthood, both of us demented from sleep deprivation, I was standing in the kitchen making up a bottle and I said to Eloïse, "How does any couple stay together after having kids?"

It must have been about two in the morning. Eloïse had crazy bedhead hair and was wearing an old black T-shirt of mine stained with baby sick. It felt like all we did in those days was mop up—or occasionally, catch—bodily fluids, sometimes with our bare hands. "I don't know how anyone stays *sane* after having kids," she said.

Of course, this was all par for the course. We had a group of friends over for dinner one night not long after and shared this story with them, and it turned out that it was a conversation *every single one of them* had had. Matt reached across the table, took Eloïse's hand, and said: "*Every* woman thinks about leaving the father of her children. All it takes is for him to stay asleep while you deal with a screaming baby at three in the morning a few times and—boom! Divorce courts."

I park in one of the staff spaces at the back of the building—it's so early and yet there's only a few spaces left. Some of my colleagues work literally a hundred hours a week, every week. They'll take a fortnight off when it's quiet and rent a yacht in the Caribbean. Few of them have young families, or if they do, they're concealing the fact. I know two female colleagues are married but leave their wedding bands at home. Family is seen as a distraction in corporate finance.

The Smyth & Wyatt building on the Victoria Embankment

is like something from *Star Trek*—Dean Wyatt spent ten million on revamping the place a couple of years ago so that the whole place would be made of glass and titanium, with leather couches imported from Italy and commissioned sculptures in the corridors. I get Dean's ethos: if you spend every day here, from six in the morning until midnight, the place has to be pretty damn nice, and nice it is.

I race upstairs and unlock my office. I can hear someone calling my name, but I ignore it and log on to my computer. The thing loads up as fast as a tortoise on weed.

"Lockie, boy," a voice calls. It's Paddy Smyth. Paddy's a Weegie, like me, though my accent has softened considerably: I've worked hard to graduate from Billy Connolly to Ewan McGregor. The London clients like it better.

"You coming out for drinks, later?" he asks.

"Can't, sorry. Got a bit of a crisis on my hands."

He stuffs his hands in his pockets and ambles into my office, looking over the photos of my children on the cabinet opposite. "Yeah, I heard about the Dubai thing. I thought Raj was dealing with that?"

By "crisis," I mean the fact that my wife is missing, but I don't say anything more. "No, I'm not involved in the Dubai thing. I've got to sign off this paperwork for the Husain account ASAP."

My computer finally loads. I type in my passcode and scroll through a list of folders. I see "Husain" and click on it.

"Oh, I saw you posted something on Facebook last night. Something about your wife. Eloïse, isn't that right?"

I find a new folder in the one marked "Husain," one my secretary has overlooked. I click on it and hit "print." The printer whirs into action.

"Yeah," I answer, moving to the printer. "She's...she didn't come home last night."

Paddy is standing right next to me, his eyebrows raised. "She didn't come home?"

The crushing feeling in my chest is beginning to return. I wish he'd go away.

"The police are involved."

The printer screams out a sound and bright white text runs across the screen. OUT OF TONER. REPLACE IMMEDIATELY. It takes all my composure not to kick the machine.

"Always running out of ink, these things," Paddy says. "You got another cartridge thingy?"

I glance at the office opposite where my secretary normally sits. She's not there. It's barely seven a.m. She doesn't come in until nine. I am apoplectic.

"Use my printer," Paddy says. "E-mail the file to yourself and open it up on my screen."

"I can't," I say, tugging my tie loose. "These files have that new security thing on them that means I can't e-mail them forward. They're locked into the computer."

Which means, of course, that I have only one option: to unhook and unplug my enormous desktop and carry it all the way to Paddy's office on the next floor. My phone is ringing and buzzing and chiming again, and by the time I set up the computer next to Paddy's printer I have twelve missed calls, eleven voice mails, twenty-seven Facebook notifications, and thirty-four tweets.

"And a partridge in a pear tree," Paddy adds. "So tell me, has your wife left you?"

Paddy has had five wives and numerous girlfriends. He

treats breakups as inevitable and women like cars, trading them in every couple of years for a younger model. He's sixty-three and is dating a twenty-four-year-old.

"No, she has not left me," I say, plugging in the computer and flicking switch after switch. "We simply don't know where she is."

"Didn't she recently have a baby?"

"Yes. A girl."

"So...who's with the kids now? The nanny?"

I don't have time to answer his questions. I finally get the thing hooked up and find the "Husain" file. I click it and hit "print," then silently beg God to let the document print. It does. I shove it in an envelope for the company courier and bring up my inbox to inform Mr. Husain that all is well. I stop mid-email, and ask Paddy:

"What time does the courier come?"

Paddy glances at the clock. "About eight. Why?"

We've recently had some new hires, and one of them was some knuckle-dragging kid covered in tats for company deliveries. Last week my secretary had to call him back because he left behind two packages marked URGENT. For the sake of forty-five minutes I could ensure that the form is picked up and sent off. I could even slip the guy a twenty-pound note and ask him to make this his first drop-off. I'm flapping. Before I realize it, I'm dialing my home number.

It barely rings before Gerda answers.

"Eloïse?"

"Hello? No, it's Lochlan."

A disappointed sigh on the other end.

"Look, Gerda, I'm really sorry about this..."

"And well you should be, Lochlan. I can't imagine what

kind of emergency forced you to go into *work* when your wife is nowhere to be found. What is going on?"

"I'm coming home soon. I've got to get something sent off and then I'll be there, OK?"

A pause. "Magnus is already driving around the area to see if he can find her. What time are the police coming?"

"I'll ring them shortly to update them, don't worry."

A resigned sigh. "All right."

"Bye."

Eight o'clock comes and goes. Eight fifteen. I walk down to the foyer and pace, envelope in hand. Eight thirty. When the guy comes, I swear I'm going to ram the envelope down his throat. Forget a twenty-quid bribe. By the time it turns nine I am sweating bullets, my heart racing. Two of my colleagues have already walked in and asked if I'm ill. I nod. Yes, yes, I am ill. It dawns on me that I expected this place to shake me back into competency, to prompt enough mental clarity to enable me to solve the mystery of my wife's disappearance. The only clarity I've acquired is that I'm an idiot.

At nine fifteen I race back upstairs, intent on arranging a private courier. I should have done this in the first place. My secretary Ramona is at her desk. I go into her office. Ramona is a genius. She's Chinese, raised by a Tiger Mother, plays the oboe at diploma level, and can solve a Rubik's Cube in under five minutes. She'll fix all of this.

"What are you doing here?" she says in a low voice. "I thought—didn't I see something online about your wife?"

I nod and flap the envelope at her before explaining the situation with Mr. Husain and the courier.

"The courier left a message with Joan fifteen minutes ago,"

Ramona says. "He's not coming in today. I was in the process of trying to find a replacement."

I thrust the envelope into her hands. "Please, Ramona. Deliver this for me. I'll pay you anything."

She takes a step back and looks puzzled. "You want *me* to deliver it?"

I move to her computer and start looking up directions to the Cauldwell Building in Edinburgh. "Here, I'll e-mail you the fastest route. Did you bring your car?"

She shakes her head. "I always come by bike..."

"OK, book a flight. Use my credit card." I take out my wallet and press a Visa card into her hand. "Just...whatever it costs, OK?"

Ramona looks a little dazed. I catch a ghostly reflection of myself in one of the glass panels opposite and realize I look like a madman. My tie is gone, my collar is open by three buttons, my hair is sticking up all over the place, and I'm shining with sweat. Plus, I'm gripping my secretary by the upper arms.

A knock on the door, the tall, lanky figure of Dean Wyatt visible through the glass.

"Everything all right in here, Lochlan? I heard shouting..."

I let go of Ramona and smooth down my hair. "Everything's fine, Dean. In light of the fact that we're down a courier, Ramona's offered to hand-deliver a very important form this morning."

He looks grave. "The Husain account?"

I nod. He raises a silver eyebrow at Ramona. "Good. This has been a very serious matter for the company." He flicks his eyes at me, a trace of disapproval there. "See you at the meeting in a half hour." He turns to leave, but I call after him. I step outside Ramona's office and collar Dean in the passageway.

"I'm afraid I'm going to have to take some time off," I say.

He turns slowly and looks deeply confused. "I'm sorry, Lochlan, but I'm not quite sure what you mean."

I explain the situation at home, and I mention the police, but he simply shakes his head as though none of this is possible.

"What about the Edinburgh branch? You can't simply up and leave at a time like this."

I make to answer, but there's an LCD screen on a wall beside us and the noise is starting to rattle my head. The news comes on, and from the corner of my eye I spy my wife's face. Both Dean and I turn to see a headshot of Eloïse enlarging on the screen until it is filled.

And in local news, charity campaigner and mother-of-two Eloïse Shelley went missing from her home in Twickenham yesterday. Her family and friends are desperately urging anyone with information to come forward.

Gerda pops up on screen. There's a microphone in her face and she's standing in the doorway of my house looking drained and wild-eyed. Her voice shakes.

"She hasn't been seen for over twenty-four hours. This really is extremely distressing and urgent. We've got two grandchildren, the youngest only twelve weeks old. We *plead* with anyone who has seen Eloïse to contact us immediately."

March 19, 2015

Komméno Island, Greece

It's morning. The sky outside the porthole window is gray and brooding. It's so cold that the bedsheets feel damp to the touch. It takes a few moments to get my bearings. Sleep seems to have made a huge difference to how I feel. The terrible pain in my breasts has stopped. My head isn't as sore, either. Still, when I move across the floor of the attic to the door, I find it locked, or jammed. Either way, it won't budge, and it takes a minute or two of pounding my fists against the wood for Joe to come and open it. He explains that the wind must have caught it and offers to help me down the stairs, but I refuse. I cling to the old wooden banister and take each step very carefully.

Eventually I find the bathroom, close the door, testing the lock several times before sinking down to the ground. There's no shower in here, just a sink and an old tin bathtub with rusty taps and a cobwebbed window. The water doesn't seem to run any other temperature than ice-cold. Sariah tells me they get their water from a cistern out by the hay barn so it's not particularly plentiful.

I peel off the pajamas that Hazel lent me and study the naked woman in the small shaving mirror above the sink. This woman who is me. She is Caucasian, slender, somewhere between thirty and forty, with thick honey-blonde hair to her shoulders. A long face, skinny arms, and round hips, the chest streaked with blue veins. Her shoulders are defined, and beneath a layer of loose skin around the belly button is a firm six-pack. Lines fan around the eyes. A small, irregular nose, light green eyes, and ears that stick out a little. No tattoos or scars. Her nails are unpainted and short, filed into neat ovals. Her left cheekbone and forehead are horribly bruised, and there are aubergine-colored splodges on her shins, her right hip, and both arms.

Why don't I recognize myself? Why isn't my body familiar? Where do I live? Do I work? Do I have kids? The white space in my mind is luminous, unyielding. *Why don't I know my own name?*

Gingerly I stretch out the arm that doesn't hurt as badly as the other and touch the mirror to confirm that this is my reflection. I want her to talk back to me, to tell me my secrets. I read this body like a puzzle, a remnant of a larger story.

There's a groove around the base of several fingers, as though I was wearing rings that have since vanished—the third and fourth fingers of my right hand, my wedding finger. Was I married? I rub my thumb up and down the faint circular indentations in my skin, willing myself to remember the ring that has vanished, if not the person who gave it to me.

I find a bar of soap on the side of the bath and slowly scrub the sour smell of brine off my skin and out of my hair, careful not to touch the cut at the right side. It stings so badly. Hazel told me she washed the clothes I was found in yesterday—a bra, pants, yellow T-shirt, and jeans—and that she put them on the washing line outside to dry. She also lent me some of her clothes.

Wrapping a towel around me, I stagger painfully to the kitchen and out the back door to the stone steps that lead down into the grassy patch at the back of the house. I find my jeans, T-shirt, bra, and pants all swaying on the line alongside the life jacket. I finger it, pulling at the straps.

A wave of dizziness forces me to sit down on a patch of dry grass. I can't bear to think that someone else died on the trip to this place. Someone I loved, perhaps. After a long while I force myself to focus on my surroundings. George asked me before why I came here. There must be a reason. I must know this place.

I sit for a while and study the farmhouse, pitched as it is on a sudden incline, subjecting it to buffeting winds. It's bigger than I expected, given how small the rooms seem inside: a tall stone building with patches of crumbling masonry, a spatter of orange tiles on the ground indicating that the roof is in disrepair, too. Metal balconies jut out from two of the upper windows that are crowned by explosions of vibrant pink flowers, lending the place a certain rustic charm. Part of the roof is flat, and there I can make out something that looks like a flat-screen TV with a huge battery attached to the top of it. Perhaps a solar panel—that would explain how the farmhouse has electricity.

A number of outbuildings are visible at the bottom of the hill, rusting and overgrown farm machinery indicating the property's former purpose. After a while, a feeling of familiarity stirs in me, a small nudge from the recesses of my mind telling me I've seen this place before. It's enough to get me to my feet to have a look around.

The island isn't what I expected. It looks neglected, abandoned, with stone relics visible in the distance of what appear to be unfinished houses. The earth is dry and parched, and the nearby trees are gnarled and overgrown and filled with thorns. There's a sense that everything here has to work very hard to survive.

I wonder how anyone would even begin to walk around the island—there's a narrow dirt path leading from the farmhouse to the trees below, but I don't imagine there could ever have been vehicles here. It's a bit of a wilderness. Beautiful, yes, but a savage beauty—not the sort of place anyone would come for a holiday.

I make out three buildings on the north side, the closest one clearly a house that someone didn't bother to finish. On the west side there are a handful of small beaches strung along the coast, but they appear rocky and treacherous. The ocean wraps itself around the island like a blue cloth dotted with the blurry outlines of boats and landmasses.

Did I really travel that distance across the sea alone? If I was drunk, did I really have the presence of mind to wear a life jacket? Did someone else accompany me? Did they drown?

It is daunting to think that the island is uninhabited. I can't fathom how Joe, Hazel, Sariah, and George don't feel marooned out here. Or maybe they do, now that their boat is gone.

I check that no one is watching before stepping into my knickers and jeans, then slip the towel to my waist and twist awkwardly into my bra and the yellow T-shirt, my muscles shrieking with the slightest movement. Both the T-shirt and jeans are good quality, both with designer labels. Am I the sort of person who would buy a designer T-shirt? It doesn't strike a chord. But then, nothing does. I have the sense of being reborn, wiped clean. The ghost of someone else.

When I turn to go back inside I see movement between the house and the outbuilding that looks like a small barn. Panic spears me, until I make out who it is: George, lurking in the shade. Did he see me get dressed?

"Hello?"

He ambles down the hill toward me, a cigarette in one hand. He looks different in the clear light. Quite tall and portly, his head shining bald. Dressed in a tatty white polo shirt and tracksuit bottoms. Mid-forties, perhaps more. He throws me a salute.

"Hello."

"Hi."

"You feeling any better?"

I try to smile. "A little."

He wiggles the cigarette at me. "You want one of these bad boys?"

I shake my head, then pause, wondering if an automatic urge will take over. It doesn't. I'm not a smoker, then.

"Thanks for the offer."

"You're welcome."

A moment passes. "You're not writing?" I ask.

He takes a long drag before answering. "Today's the day I usually head over to Chania for supplies. I might go take a look at the beaches on the west side, see if our boat turns up."

"I'm sorry about your boat," I say. "If it turns out I'm rich, I'll buy a replacement."

George offers a laugh. "Hardly your fault. Pretty sure the insurance will cover it."

This brings a great deal of relief. Maybe I misread his mood before—I felt he was irritated with me, that he blamed me for their boat sinking. He seems less brooding in this light, less intimidating and not as tall. I'm about to ask about getting to Crete, when he says:

"I contacted Nikodemos half an hour ago."

"Nikodemos—the man who owns the island?"

He nods. "Well, I spoke to his wife. She says he's out of town for the next couple of days but she'll get him to come out here and pick you up on Monday evening."

I give a gasp. "Thank you *so* much. That's fantastic news."

George grins. "And he's bringing food. You ever tried mizithropita?"

I shake my head, only half hearing what he's saying, but he persists.

"*Gorgeous.* Ah! No food like Greek food, I'm telling you. It's why all the Greeks live so long. I've put in a special request for him to bring squid, too. Sounds disgusting, doesn't it? *Squid.* Not something I've ever tried in England, but here, you don't want to miss it."

He's still talking but I'm thinking about this man, Nikodemos, trying to figure out if his name sounds familiar or not. I decide that it doesn't, and so I wonder if he will help me contact the embassy and explain to them what happened. From there we can work out how I ended up here, and more importantly how to get back to whoever may be going crazy looking for me.

"You're sure you want to leave this place?" George asks. I notice he's standing closer, studying my body language. The wind carries a sharp smell of his body odor. I turn my head but he doesn't notice, pointing at the hills ahead. "Paradise, here."

The island is more of a wilderness than a paradise.

"Yeah, yeah, I know, a bit shabby," he says, as though reading my mind. "Well, there are some interesting ruins around. Trust me, you've hit the jackpot, coming here."

"Have I?"

"Mmmm. Archaeological treasure trove, this place. Real mythology to it."

I give him a look that says I have no idea what this means, and he grins, pleased that he gets to fill me in.

"You see that?" He leans toward me and points at a cave in the distance. "Apparently, that there's the actual cave that King Minos used to send boys and girls into as food for the Minotaur. Thousands of years old, that is."

I glance at him. "Minotaur?"

"Ah, forgotten your Greek myths, too, then?" He chuckles. "They say King Minos had a son who was half-human, half-bull. Instead of killing him, he built a network of caves, a labyrinth, and put the kid at the end of it to make sure he never got out. Then Theseus, the hero, said he'd go in with a ball of wool to help him retrace his steps. And he found the Minotaur."

It crosses my mind that he's telling me this to unnerve me, and if I'm honest it does. Perhaps I sense that this place has been abandoned for a reason.

"They found some helmets not so long ago, couple of swords, I think," George says when I don't react to his myth. "Bigwigs from the museums came over, took the lot."

He's still trying to convince me not to leave. I say, "Thank you, and it's tempting, but no. There must be people who are going frantic without me."

He sniffs, glances down, like a rejected schoolboy. "Well then, you've got a little while to enjoy this place. Six miles square. That's how big the island is. Or small, depending how you look at it. The dock's about a fifty-minute walk in that direction, by the old hotel."

A small flicker of hope stirs in me. "Hotel?"

"Don't get your hopes up," he says. "Went bust a while back, so it's nothing but a shell. Investors stripped it bare. The recession hit this place very hard. There are derelict apartment buildings to the east side, too. Money ran out. Builders packed up and left before they got finished. Now the carcasses are just sitting there, empty. Shame." He nods ahead in the distance. "Some interesting things to see round here, though. Loads of interesting flora and fauna, if you're into that sort of thing. Sariah can tell you all about the plants and flowers. Animals, too. All sorts here. You got your geckos, your tortoises, rabbits, hedgehogs, snakes..."

I shudder. "Snakes?"

"Not fond of snakes?"

"Not particularly."

"Pretty harmless round here. It's the spiders you want to watch out for. Oh, and wild goats. I reckon they keep to the hills over there to the right, near the hotel. Wicked things, they are. Kri-kri goats. More ibex than goat. Big looping horns." He makes the shape of the horns with his hands, swooping from the base of his skull to his chest. "According to folklore, they're the offspring of the Minotaur."

"I'll take that with a pinch of salt."

He winks. "Stay well clear if you see them."

I squint into the distance at the hills veiled with blue mist. "I will."

"Hey, guys."

I turn to my left and see Joe coming down the steps from the kitchen door, a laptop under his arm. He is tall, thin as a string, and walks with a loping gait.

"You off to find a writing spot?" George asks him. Then, to me: "Joe doesn't like writing in the same place every day. Weirdo."

Joe stops next to us and looks out. "Think I'll try one of the beaches."

I ask if I can come with him, if I can see the beach where my boat landed. "Perhaps we might even spot the boat that got unmoored," I say, turning to George.

Joe frowns and looks me up and down. "I mean, I *guess*. It's a fair walk, though. Are you sure you're feeling up to it?"

I nod, though I'm not sure I am. I can't quite believe that the *whole* island is uninhabited. Sariah—or maybe it was George—said it was only a couple of miles long. I can make that if I take it slowly.

We veer off the path toward a bank covered in tall reeds, stiff and unyielding as horse whips, then pick our way through an overgrown lemon grove. I suspect Joe is keen to march a good deal faster, but he waits patiently for me to keep up, holding back the branches and vines for me to pass through. This part of the island resembles a jungle, all tangled branches and rotting citrus fruit underfoot. I reach up and pluck one of the fruits that looks like a small green plum. It has a sour taste, and when I bite into it a walnut drops out. There are mounds of cacti with spiny paddles, and despite all my efforts to give them a wide berth I end up getting pricked in the legs.

I'm still barefoot—my shoes must have been lost at sea—so I have to tread carefully across the soil, which is surprisingly warm. What I do wish for, though, is a pair of sunglasses. The sun is piercingly bright out here, with virtually no shade.

"Do you think you'll publish a book after this?" I ask Joe, more to keep up the conversation than anything else. "Is that what the retreat is for?"

He shrugs and tosses the rind. "I don't know." He stops and looks down at me, then removes his sunglasses. "Here," he says, handing them to me. "You seem bothered by the light."

"Are you sure?" I say, reluctant to take them.

"Absolutely." He plucks his spectacles from a pocket and puts them back on his face. "Can hardly see without these on, anyway." He surveys the coast behind me. "I think I'll try one of the caves to write in today. I won't need them in there."

He stops and points at an inlet on the west side of the island. "You might not see them, but if you look past the Cyprus trees there's a row of black dots. They're ancient caves. Pretty cool. Atmospheric. I can take you, if you like."

I'm already feeling a lot weaker than I expected, so I tell him that maybe I will in a day or so.

"Well, we're close to Bone Beach," he says.

"We are?"

A nod. "It's a bit of a climb down. I'm not sure you're well enough to manage it."

I tell him I can manage, but he insists on my taking his arm before negotiating a narrow pathway that leads down to a rocky outcrop. A few moments later, I'm gazing down at calm, azure waters, gently lapping at the rocks below.

"The tide is in," I say, straining to see any sign of a boat.

He grins. "No such thing as a tide here."

"No tide?"

"Not really. Something to do with the Mediterranean not being affected by the Atlantic."

I think back to the other night. "I definitely saw waves crashing against the rocks."

He nods. "Yeah, it's the currents between Crete and Libya. We get big cruise ships passing by every now and then, too. Causes waves. Or it might have been the storm. Here, take my arm again." He crooks a pale elbow at me. "Bone Beach isn't much farther."

He reveals a path to the right of the outcrop that drops down to another level. He tells me to be careful and follow behind as he presses against the rock face and moves along. Finally, he stops and turns carefully.

"There is a faster route, but I don't think you'd make it today. Some climbing involved. Look down to the right."

I see a chalky beach about twenty feet below. The name of the beach is immediately clear—the rocks do resemble bones. They are muscular and ribbed, the color of old teeth. From here it looks as though a giant is pushing upward out of the ground, two white rocks the shape of shoulder bones on either side of a strip of small rocks mimicking a spine. And there, right at the edge of the water, is a wooden boat, two long masts jutting from the center. Red sails splay out across the milky sand like the huge wings of a Jurassic butterfly.

"Does that help you remember?" Joe asks.

"That's the boat I came in?" I say, and his silence confirms it. Astonishment doesn't even begin to cover how I feel. I have no memory, nothing, that indicates a link between me and that boat. It may as well be a spacecraft as a boat.

"Are you all right?" Joe asks.

I tell him that I'm fine, but I feel scared and dazed. I guess I'd expected everything to come together upon seeing the boat. The fact I feel nothing, remember nothing, despite being able to see the very vessel that brought me here, is deeply troubling.

I turn and look up at the cliff path that leads back to the farmhouse. It looks treacherous.

"How on earth did I get up there?"

"George carried you," Joe explains. "I gave you mouth-to-mouth." He shrugs. "Like I said, you were lucky."

Farther out to sea are shadows of other islands, boats, a cruise ship. The possibilities for my origins are daunting, endless. I feel panicky again, like I can't get my breath.

"I'm glad Nikodemos is coming," I say. "I need to find out where I've come from. Who I am."

"Still no memory of your name, then?"

I shake my head.

"Have you considered that perhaps you don't want to remember?"

I turn and try to read his expression, the tone of his voice, but I don't know him well enough to work out whether he's joking.

"That sounds dramatic. Why wouldn't I want to remember?"

He shrugs and looks back down at the boat, unaware of how stricken I am.

"I'd say that the fact that you were on a boat in the middle of nowhere suggests you were running from something. Or sailing, rather. And there's no other island nearby that you might have been headed for. Why would you come to *this* island?"

I think about this for a long minute, willing the answer to come to mind.

"I really don't know."

"Can I make a suggestion?"

"Of course."

A smile. "Why don't you try writing?"

"Writing?"

He nods. "It really does stir up the subconscious. As therapy, for want of a better description. It's helped me with a lot of stuff. Childhood stuff." He bites his lip and looks down, a shadow passing across his face. "Anyway. It might help you remember your name."

"I'll give it a go," I say with a shrug.

He brightens. "I'll give you a notebook and pen. Get you started. Come on, then. Let's get you back on higher ground."

The climb saps the last of my energy. By the time I reach the top, I'm so out of breath that I want to be sick.

"Sit down," Joe instructs me. "Lean forward, like this."

He sits beside me and demonstrates. I copy him but still feel awful. My hips and shins ache and I'm weak from thirst. I decide to head back to the farmhouse and tell Joe to go on, but he insists on accompanying me. This time I head for the other route past more trees and shrubs surrounded by grass. Grass is easier on my joints. The ground rises up sharper than I'd realized, affording me a view of an elephant-shaped headland on the west of the island, a clean cleft of shimmering white rock.

A rhythmic gust of wind keeps me from feeling like I might drop to my knees. Joe steadies me.

"Keep back from the cliff," he warns, though the wind is so strong his voice sounds far away.

I sit down again, pressing my hands behind me and lifting my face to the sun.

"You don't look well," Joe says. "Why don't you stay here? I'll run up to the farmhouse and bring you some water. Maybe I can get George and we can carry you, save you walking?"

I shake my head, but even this small movement makes me feel woozy. My vision is beginning to blur at the edges. Joe doesn't wait for any further prompting but gets to his feet and begins to run up the hill.

It's then that I hear it: a raw, desperate cry, almost human. It's coming from the other side of the cliff. I crawl on all fours to the rocky edge and look over. The sea is below, licking the rocks. Dozens of nests dot the narrow ridges of the rock face at either side of me. Black birds with white faces sway against the wind, wings impressively wide, attending to white fluffy chicks bobbing in the nests, ravenous.

The shrieking rises to a clamor, a piercing wail. The sound of a cat or perhaps an infant. I sit back on my hips and all at once there is a burning sensation in my breasts, a sudden pain searing through them. I am alarmed—it's as though the noise is causing it. I have no idea what is happening.

I pull my T-shirt forward and peer down, expecting to find blood there. There's a slight wetness around my breasts, but no blood. A sugary smell rises up. Sweet and milky.

I turn and stagger back up the hill, hot, sharp stones digging into the soles of my feet and my breasts leaking, soaking my shirt. Something is terribly wrong, and I barely know how to describe it.

March 18, 2015

Potter's Lane, Twickenham

Lochlan: When I pull into our driveway with a screech of tires there is already a police van on the curb opposite, and a silver Mercedes facing me has a man and a woman in the front seats who jump to attention when they see me emerge from my car. I stride toward the front door and they race after me with that surprising paparazzi speed, calling out, "Mr. Shelley! Mr. Shelley!" And I say "not now" and shut the door in their faces.

Inside I can hear Cressida screaming and Magnus barking at someone down the phone. There is a man in the front room in my favorite armchair and a woman wearing a crisp white shirt and trouser suit. She rises to her feet when she sees me, and I hold up a hand to tell her to wait a second while I search out my screeching daughter in the kitchen.

Cressida is in Gerda's arms, fighting off a bottle. I pluck the bottle from Gerda's hand—it is ice-cold—and toss it in the microwave.

"It has to be warm, otherwise she won't take it," I say. How much I've learned in the last twenty-four hours.

"Well, it would have been nice to know that *before* you left," Gerda snaps.

I take Cressida, struck by a sudden affection for her, so small and fragile in my arms, her cries turning to whimpers when I hold her. She roots at my chest, as though expecting to find a nipple there. Not finding it, she's back to shrieking within seconds.

The microwave bleeps. I take out the bottle, give it a vigorous shake, and place the teat into Cressie's mouth. She sucks greedily, making piglet noises and bunching her fists tightly against the bottle. The milk foams against the sides of her mouth and her eyelids flicker, as though she's spent all her energy railing against cold milk and is now about to fall into a cloud-cushioned coma of satiation. She drains the bottle in about five minutes, but as soon as she's done she starts to cry again.

Frustrated, I pass her back to Gerda, who kisses the crown of her head and manages to console her. I head back to the living room to speak with the police.

The male detective leans forward and offers his hand. He is tall, serious looking and broad shouldered, early to mid forties, pale haired, dressed in a gray suit with a navy tie. He reminds me of Archie Sims, one of the posh kids from Year Ten who used to throw wet paper towels at me in the playground. He doesn't smile but gives me an iron handshake.

"Detective Sergeant Roy Canavan. I'm the OIC. Officer in charge. This is my colleague, DS Welsh."

The female detective is young: mid-twenties, soft face, light brown hair wrapped up in a bun. She extends her hand and nods out the window. "Seems we've already got some attention from the press."

"Yeah."

I'm not quite sure where to sit, and it occurs to me that my own home has become rearranged by the situation, this thing that shouldn't be happening, by these people who I shouldn't be encountering. It's like I'm visiting a place that reminds me of my house, and I'm waiting for someone to tell me where to put myself and how to act. I almost offer Detective-Sergeant-Canavan-the-OIC a stiff drink, and only as the words are about to tumble from my mouth do I realize this is probably not wise. He and DS Welsh sit on the sofa and each pulls out a notepad, ready for business. I take a seat in the armchair adjacent to them.

"Mrs. Bachmann—your grandmother-in-law?—said that some of the neighbors came forward this morning," DS Canavan says. "Mrs. Shahjalal's the one who raised the alarm, is that right?"

I nod. "She called me at work yesterday afternoon. She'd thought to check in on Eloïse after a delivery couldn't be made. Good job, too, otherwise Max and Cressida would have been alone all night and I wouldn't have known."

It's the first time I've said this aloud. What would have happened if Mrs. Shahjalal hadn't spotted Max? Cressida's so young that she could have become dangerously dehydrated in a matter of hours. Max is too young to know how to contact anyone. He might have tried to feed himself and Cressida. I can't bear to think of it. The tragedies that might have unfolded are too great.

"She mentioned that UPS tried to make a delivery here," he continues. "We're trying to locate the driver involved in case he heard or witnessed anything. One of your other neighbors from this side of the street—Mr. McWhirter—said he saw a car pull up outside your house yesterday around eleven o'clock in the morning."

I straighten. "Did he get the registration details?"

"No. He said it was a white saloon, not sure of the make or model. He's certain it mounted the pavement and remained parked for ten or twenty minutes. We'll make enquiries with local taxi companies. Another neighbor, Mrs. Malvern from number twenty-nine, said she thought she heard a shout sometime in the morning but couldn't be sure."

"My colleague noted that you had a faulty lock on the back door of this property, is that right?"

I nod, crushed. I should have fixed it. "Yes."

"There's been a couple of incidents over the last month in this area, so we'll make enquiries about that."

"Incidents?"

"Burglaries. You said no valuables were taken, correct?"

"As far as I can tell."

He searches my face, so I add: "I work away Monday through Thursday. So I suppose I'm not completely up to speed with everything in the house."

"We'll do a sweep of the door for prints."

DS Welsh tells me they want to ask me a few more questions, although a "few" in this case means so many I lose count. Medical numbers, insurance company details, schools we went to, everyone and anyone we have contact with. They want to know more about my job, about Eloïse's job, and I tell them that eight years ago she set up Children of War, a charity that offers emotional and educational support for refugee children. The detectives are deeply interested in this and take copious notes. When she set it up, what kind of work it involves. Their questions make me realize how much I don't know about the charity.

"Any colleagues holding a grudge against her?" DS Canavan asks. "Anyone who owes the charity money?"

"I'm afraid I have no idea."

He lifts his eyebrows. "She didn't talk about her job? The people she worked with?"

"I guess that Eloïse was so good at her job that everything looked to be very smooth." Even to my own ears I don't sound very convincing. Right before I go dig out my Bad Husband sackcloth, I remember that she really did make most things look effortless. That's why I didn't tend to ask. If anything was good or bad, I expected that she'd tell me. And of course, she's currently at home full-time with the kids.

He taps the pen against the page. "Even so, it's important that we get a complete picture of the events leading up to her disappearance. Any media interviews she might have given, anything work related at all, could prove extremely useful."

"What about her mental state?" Welsh asks from the other armchair.

"Eloïse's mental state?" I say. "What about it?"

"Well, she gave birth recently. Sometimes women can experience mood swings and depression."

I shake my head. "She was fine."

"Has she ever had any signs of depression or emotional instability in the past?"

A memory rises up. "Well, she saw a counselor for a while after Max was born, but other than that she was fine."

"What counselor?" Canavan says, and I can see he's writing down everything I've said and underlining it.

I rub my face, trying to think. "I honestly don't remember the name. I mean, it was over four years ago. A health visitor kept going on about El's moods after our son was born. Despite El saying she was fine, a bit tired, she had to go talk to someone. But she was discharged very swiftly. It was nothing."

"We'll look into that," Welsh says, throwing a look at Canavan.

"I really don't think this has anything to do with her going missing," I say, fearful that they'll waste time looking into something completely irrelevant. There's no way this has anything to do with El having a bad day.

"We need to rule this one out," Canavan says firmly. "We see a lot of cases where a loved one goes missing because they don't want to admit that they're struggling and don't know where to turn to for help."

"I'm pretty sure my wife doesn't fall into that category."

He ignores me. "Anything else you can think of? Anything missing, any personal belongings gone? Even a single credit card can make a huge difference to the investigation."

I shake my head, but then an image jumps into my mind: the Swiss passport. I tell Welsh and Canavan that it's gone, but that I haven't seen it in a long time anyway. "She never used it," I say. "More a token of her heritage than anything. Besides, if she'd used it to travel overseas I'd see it on the credit card statements. But I thought I'd mention it."

Both Welsh and Canavan react to this a lot stronger than I'd have anticipated. "She could have used cash to travel. You don't keep any at home?"

I tell him we do, but it's all still there.

Magnus and I begin to draw up a list of everyone El's ever had any association with, while Canavan writes up his notes. He interrupts Magnus and I to ask more questions: addresses and telephone numbers, a list of Eloïse's support network. I'm embarrassed to say that I can't recall the names of many of her friends and have no idea where they live. I promise to get the information off Facebook, but he tells me there's no need: they'll do their own investigation of my wife's social media activity and check out her e-mails. For this, they require every device she has access to: her laptop, tablet, and mobile phone. They'll check our bank accounts, Eloïse's charity, and they'll be speaking to our GP.

"So, what happens now?" I ask as the interview comes to an end. I feel wrung out.

"There are a number of steps in cases of missing persons," Canavan answers. "Eloïse is what we call high risk, given that she may not be fully recovered physically from the birth of your daughter. First, we'll need to do a search of the property."

I stare at him. "A search of the property?" Is he insinuating that I've murdered my wife and buried her under the gladioli?

DS Welsh must spot whatever crosses my face because she jumps in to explain. "We're aware that two small children are without a mother right now, and that Eloïse recently gave birth. Both things combined make this case a high priority. We really want to make sure we can locate her as fast as we can. Searching the property is standard procedure."

Welsh is convincingly sympathetic, and her role in this partnership becomes clear. She has a soft manner, the kind I usually associate with early years' teachers and childminders.

Once I've ascertained that I'm not about to be dragged from my children in handcuffs, I step away from the doorway, granting them entry to the stairs. Swiftly and efficiently they move throughout the house, peeling back the layers of our lives.

The search takes most of the afternoon. After some debate over whether or not I should send Max to nursery, Gerda and Magnus drop him off on the basis that his routine ought not to be too disturbed. Then they pack a baby bag and take Cressida to the park while I pace back and forth from the playroom to the kitchen, listening to the noises of strangers upstairs trawling through our cupboards and drawers, emerging every now and then with a box of toys or paperwork.

In the kitchen, I go through our family paperwork in the oak dresser to find anything that might indicate a reason for all of this, something concrete and reasonable. Receipts, birth certificates, Max's paintings from nursery. Still no sign of the Swiss passport, and so I phone our bank to make sure that there aren't any payments pending, no airline tickets booked. Then I turn yet again to El's laptop and phone, before the police have a chance to take them away. It takes me a while to work out her e-mail password, but finally I crack it: MaxJan11. I spend ages searching carefully for train or flight tickets, but there's nothing. I sign into her Facebook account. Her most recent status update hardly suggests anything out of the ordinary:

Big smiles from Cressida all morning! Love this girl ☺

She had sent text messages to her friends Rachael, Mimi, and Niamh about meeting up for coffee and the park and an eBay offer for a toddler bed. She'd made recent calls to the dry cleaner's, Gerda, and me. Her phone contains hundreds of photographs, a vast percentage taken by Max, it seems—these images are mostly of Max's nose, hand, and the carpet, with a few blurry shots of Cressida in various states of discomfort. There are several blurry ones of Eloïse, too, and on seeing these images I can't help but fall into a chair and wrestle with the urge to turn into a big mushy puddle of emotion. It's more out of frustration, or perhaps a concoction of extreme emotions, that I find myself with tears running down my face.

Max must have taken these. El seemed unaware that they were being taken. In one she is asleep in Max's bed, his *Thomas the Tank Engine* bed covers visible. In another she is sitting cross-legged on the floor by his *Peppa Pig* set. In another she is captured from behind as she stands at the back door, her head turned to the right. I flick to the next image, then go back.

She is holding something in her hand.

I zoom in to it. The image is blurry, and at first I dismiss the small white object as a pen, but on closer inspection I can determine that the ghostly white spiral above her hand is smoke winding upward like a thin white ribbon. A cigarette.

The date stamp is February 7, 2015. This year. A month ago. I study it for a long time, wondering if it is Eloïse in the picture or someone else, maybe one of her friends. El has never smoked. She was staunchly opposed to the whole concept of smoking, would choke and wave her hands if anyone lit up close by. It was actually embarrassing how vocal she'd get about it. I quit soon after we got together because she threatened to dump me if I didn't.

If for some reason she suddenly decided to take it up, surely she would have told me, of all people? And why when Cressida was barely eight weeks old? Eloïse decided to become more or less vegan to ensure that Cressida got the best nutrition while being breastfed—so, *smoking?* I'm amazed. It doesn't seem to fit the picture, and yet here she is. Smoking. I almost want to laugh, it's that bizarre. I have no way of even beginning to interpret what this discovery means.

I flick through all the images, studying them for any signs of anything equally mis-fitting. One of the videos shows El laughing and clapping as Cressida kicked her legs on the play mat. This is consistent with the woman I know and love, and so I give a big sigh of relief, as though I've found her again. Another clip shows her in the living room sleeping as Max tells the camera to be very quiet and not wake Mummy up.

I make a mental note to think carefully about how to ask Max about Mummy smoking.

As I'm figuring out how to work the dishwasher, DS Canavan comes into the kitchen holding out a baby monitor. "We're going to have our technical team look over these, if that's OK?"

I nod. "Yes, of course." I tell him I've already checked them in the hope that they might tell us where she's gone. He perks up at this, and I feel gut-kicked all over again when I tell him they were turned off.

"Have you the one set of monitors, or are there any more around the house?"

This, I *can* answer.

"We have four. A camera in each of the kids' bedrooms, one in the playroom and one overlooking the landing upstairs. They're wireless."

"And did you link up the babycam to any online account?"

"My wife had them synced to her phone. I've already checked. She had the monitors switched off."

Canavan nods.

"We'll get our tech team to check it out."

March 20, 2015

Komméno Island, Greece

My dreams are strange and vivid. I dream I am holding a ball of red wool and walking from the back door of the farmhouse toward the outside. Only, the island with its vast blue sprawl of ocean is not to be found beyond the threshold—instead, I step through the door to a dark cave.

I am terrified of the dark, of the cave entrance marked with fang-like stalactites and jagged walls, but somehow I know I have to go in. I have no choice. I find a cigarette lighter in my back pocket and flick it to illuminate my path. At my feet I can see shallow puddles of muddy water. The cave is narrow, though the ceiling is high—about fifteen feet. The cave does not stretch very far ahead but seems to twist and bend around many corners, widening at some parts to ten or twelve feet and then narrowing again to three or four. I keep the ball of wool in one hand and the flickering lighter in the other, my mouth dry with anticipation.

At one point I notice the wool has started to unravel on the ground behind me. I stoop to pick it up, and as the light struggles to remain it occurs to me that it isn't a bad idea to let the wool unravel—when I need to return to the entrance, I will be able to find my way, even if the light dies out altogether.

So I press on, deeper into the cave, the small flame from my lighter gradually washing my surroundings in a yellow haze. The stalactites grow longer, wider, dripping with moisture, an occasional rustling sound signaling the presence of bats. My skin crawls, but I close my eyes and whisper to myself. *It's OK. You can do this. Don't be afraid. Keep going and you'll find your way back.*

After a long while I seem to reach some kind of central point, a circular space with several pathways leading off it. I find a large round rock and sit down with my ball of wool, which is now no bigger than a plum. I have very little wool left, and my lighter is running out of gas. I'll need the wool to find my way back, but I know I have to keep going until I find the end. There is something there, waiting for me. I have to find it.

As I stand up to choose a path, a loud noise shakes the walls of the cave. A deep, muscular growl, belonging to something larger than a dog or wolf. A rhino, perhaps, or an ox.

I drop my lighter and the cave plunges into soupy darkness. I scramble around on the ground trying to find it, splashing my knees, hands, and face in pools of stagnant water. The growling has started up again, a rumbling sound about a hundred yards away. Finally, my fingers hit against a small plastic object, and I scoop up the lighter. But no matter how much I thumb the switch, the light won't return.

"Hello? Excuse me?"

I wake to someone shaking me, a pair of bony hands gripping my arm and a voice hissing something I can't make out. It takes a handful of seconds to gather where I am: bright sunlight from a round window, the smell of damp. I'm in the attic and a reedy figure with a wooly head of hair is standing over me. Hazel.

"Hello?" she says. "Hello, hello, hello?"

"What?" I whisper.

"Gosh, it's really weird not having a name to call you by. Should we make one up for you?"

I look at what she's holding: a saucer and teacup that is filled to the brim with a watery green liquid. I catch a whiff of it—chemical and herbal at the same time.

"What's that?"

"What? Oh, it's sage tea."

"Sage tea?"

"Sariah said you need to drink all of it. She said it would help."

I struggle to sit upright. My arms have no strength in them and I feel dizzy, even though I'm lying down. Hazel sets the cup and saucer on the ground and helps me, propping a pillow between me and the bedhead.

"There. Better?"

She lowers and retrieves the cup and saucer. I take them from her and inspect the contents: hot water tinted pea green, two oval leaves visible at the bottom of the cup. I sniff it. It smells foul.

"I'm OK," I say, handing it back, but Hazel looks alarmed.

"No. Sariah said you have to."

"I have to?"

Hazel has pulled up a chair beside my bed, her hands folded in her lap.

"It's for your—you know."

"My what?"

She tuts as though I'm being silly, then leans forward and whispers, "Your *boobs*."

I wonder for a moment whether she's joking, but then the pain stirs again: a deep, sharp invisible wound, as though someone is pushing hot pokers through my nipples. My T-shirt is stuck to my chest, like something has oozed out and dried. It's not blood.

Hazel is wide-eyed and solemn, like a toddler that's said a naughty word for the first time. She's like a very young, mischievous child trapped in a fifty-year-old's body.

"Sariah said you must have engorgement because your boobs had too much milk. You know, after the walk you went on with Joe? She said the sage tea will make it go away and you'll be better again."

I raise a hand to my breasts, though they no longer feel connected to me. They feel like hot stones someone has placed on my chest to weigh me down. Hazel watches me silently, her head cocked in curiosity, as I drink the disgusting tea. When I finish, she says, "Did it work?"

"Hazel, did you say I have breast milk?"

"Huh? Oh, yes. That's what Sariah said."

A chill runs over me. This means I have a child. A young child. Why can't I remember this? Was the child in the boat with me? Did he or she drown?

"Hey, calm down," Hazel says, standing up and stroking

my hair. "Come on, now. Stop crying. You've got to stop crying, it's not going to make anything any better."

I can't speak. My mouth is filled with terrible noises. I feel so angry and confused. Why am I here? Why can't I remember what happened?

Eventually Hazel wraps her arms around me and holds me until I calm down.

"There, there," she says, and even though her arms are like twigs, I feel myself beginning to take deeper breaths.

"It's all right," she says. "We're here for you. We're looking after you."

I wipe tears from my face. Crying has whisked away the last of my energy.

"Which reminds me: you need to take these as well."

I find two small white pills in my hand. "What are they?"

"Painkillers, I think. Joe sent them up. He said you need to keep taking them until all the muscles in your neck start to heal."

I toss them back with the dregs of the tea. Hazel remains seated, one leg folded over the other, giving off eager vibes. As much as I'm grateful for her bringing these up, I want to sleep. I tell her thank you and shuffle myself gently downward into the bed, sleep already pulling at my eyelids.

"What shall we call you, then?" Hazel asks breezily.

I give a deep sigh. I don't care what she calls me.

"How about 'Hazel'?"

I give her a look. "Isn't that *your* name?"

"Don't you like it?"

"Aren't you writing today?" I ask weakly.

She shakes her head. "Hate it."

"You hate writing?"

"Yes. Hate it," she says, with a weird little smile on her face, a kind of smirk. "But I told Sariah, Joe, and George that I'd go along with it and behave myself." She pouts, then bites her lip.

Go along with what? I don't know what to say.

"Are you really not able to remember anything?" she asks, petulant. "Or are you pretending?"

"Pretending? Why on earth would I pretend?"

Her tiny gray eyes are fixed on me, checking I'm telling the truth.

"I don't know," she says with a shrug. I thought you might be. Weird, not to remember who you are. You'll stay here a little longer, though, won't you? It's nice having another person here."

I'm flattered, but frankly I'm not staying here a minute longer than I need to. If I've got breast milk it obviously means I must have a child. I need to get off this island as quickly as I can. I ask her, "Did George hear anything from the police on Crete?"

"No. Nothing." She bites her lip. "Look, I want to tell you something."

"About the police?"

"No, not about the police." She turns to look behind her. From where I'm sitting, the door appears to be closed. Then she leans forward and whispers: "I've got a secret."

"A secret?"

She grins, a light coming on behind her eyes. "I'm not supposed to tell."

I fall quiet. Her words have riven me with fear.

"What aren't you supposed to tell, Hazel?"

"You promise you won't say anything?"

"I promise."

She looks suddenly afraid. "'Cos if you do, George would..."

"George would what?"

She draws back. I can feel my heart racing. What is it she wants to tell me?

"You're not leaving this island."

"What?"

A sharp knock at the door makes us both jump.

"Hazel?" a voice calls. "Are you in there, Hazel?"

Hazel darts across the room. "Coming!"

At the door she turns to me, drawing a finger against her lips, and my mouth falls open. She said I'm not leaving this island. Why would she say that?

Sariah steps into the room. She eyes Hazel, then glances over at me.

"Are you all right?" she asks, and I say I am. I see that she's carrying a tray of food, the smell of it winding toward me and making my mouth water.

I sit upright again, part of me energized by the prospect of food, the other anxious to ask Sariah why Hazel would say such a strange thing.

"Here we go," Sariah says with a warm smile, sweeping across the room in a long turquoise dress. She always looks like a Moroccan queen, all vibrant colors, beaded jewelry, and a kind of gracious manner that I find very soothing. She brings the tray close to the bed and searches for somewhere to set it, opting to make do with the chair that Hazel was sitting on. Then she turns right the way around and glares at Hazel, who is still lurking in the doorway, biting her nails.

"Is everything OK, Hazel?" Sariah asks.

The sound of floorboards creaking announces Hazel's departure down the stairs. Sariah turns back to me, her smile returning.

"Now, then. No, no. Stay where you are. I can help you eat this, OK?"

She stirs a bowl of red, fragrant soup, spooning some of it into my mouth. She asks about the tea, if I drank it, then asks how I'm feeling, where it hurts, and how badly. When I tell her, she listens and nods and strokes my hand.

"What was Hazel saying?" she asks.

"She said I'm not leaving this island."

She looks up and studies the air ahead of her, as though my words are written there. "Hazel said that?"

I think back, questioning myself—did I misread Hazel's tone?—and Sariah sighs and shakes her head.

"Ignore her," she says, spooning more soup into my mouth. "She's a head full of crazy, that girl. She's fascinated by you. That's what this is."

"Fascinated?"

"Leave it to me," she says, straightening. A flicker of a smile. "I'll tell her not to bother you."

I'm caught in a sudden flurry of questions, and as though sensing this Sariah says, "You're probably wondering why on earth the four of us would come all the way out here to a Greek island with nothing but goats and sunshine."

It's not an invitation to respond, so I stay quiet.

"Now, I'm not one for making anyone do anything against their will," she says, her accent thickening. "But I did put a little pressure on the guys to come to this place. Part of that reason is owed to the solitude, yes, but the rest of the reason lies in the stories my mama told me when I was a little girl. My mama had been to Greece loads of times, and she loved the myths. The building blocks of every story we ever learned, those myths. And her favorite was Pandora. You know, the box?"

I nod.

She continues, offering me more soup. "The story goes that Pandora was told not to open a box and her curiosity got the better of her, and of course she went ahead and opened it and out flew all life's bad stuff. Right?" She pauses, shakes her head: "Wrong. This is the version of the myth that's been passed down. The original myth states very clearly that Pandora knew *exactly* what was in that box. At least, that's what my mama said. I don't know. That version stuck with me my whole life." She stirs the soup with slow, thoughtful strokes, scooping a small amount and spooning it into my mouth. She waits until I've swallowed, until I'm listening.

"Lately, I've been thinking about it more and more. It seems to me, that addition, the fact that she knew, changes the whole story. It makes Pandora brave. A tigress. She hesitated not because she was obedient, but because she was weighing it up. Better to live a life free of trouble, or face up to the way things are and grow from it?"

She pauses, searching my face. "What I'm saying is, if you suspect you might be hiding from something, if you think you might not want to face up to something, my advice to you is: be a tigress."

I give as much of a nod as my neck will allow, and she remains thoughtful and intent on making me finish the soup.

March 18, 2015

Potter's Lane, Twickenham

Lochlan: Magnus and Gerda should be back by now. Max finished nursery at half past three and it's after four. I ring Gerda's mobile and there's no answer. I feel sick as I try Magnus's number again. They've had a car accident, I know it. I don't think I can take much more of this.

"Hello?" Magnus answers.

"Magnus, where *are* you? It's twenty past four."

"Wait a minute, I'll pass you on to Gerda." A muffled sound as the phone passes between hands, then Gerda's nasal tones.

"Who is this?"

"Where the hell are you? Where are my children?"

"We're coming up your street now, darling, keep your pants on."

I stride out into the street to see Magnus's silver Bentley

driving at a snail's pace toward me. He parks on the curb and gets out while I shake out my hands, sick with nerves. I open the passenger door and reach in for Max, who has already unclipped himself out of his child seat and is pulling a wad of paper out of his backpack.

"Daddy! Daddy! Look what I made at nursery! It's for Mummy!"

He thrusts a folded card covered in paint and glitter at me before racing toward the house, his *Thomas the Tank Engine* raincoat trailing after him.

"Max!" I shout. "Come back!"

My voice startles Cressida, who begins to shriek in her car seat, but I chase after Max, fearful that he might deviate from his course toward our house and sprint on to the road, or trip.

"I'll get the baby, shall I?" Gerda snaps as I race past her.

Inside, Max calls frantically for Eloïse. His first port of call is the kitchen, where the red tulips I bought on his behalf to gift to Eloïse for Mother's Day are still going strong in a vase by the window, the cards we painted for her attached to the fridge with magnets.

"Is Mummy not back yet?" Max asks, looking under the kitchen table.

I'm too flustered and exhausted to come up with a decent lie.

"Come here, Maxie. I need to ask you a question."

I squat down, waving my hand for him to come, but he continues searching, finally making to rush past me into the other rooms of the house. I catch him and put my hands on his shoulders.

"Maxie, I need to ask you about Mummy," I say. A part of my brain is demanding that I take a moment to plan what

I'm going to ask, to take time choosing my words. It's a delicate thing to be asking him, especially when he's so perplexed by her absence. The other part of me is in knots from the police searching through our house, and from seeing the photo of Eloïse with a cigarette in her hand.

"Max? Max," I say, because although I've managed to get him to stand still, his eyes are searching behind me and he's standing on his tiptoes scanning the house for anything that might signal her presence. At last I manage to get his attention.

"Max, do you know how Granddad Angus smokes?"

He thinks about it, then nods.

"Well, I was wondering if maybe you had spotted anyone else smoking?"

His eyes light up. "Yes. I saw a lady with a cigarette."

"Yeah?"

"Yeah, and she dropped it on the ground, Daddy, and she didn't pick it up, and that's naughty, isn't it, Daddy?"

"Yes, but... OK, I mean, here. In our house. Mummy didn't smoke, did she?"

"Smoking puts black stuff in here." He points at his chest. "That's what Granddad Magnus said."

"OK, but..."

"Daddy?"

"Yes?"

"Does that mean Granddad Angus has black stuff inside him?"

"Max? I need you to listen. Can you do that?"

"Yes, Daddy."

Fear edges his voice, and the fright on his face makes me chide myself. I mustn't be too harsh with him. I need to be gentle.

"Max, did you ever see Mummy smoking?"

"Ummm, no. Yes."

"Yes?"

"Well, I think Mummy had one, didn't she?"

I'm stunned all over again. "Mummy smoked a cigarette?"

He leans forward and whispers, "Yeah, but don't tell anyone. It's a secret."

"Why?"

"It's naughty to smoke a cigarette."

"Did Mummy say why she smoked one?"

"Can I have Netflix, Daddy?"

"Absolutely. But can you tell me why Mummy smoked one?"

"Can I watch *Peppa Pig*?"

"Max? Why did Mummy smoke?"

"I think...to help her feel better."

Gently I push his hair back from his face, trying to keep eye contact. "What about when you woke up and Mummy was gone? Can you remember that, Maxie?"

I know it's the wrong thing to ask the moment the words are out of my mouth. His expression changes from playfulness to worry, his eyes turning from mine to search her out.

"Can you get your phone and tell Mum to come home now, please?"

"She'll be back soon, Maxie."

He looks up at me with wide, hopeful eyes.

"When?"

"I don't know."

Stupid, stupid, stupid.

His face drops. "You said she was coming back."

I kneel down and, despite every instinct that tells me to

change the subject back to Netflix, I say: "She's had to go to a conference for her charity, Maxie. You know the way she helps boys and girls who don't have a home anymore?"

It's working. His expression lifts in thought, mulling over the image of his mother off doing work on behalf of children who don't have any toys or Netflix.

"Mamie said Mummy was staying with a friend for a little while."

The front door slams and Gerda and Magnus's voices creep through the hallway. Max turns and pulls open the kitchen door, running to them.

"Mamie! Is Mummy with her friend?"

Gerda turns at the doorway to the living room, Cressida in her arms, punching the air. She frowns at me.

"Um, yes. Mummy's with a friend, darling," she says to Max. Her tone fails to convince him and he turns back to me.

"But Daddy said Mummy's...Where did you say Mummy went?"

"Your mother's had to go away," Magnus barks from the other room, stepping forward to take Cressida from Gerda only to bounce her up and down. Moments later, she pukes on his shirt.

Max bursts into tears. He turns and races up the stairs, yelling, "Mummy! Mummy!"

"Smooth, Magnus," I say, striding up the stairs after my son. "Bloody brilliant."

"Pardon?"

I turn, halfway up. "Why did you have to yell at him like that?"

"I never yelled at anyone," he yells, his deep voice magnified by the tiled hallway.

I head across the landing toward the sound of Max's weeping. He's in his bedroom, both hands deep in the plastic box full of wooden train tracks. One by one he pulls them out and throws them around the room.

"Max, stop it!" I say, but he gets more frantic as I approach him. I can't think fast enough to calculate my moves, so I end up trying to pick up all the wooden pieces of train track that he's dumping on the ground and setting them back into the box.

Gerda comes in, hand on her hip. "Didn't you sterilize the baby bottles?"

I hold my face in my hands and groan. "No, I forgot."

"Go away!" Max screams at her.

"Now, now, Max, that's not what nice boys say," Gerda chides him.

"Come here, Maxie," I say, but he tips the box of train tracks all over my lap and flings himself to the floor. I try to pick him up but he writhes and shouts.

"Don't want you! Want Mummy!"

I lift him by the waist and try to carry him into my bedroom. He is remarkably strong, almost throwing himself out of my arms when I change position. I turn him around so that his back's to my chest, my arms wrapped around his waist, but all of a sudden he kicks me hard with his heel in the balls. I cry out and fling him onto the bed.

He lies still while I cup my testicles, holding back the urge to smack him. I hobble beside him and sit down, but immediately he turns his face away from me.

"Want Mummy," he sniffles into a cushion.

It's a struggle not to yell, *Where is she? You must have seen something!*

"Max, before Mrs. Shahjalal came, did you see Mummy go somewhere?"

"Want Mummy!"

"Can you tell me, Maxie? Did someone come to the house?"

Gerda watches from the doorway.

"Magnus has already tried asking him," she says. "He can't understand, he's too little."

"I think I know my own son, thank you," I snarl. Her face tightens. I turn back to Max, stroking his head. "Maxie, you can tell me, OK? Please tell Daddy. Where did Mummy go? Did someone take her?"

Max sniffles and glances back to me. For a moment he looks like he's going to answer, but then he scrunches his face up in anger and screams, "Hate you!," before running to Gerda. She throws me another withering look before walking away with Max clinging to her leg.

"Why's Mummy not here?" he cries. "Where's Mummy gone?"

April 11, 1983

Geneva, Switzerland/London, England

"Where are we going, Mummy?"

The girl was half-awake, having been carried out of her bed by an unseen pair of arms and dressed hastily in the cold dark of the bathroom. From there she was bundled into a car, the sound of someone scraping ice off the windscreen bringing her to her senses. She started to grow upset when the car pulled away, but then she realized her teddy, Peter, had been inserted into her coat—between the coat's zipper and her chest—and she fell quiet. Her mother was in the front seat and a man with black hair and brown hands was driving. The girl had been introduced to the man some weeks ago but she couldn't quite connect this brief introduction to the reason why he seemed to be taking them somewhere at a very strange hour.

They'd driven until morning, when the sky was sparrow's

egg blue and people's breaths sailed upward like clouds. Then they'd parked the car and her mother had taken some big bags out of the back of the car and told her to hurry. They were at a train station, lots of people rushing past, lots of noise and urgency, and they were approaching a gateway that reminded her of the sheep stalls at that farm they sometimes went to, where all the animals had to push through a kind of gate. Her mother and the man had tickets and were observing the large clock overhead.

"Mummy, where are we going?" the little girl asked. This time she spoke in French. Her mother looked down at her.

"London, Ellie. We're going to London with Orhan. Isn't that exciting?"

A sharp whistle sounded close by, making the girl jump. She felt herself being pulled forward, her mother transformed by a rush of strangers into a pair of bodiless feet in brown lace-up shoes. The girl clutched her mother's unseen hand and felt the cool licks of morning air as they made it to the platform, where a train sat like a serpent, waiting.

The girl saw the man—Orhan—climb on board, before turning to take her mother's hand. The girl stopped.

"What's wrong?" her mother asked.

"What about Mamie?" the girl asked, and she started to cry. "What about Papa?"

"Come on, Jude!" Orhan called from the train, but the girl's mother bent down and brought herself level with her daughter's face.

"Orhan says London is better for us, OK?"

The girl shook her head. In the book that Mamie read to her last night, trains took people far, far away. She didn't want to go far away. She wanted to go home.

"You'll like it," her mother said, before disappearing onto the train.

A queue of people brushed past the girl to take their seats. She was still on the platform, her mother apparently leaving it up to her to decide whether or not she was coming. She turned and looked back across the platform, at the skirts and trousers that were at her eye level and the roof of the station where pigeons roosted along the girders.

A sharp whistle rang out, indicating that the doors were about to close. Just then, something knocked against the girl, bringing her back to her senses. She had to get on the train. She spied the something that had knocked into her—the large backside of a woman as she bustled onto the train. From the corner of her eye, the woman spotted the girl, then turned and extended a hand to her.

"Come on, now. Get on quick before the doors close!"

Without thinking, the girl took the woman's hand and felt herself lifted through the air onto the train. The doors slammed tightly behind her, a whistle sounded, and the jerk of the train knocked her to the ground. But the woman was there again, lifting her up. She bent down and smiled.

"You OK?"

The girl nodded.

"What's your name, sweetie?"

"Eloïse." *El-wheeze.*

"You on your own?"

Behind the woman, Eloïse spotted her mother, waving at her impatiently from the row of seats ahead. She shook her head.

"My mummy's there."

"OK. Be careful, now."

Eloïse headed in the direction of her mother, swaying from

side to side along the aisle as the train juddered over the track. When she sat down beside her mother she saw the woman take a seat a few rows ahead of them on the other side of the train. She seemed very capable, and there was an element of difference about her—different than Eloïse's mother, at least. She studied her for a long time, noticed the peculiar way her black hair was twisted, like ropes, admiring the brown shade of her skin. She had liked the way the woman was built— broad shouldered, like a man—and even the tattoo on her wrist had seemed to indicate strength. Eloïse felt set adrift and wrung with fear. She was four years old, still sucking her thumb, but she sensed that her mummy did not know how to care for her. There had been that time at the shopping center when she'd allowed Eloïse to go wandering off, and even when they called her mother's name over the loudspeaker it took over an hour before someone came for her. And it wasn't her mummy that came but her grandfather, his face flushed with anger and worry.

Eloïse kept her eyes on the woman who had helped her on the train. She would have given anything for the woman to venture over to her and persuade Eloïse's mother to let her look after her. But that wasn't going to happen.

When she woke up, she was in a strange house. It was small and very messy, clothes and papers strewn across the floor, and it smelled different. A large window behind her overlooked the backs of redbrick houses. It wasn't like her grandparents' house, which was surrounded by beautiful hills and lakes and had chickens in the garden. And where was Peter, her best teddy?

She could hear a noise in the room across from her, a tap-tapping noise like a bird or small animal. She got up and

103

tiptoed toward it and whispered, "Peter?" She knew when Peter was sad and when he was happy, and even when he was feeling mischievous or cheeky. There was a difference in his expression that only she could read, and besides, she could sense his mood deep in her bones. When she found him, she said, "Never leave me, Peter. Promise?"

She stood at the threshold of the room and saw what was making the sound: the man who'd been driving the car was putting stickers on the windows. He turned and gave her a broad smile, and she instantly smiled back.

"Hello, Eloïse," he said, and she remembered his name. Orhan, that was it. *Oar hand.* His voice was different from her mummy's and she couldn't work out why. "Are you still sleepy?"

She shook her head, translating his mood like a weather vane reading whispers in the sky. He seemed bouncy and happy, not like her mummy, who seemed to be covered in invisible prickles.

He waved to her, gesturing for her to come and see what he was doing, but she was hesitant. "Where's Mummy?" she said.

"Mummy's sleeping," he said. "She's a little tired after the journey. Oh, but look what I found."

He picked something up from the ground—Peter—and she ran to it, clutching him tightly.

Orhan grinned. "I thought you'd be missing him."

She looked at Orhan deeply, noticing how his eyes were big and chocolatey like Princess Leia's. There were cuts on his face with tiny pieces of toilet paper stuck to them, red dots of blood in the center, and he had very yellow teeth.

"You got hurted?" she said, touching the paper delicately.

"Oh. No, that's from shaving."

She looked at him deeply. "It doesn't hurt?"

He shook his head. "No, no. It's fine." Then: "You like your new room?"

She looked around. There was a small bed in the middle of the room with a fluffy pink quilt on it. A white chest of drawers, white walls, and a lampshade with pink fairies on it.

"*My* room?" she said, and he nodded. "What about my old one?"

"This one's much better. We're in London, you see, which is better than Geneva, and you're going to make new friends and get lots of toys."

Despite his excited tone she felt a tightness in her chest at the thought of this. Mamie and Papa didn't seem to be part of her new life. She wanted to ask when she'd see them again, but she sensed this would make the man disappointed and she didn't want him to be disappointed in her. He had already turned back to the window of the room and was pointing out long white bars that looked both pretty and odd against the window frame.

"...to protect you," he was explaining. "I put these up to keep you safe. You see?"

She reached out and gripped one of the bars, running her hand up and down it. It felt cold and smooth, like the bars on her cot. She had still slept in her cot at Mamie's house, even though they'd offered to buy her a big girl's bed, because in the cot felt safe and secure.

"To keep me safe," she repeated, and Orhan nodded.

"How old are you, Eloïse?" he asked, and she held up four fingers.

"I think you turned four, didn't you? What would you like for your birthday present?"

She made to mention that her birthday was some time ago, but Peter interrupted.

"Peter says he'd like a bicycle."

"Who's Peter?"

"My teddy."

He grinned. "Isn't Peter too small to ride a bike?"

"A bicycle with a basket on the front so Peter can sit in there and I can ride it."

When she turned to him again she could see flashes of silver at the sides of his head, like Papa. Orhan seemed lots older than Mummy, more Mamie's age than Mummy's age.

"OK. If you're a good girl, you can get a bicycle for your birthday," Orhan said, setting her back down to the ground. "Now, why don't you go and play?"

She took Peter and began to introduce him to the new room, to the lampshade and the new bed, which she promised he'd find very cozy. Peter was very, very nervous, and he wasn't so keen on Orhan, but she told him in her head that Orhan was nice and was keeping them safe. Then Peter saw Orhan take something out of a bag and begin screwing it to the inside of the door.

"What's that?" she asked Orhan.

"It's a lock."

"A lock."

"Yes. It locks the door, see? To keep you safe."

Peter asked her why Orhan was putting the lock so high on the door. Surely she wouldn't be able to reach that? What if she wanted to get out of the room?

And then, Orhan reached up and locked it. She watched him, puzzled, as he sat down on the bed and watched her.

What do you think he's doing? she asked Peter in her mind.

I don't know, Peter answered. *Maybe he's tired.*

Orhan turned and said, "Do you still feel safe?"

Do you feel safe, Peter?

I guess so.

She nodded. Orhan moved closer and crouched down beside her. "But do you feel safe with me?"

"Yes," she said, not wanting to hurt his feelings.

He smiled, and she was happy because he was smiling.

March 23, 2015

Komméno Island, Greece

Today, Nikodemos, the man who owns the island and the missing boat, is coming from Chania in Crete to collect me and take me to the police station there. I'm excited and nervous. Excited to find out where I came from and who I've left behind, and hopefully to get treatment to restore my memory. Nervous in case the police have no report of anyone missing and they aren't able to help return me to wherever I've originated. Nervous in case they say they can't help someone who doesn't remember her own name. Terrified in case I uncover a terrible truth. I know I must have a son or daughter. What sort of person forgets their own child? What if I find out I've done something so terrible that I'll never be able to live with myself?

It's almost five right now, and I've had a shower and washed and dried my clothes. The next step is to say good-bye to everyone and head to the dock for the boat to arrive. It's only been a few days and yet I feel as though I'll be lost without them. And I guess they were the ones that found me. The only people I remember.

I spent the weekend sleeping and it seems to have helped me recover. The bruises on my legs and back are starting to improve and I'm not in as much pain. The awful agony of my breasts has gone and I also have better mental clarity, but the real damage must be very deep—I still can't remember who I am. I am pretty certain that I have a degree in art history, though I have no idea where I studied or when: the fact that I have this degree is simply in my brain, like knowing that red is a primary color. I was pretty excited when the knowledge of my degree appeared, completely out of the blue, and I was confident that other memories would follow on the heel of it. But they haven't. I've felt waves of familiarity washing over me, and when I try to summon my name to mind I can make out letters: an L and an E. I have a strange déjà vu that I try to seize upon, and when I woke this morning I was certain that I had remembered: it was right there in my mind, solid and sure, but the harder I tried to recognize what it was, the more it slipped away from me.

I haven't been able to place the sensation of familiarity or work out *why* something should feel familiar. But there is one thing I seemed to recognize that has bothered me. Joe is familiar. He said he was a first-aider, and that he'd resuscitated me. Maybe that was why he seemed familiar to me? Because he was the first person I saw when I regained consciousness? I even wondered if I was *forcing* myself to remember life before this island.

I have really struggled to work out why he seems familiar. Perhaps he looks like someone I know in real life? I can't quite explain it. In any case, he obviously has never met me before I washed up on Bone Beach.

Yesterday, I slept all day and woke when it was dark with a pounding headache. I staggered downstairs and found all four of my hosts around the dining table, holding wineglasses and enjoying dinner.

"Good evening," Sariah greeted me. We never settled on what to call me until I find out my real name. "Would you care to join us?"

I hadn't seen Sariah since she came up to the attic and fed me soup. I'd told her about Hazel's strange comment to me—*You're never leaving this island*—and she dismissed it. Crazy, that's what she'd called Hazel. Still, Hazel's words have stuck with me and in between periods of deep, enveloping sleep I've wondered about what she said.

It's a callous and deeply sinister thing to say to someone who has amnesia, and who is dependent on strangers to figure out a way home from a wilderness in the middle of the ocean. I decided that I had to confront her about it, that there had to be a meaning behind it, but as I was gearing myself up to go downstairs I saw her through the window, doing some kind of weird dance in the garden. She was flapping her arms like a bird and doing cartwheels, then swaying and pulling her skirt up over her knees. I picked over her comment again in my mind and decided that the words held no threat, and no promise of any mystery. It was just Hazel being dramatic.

At the dining table she avoided my gaze. Joe and George were sitting at the table on either side of her. Sariah had

110

prepared lamb kleftiko with an apricot and honey dressing, potato and feta skewers, and pita with plenty of olive oil.

"Your bruises don't look as bad," Joe said, stuffing his mouth full of pita. "What about your memory? You remember your name yet?"

"No."

"What about your age?" George asked gruffly. "Or where you've come from?"

I shook my head.

"Crikey."

"That must be very frustrating," Sariah added.

I nodded, but Joe said: "Depends on how you look at it. If you forget everything, you don't have any regrets, do you?"

Sariah laughed lightly. "I guess I'd rather have my memory in full working order."

Hazel seemed to contemplate this. "Selective amnesia would be nice. Wouldn't you think they'd invent a kind of surgery that would take away all the bad things that happened to you in the past?"

"They have—it's called a lobotomy," George said grimly, lighting a cigarette. I felt as though I was no longer part of the conversation.

"There was a film about that," Joe chipped in. "Jim Carrey was in it."

"I'd like amnesia," Hazel said. "Just a little bit, you know. I reckon I wouldn't have had to go to therapy for all those years if someone had smacked me hard on the head."

"It can still be arranged," George said with a grin, and she gave him a twitchy look.

"I think we *all* have amnesia to a degree," Sariah offered, pouring me a glass of wine. "I mean, does anyone recall being born? The most significant moment of your life and not one person remembers it."

"Or do they?" Hazel whispered conspiratorially.

"I think it says a lot about the human condition," Joe says.

"What does?"

Joe paused, looking blank. "I've forgotten."

"Touché!" Hazel chirped.

I watched Hazel and George carefully, trying to fathom the dynamic of their relationship. It was hard to place. As I watched them chat that white space in my mind flickered with an image, just for an instant—I was in a room with four other people, and we were sitting around a long table, writing. I tried to think what I was writing, who the other people were. Where the room was. But just as quickly as it had arrived, the memory faded.

"How did your writing go today?" I asked.

Joe frowned and ran his fingers through his hair. "Some days it flows, others it's like breaking rocks with a fork," he said with a sigh.

"I would have thought the muse would give generously in a place like this," I said.

The others made noises of agreement. Joe took off his glasses and rubbed the lenses with the hem of his T-shirt. "I got a lot done today, even so. Some editing. A new villanelle. Some ideas scribbled down for tomorrow."

George arched an eyebrow. "And how many words is a villanelle?"

Joe shrugged. "It's not about word count with poetry."

"Well, how many *lines* is a villanelle?"

Joe counted on his fingers. "About nineteen?"

George made a "ppssh" sound, as if nineteen was nothing, and Hazel started to chuckle.

"What?" said Joe.

George leaned toward me in confidence and tilted his chin at Joe. "Last year, me and Hazel finished a whole novel each while we were here. Ask Joe how many poems he wrote. Go on, ask him."

Joe rolled his eyes.

"Fifty?" I said.

"Six," Joe said, and everyone burst out laughing.

"Six poems in *a month*," George said, shaking his head.

"Hey, they were intricate poems," Joe said, matter-of-factly. "Poetry is about the economy of language. Each word has to be weighed—"

"—and measured," Hazel finished. "Yes, you've told us."

Joe plucked a leather notebook from the worktop and handed it to me, the page opened to one of his poems. It was handwritten in a spidery scrawl with black ink.

Union
I heard the creep of ice.
I heard the wolf-cry of the sea.
I heard the slowing dawn.
I heard the night drown in the trees.
I heard the return in the bend.
I heard the whisper of amends between darkness
and light.
I heard what the silence confessed.

I didn't really understand the poem—or if I was meant to understand it—and I was keen to keep up the slightly elevated mood. But as I read it, a deeper instinct told me that I had read this poem before. I looked up at Joe.

"This is one of your poems?" I said.

He nodded. Then, detecting the edge of disbelief to my voice: "Why?"

I looked at it again. Yes, I had definitely read this poem before. I *knew* this poem, the flow of the sentences, the rhythm of the lines.

"I thought I recognized it," I explained. "Like maybe it was written by Alexander Pope, or Shakespeare."

Everyone laughed, and Joe looked hugely flattered.

"Gosh, thank you very much," he said.

And it was then, right as Hazel was asking me how I knew who Alexander Pope was and whether that meant I was beginning to remember, right as George lit another cigarette and Joe leaned toward me to read the poem for himself, as though he might see it anew, that it struck me: not only did I know the poem, but I also knew Joe. Something about his smell, his long, pale fingers...I stared at him until he caught my eye, and I struggled to form a context for this recognition. Was it the square glasses, the heavy black frames obscuring his eyes? Or the way he always looked down when he smiled, bashful? It didn't come, but it was there, deep in my bones: an unshakable sense that somehow I knew him from before.

But as I tried to remember how, there was that white space again, a sprawling desert in my mind.

It's five o'clock: time to head to the dock and meet Nikodemos. I make the bed I've been sleeping in, then head downstairs to say my good-byes to Hazel, Joe, Sariah and George. Sariah is by the range oven preparing a dish that smells divine. When she spots me in the doorway she sets down the oven glove and stretches her arms out for a hug.

"You're leaving already?" she says.

I nod, suddenly anxious. I wish she could come with me, but it would be wrong to ask. She pulls me into a deep embrace and kisses my cheek. Then she leans back and looks me over.

"You're going to be fine," she says warmly, her dark eyes twinkling. "Just fine. What time did George arrange for Nikodemos to come?"

"Six, I think. I'm guessing he'll take a little while to search for the missing boat, and then hopefully he'll take me to the police station."

"You want food before you go?" she says, turning to the pan on the stove that's emitting steam and a heavenly smell. "It's at least an hour to Chania, maybe more, depending on how the wind's blowing."

I shake my head. "I'm OK."

She looks doubtful. "You're sure?"

I nod. My stomach is in knots over leaving the farmhouse and, as delicious as the food smells, I can't face eating it. I am, quite literally, heading into the unknown—everything I know is right here.

Hazel comes in and sees us embracing. "What's going on?" she says, then raises a hand to her mouth and widens her eyes as the penny drops. "You're *leaving.*"

To my surprise, she opens her arms and joins us in a group hug. When she pulls back—Sariah taking both my hands in hers—Hazel folds her arms and flicks her eyes across me, studying me.

"You're really leaving? I thought you might have stayed a little longer."

"It's for the best," Sariah answers. "Remember," she tells me in a low voice. "Be Pandora."

115

"Be what?" Hazel says, glancing back and forth at Sariah and me, but neither of us answer.

Joe comes in then, deep in a yawn. "Oh, man! You're going!" he says suddenly, and I feel tearful. He throws his arms around me and lifts me off my feet. When he lowers me, he tells me to wait right here and races out of the room. He returns with a small jotter and a pen.

"I said I'd give you something to write in," he says, smiling. "So here you are."

"Thank you."

"I wrote in it," he says, bashful. "In the front page. A gift to remember us by."

He's a sweet boy—a gentle giant—no more than twenty, with a huge, caring heart. I will miss him dearly.

"Thank you, Joe."

"Are we ready to go?" George says, emerging from the stairway with a long wooden walking stick in one hand and a coat in the other. He hands it to me: an old man's fishing jacket. It smells foul and is covered in dust. "Gets nippy down by the beach. Bit big for you, but beggars can't be choosers, eh?"

"Thanks," I say, putting it on. George straps on a large, empty rucksack to hold the food that Nikodemos is bringing for the others. Joe insists it isn't big enough, but George tells him to shut up, he'll be fine.

Sariah insists on giving me food in a paper bag and Joe makes me sit down and have my blood pressure checked before he decides I'm well enough to walk the distance. Then Hazel studies me to ensure I'm organized, though all I have is the clothes on my back and the food Sariah gave me. But Hazel reminds me about the jotter and pen Joe gifted me, and puts them in my pocket with a bunch of tissues. I can't help feeling like a child going off to school for the first time.

It's already beginning to darken outside when George and I head down the steps of the farmhouse and take the path through the olive trees toward the far end of the island. The sky's navy and lilac silks lift my spirits, as do the call of birds and the shapes of boats in the distance, dotted on the clothy texture of ocean like white party hats. Maybe the language barrier won't be so much of a problem. Maybe the police in Chania will have some sort of database that they can look up and find out who I am, and who is looking for me.

It takes almost an hour to reach the small dock, for the island has virtually no straight paths and the only flats are the dramatic stone banks near the cliffs. The wind grows so fierce that George insists we stay close to the trees, his faint torch picking out a rugged path and scaring off small creatures.

George doesn't talk much along the way. He hums occasionally, his walking stick knocking against rock and his heavy boots thudding against the dirt path, the empty rucksack making whispers against his back. I'm glad of the quiet; it gives me time to take in the sight of the sunset.

The abandoned hotel is located close to the beach, along with the wind-scrubbed shell of a restaurant and some derelict buildings. Their signage blown away, it's difficult to pinpoint what their purpose was, though George's torch picks out evidence: broken pint glasses; a handful of toy dolphins with "Komméno" stitched along the fin, the price tags still attached; a flip-flop; a menu, Greek and English lettering indicating the intended customers.

"Sad," says George, rubbing his nose. "They had high

117

hopes for this place. The whole island. Said it was going to be as big as Kos."

He points out a small wooden pier beyond a cluster of towering palm trees. "He'll dock there." He begins to head toward it. I follow.

Now that I'm here, waiting for Nikodemos, I feel terrified. What will happen in Crete? Will the police help me or abandon me? Where will I go? I have no money, no phone, no friends or family that I remember. I look out over the darkening sky, the skyline populated with shadows of distant ships and islands, and take a deep breath. Six o'clock passes. I take off my shoes and sit down on the end of the pier, dangling my feet toward the sea below. The water is so clear that I can spot slivers of fish in the water, nibbling my toes. The sky bruises, first stars jeweling the clouds. For the first time in a long while, George speaks.

"Chilly, see? Aren't you glad of that coat now?"

I nod, pulling it tighter across me. I turn to climb on top of a boulder beside the pier for a better view of the horizon, squinting for any sign of a boat coming to the island.

"Do you see him?" I ask George.

"Who?" he calls.

"Nikodemos."

He clicks his teeth with his tongue, his gaze straight ahead. "How will you know it's really Nikodemos?"

"What?"

A shrug and a strange curl at the side of his mouth. "I said, how will you know it's really Nikodemos? You'll be getting in that boat, sailing off. It could be a smuggler. Could be anyone."

I laugh it off, but when he doesn't laugh back I wonder

whether he's joking after all. The cold has set in now, making my eyes stream. I rub my eyes and reach into my pocket for a hankie to wipe away tears and snot caused by the cold wind, but all I find is Joe's notebook. I pull it out, remembering with a smile that he said he'd written a note inside to remember him by. Turning to the first page, I can make out his spidery handwriting, though it takes me a moment to work out what I'm reading.

Your name is Eloïse Beatrice Shelley.

The letters on the page are meaningless and abstract, and I tell myself this is a name he has assigned to me, made up for me, like a character in a novel. But then there is a chime, a ripple in that white space, announcing that this *is* my name. Eloïse. This *is* my name. I am Eloïse Beatrice Shelley.

But how does Joe know this?

George has started to walk back up the pier. I expect him to come toward me but he continues walking. I shuffle down off the boulder and walk after him.

"Has Nikodemos contacted you?"

He keeps walking.

"George?"

He won't respond, but simply lumbers on through the tall blades of grass. With great loping strides across the rocky ground I manage to catch up with him, keeping pace while he prods the earth with his walking stick and whistles.

"Where are you going?" I ask him.

"I'm going back to the farmhouse."

I'm already out of breath, my heart racing.

"But . . . what about Nikodemos?"

"What about him?"

"George!"

He stops. I step in front of him, one eye on the pier in case the boat pulls up.

"Where is Nikodemos?" I pant. "He's bringing food, isn't he? And taking me back. Where is the boat?"

George sighs and smiles down a time. "Look, it's for your own good."

"What's for my own good, George?"

"You've got to stay here until you get your memory back."

My mouth falls open.

"But—you called Nikodemos. On the satellite phone. You said he was coming today, that he was bringing food for all of you, and that he'd take me to Crete."

George shakes his head and gives a stupid little laugh. Like this is all a game.

"It's for your own good. Trust me."

"*What?*"

"I have *always* watched your back," he says. "Always. And that's precisely what I'm doing now."

"What the hell are you talking about?" I shout, and my gut is tight and my heart is beating in my throat. He ignores me and walks on.

"I have to go back to Crete, George. I have to!" I shake the notebook in the air. "I know my name! I know who I am!"

In one quick movement he reaches out and loops his thick arm through mine, pulling me along with him. I reel at his strength.

"George, let me go! I want…please, let me go to Crete. They'll be able to contact the Embassy. Please, let me go!"

March 23, 2015

Little Acorns' Playgroup, Twickenham

Lochlan: Eloïse has been missing now for six days. It doesn't sound that long. Not even a week. Yet it feels like I'm falling through time, each minute a century. My nerves are flensed. It's like being on LSD, but with the pain of an amputation without anesthetic. I spent a while last night googling space-time wormholes and considering whether El might have time traveled. I leap from one extreme to another, like a monkey from branch to branch: black despair to a strange, cocky certainty that she's about to walk through the door. Every instance that I realize she's not here, that this is not a dream, is an electric shock to the system.

And then there's the anger. I have moments, usually in the middle of the night, when fury envelops me and I'd give anything to fight someone. I mean, it's staggering that someone can go missing in this day and age, given that she's been on the news, we have a dedicated Facebook page, "Help Find Eloïse Shelley," with over fifty thousand shares, and the hashtag #findEloïse went viral for half an hour last night on Twitter after being retweeted by Lorraine Kelly. I read somewhere that the average man or woman is captured by CCTV fourteen times a day and yet all the CCTV cameras that the police have checked show no sign of Eloïse. The whole neighborhood has been involved in the search. There are posters in libraries, on lampposts and school gates, at the entrances of our local Waitrose and Sainsbury's and throughout London. And yet it has all amounted to nothing. As though she evaporated.

The thought of her running off with another man now seems at once unlikely and an outcome I almost wish for, given the other possibilities for her disappearance, because at least if she has left me for someone else she is safe. Logic is no longer what I thought it was. The air in our home is stagnant. Her coats hang in the utility room like bats. Her underwear sleeps in the top drawer of her dresser. Envelopes flit through the letterbox bearing her name. Each minute is weighted with unanswered questions.

Magnus, Gerda, and I have cobbled together a routine for Max and Cressida. Dean Wyatt reluctantly signed me off on compassionate leave from work. There's a huge part of me that wishes I could go to work for the normality, the chance to dive into investment forecasts and forget about this hell. Anyway. Having had no real clue where exactly El has been taking our children every day, I managed to get some information from her friends. Max goes to preschool every afternoon from half past twelve to half past three, and in the mornings he attends playgroups, including a singing group, toddler Spanish, and a baby massage group for Cressida on Fridays.

I have finally managed to convince Max that Mummy has gone on holiday for a little while, and that Mamie and Grandpapa are here to spend time with him. He seemed more settled by this, more accepting, and it struck me that perhaps he had picked up on how worried I had been, that he'd been reacting to the chaos surrounding her absence. I forget sometimes how sensitive he is, and how intelligent, despite being so young. I've promised him that we will go to Thomas Land to see *Thomas the Tank Engine* as soon as Mummy gets back, and the words were out before I realized the problem in this promise. What if she doesn't come back? What then?

This morning Max wanted me to take him to playgroup, so I left Cressida behind and brought Max to playgroup. Talk about feeling like a square peg in a round hole. I'm sitting in a long room in a church with a cup of watery tea by my feet watching Max as he runs around the room wearing a Darth Vadar helmet and a tutu, wielding a plastic sword.

A part of me is starting to realize that I don't know all that much about Eloïse's life, not anymore. The detectives were very keen to know what clothes were missing, as she'd hardly have left the house naked, and if she left certain items behind—shoes, coat, that sort of thing—it could possibly indicate a forced exit. An abduction.

This made me feel sick. I looked and looked through her clothes, but I had no idea if anything was missing. She had some stuff I'd not seen before, some new shoes, dresses, coats. DS Welsh tried to make light of it, saying her boyfriend's the same, never notices anything, but the guilt is crippling. I haven't been present, physically or emotionally. When I was moved to the Edinburgh office we planned to make sure that it didn't affect things. We would Facetime at least twice a day and I'd speak with Max and read bedtime stories to Cressida virtually. It worked at the beginning, but then I got more and more sucked into work and the week would zoom by without a single Facetime. I guess it's easier said than done, maintaining a relationship properly via a laptop screen.

I took it for granted that her world was my world, because for a long time that was the case. But after we had Max, my world had become ten-hour days talking investment plans with corporations, business trips to Dubai, networking events. Even on weekends and holidays, I have been mentally "at work." Looking at Eloïse's calendar, it seems that playgroups such as the one I'm at now have been how she has spent much of the last four years. I can hardly imagine it.

A plump woman with an infant strapped to her chest sits next to me, and I know before she speaks that she's going to ask about Eloïse.

"Any word?" she says quietly.

I clear my throat and put away my phone. "I'm afraid not, no."

She gives me the same kind of pained sigh that I'm almost used to now, her face so creased with pity that it turns me inside out. She sighs contemplatively and looks on at Max as he clambers to the top of the plastic multicolored climbing frame, shouting, "Aargh! Me hearties!"

"Poor little mite," she says. "You never know what's around the corner, do you?"

"The thing is, so far my life has been very much about knowing *exactly* what's around the corner," I find myself saying. "Everything's been planned and worked out. I've never really had to deal with any disasters."

I hear myself saying these words and wonder why I'm saying them to this woman. She nods and murmurs in agreement. Suddenly she glances up sharply.

"Elvis! Elvis! Don't shove your fingers in Harry's mouth, please! You've got worms, sweetheart, we don't want to pass it on!"

I have a vague sense that this kind of shouted statement might ordinarily make me squirm, possibly even motivate me to move swiftly to another corner of the room. Then again, I have never been to a playgroup before, and the chances of me having a heart-to-heart with a woman like this were, pre-disappearance, slim to none.

"I don't think anyone can prepare for a thing like this," she says. "It must be very hard, not knowing." She kisses the infant's head, strokes the fine strands of black hair. "I didn't come to this group for a while because madam here decided to develop a kidney infection and spent a while in the hospital. But I remember Eloïse. She was so lovely, especially with little Max. She lit up whenever she spoke about him. She seemed like such a good mum."

Seemed. More and more I'm noticing people speaking about my wife in the past tense. *She was always so sweet.* I wonder if they realize how much it deepens my despair.

Another woman comes and sits down on the other side of me, an older woman with white hair and glasses on a chain, her face fixed in condolence. "Oh, you're Eloïse's husband," she says, and I smile, guilty as charged.

"How are you doing?"

"All right," I say automatically, but this only serves to make her expression droop and she flicks her eyes at Worm Lady, who sits at my right.

"I was saying to Sandra over there how lovely Eloïse was," the older woman says. "Nicest person. Such a wonderful mother, too. Always so happy and cheerful."

Worm Lady leans in. "If I'm honest, me and a few of the other mums were a tiny bit envious of Eloïse. She was *so* perfect! Her hair and makeup always done to perfection. And so skinny! Honestly, you'd never have thought she'd had two babies." She gives a shrill laugh.

The older woman nods, gravely. "I was a wreck after having my two. Two were enough for me. One would have been enough, but then I thought it weren't right for Claudia to be an only child, so we had Martin. Hadn't even heard of colic back then."

"Both mine had colic. Madam here has colic *and* reflux. The health visitor tried to tell me not to drink Red Bull if I was breastfeeding. I said, are you mental? How am I supposed to get through the day on half an hour's sleep?"

"I've been bringing me grandkids to this group for years now," the older woman continues. "Lots of mums struggling, especially during the early days. Not her. Not that Eloïse. I told the police, I said, she didn't walk out on those kids."

"Frankly, some of the other mums thought Eloïse was up herself, but not me."

I flinch at this, but Worm Lady doesn't see.

"I thought she was one of those lucky people who managed to have their cake and eat all of it. Elvis! My love, that's a potty, not a hat!"

"She had it together. Nothing fazed her."

Max runs up to me, his Darth Vadar mask replaced by a

tiara. "Daddy, why are you talking to Elvis's mummy?" He gives worried looks at Worm Lady and the older woman.

"I was telling your dad what a big boy you are, Max," Worm Lady tells him.

"My mummy smokes cigarettes!" he announces, and Worm Lady throws me a puzzled look.

"It's OK, son," I tell him. "Everything's fine. Go and play."

He leans on my thighs and gives a sigh. "Want to go now."

One of the leaders of the playgroup claps her hands and calls all the children to a table, where plastic plates of sliced apple and sandwiches are being set out.

"There's food, Maxie. Go and eat."

"I'm not hungry," he mumbles sadly. "Miss Mummy."

"I know. I do, too."

"Can we go and get her, Daddy? Maybe she would like to come home, now."

This breaks my heart.

"Maybe, Maxie. Maybe."

I think back to the first day Eloïse returned to work after Max was born. He was seven months old, determined to crawl, and dragging himself around the floor like a baby seal. I'd booked some holiday time to take care of him for the first week, and then Eloïse had already interviewed and hired a nanny. She put on the new dress she'd bought and walked to her car, and I held up Max and got him to wave. He was a little perturbed by her leaving, but I think it was harder for Eloïse. She tried hard not to cry.

Later that day she phoned. "How's Maxie doing?"

"He's having a nap," I told her. "He's absolutely fine. Stop stressing."

She took a deep breath. "I blended some carrots and butternut squash last night. It's in the bowl with dinosaurs on it. In the fridge, remember? You have to stir his food after taking it out of the microwave. Not a couple of times—you have to stir it loads to make sure it doesn't burn his mouth..."

"Eloïse. I know how to stir food. I'm not completely useless..."

"OK. Oh, and don't use the nappies in the nappy basket, I think they're giving him a rash. I bought a pack of new ones, they're in the utility room..."

"Anything else? Shall I hire a chamber orchestra? A petting zoo?"

"Please...tell me you'll use the new nappies."

I laughed ruefully. Was she seriously this wound up about Max?

"Say it, Lochlan. I'm not hanging up until you say it."

This was the difference between the sexes, I thought. One morning at home and I was already at a loose end, bored, restless, feeling that childcare was beneath me. At work, I didn't think about whether someone was stirring our son's food enough or putting him in the right nappies. El, on the other hand, was clearly unable to insert herself back into her working life.

"This is hard for me, you know," she said, her voice wobbling. "I miss him so much. I know it's silly..."

"It's not silly," I said, suddenly remorseful, though I still couldn't quite grasp why she couldn't simply *enjoy* being at work and leaving him at home. I felt guilty for snapping at her. She loved our son, and she was so dedicated to looking after him. A different person seemed to step out of her when Max was born. Yes, Eloïse had always been a 100 percent kind of girl, hardworking and passionate, but the way she took on motherhood was unexpected. If I'm honest, I felt a little in the shadows when Max came along. And sometimes I wondered if I didn't love him as much as she did. Perhaps I didn't.

I shifted tack. A voice in my head nagged at me to stop giving her a hard time and reassure her, otherwise she might quit her job altogether when there was no need.

"Darling, I promise you—Max is absolutely fine. We've had a great morning. I read him that peekaboo book he likes about fifteen times."

"Oh! The one with the mirrors? He loves that!"

I nodded. "Yep, and the little flippy-out bits where he has to open the door..."

"Did he laugh at the end?"

"Every time. And then I took him out to the sandpit and we played. Now he's having a nap. He is completely fine, I promise."

She fell silent. "Thank you, Lochlan," she said after a while, her voice shaking.

I told her to enjoy the rest of her day. I made her promise to get herself a caramel macchiato and revel in the fact that she could drink the whole thing without having to wipe up snot or poo in the middle of it, or indeed out of it, and she laughed.

But the night before the nanny was due to start, Eloïse woke me and said she couldn't do it. She couldn't face leaving Max with a stranger all day, every day. I tried to get her to consider working part-time, but it didn't seem to be enough. She wanted to be at home, end of story. And so she stepped down as CEO and Danny Holland took over.

Eloïse's absence is so much more powerful than her presence. The kids feel it. I lied to Max and made everyone else lie, too. I figured it would be best if we told him that Eloïse had gone to America for her job. He knows about Mummy's job, she's told him all about it with pride and even took him into her office a few times. I thought he'd buy this, but he clapped both hands on my cheeks and studied me. Then he said, "Are you telling troof, Daddy?" And I tried to nod but I started to sob and now he's more unsettled than ever.

And for all of Cressida's short time on this planet, she certainly senses that something is up. She hates taking her bottle, fighting with it as though it'll give in and morph into her mother's breast. I found some of Eloïse's clothes in the laundry basket and put one of her tops in Cressida's crib, and she slept right through the night. But when she's awake, she cries and thrashes and won't be comforted. Gerda and Magnus are still staying here, filling the endless barbed hours with Max and Cressida's routines. Magnus was crying in the garden yesterday. He was watering Eloïse's rosebushes and trying to hide his tears. I didn't know what to say to him, and neither he nor Gerda seem to know what to say to me. We're all pretty civil but I can't say I have much of a relationship with them. I don't ski and I don't have a massive property portfolio like they do, so we've never had much to talk about. In this instance I suspect that, like me, they are stunned into silence, mentally turning over every memory in case it yields a clue to El's whereabouts.

The house has been full of visitors—my father, brothers, and Susan, my stepmother, our friends, a group of women I've never met but who apparently are very close to my wife from meeting at toddler groups. Events like this tend to show up the people you thought you knew in odd colors.

My father, for instance, always the person rooting for me and the one person I would have expected to understand intimately the kind of hell I'm in, gave me a manly slap on the back and muttered a few words of comfort before telling me that he and

Susan were heading off to the Bahamas in the morning and to keep him updated. I suspect he believes that El has walked out and left me with the kids, just like my mother did to him. Mrs. Shahjalal has popped back and forth, relaying over and over again the same story about how she found Max alone at home. Mr. McWhirter, our weird, irritable neighbor from the other side of the street, who hasn't spoken more than two sentences to me since we moved here, spent an entire morning on our sofa telling us about his life as a commander in the army. Turns out he's a widower, bitterly lonely since nursing his wife through cancer. He was sincere in his consolation and made some solid suggestions for a search campaign.

Now I realize that the one person I really, really need to help me navigate this hell is the one who is missing.

I clip Max into his car seat and drive him to preschool. I have to google it for the postcode and then satnav my way there. I feel ashamed that I've never actually dropped him off. I haven't even met his teacher. And then Max says, "This is a nice car, Daddy," and I realize that he's never been in my car. We use Eloïse's Qashqai whenever we go anywhere as a family, but still.

We pull into the car park across the road from preschool—Willowfield First School and Nursery—and Max waves to a little boy climbing out of a Range Rover next to us.

"Hi, Wilbur," Max says, before turning to me. "Daddy, Wilbur brought his scooter. It must be Scooter Day. Is today Monday, Daddy?"

"Yes, today is Monday." My phone has started to ring and I'm searching for it in my pockets.

"Monday is Scooter Day, Daddy. It's Scooter Day. Daddy, Daddy, Daddy."

"Hold on, Max."

By the time I find my phone, the call has rung out, straight to voice mail. Number withheld.

Max is still going on about Scooter Day when we arrive at the front doors. An older woman greets Max and he attempts to enlist her in the scooter cause, though mercifully she manages to cajole him with a promise of a spare scooter. She holds my gaze, and I figure that I need to mention the situation at home. I wait until the other parents have dropped off their children before speaking, but before I get a chance the woman says: "We've heard about Max's mother. I'm so sorry."

I shut my mouth and nod, stricken. Every time someone tells me this it feels like a condolence, and though I know it's offered out of kindness it only adds to my fear that I'll never see my wife again.

"Max is very unsettled, as you might expect," I say, and it takes a fierce amount of effort to keep my voice from shaking. "He misses his mother and it's difficult to know what to tell him."

She has a look of deep understanding on her face. "You've done the right thing by trying to keep his routine nice and consistent," she says, and I breathe a sigh of relief. How much I have needed to hear someone say those words. *You've done the right thing.* This week has been one of crazy introspection and I've felt like all I've done my whole life is the wrong thing.

"I'll keep you informed," I say, and I don't finish the sentence. She reaches out and squeezes my hand. Inside, I catch a glimpse of Max chatting animatedly with a group of friends, and my heart swells.

I'm getting back into my car when the phone rings again. This time I answer on the second ring.

"Hello, Mr. Shelley?"

"Yes?"

"DS Canavan speaking."

My heart beats in my mouth. Is he phoning with news of Eloïse?

"I have a question for you."

"Yes?"

"About the baby monitors."

I allow myself to breathe. "What about them?"

"Our tech guys say that the footage was rerouted to another ISP. Do you know anything about this?"

I have no idea what any of this means. " 'Rerouted'? I don't know . . . Eloïse had it set up to her cloud, or something."

It strikes me that neither of us really understands what we're talking about.

"OK," he says. "I'll pass this back to the tech guys and see what they say. Meantime, we've received the forensic report on your back door."

"And?"

"We found your prints, your wife's prints, and your son's. No one else's."

"So that means a break-in can be ruled out?"

"It's unlikely. Not ruled out." A beat. "We've also spoken to Eloïse's health visitor and midwives. There's a difference of opinion in terms of her medical history, so we'll be investigating that further. We do have some footage from the babycams, though. Perhaps you'd like to review it for anything that seems significant."

I nod at the phone.

"When can I see it?"

March 24, 2015

Komméno Island, Greece

I spent last night on the wooden pier at the edge of the island in front of the derelict hotel, wrapped in the smelly fisherman's jacket that George pulled out of the pantry in the farmhouse. Still, it kept me warm. I must have fallen asleep briefly several times, and twice I woke up to the sound of an engine ripping across the waves.

It was the oddest thing: I swear I saw a speedboat pulling up toward me, the surface of the water parted by the stern as though unzipping the ocean, a man with gray hair and sunglasses standing by the wheel. I saw the glint of moonlight on the side of the boat and heard the engine roaring louder as it got closer. And both times my heart started racing and I ran to the very edge of the pier, only to find that there was no sign of a boat out there. Nothing but the sway and roll of waves.

I imagined it. It's the only explanation.

For most of the night I sat cross-legged, looking up at the galaxies to distract me from the sounds of the island. Night doesn't simply blanket the island in darkness; it replaces it with an inversion, an ink-dark place that seems on the cusp of another realm. The olive groves and cacti morph into grotesque figures that emit weird shouts, clicks, and cries that sound fearfully human.

So I kept my eyes on the galaxies, forcing myself to count them, describe them. *Fireworks suspended at the moment of exploding. Diamonds, rubies, and sapphires scattered across a black velvet quilt.* The knowledge that each of them was a star or planet or constellation with a name and a gravity that I did not know, just as I did not know where I had come from or who I had left behind, was at once comforting and frightening.

Though, now it appears I know my full name. Eloïse Beatrice Shelley. I've said that name out loud a thousand times, as though the sound of it is a line I'm casting into the waters of memory to hook some other clues. *Eloïse. Eloïse.* Nothing yet, but maybe it'll take a bit of time. When I get to Crete, I have much more of a chance of finding out where I came from. I could possibly locate myself via Google or Facebook. If only the farmhouse had Internet.

George tried to pull me along the path toward the farmhouse. His grip on my arm was like an iron vise, and he's so strong that he managed to drag me along behind him for a few feet without breaking pace. I shouted at him to let me go, then resorted to kicking the back of his legs, which felt very unnatural for me—I must be a fairly placid person in real life. Even so, it seemed to have little effect. It was only when I blurted out about the notebook, how Joe had written my name inside it, that he stopped and turned around, his eyes wild.

"Show me," he shouted. "Show me what Joe wrote."

I dug the notebook out of my pocket and opened it at the first page. He snatched it from me and stared down at the writing, then looked up at me one last time before stalking off, flinging the notebook to the ground. His reaction to it was so furious that I was worried for Joe. But why would he be angry? What would be wrong about telling me my name?

All night I fought sleep, questions rolling around my head. Along the horizon were the lights of cruise ships and the distant shadow of an island. I tried to allay my fears that I might have missed Nikodemos by recalling Sariah's words: Nikodemos was bringing them food, and then he was taking me back to Crete. George had to have called Nikodemos about the missing boat, didn't he? Nikodemos would want to check that out. The others would need food as they had no transportation to Chania. Nikodemos wouldn't simply turn back if we weren't on the pier. He would wait, surely. And I would be there.

But no one came.

When I wake up, my backside is soaked from water surging through the slats beneath me, the sky is bright, and the sun hot against my face. I stand up and stretch, revived by the wind and the scenery. When we arrived at the pier last night it was too dark to make out much of the landscape but now, in this gold, mellow light of morning, the vision before me is postcard worthy. The water licks at my feet, perfectly clear. Behind me, the hills are a rich, lustrous green. I'm amazed by how many cacti are nearby. Towering green sculptures edged with sharp prickles. A good job I didn't stumble into those last night. What a difference light makes. The only sign of the commercial past of the island is the delapidated hotel to my left, even more ugly and sad in daylight. Litter blows across the pale sand and the broken windows and torn signage is hard on the eye.

I try to work out what to do. There's no sign of anyone for miles around and I can't make out the farmhouse from here, though I can probably find my way back easily enough. I'm hungry and thirsty. And I need to get one of the others to contact Nikodemos on the satellite phone.

I begin to head back, keeping my pace slow to conserve energy. I find some trees and fill up on fat, overripe peaches until I feel slightly ill. Then I keep as far away from the hills as I can, recalling George's warning about the wild goats, but my detour leads me to a path along the cliffs, and before long I find myself on a course that I recognize: I'm heading toward Bone Beach.

Finding the path that Joe had taken, I make my way to the first outcrop below, then the second. Looking down, I can see it's quite a drop to the third, with virtually no footholds in the rock.

The birds are crying above, swooping and diving from the nests along the upper ledge. My breasts burn again but I stay focused on my breath and on finding a way down to the beach until the pain dissipates. Gingerly I press my left foot into the rock, then find a small ledge and grip it tight with my fingers. From there I'm able to lean against the rock and reach lower, scaling down to the lower outcrop, then it's a leap of about six feet on to the clean white sand of Bone Beach.

The boat looks much bigger from this vantage point,

about thirteen feet long. An old wooden sailing dinghy. It is lying on its side in the water against a cluster of rocks, pale blue paint flaking from the sides. A name—*Janus*—is painted in black cursive on the right flank. Inside, I can see a cupboard door flung open, a series of handles and ropes. The oars are gone.

An idea strays into my head: maybe I could sail back to Crete. If I managed to sail here, surely I could sail back? I walk slowly around the boat, inspecting it for damage. And then I see it: both the rudder and centerboard—the bit that hangs down from the base of the boat like a dorsal fin—have been ripped off, fragments of them lying across the stones. The stern is pretty damaged but looks fixable. Without the rudder and centerboard, though, somehow I know the boat isn't fit for purpose.

I climb back up the steep cliff, nauseous with fatigue. A tree nearby has fat green fruit hanging from its branches. I reach up and pull one down. A fat, ripe pear, the skin a smooth jade with bronze blotches. When I bite into it, the juice runs down from the corners of my mouth. I stop and look down at the beach, remarking again on how George had virtually risked his life to save mine. Why, then, was he so insistent on keeping me here? And what did he mean when he said he had always looked out for me?

I'm apprehensive about going back to the farmhouse, but I have no choice: I have to get in touch with Nikodemos. Perhaps he ran into difficulty and tried to call the satellite phone. Or perhaps George was lying to me.

At the farmhouse, Joe and Hazel are sitting at the kitchen table, silently writing in notebooks. I notice that Joe has a black eye. I take a seat beside them, exhausted from my trek back to the farmhouse. Joe takes one look at me before rising to get me a glass of water. I tell them about George, how he told me Nikodemos wasn't coming and that I wasn't going anywhere until I got my memory back. I don't mention that I know my name, now, nor that Joe was the one who told me it.

"Wait, so Nikodemos didn't show up *at all*?" Hazel says, rising sharply from her chair. I nod, and she begins to pace, agitated. "But...this doesn't make any sense. Nikodemos said he was bringing food."

"I think we've got enough for another week," Joe says, but Hazel begins to argue. I watch her carefully, trying to work out whether she's pretending.

"We can phone Nikodemos and ask him to come tonight, or even tomorrow. OK?" Joe says. "He's retired."

"George has the satellite phone," Hazel says, swiveling her eyes to me.

A set of footstep noises from the stairwell. For a moment I think it's George, and I break out in a cold sweat. But it's only Sariah, singing to herself and covered in pastel smudges, blue and pink streaks on her arms and all over her white dress. She spots me and crosses the room, a worried expression on her face.

"What's happened?"

"There was a problem with Nikodemos," Hazel says.

"What do you mean?" Sariah says, and I tell her about last night. About George telling me I couldn't leave, though when I try to repeat exactly what he said, I can't remember. Did he say he called Nikodemos, or that he didn't? Either way, he has the only means of contact with the outside world. Then I remember what he said about me having to stay on the island "for my own good," and Sariah's expression changes. She flicks her eyes at Joe.

"Where is George?"

Joe lowers his eyes.

Hazel says, "He's off writing somewhere, I'm guessing."

"Well, when he comes back we'll tell him that he must call Nikodemos immediately," Sariah says, glancing at me. "We'll get you home soon enough," she says. "Whoever you've left behind must be frantic by now."

"We'll talk about it over dinner tonight," Hazel says, clapping her hands together. "We'll make George's favorite meal and give him plenty of raki. Trust me, raki turns George into a pussycat. Then we'll ask him very nicely to call Nikodemos and tell him it's an emergency." She glances nervously at me. "That sound all right?"

I nod, but I'm now watching Joe, trying to work out why he seems so afraid of George, and how on earth he could possibly know my name. For a sinking moment, I wonder if he made it up, if it isn't my real name at all. Maybe I wanted it to be my real name because I'm so desperate. After all, how would he know my name if none of them has ever met me before?

I wait until Hazel and Sariah are out of earshot, making plans for this evening, before approaching Joe at the table.

"The notebook you gave me," I say in a low voice. "You said you wrote a message in the front page. It was my name. Eloïse. Is that my real name?"

He continues writing in his notebook—a poem, it looks like—pointedly ignoring me.

"Joe?"

He won't look up. I notice sweat gathering at his temples and his writing becomes faster, more agitated.

"Joe, did George give you that black eye?"

Now he stops and raises his head, but he won't meet my gaze. The notebook slides off my knee to the ground, still open. Hazel stoops and picks it up before I can get to it.

" 'Your name is Eloïse Beatrice Shelley,' " she reads, before glancing at me with wide eyes. "Is that your name?"

I nod.

"That's not my handwriting," Joe snaps, gathering up his notebook and rising from his seat.

"What's this?" Sariah says, wiping her hands on a towel.

"Her name's Eloïse," Hazel says, watching Joe with narrowed eyes. "Did you write this, Joe?"

Sariah says, " 'Eloïse'—pretty name. Does it ring a bell?"

I nod, and she smiles. "That's progress."

"I think she suits 'Hazel' better," Hazel says.

"It sure does look like your handwriting, Joe," Sariah says, craning her head to see it better.

"Well, it isn't," he snaps from the other side of the room. "I don't know who wrote that."

Sariah steps up as the voice of reason, her hands up to bring the debate to an end. "Let's stay focused. You—Eloïse—need to get off this island, we need to get food. Or a mode of transport, at least. It seems you have more than a first name now to take to the British Embassy, yes?"

I nod in agreement and she glances at Hazel. "Well, then. Let's get that phone and call Nikodemos. Or *somebody*. The police should be able to run a few checks and narrow it down."

The back door clangs shut. A set of heavy boots on stone. A throaty cough. We all turn to find George in the doorway, a long and heavy object in his hand. Brass gleams in the light.

"George," Sariah says firmly. "Please can you call Nikodemos?"

He ignores her, removing his boots and admiring the object he is carrying.

"Is that a...gun?" Hazel asks nervously.

"A rifle," George replies, holding it up to look at it. He glances ahead of him, catching Joe's eye as he stands, rigid, on the threshold. He seems too scared to make a run for it.

"Why have you got a rifle, George?" Hazel asks.

"Gorgeous, isn't she?" George hefts it upright to inspect the wooden stock. "A real looker. Found her in one of the barns the other day. From the Venetian invasions, I think. Maybe Turkish. An old box of bullets there, too."

The weapon in George's hands makes my blood run cold. I glance at Sariah, but she is unmoved. "Could you try Nikodemos's number, please?" she says casually.

George lowers the rifle and squints through the sight, waving the barrel in our direction.

"George, *please*," Sariah says, bringing her fist down on the table.

He looks up. "What?"

"Call Nikodemos. We need to get food, and Eloïse has to go to Crete."

He lifts an eyebrow, the gun still casually raised. "Eloïse, eh?"

I nod.

He sniffs. "Eloïse needs to stay here."

Sariah gives a sigh of frustration. "OK. OK, everyone. Let's...reset, shall we? Let's have dinner, relax, and talk this through. And—George?"

"Yes?"

She gives him a hard look.

"Please put the gun outside."

Mercifully, he does, and we eat around the large kitchen table, a heavy shower of rain clapping at the windows. But there is still atmosphere so charged that I can hardly think straight. Sariah speaks in clipped tones and serves the dinner with barely suppressed irritation. Joe won't look at me and my mind races with possible reasons for his secrecy. Nobody answered my questions about Hazel's secret, and George seems determined, for whatever reason, to keep me here. Is it sexually motivated? I don't know. If it wasn't raining so hard I'd try to escape, maybe take shelter in the hotel. But then, there's no food or water there, and the satellite phone is here.

I glance every now and then at Joe, whose black eye serves as a reminder of last night. What happened when George came back? Did he punish Joe for writing in the notebook? Whatever took place is not aired, and I sense deeper layers to the group's dynamic. A hierarchy, where George is the chief, a tyrant. They are not friends at all.

I have no choice but to pretend. I sit at the table and make small talk about the weather, about their writing, and neither George nor I mention Nikodemos. Sariah cooks her most fragrant meal yet—griddled halloumi, fat green olives, artichokes drizzled in olive oil, and a creamy sauce topped with sprigs of rosemary. Still, it doesn't so much as tempt me, nor does it remove the stench of chaos in the air.

"Raki, Eloïse?" Hazel asks me, holding a bottle over my glass. She winks, and I nod. She pours for everyone and we toast.

"To remembrance," Sariah says, taking her seat. George

143

gives her a weighted look, and I sense something shift between them, a new color entering their friendship.

After a few minutes, Hazel glances at me and Sariah before saying, "George, I think we've run out of wine for the rest of the week. There's not much food, either. Why don't you give me the satellite phone and I'll call Nikodemos to make a delivery?"

George is laughing hard with Joe over a joke I can't quite hear, slapping the back of his head, and spitting as he talks. He rolls his eyes to Hazel. "What delivery?"

"Food, George," Hazel says flatly. "Why did you tell him not to come last night?"

"I didn't," he slurs. He nods at me. "She did."

"Don't be ridiculous," Sariah says. "You're the only one with the satellite phone. Come on, George. Pass it over. Let one of us call Nikodemos."

George grins broadly, sets down his glass with a wobble, and looks at Sariah unsteadily. "What's Nikodemos's number?"

Sariah opens her mouth but looks stumped. She glances at Hazel. "I knew it before...I'm sure I did. You know it, don't you, Hazel?"

Hazel looks equally stumped. "George always rang Nikodemos, so I never bothered writing it down. Joe?"

Joe is slumped forward, his head on the table, unresponsive.

"What did I tell you?" says George triumphantly. "She's not leaving. She's staying here, safe and sound. It's not right, letting her go. I won't have it." Suddenly he is off his seat, lumbering toward the back door. He lurches into the pantry and grabs his rifle from the corner.

"Don't worry about food," he shouts. "I can hunt for us all."

It happens so fast.

One minute George is in the kitchen, the next he has raced out into the night, his footsteps clattering down the steps at the back door.

"George! Come back!" Hazel shouts, racing to the back door. We all follow and look out over the darkness. Outside, the moon is a silver disk, and there's a velvety fog creeping over navy hills, the trees and grass trembling in a forceful wind. A shadow moves near the barns to the left of the farm-house.

"We'll have to go after him," Sariah says. "He was heading in the direction of the barn, so he must be planning on taking the shortcut through the ravine—not the smartest move when you've just drunk half a bottle of raki."

"I'll come with you," I say. Hazel makes to join us, but Sariah waves her away.

"You and Joe need to stay here in case he comes back."

Far out to sea are tiny shimmering lights—from boats, or perhaps neighboring islands—and the full moon flings a long strip of silver across the ocean, which looks tantalizingly like a causeway. I hesitate when I hear the usual shouts and barks that swell when darkness falls. "Nocturnal animals," Sariah assures me when I hesitate, and she tells me that the creatures won't bother us. But the noises are utterly chilling.

Even so, we head down the bank toward the barn, grasping at fistfuls of reeds and shrubs to keep from tumbling down. There's a lip of rock where Sariah is concerned that George might have fallen and injured himself, but we don't see him. Exhausted from the descent, we head slowly to the barn.

The barn is a long wooden building with a tin roof that lifts and whines in the wind, and inside are old cubicles curtained off by rusting sheets of tin. There's virtually no light inside, though moonlight trickles across the remains of farm tools: forks, scythes, hooks hanging from the ceiling, and the blades of old machines. I'm wary of going any farther, but Sariah strides ahead, through the barn door, and is immediately swallowed by the darkness.

"We need a torch," I say loudly. "Let's go back."

"Might as well check the barn first, in case he's passed out somewhere."

I bite back a refute and start to search the area around the barn, walking slowly and carefully, my feet connecting with cold stone. Moonlight pulls the occasional rock or olive tree into visibility, but mostly it's so dark that I'm having to rely on my sense of smell and hearing to guide me. I keep my eyes fixed on the small illuminated spots on the ground, hopeful that I'll find George unconscious nearby, and the phone in his pocket. I don't care if no one else knows the number for Nikodemos—I'll dial every number I can think of until one of them connects.

Suddenly there's a loud bang, followed by a pained cry. I shout out, "Sariah!" and there is another noise, an object connecting against stone, but no reply. I call her name again and hurriedly retrace my steps inside the barn, toeing a tight line of rope so that I don't trip over and miss her. But as I do I hear a whimper, close to the stalls.

"Sariah? Are you there?"

"Eloïse."

I recognize the low, rumbling voice immediately. It's George. My heart leaps in my chest. I spin around but it's so dark—impenetrably dark—and I can't see anything.

"George? Where are you?"

"Take a step to your left."

146

I do this, stepping across the wooden floor.

"Now turn forty-five degrees to your right."

Immediately a shaft of light reveals the figure of George crouching over Sariah, who is lying on the ground on her side, arms over her head. She doesn't move.

George straightens to his full height. Then he produces his rifle and lowers it, pointing it at her stomach.

"She wouldn't feel a thing if I pulled the trigger," he says mildly. "Best way to go, really."

"George, please put the gun down."

It's as though time has slowed down. His face is vacant and serious, no sign of the drunkenness I saw clearly before. I flick my eyes down to Sariah to work out the cause of her injury but it's too dark. With a sickening twist in my gut, I consider that she might be dead.

"Sariah is your friend, George," I plead.

"You think I won't do it," he whispers, his eyes wide.

Joe and Hazel are too far away to be alerted. I can't think fast enough. There is no way of escaping him without abandoning Sariah, and there's no way of helping her without risking my life. I have to talk to him, persuade him.

"I know you wouldn't dream of it, George. Come on, now. It's late. Let's go back inside. Put the gun down..."

His expression is eerily composed and sincere, as though he's offering to help me out in some way.

"I would do it, you know," he whispers. "I've seen people die. It's not as bad as they say."

I take a small step to the left but he lifts up the rifle and points it at me, his manner agitated.

"Don't you move. Don't you dare think about leaving this island."

"OK, George," I say, anxious for him to move the gun away from Sariah. One slip and he could shoot her by accident. "OK. I'll stay."

I raise my hands by my head and he moves the gun away from Sariah. But she still isn't moving.

"Now," George says, visibly appeased. "I think we ought to establish a few ground rules, don't you? First of all, no more trying to leave." I nod but he seems unconvinced. "I'm telling you, it's for your own good. You say you can't remember anything, and that's as may be. But what I know for certain is that you haven't got any *money*. There's a rumpus going on in Greece right now. Riots on the street, tear gas, and stuff like that. The police aren't going to give a monkey's about your so-called amnesia with all that going on, so I hardly think it's wise to go running off there."

I start to speak, but he raises a hand and points at me.

"Shut it. OK? No more questions. Two rules, think you can manage that?"

I nod in earnest but don't speak. I'm too terrified. Sariah is starting to move her fingers and I can hear her moaning. It looks like she's taken a terrible blow to the head.

George grins. "Good. Now remember, when you disobey George, bad things happen. Understand?"

"I understand."

He hoists the rifle onto his shoulder and stumbles off into the darkness, the swishing sound of reeds indicating that he's climbing back up the hill. I wait another long handful of seconds before racing toward Sariah. There's a dark patch of blood on the left side of her head. I take off my T-shirt and press it against the wound, and she jerks.

"Are you OK?" I say. "Sariah, are you all right?"

She sits up slowly, moaning.

"What happened?"

"I think George hit you," I say, helping her sit upright. I wrap the arms of the T-shirt tightly around the wound, watching it carefully to check that the bleeding is slowing. She is in serious trouble if not.

"We need to leave," I say. "You need to get out of here."

She is woozy and disoriented, and I'm terrified in case she falls unconscious again. I drape her arm over my shoulders and help her rise slowly to her feet. She begins to moan from the pain in her head.

"It's OK, Sariah," I tell her, moving us closer to the barn entrance. "It's OK."

"Take me...take me to Joe," she mumbles.

We both walk carefully, hip to hip, toward the light of the farmhouse. I begin to tremble, the shock of the events just before and the icy wind against my bare skin making it hard to climb the hill. The wind is so strong it almost lifts us off our feet, and we have to hold fast to each other to keep grounded. I glance around again and again in case George lunges out of the shadows, but he is nowhere to be seen.

It seems to take an eternity to make it back, the wind strong in our faces, the stars bright above and on the black sea. At the back door of the farmhouse, Sariah seems steady enough to walk inside by herself and I tell her to get Hazel to look at the wound.

"Where are you going?" she asks.

I tell her about George's threats to me, how he made me swear I wouldn't leave. It's much too risky for me to go back inside the farmhouse.

"You can't," Sariah says. "You'll not last in this weather."

Somehow I persuade her, and she reaches inside and hands me the fisherman's jacket.

"Thank you."

I wait until she closes the door before heading into the night, utterly terrified. As I feel my way across the bracken and stones, I turn and look back.

At George's bedroom window, I can see the form of him in silhouette, hands in his pockets, looking down at me.

March 24, 2015

Potter's Lane, Twickenham

Lochlan: I dream all night of dark tunnels lined with CCTV cameras. At first I think I'm in the Channel Tunnel, only I'm on foot and there are no cars. I can sense someone is at the end of the tunnel and that's what keeps me walking. But every time I reach the end, the tunnel veers sharply to the right or left. I never reach the end.

I wake in the bathtub. It takes me a solid minute or two to work out where I am and how I got here. I vaguely remember drinking last night, then going somewhere in the car. I think I might have crashed it into the garden gate.

I struggle out feetfirst and fall forward on my hands and knees. There's a puddle of vomit on the tiles close to me. I straighten painfully and splash cold water on my face at the sink. The face that looks back at me in the mirror is haggard and sunken eyed. I haven't shaved in three days and the stubble that has emerged is patched with silver. I feel fragile, in the exact way I felt the morning my mother walked out. I couldn't tell you what day it is, or even the month. There is so much chaos in my head right now that it seems wrong for things to go on being ordinary: the hairline fractures in one of the tiles that Eloïse asked me to fix. She threatened to do it herself if I didn't. I brush my teeth and clean up the sick on the floor and make a plan to fix the cracked tile.

I bump into Gerda on the landing. Her blonde hair is flat at one side from where she's been sleeping, her face bare and pinched. She's wearing a white cashmere robe and has her arms folded.

"Morning," I say.

She squints at me and frowns. "You were in quite a state last night. You've wrecked your poor car."

How can a car be poor? Does it have feelings?

"It was an accident."

"This isn't the time to fall apart, Lochlan."

Childishly, I make a show of patting myself all over. "I think . . . yes, I think I'm still intact."

"Where are you going now?"

I nod at the bathroom. "Got a cracked tile. Got to fix it."

"Lochlan—"

I'm halfway down the stairs. "I'll get Cressida's bottles sterilized and set up for the day while I'm downstairs," I tell Gerda.

"Lochlan," she calls again, a firmer tone. I turn and glance up at her.

"Yes?"

She sighs. "It's five in the morning. Go back to bed."

"Can't," I say, mildly aware afterward that I sound childish. "I've loads to do."

"Like what?"

"The cracked tile in the bathroom, for one. And Eloïse wanted the dining room painted. I'd best get a move on."

There's a stack of newspapers on the kitchen table, purchased by Magnus, who seems to spend his days pacing our street and angrily scrutinizing media reports of Eloïse's disappearance. Despite myself, I find my eyes straying to the paper on top of the pile, a page folded over at a headline: **Refugee Activist Amidst Racist Row in Abduction Hoax.**

Don't read it, Lochlan.

I have to.

Continue doing the tiles. Ignore what the media says.

I need to know what they're saying about my wife.

...Eloïse Shelley (37) recently walked out on her charity, Children of War, where she had campaigned against immigration reform and condemned the Rt. Hon. Giles McBratney MP as racist. Now it seems Ms. Shelley has also dumped her husband and young children and absconded from their plush Richmond home, but a close source revealed that this so-called disappearing act is a calculated move to draw attention to her charity and breathe some much-needed fresh air into her media career...

A large photograph of Eloïse in a short red dress and gold stilettos with a glass of champagne in her hand sits at the top of the article. They've pinched it from her Facebook page, overlooking all the ones of Eloïse with Max and Cressida in her arms for the one that seems to portray her as a ruthless career woman, someone morally lax enough to fake her own disappearance.

You see? It's all lies. No one's interested in helping to find her. You shouldn't have looked.

I head into the kitchen and flick on the espresso machine. There are flowers everywhere: five bouquets in the kitchen, two of them standing in plastic B&Q jugs as we only have three vases; and I can make out a number of new potted plants in the family room. The place is a mess. Why did Eloïse ever get rid of our housekeeper? I pull out a pair of gardening gloves from a cupboard, and even though they're far too small and have roses on them, I keep them on as I gather up the flowers and take them into the back garden. A part of my brain tells me that these gloves last held my wife's hands, that there are traces of her there and on my skin, all through this house, so many traces and remnants, and yet no sign of her. It would make your head spin if you thought too much about it.

Gerda comes out into the garden, her expression oddly sympathetic. She glances up at the pink sky and stifles a yawn.

"Can't sleep?" I ask her.

"What? No, I...Lochlan, this behavior is not helping anybody. I know it's difficult but...the children, Lochlan. The children need you to be strong. This isn't the time to be silly..."

"No one's being silly, Gerda. I'm just...dealing with things until my wife gets back, that's all."

She begins to cry, and I watch her, that same sense of ghostliness coming upon me, as if I'm no longer here but part of the atmosphere. I hear myself tell her it's OK, I know this is hard on everybody, but the words are no more than sounds my body is making. The part of me that I can feel and identify as me is somehow detached, looking on.

Gerda takes her mobile phone out of a pocket and checks it, sniffing and mumbling in German.

"I'm still waiting for her to call," she says. "I have to charge it twice a day to keep up with how often I'm checking it. Looking at the Facebook page, checking the news. Every second, every minute, I'm expecting her number to pop up on the screen. It's agony, all this waiting. All this unknowing."

A long silence.

"For the first time in my whole life, I feel utterly helpless," she says, folding her hands between her legs.

I am about to agree when I feel a pain in my chest and a tightening in my throat, and so I push the thought of my own helplessness away and set about planting the tray of small seedlings Eloïse has placed beneath a plastic shield on the ground nearby. My thoughts are a mishmash of clichés and their terrible truths. *Missing a limb. Half a person.* Keep working, that's the trick. Work provides structure and squashes those spiraling questions that have no answer. Right now, my wife is a question mark, and I'll tear down the house and rebuild it with my bare hands if it distracts me long enough.

Eloïse would fall on the ground laughing if she saw me now. I don't think I've been into our garden since last summer. I leave the house at seven each morning, except Sundays, and I'm not back until seven at night, at the earliest. No time for the garden. It was just a long strip of soil and concrete when we bought the house, but Eloïse has transformed it. There's a playhouse at the very bottom, a plastic castle for Max, and six raised beds. I have no idea whether I'm pulling plants or weeds, but being out here among the things my wife cultivated, in her space, brings a small amount of comfort.

"I can't help but feel this is a punishment," Gerda says.

Tears are streaming down her face and she catches them at her jaw with her fingertips. "We never knew, did we? We were in Switzerland. I mean, when she contacted us at—what? Thirteen? Twelve years old? We came back and took her in immediately. We did all we could to...you know. Rectify the damage that had been done."

She glances at me with large wet eyes.

"What damage?" I ask.

She tuts impatiently and glances away.

"You know fine well 'what damage.' It's hardly something I feel proud of, is it? Jude. Our only child, a heroin addict."

She presses her fingertips against her mouth and shakes her head, as though suddenly overwhelmed by letting the words come out of her mouth.

"El never says much about her mother," I say. "She counts *you* as her mum. Even though she calls you 'Mamie.'" Mamie's Swiss for "Granny," apparently.

"I can't stop thinking of all the things I regret doing, the things I regret *not* doing," she murmurs. "I should have helped her more. I know it's pathetic, but...When Jude left, I had an instinct that we should have insisted that she left the baby behind. But Eloïse was three. Maybe four. I told myself she needed to be with her mother."

Eloïse rarely mentions Jude, though from snippets of conversation I know that she fell pregnant with Eloïse at the age of sixteen. When El was four, Jude looted her parents' safe and ran off to London with an older man. Eight years later, she died of a drug overdose in some squalid flat. El found a telephone number for Magnus and Gerda and rang them. To their credit, they flew straight to London, picked Eloïse up, brought her home, and raised her.

I say, "I really don't think this has anything to do with all that."

But she's not listening. She's caught up with her memories, with the chapters of El's life that I don't know how to translate.

"Why Eloïse?" Her voice shakes again and she presses her fingertips to her lips to control her emotions. "Of all the people to go missing, why her? She's done nothing to deserve this, has she? Two darling children. Puts her heart and soul into raising them. A charity campaigner, changing the lives of thousands of poor refugee children."

For a moment it crosses my mind to record this to play to Eloïse when she returns. Gerda does nothing but criticize Eloïse and order her about like a drill sergeant. I've lost count of the times that El has complained wearily to me about her grandmother's words of disapproval, how she seems to do nothing right in Gerda's eyes. It was Gerda who persuaded her to give up her job when the children came along, if I remember correctly, only to chide Eloïse for handing in her notice.

"When we lived in Geneva, she was too afraid to go more than ten feet away from us," Gerda continues. "I gave her so much freedom and yet she was a timid thing, always by my side. She'd climb into our bed some nights, even as a teenager. It's wrong, all of this. She shouldn't be gone."

I say nothing more but go about digging and planting until my muscles ache. When I'm done, I leave Gerda in the garden and go upstairs to tackle the tiles in the bathroom.

The crack is still too apparent, so by the time Max wakes up I've hacked all the tiles off and am ordering replacements online. Max saunters into the bathroom, bleary-eyed and half-asleep, his blanket trailing after him.

"Morning, Daddy," he says. He frowns over the mess on the floor. "What you doing?"

"Making the house nice for Mummy when she comes home," I tell him.

He holds me with those beautiful blue eyes of his and shakes his head disapprovingly. "You've made a *big* mess. Mummy will be *very* cross."

"But Daddy's going to buy new tiles, you see? Nice shiny ones. And Mummy will be happy, won't she?"

He considers this, then gives a nod.

"You tell Mummy she has to come back now. OK, Daddy?"

I stroke his face. Helplessness is one thing. Lying to your boy like this is something else entirely. I clear my throat and make a tight fist behind my back. I have to keep it together.

"Yes, of course, Maxie. How about we make some cookies for Mummy, shall we do that?"

His face lights up. "*Thomas the Tank Engine* ones?"

"*Thomas the Tank Engine* cookies."

Both Cressida and Max have rejected the sleeping routines that Eloïse worked so hard to create and are still asleep in my bed. Max has started wetting the bed again, though luckily I managed to find an old packet of swimming nappies, which has prevented our bed from getting soaked. Cressida refuses to sleep unless she's touching me. I go and check on her, wedged in between two pillows in the middle of the bed. I'm struck with a sudden tenderness for her, a gladness that I hadn't felt at her arrival. I mean, of course I love her, she's my daughter. But I guess I felt we had enough on our plate with Max and my job and El's charity. I had to force myself to get used to the thought of double that amount of work.

Cressida is lying flat on her back with her head turned to one side, her lips puckered, and her fists bunched at either side of her head. Her hair has thickened over the last week, a little downy Mohican forming on her head. She has dark hair, like me, and the familiar Shelley dimple sits in the middle of her chin. I hadn't noticed this until Eloïse went missing. I tried to tell myself that it's only recently appeared, until I spotted Eloïse's Facebook pictures of Cressida in the hospital, barely a day old, and the dimple is there.

I tiptoe out, letting her sleep as long as she needs.

Oddly, from the ashes of this nightmare has risen a renewed relationship with my younger brother, Wes. We haven't really spoken in about six years, give or take the odd grunt at a family do. Wes is the black sheep of the family, my parents' late-in-life child who wreaked havoc from being knee-high to a grasshopper: expelled from primary school for biting another kid, expelled from high school for drugs and fighting, then locked up for the same things in his early twenties. He drives far too expensive a car for someone without a job. My dad blames it all on my mum leaving when Wes was only a baby. He was four, so not technically a baby, but the age that Max is now. The thought of my wee lad turning out like Wes has added a new layer of fear to the present situation.

Anyway, Wes phoned me this morning and asked how everything was, and I did the very manly thing and broke down on the phone. I told him about the baby monitors and he asked all kinds of questions, which I attempted to answer. Then he said, "Don't talk to the police, mate. The police'll do nothing. You find out anything, you come to me. No one else. I'll get this put right, trust me."

I told him I would, but my gut feeling is that if I took Wes up on his offer, several people would end up with their throats cut and I'd be locked up as an accessory to murder.

At ten, one of Eloïse's baby group pals, Niamh, a polite Irish woman with dark curly hair and glasses, comes over to take care of Cressida and Max while her own kids are at school. I spend a couple of minutes showing her how to sterilize a bottle and explaining how important it is to do it properly, otherwise Eloïse will go mad, until Niamh places a hand on my arm and looks at me with unveiled pity. "I've done it a few times before," she says.

The plan is that Niamh will look after Max and Cressida in the family room while Canavan and Welsh brief us on the latest developments in the living room, but Cressie develops a dire need to practice her finest yelling voice. We all take turns trying to decipher the reason—Gerda cuddles her, Magnus bounces her against his shoulder and sings the Swiss National Anthem, I change her nappy and let her kick her legs against the mat. She lies there waving her clenched fists, her mouth wide open and her tiny chest heaving out pitiful yells. Max lies down beside her at one point and mimics her. It almost makes me smile.

Niamh eventually sets up the double buggy and discreetly wheels Max and Cressida through the front door to, presumably, the park a few streets away. I watch them disappear down the street through the living room window, my heart in my mouth.

When Welsh and Canavan arrive, they bring a guest. The woman in the navy suit walks toward me with an outstretched hand. She's black, tall, and slender, a look of sympathy on her face. I don't look her in the eye in case that sympathy makes me emotional.

"Call me Lochlan," I tell her, returning her handshake briskly.

"I'm Sophie Ojukwu," she tells me, lowering onto the sofa as I sit in the armchair opposite. "I'm the Family Liaison Officer. I'll be helping you while the police carry out their investigation."

"Good to meet you," I say, tempted to ask if by "helping" she means that she has a special ability to find my wife.

We take our seats; I ask if anyone wants tea, but no one does. Gerda looks shrunken into herself, and although Magnus greets the detectives in his characteristically brusque manner, I notice he's quieter than usual, and when he sits he bounces one knee until Gerda places a hand on it, forcing him to stop.

Canavan goes about setting up a laptop on the coffee table, which I presume is to show us the footage they've managed to download from El's phone. But then he says, "Our tech team has found evidence of 'tampering' with the baby monitors they'd taken during the search."

I can't quite believe what I'm hearing. "Tampering?"

Welsh nods. "Unfortunately, the kind of baby monitors you owned are vulnerable to hacking. It appears that someone has hijacked them."

Gerda says, "What do you mean, 'hijacked' them?"

Canavan explains that their technical guys located several IP addresses that had been used to download data from the babycam. It's no easy feat, he says, not like a channel or website someone could stumble upon by accident. In fact, the tech team say that our babycams were installed with firewalls to protect them from possible intrusive activity, but this had been circumvented. Whoever has done this has significant technical skills and would have had to search out our own IP address in order to access the footage. It was a deliberate, calculated effort to spy on our family.

"How long have you had the monitors?" Canavan asks. I'm still processing everything he's said, so it takes me a moment to realize he's asked me a question. The irony. When Max was born, Eloïse insisted on getting top-spec baby monitors. Despite my suggestion that we go for the standard audio-only versions available in the likes of Mothercare or Mamas and Papas, El purchased four wireless monitors with high-quality video cameras. And whereas ordinary people might place the monitor on a cabinet or sideboard and point it in the direction of the crib, our monitors were set up Eloïse-style: mounted high on the wall, connected to the mains so they wouldn't switch off, synced together by a technician to provide one continuous video stream throughout the house, all the way from the children's bedrooms, right down the stairs, into the hallway and reception rooms and the kitchen.

Eloïse was able to link the footage to her phone and record it. Completely unnecessary, I told her, but she had planned to hire a nanny for Max and wouldn't dream of leaving him without surveillance. She argued that the monitors made it possible to check on Cressida and Max at night without having to get out of bed: all she'd have to do was turn on her phone. The monitors also synced to some kind of heartbeat-monitoring app, a preventative against cot death. If Cressida stopped breathing for more than fifteen seconds, the phone would sound an alarm.

"I guess we had the cameras for four years," I tell Canavan. He looks grave. "Then I'm afraid it's possible that whoever was hijacking the babycams could have been watching you for that length of time."

"But what does this mean?" Magnus shouts. "Are you saying that someone was spying on Eloïse?"

"Why would anyone do that?" Gerda cuts in, her hands at her mouth.

"That's precisely what we intend to find out."

"So—you're saying that whoever hijacked the cameras is likely to have taken Eloïse?" Magnus says, tripping over his words a little. I've noticed that his left hand has started to shake.

Welsh and Canavan share a look. "It seems highly coincidental, at the very least," Welsh says gently. "Once we get the address of whoever was spying on your family, we'll be speaking with them in connection with Eloïse's disappearance."

"How long will that take?" Gerda asks.

"We're working on it," Canavan says. "For now, though, we'd like you to look very carefully at the footage we've retrieved and let us know if there's anything here, anything at all, that seems out of the ordinary."

He turns on the laptop. Max's bedroom appears on the screen, albeit at a slightly convex angle. The image is strikingly clear—I can see Max sitting on his mat, his little legs splayed wide as he rolls a toy train along a small wooden track looped in a figure eight.

After a few moments, Eloïse comes into the room carrying a basket of laundry. The footage is so raw, so real, like Facetime. It crushes me that she is behind that screen, in the past, anywhere but here. All of us cover our mouths. The air in the room is suddenly thick with emotion.

"What you doing, Mummy?" Max says as Eloïse folds his

clothes and puts them in his drawer. He sounds and looks so much younger, his pronunciation looser and awkward. This footage must be from last year, before he turned three.

"I'm putting your clothes away, darling. Do you want to help me?"

"No fanks."

Eloïse laughs. There's a sound elsewhere in the house that makes both of them stop what they're doing and glance at the door.

"I think that's Daddy, back from work," Eloïse says. "Shall we surprise him?"

Eloïse stands close to the wall behind the door, as though ready to leap out onto the landing. Max runs toward her and clings to her leg, peeking out from behind the door.

They wait a long time, but I don't appear. Eventually Max calls out, "Daddy!" and Eloïse tells him gently to be quiet.

"I think he's coming upstairs," she says. The screen flicks to the camera positioned at the top of the stairs, showing me heading upstairs with the *Financial Times* tucked under my arm, my free hand tugging at my necktie. I don't remember this at all.

"Come and get us!" Eloïse calls, and Max claps his hands to his mouth and giggles.

"Not now," I say. "I've got to catch up on some work."

My heart sinks as I watch myself on the landing camera, heading for the office at the end of the hall. The screen flicks back to Eloïse and Max, who asks: "Daddy not coming?"

Eloïse picks him up and kisses his forehead. "He's busy. Why don't we finish putting away your clothes, eh? You can give Mummy a hand."

The video cuts to Eloïse and Max in the family room, sitting on the floor singing nursery rhymes. Eloïse is pregnant, about five or six months. I recognize the floaty white top she's wearing; she bought it shortly after the anomaly scan. She stops singing "Row, row, row your boat" and Max continues. Then he says, "Why you not singing, Mummy?"

Silence. Then, "Mummy feels a little bit sad, Maxie."

"Why you sad, Mummy?"

"I don't know, Maxie."

"Did you hurt yourself?"

"I don't think so."

"'Cos I cry sometimes when I hurt myself."

She laughs. "I know you do, Maxie. But then Mummy always kisses it better."

"Maybe I can kiss your ouchie better."

He leans over and kisses her on the arm with a loud *mwah!*

"Now you should be all better."

"Thank you, love."

He starts another nursery song and she tries to join in, but I hear the tremble in her voice. I try to think back: Why was she upset?

Other scenes briefly show El and me discussing schedules, work arrangements, family holidays—normal stuff. One scene makes me laugh: Max throws an epic tantrum about getting dressed, and even after Eloïse manages to pull his T-shirt and trousers on him he strips naked and runs down the stairs. When he was potty training, he went through a phase of several months of taking his clothes off anywhere, anytime: supermarkets, friends' houses, playgroups... The camera angled down the stairs captures him heading for the front door right as the postman is delivering some letters. He pulls it open and blows a raspberry at the postman before turning and racing back into the family room. Eloïse apologizes to the postman, then races after Max and scolds him. He lies face-down on the floor and screams his lungs out in protest. I know his tantrums drove Eloïse to tears at times, but it makes me chuckle.

I soon realize, however, that everything that seems to come out of my mouth in the footage is work related: clients, investment cases, stock. Was I always so dull? I seem perpetually tired and long faced.

Forty minutes in, Eloïse and I are waltzing in the kitchen late at night, laughing. Her hands are clasped at the back of my neck, her head angled up to mine.

I'm grinning like an idiot and have my gaze fixed on her lovely breasts. "What are you thinking?" she says, smiling up at me.

"Happy thoughts."

She turns and loops her hands around my neck from behind, and I slip my hands beneath her swollen belly, cradling it. A few seconds later, Max runs in and wraps his arms around her legs. She picks him up, setting him on her hip, and we all sway to the music together. Welsh passes a box of tissues around and it's only then that I realize that Gerda and Magnus and I are all in tears.

The next scene shows Eloïse walking across the landing, talking to someone. At first I think it's me or Max, but then the nursery camera picks her up and she turns, as though someone is standing behind her, and addresses thin air. She is no longer pregnant, but her stomach still protrudes, as though she has very recently given birth. I watch closely, utterly confused.

"But what about Lochlan?" she is saying. "I don't know..."

It's strange, completely unlike her. Her whole manner, I mean. She puts her hands on her hips and looks as though she's mulling something over, but occasionally she says "yeah" or "I guess so," as though she's having a conversation with a ghost.

I hit pause to take it in.

"What do you make of that?" Cavanan says.

I look to Magnus and Gerda. "I've no idea. Can you play it again?"

He rewinds it and zooms in slightly closer, rendering El's silhouette in pixelated fuzz. Eloïse laughs and nods this time, then says "thanks," before walking out of the room.

"Maybe someone out of shot?" Welsh says.

"That's my thinking," Canavan says. "I'd like to see if we can get this image enhanced. We might be able to pick up a reflection from that window, there."

"Maybe her mobile phone was in her pocket," I say, squinting at the screen. "And she had someone on speakerphone but the microphone on the babycam didn't pick it up?"

Canavan nods. "Possibly."

But when we play it again, and then again in slow motion, we all agree: there is no one else in the room. I find myself wanting someone to explain it, for a shadow of another man to appear in the corner. Even if it turns out that she's talking to a lover, I don't care: it's too preposterous for me to ignore.

But Canavan and Welsh are keen to move on, to find more clues. Other scenes show Eloïse getting up during the night and going into the nursery to check on Cressida. Cressida is not crying and remains asleep, but Eloïse paces and paces, going in to check on Max. Then she checks the front door and the back door. The clock in the family room reads two twenty.

Several more scenes show the same—Eloïse wandering around the house in the middle of the night while I lie snoring in bed. Cressida was only a couple of weeks old. Why was she up? She must have been exhausted. Why didn't she ever say anything about not being able to sleep?

Fifty-four minutes in, the footage cuts to the sound of shouting and a child screaming in the background. We are both walking between the kitchen and the family room. It is late—the large round clock on the wall reads half past twelve. I know it's February from Max's hand-drawn Valentine cards on the mantelpiece. Six weeks ago. Eloïse is barefoot, her hair loosely gathered up, a long white nightdress brushing her calves, Cressida in her arms producing such a loud shriek that the laptop speakers vibrate and I have to turn the volume down.

"What's your problem?" I seem to be saying, angrily gathering up clothes and toys and throwing them into corners. "It's only a week! That's all!"

"It's not about the conference!" she shouts back. "I understand you have to work long hours six or seven days a week, but you don't *have* to go to the conference! Cressida's not going to know who you are at this rate."

"Don't be stupid."

"It's like you're determined to be away from us as much as possible."

"And that's fair, is it?"

The anger retreats from her voice, turning into a plea. "I *need* you, Lochlan. I need you and you're never here."

I'm mortified at how I come across, and there's this strange feeling nagging at me that this is not how it happened, or that the cameras are somehow making me seem angrier than I really was. I didn't go to the conference, and Lincoln Kavanagh got the Pinco deal. But no, I shouldn't have resented El for it.

"Mummy, what's all the shouting about?"

Max isn't visible but his voice carries all the way to the microphone, and I remember him then, standing in the doorway in his *Gruffalo* pajamas, bleary-eyed and yawning.

Cressida's wailing reaches vibrato; Eloïse pulls a dining chair from the table and sits down, awkwardly positioning Cressida to her breast for a feed. She gives a loud gasp as Cressida latches on, and I recall how painful breastfeeding was for her. I see her curl up her toes, her face tight with agony. In my worst moments, I wondered if she was exaggerating, trying to make me feel bad.

I am barely visible at the corner of the screen, still in the kitchen, still shouting.

"Why don't I do what you did, eh? Why don't I damn well jack in the job and move us all into a council house? Though I've a feeling you wouldn't like that very much, El."

She stares at me. "What are you saying?"

"I'm saying you've been used to better than what I've got to give, haven't you?"

"You're saying you've got something to give, Lochlan?"

At this I slam my fist into a door, making Eloïse jump and the baby start to cry. I feel Magnus and Gerda's eyes turn to me. On the screen, El continues breastfeeding, one hand covering her eyes, biting her lip and making whimpering sounds. Cressida unlatches and starts to scream again. El swipes the tears from her face and lifts Cressida to her shoulder as she makes for the kitchen.

As she moves out of shot, there is a loud slapping sound, followed by a yell.

The screen flicks to Eloïse entering Cressida's bedroom and settling down into the nursing chair, where she continues to feed Cressida with a bottle. She is crying.

I stand up and begin to pace. No one will meet my eye, and the exhausted, wrung-out part of my brain interprets the whole situation as a setup, designed to point the finger of blame for her disappearance at me.

"I didn't hit Eloïse," I say, though a voice in my head tells me I sound guilty. "It may have looked like that, but it wasn't the case. Neither of us would ever hit the other. The sound you heard was Max's train rolling off the edge of the worktop and landing on the floor. Eloïse stood on it."

Gerda glares at me. "She had recently had a baby, Lochlan. Did you have to be so cruel?"

I look at everyone in the room, skewered with regret. "I've never hit her. I would never do that, honestly. Watch it again."

We do, but I don't come across as any less callous. I hang my head, stung by the note of pain in El's voice when she tells me she needs me. I recall the argument now, but it played out differently in my memory. She had had a rant at me earlier for not pulling my weight around the house. I'd felt hurt, too, when she ignored a romantic text that I'd sent her, and she had seemed distanced for weeks, flinching from my touch. I didn't believe her when she said she needed me. At least, I'd interpreted it as a need based on doing my share of laundry and dishes, not emotional need.

Welsh and Canavan share a look. Then Canavan clears his throat and says, "Anything else there that seems out of the ordinary?"

March 24, 2015

Potter's Lane, Twickenham

Gerda: I have asked myself many questions since the telephone call from Lochlan, telling us that my beloved Eloïse was missing. I suppose anyone would ask questions in the face of this. It's not the questioning but the failure to reach answers that I find most maddening.

We lost Jude, our only child. Our only daughter. Both she and I had escaped death when she exploded into the world three months before she was due. The doctors told Magnus to say his good-byes to both of us. I was unconscious during it, of course, half my life's blood on the tiles of the operating theater and our tiny little sparrow fighting for her life in the ICU. A nurse asked him to name her before she died, and he couldn't recall any of the names we'd discussed for our first child. I'd particularly liked Amandine or Bastien for a boy, but his mind turned to Jude, the patron saint of the impossible.

We both survived. The doctors told us we would never have any more children, but this news paled into insignificance compared with the fact that we'd been given a second chance.

We had a wonderful life in Geneva. Jude thrived and excelled at school. She was naughty, yes, and it is possible we spoiled her. She was a lazy child, too. I was always troubled by this side of her character. Perhaps it was bad genes. I'm not sure. Willful from the moment she was born. Wouldn't sleep, wouldn't eat. Refused to walk until she was almost two, didn't utter a word until she was five. It was probably a blessing that I couldn't have any more children—Jude was as demanding as six children put together.

And then, when she was twenty, she left home with her boyfriend, Orhan, and Eloïse. I was married at twenty, and it's certainly not a young age to be trying to carve a place for oneself in the world, but Jude seemed younger. Less mature than I had been. She stole a lot of money from our safe, so we knew that, at the very least, she'd be able to take care of herself for a while, until she figured out what she wanted to do. Still, I worried terribly, and I blamed myself. Deep down I knew she was too selfish and chaotic to be a good mother. Had I acted upon that instinct, perhaps I could have changed things. But I didn't.

We wrote to her and Orhan as much as we could, sent them money. She had brought him over for tea shortly before their dramatic departure for London. He was a university student, she said, but I didn't believe a word of it. He was much older than I expected. Around thirty. A little quiet, but handsome. Dark haired, a tendency to hold a gaze longer than was comfortable. His father was Turkish. Magnus didn't like him. I remember that Jude had fallen in with a crowd of girls at college that I didn't like, and anything that distracted her from them was a good thing in my book. When Orhan came on the scene, she stopped seeing those girls, and I was happy with that. But, from the fire into the frying pan, as they say.

When the Officer in Charge, Detective Sergeant Canavan, told us that someone had been spying on the family via baby monitors, my first thought was bitterness at modern technology. *Baby monitors!* I'd exclaimed when El told me about her purchase. *You're the baby monitor, darling! You're the mother!* But she laughed it off.

Which brings me to my second thought: this generation of parents seems under some kind of spell that compels them to achieve complete and utter perfection. That's the impression Eloïse always gave me when we spoke on the phone and whenever she would come and visit with the children: that she was competing against every other parent alive and that this was entirely normal and expected. The baby-monitor issue was one of many indicators of the frenzied effort Eloïse made to *win* at motherhood. As if it was a competition.

I think what I'm saying is that, whilst my anger is of course directed at the villain who saw fit to hack into the baby cameras, I can't help feeling that, had Eloïse taken a more traditional approach to parenthood, had she resisted the social pressure that is undeniably bearing down on today's parents—particularly mothers—then this terrible situation would have been avoided. But I can't tell this to a soul. And anyway, it's hardly going to bring my granddaughter back, is it?

I came to this house believing that Eloïse had walked out on her marriage. Lochlan is dependable, and they make a nice couple, but he's not exactly what I wanted for her. He's fond of alcohol and on one occasion she turned up on our doorstep asking to stay with us for a couple of nights. I pressed her to tell me what was wrong, for she seemed withdrawn and ill at ease, and Max was starting to walk. It seemed a time when any wife would want to be in her own home with her husband and child, but she was reluctant to go back.

After watching the footage from the baby cameras, I don't know where to turn. Lochlan isn't quite the decent fellow I had come to believe he was. Certainly not the husband and father I had assumed him to be. He was so nasty to Eloïse, so explosive. I had put all my fears aside and given him the benefit of the doubt, but after seeing him yelling at Eloïse like that, and then crashing his lovely car . . . I have a mind to tell the police that he was drunk driving.

I tried to speak my mind to Magnus earlier, as we were getting ready for bed. We're staying in the spare room on a blow-up mattress. It's not very comfortable and Magnus has to sleep upright due to his angina, so he's spending his nights on a camping chair by the window until the leather recliner I ordered for him arrives from Switzerland. I don't trust anything mechanical made outside Switzerland.

"I read that most disappearances are linked to family members," I said. "Do you think this is anything to do with Lochlan?"

He sighed and settled down into his chair. I felt irritated at him. We've been married for over half a century and in all that time I doubt I've ever felt as angry as I did right then. He didn't seem to be as concerned about Eloïse's disappearance as I was. He seemed blasé, as if everything was normal, and he was ready to believe anything that came out of Lochlan's mouth. Why wasn't he *doing* more? Why wasn't he calling his old contacts for information, or hiring a private investigator? Didn't he care?

"Leave it alone, Gerda," he said simply, rifling in his medicine bag.

I suppressed the urge to scream. "Eloïse said they had an argument the other week. What if he...you know."

"What?"

I sighed. It made sense as thought but sounded silly when spoken. Every couple has arguments, I know that. Especially when children come along. Goodness knows, Magnus and I argued over Jude.

But then I remembered something I hadn't thought of until then. Not long after little Cressida was born, I came to spend a few days with Eloïse and the children while Lochlan went back to work in Edinburgh. She seemed to be coping rather admirably, until one night I came down and was surprised to find her sitting in the garden. It was January, far too cold to be outside in the middle of the night, and at first I thought she was up because of the baby. But Cressida was still asleep in the Moses basket. And Eloïse was acting rather oddly, now that I think about it. She was muttering as though carrying on a conversation, and reaching out to someone ahead of her, but there was no one else in the garden.

"Eloïse," I said, throwing a blanket around her shoulders. "Whatever's the matter?"

She didn't respond until I laid my hand on her arm. And then she snapped her head around. She didn't look like herself. I don't know how to explain it. It was Eloïse, of course, and it wasn't that she was pulling any particular face. She simply looked unlike herself.

After a moment or two she gave a little shiver and seemed to recognize me. I asked if she was all right. And what she said was every bit as odd as her appearance.

Sometimes my life feels like it's happening on the other side of a window.

I didn't ask her what she meant. We went inside and she got back into bed and in the morning everything was back to normal.

But now—now, I wonder if I missed something at that moment. If there was something more to that night than I'd recognized at the time.

And perhaps I'll never know.

March 25, 2015

Twickenham Police Station

Lochlan: Magnus, Gerda, and I have all prepared for today's press conference by dressing defensively—both Magnus and Gerda wear similar pin-striped shirts with silk navy scarves wound tightly around their throats and I find myself drawn to a gunmetal gray shirt with a black tie and chinos. My belt slips easily into a tighter notch—stress has made it difficult to eat and turned my guts to mush.

Gerda's blonde hair is hairsprayed and moussed to petrification, her lips slicked blood red, and her mascara visible from a distance. Magnus has cut himself shaving in several spots and his lips are tight and thin. I would give anything for a drink.

Sophie and Welsh show up in similar trouser suits, both of them looking official and authoritative. We all sit around the table and Sophie and Welsh talk us through the format of the press conference with calm, slow voices, as though they're addressing a group of two-year-olds. I appreciate the slowness. It is still so daunting and unbelievable that we should be doing this. Several times Gerda has to ask Sophie to repeat herself.

The format is this: at noon there will be a group of reporters from the national and local newspapers, TV and radio channels, and a handful of web broadcasters who will gather in the conference room at Twickenham police station to disseminate information so that the public can be informed about the investigation.

"I have a speech prepared," Magnus announces, pulling out his reading glasses with one hand and flicking open a sheaf of folded paper with the other. He begins to read, but Welsh cuts him off.

"I think perhaps we should keep it quite concise."

"I want to address whoever was doing the spying," Magnus says angrily. "I'm her grandfather! I damn well raised her!"

Sophie smiles and nods. "We need to be careful how we put our message across. Remember, everything you say is going to be recorded and picked apart. Naturally, you want to say that you are missing Eloïse terribly and we all want her home safe and—"

"Of course I want that!" Magnus pounds the arm of the chair with his fist. "That's why I've written the speech!" He begins to cough. Gerda rubs his back and urges him to take it easy. I notice he is shaking. Spit forms at the corner of his mouth and his ears are burning red.

Welsh turns to me, emphatic. "We think it would be good if you take the lead in the conference, Lochlan. You're her husband, so people will likely respond to any comments you have about Eloïse. The request for information has to have a solid human context. You might tell people how dedicated Eloïse was to her work, to her children. What she was like as a wife, as a friend. How long you've been married. That there are people out there who are desperately missing her and need her back."

Gerda clears her throat and throws a meaningful glance at Magnus.

"We'd like to offer a reward for information. Magnus and I want to offer fifty thousand pounds to anyone who comes forward with anything that can lead us to Eloïse."

DS Welsh looks wary at this announcement, glancing at me for what I interpret as an intervention, but I don't offer it. I'd happily give a kidney for information on El's whereabouts.

"I think we have to be careful with that kind of thing," she says. "We've found that it can absorb precious time and resources with frankly useless information."

"I thought it might inspire anyone who feels afraid or reluctant to come forward…"

Welsh backpedals. "It *might* do that, but in the past it has tended to muddy the waters. Let's put out the appeal for now. We'll obviously assure viewers that all information will be held in strictest confidence." She glances at her watch. "I think it's time to go. Are we ready?"

We file out to the police car parked by the curb. A constable pushes back a couple of haranguing reporters, but as we get inside the car, flashbulbs strobe off the glass and I imagine my face splashed across the middle pages of some right-wing newspaper, cadaverous and shaken.

The press conference is held in an oppressive room with a low ceiling, blank walls, and a large banner bearing the Metropolitan Police logo. A Crimestoppers banner declares the national phone number in black and white, a directive to *TELL US WHAT YOU KNOW, NOT WHO YOU ARE* emblazoned across the top. At the far end of the room there is a row of tables, six microphones, and a jug of water. Gerda and Magnus seem frail and alien in this environment, both visibly anxious at the scene of thirty-odd strangers sitting a few feet away with camera lenses as long as my arm. The sight makes my own stomach churn. It suddenly feels less like making a plea for information than offering a plea for "not guilty."

Welsh reappears, her brown hair scraped back from her face and pulled into a tight bun. She has applied pale pink lipstick and blusher, her composure more authoritative than before. She gives me a firm nod.

"Ready?"

I say that I am, but as I go to walk up the room toward the table, Sophie waves me back. I tell Gerda and Magnus to go ahead and they follow Welsh, glancing at me with concern.

"What's wrong?" I ask Sophie.

She seems out of breath. "The police have located the person who was registered for the IP address associated with the baby monitors. That's where DS Canavan is now. He's about to make an arrest."

She signals someone behind me, and I turn to see Welsh motioning me to join them at the tables. The news that Canavan is about to arrest whoever was spying on my family for the last two years sends my heart racing and a cloak of ice descends on my shoulders. I ask Sophie if I can go with her, if I can make my way to wherever Canavan is and find out who he's arresting, but even as I'm spilling out my plea someone is pulling at me and telling me I have to go, I have to go and talk to the press conference about my wife.

In a daze, I take my place beside Welsh and watch Sophie disappear through a door. This all feels like a parallel universe. Like this is happening to someone else.

Welsh remains standing and addresses the crowd over a whir of clicking shutters and fuzzy-headed microphones.

"Thank you all for coming to the press conference here at Twickenham police station. We are here in relation to the disappearance of thirty-seven-year-old Eloïse Shelley, who some of you may know as founder and former CEO of Children of War, a charity for refugee children. Others among you may recall her as a public speaker, media broadcaster, a passionate advocate for equality and human rights."

Welsh nods at someone at the far end of the room, and suddenly an image flicks up on the white screen behind us. We all turn to see a projection of Eloïse on the seat of a morning TV program, mid-sentence. She looks great. Her hair is finely tonged into loose tumbling curls, and she wears a white jacket and matching skirt. She clasps her hands and crosses her feet at the ankles to one side as she chats with the TV host.

. . . well, to anyone who still feels as though migrants should be treated like second-class citizens in this country, I say— we're all of us human. We are all of us the same underneath our class, whatever language we speak or whatever accent we have, the clothes we wear and the car we drive. If we happen to drive a car at all. There are two hundred thousand children under the age of fourteen in this country who will not sleep in a bed tonight. They'll sleep on the cold hard ground outside, whether it's raining or snowing. Not only that, but we know that eighty percent of children without a home will be subjected to sexual or physical violence. That's unacceptable.

Think of how this experience affects them for the rest of their lives. If and when they are granted citizenship, the terrible damage is already done. We have a duty, a responsibility, to protect them. We have to remember that politics is only about labels, about barriers. We're all of us the same…

The footage cuts out as she's warming up and beginning to talk with her hands in that way she does when she's passionate about something. When I turn back to see the glow of the projector overhead, I see that Eloïse is all over me, her image caught on my sleeves and chest, as though I'm wearing her.

The screen goes blank and Welsh continues her speech: "People who know Eloïse describe her as loving and kind, the sort of person who would give a stranger the shirt off her back or the last coin in her purse. But beyond her roles as activist and CEO, she was also a loving wife and mother of two very small children. Max is only four years old, not yet at school, and her baby girl, Cressida, barely three months old. Both of them miss and need her greatly, so this request to the general public for information about her whereabouts is very urgent."

She pauses to allow the message to sink in. Gerda has started to weep and is reaching for the box of tissues in front of us. Magnus puts his arm around her. I can hear him making hiccup sounds, as though trying not to break down.

I make eye contact with a man wearing headphones and holding a large feather-duster mic in my direction. He throws me an odd grin, and panic grips me. *There could have been more than one person involved in hacking the babycams. Are they here, right now?*

Did they record our conversations?

Did they plan to blackmail us?

"Eloïse Shelley was not erratic or prone to abandoning her family," Welsh continues in a grave tone. "Eloïse was a devoted mother who stepped down from her role at the charity because her children needed her more at that time. We appeal to anyone with information pertaining to her whereabouts as of Tuesday the seventeenth of March to contact us on the number given here. All information will be held—"

Suddenly Magnus leans forward and roughly thumps his mic, causing a surge of ear-bursting feedback. He clears his throat and says, "I would like to offer a reward of fifty thousand pounds to anyone who has information about what has happened to my granddaughter. Anything at all."

"Mr. Bachmann—" Welsh interjects, but he waves her away.

"And to anyone who is able to bring her back to us within the next twenty-four hours, I pledge two hundred thousand pounds in cash."

Was that it? Was El blackmailed?

Reporters begin thrusting arms into the air, clamoring to ask their questions. "Mr. Bachmann! Mr. Bachmann!"

Welsh steps forward and instructs the press to remain quiet until she has finished her address.

"We will be taking questions in a moment. Please bear with me whilst I relay the necessary contact information and details that will assist us in locating Eloïse. We urge *anyone* who may have seen Eloïse in the hours leading up to her disappearance to make contact via the number provided on the press release. We guarantee that any information relayed will be treated sensitively and in confidence."

She nods at me. I can tell she's keen to distract the media from Magnus's offer of a reward, but the men and women in the front row look poised to follow up on it.

I glance over the cameras and mobile phones and microphones, then pull out a folded photograph of Eloïse from my shirt pocket. She is standing in our back garden in denim shorts and wellies, posing with a flute of champagne in one hand and a giant weed in the other, a saucy smile on her face and her blonde hair caught by the wind. On a deep exhale, I hold it up in front of me.

"This is my wife," I say. "Eloïse is an incredible woman. My son and daughter miss her so very much. We are lost without her." I begin to well up, my voice becoming tighter with each word I utter. I have never felt so exposed in my life, so completely naked. The words on the page swim and merge and I swipe my eyes with my hands. "Please, Eloïse. Please . . . anyone . . . just tell us she's safe. Please bring her back to us."

A hand shoots up. "Mr. Shelley, was your marriage in trouble? Do you think Eloïse may have walked out on your family?"

The question catches me off guard. "No," I say in disgust, which seems to trigger every hand in the room to rise.

"Mr. Shelley! Mr. Shelley!"

"Please, let him finish!" Welsh shouts, but her voice is drowned out.

I pull at my collar. Sweat pools in my armpits and runs down my back. I try to regain my composure, reminding myself of the many thousands of eyes that are watching. My colleagues. My bosses. Whoever may have taken my wife. I try to speak. But the thought that whoever has been arrested for spying on us is at this moment confessing to her murder overwhelms me.

"Mr. Shelley, do you have a message for your wife?"

I take a deep breath and stare into the lens ahead. "If you're watching, Eloïse, I promise that I'll find you. I won't rest until I bring you home."

January 21, 1986

Brixton, South London

Eloïse was in her mother's bedroom, trying to wake her up. She held Peter tightly in one hand and shook her mother with the other.

"Mummy," she said. "Mummy, please wake up!"

Eventually her mother stirred. She had bruises all over her pale arms and Eloïse noticed that her mummy's arms were becoming very thin. Her legs were skinny, too. Eloïse knew what Mamie would say if she saw Mummy. She would make her a big pot of potatoes and meat and tell her to eat the lot.

She looks sick, Peter said. *Maybe she needs to sleep.*

"But it's my birthday, Peter," Eloïse said. "I'm seven. I'm not six anymore. I want Mummy to wake up."

You've still got to go to school, though.

On the bedside table Eloïse could smell the funny stuff that made Mummy go droopy, or sometimes very happy, or occasionally very silly. She suspected that Orhan gave Mummy that stuff but dismissed the thought even as it prodded her, because Orhan was nice to her. Orhan was the one who bought her toys and sweets and sometimes pretty clothes. When Orhan hurt her, he always said sorry.

She looked over the spread of dirty spoons and paper wrappers on the table with a stab of anger. Peter was wrong. Mummy wasn't sick. She was floppy because of the stuff she took.

She took Peter back into the bedroom. The front door slammed downstairs, making the toys on her windowsill shake. She felt a familiar slick of cold running up her back and all down her arms, a tightening of her chest.

It's Orhan, isn't it? Peter said.

She held a finger to her lips and closed her eyes. She wished, without understanding why, that she could become invisible.

She held off getting changed until she thought it was safe. Then she did so quickly, first climbing on top of her chest of drawers and reaching across to the lock on her door. Orhan had moved the lock twice before, higher, and then higher again, to ensure that she couldn't lock it herself. He had to do that, he said, because he was in the room with her and she might unlock it and find that there were intruders out there. People who wanted to hurt her in different ways.

"Happy birthday, princess," a voice said. She gave a jump and spun around. Orhan was standing in the doorway of her room, both hands in his pockets, smiling.

He wasn't wearing his factory uniform: just jeans and a black T-shirt.

He walked in and sat on the edge of the bed. She had managed to get her skirt and shirt on but not her tights. She opted for socks. He watched.

"I got you some presents," he said, and she lit up.

"Presents?"

He glanced at Peter. "I got you a new teddy. That one there's looking a bit old and grubby. This one's white, too, instead of brown."

She couldn't hide her disappointment. Peter said nothing, as he was wont to do when Orhan was in the room. She wondered sometimes if Peter was scared of Orhan, or if he didn't like him.

"You don't like your present?" Orhan said.

She looked at the new teddy in her arms. "No, no. He's nice. Snowball. I'll call him Snowball."

Orhan grinned. "And your *big* present is downstairs."

She went to race out of the room to see it, but Orhan said "ah, ah, ah," making her stop.

"What do we do before getting a present?"

She turned. "We say please?"

He shook his head, rising to his feet and stroking her cheek. "Remember what I told you? It's nice to *give* presents, too. Isn't it?"

There it was again, a horrible feeling in her tummy when he said that, the same feeling she had when he needed a cuddle in the middle of the night. She wanted to say no, she didn't want to anymore, but he was already standing, and Peter was sagging on the windowsill, sad and empty, and there was no one anyway, no one anywhere to come and unlock that door.

March 28, 2015

Potter's Lane, Twickenham

Lochlan: The atmosphere at home is unbearable. Gerda has decided that *she* is in charge of the children and won't make eye contact. When I try to intervene in the militaristic schedule she's created for Max and Cressida she becomes upset and I feel pressed to back off. Magnus has taken to wandering the house or neighborhood, unshaven and disheveled. I keep finding him at odd hours in the garden in his pajamas, looking under the hedges. At two this morning he came downstairs with a torch and a cardboard box that had arrived from Amazon—a home fingerprinting kit that he insisted on dusting all over the back door and kitchen. We both stayed up all night, Magnus in the kitchen on his hands and knees, muttering to himself in German, me in the family room, cross-legged on the floor in one of El's dressing gowns, checking the #find-

Eloïse Twitter campaign and the Facebook page we set up. I came across missing person statistics. Apparently, over seven hundred and fifty people go missing in the UK *per day*. It's staggering. Selfishly, that figure depresses me because it makes El's disappearance less significant in the public domain. Seven hundred and fifty a day. Over five thousand a week. I've been badgering the police all weekend for information, wanting to punch the walls in frustration when they say they're working on it. *How could anyone have hijacked the babycams? Why would they do that?* They have no answers.

Last night I had a long conversation with Niamh about El and I was left more confused than enlightened. I went to pick up Max and she invited me in. All of El's friends and associates have been really helpful in trying to compile some insights from the last few months—and particularly the days leading up to her disappearance—in order to nail down possibilities, so I sensed she wanted to give me some info to add to that.

Niamh told her little boy, Daniel, to take Max upstairs again and play with his new train table while she sat down with me in the front room. They live in a tiny flat not far from us. I know Niamh's partner walked out on her a couple of years ago, so she's been especially sympathetic to my situation.

"I wanted to mention something that has been bugging me," she told me, keeping her voice low in case the boys burst in. "It's probably nothing, but after I watched the press conference...well, you'll agree that something's better than nothing."

I nodded, suddenly feeling sick at what she might say.

"I'm sorry." She started to explain why she hadn't said anything before, and I saw she was growing upset. I tried to reassure her that it was fine, that I wanted to know whatever it was she had to say. She took a deep breath and laced her hands together, bracing herself for the terrible information she was about to set loose.

"About six months ago, El said she'd joined a writer's group."

I waited. "OK."

She looked to the ceiling and sighed. "I knew this was a stupid thing to tell you..."

"No, no, please. Go on."

"I'm not even sure where the group met, or *why* she joined. But she seemed different while she was attending it. She even said she might publish a book."

I wasn't sure why this was such a big deal, or why it might bother Niamh so much that she had to tell me. In the brief amount of time that I had got to know her, Niamh had struck me as a thoughtful, quiet woman. Not the type to exaggerate or cause a fuss. I asked her when El joined the group—she'd never mentioned anything of the sort to me—and Niamh said September last year. I told her I'd search El's e-mail account again, see if I could find any details. She had a hunch that something had been off, and that it had happened around the time of this mysterious writer's group. Maybe El had been seeing one of the other writers. At this point I was still in the dark about who Canavan had arrested for hacking the babycams, tortured by all the waiting and silence, and so I quickly imagined whole scenarios involving El and a sonnet-writing lover who tried to blackmail her into staying with him. Maybe he threatened the kids and she tried to protect them.

"When you say El was acting different," I asked, "what do you mean by that?"

"She didn't seem herself," she said. "We'd make plans to meet—here, or at the park—and she'd not turn up. Wouldn't call or text to say her plans had changed. It was...unlike her. And our friendship suffered." She lowered her eyes to the floor. I tried to offer words of reassurance, to coax it out of her. She nodded and cleared her throat.

"I can't help feeling guilty," she said in a cracked voice. "We were close, as you know, and then...when she kept ditching me, especially at a time when I was so stressed, what with Paul messing me around with child payments..."

"I understand."

She wiped her eyes. "I assumed she was at the writing group because whenever I saw her it was all she talked about. She even said she'd resign from the charity permanently to write."

I made a face at this. "That doesn't sound like El."

She laughed. "I know, it sounds crazy. I mean, she stopped talking about it once Cressida was born."

"She did?"

"Yeah. I didn't want to bring it up again in case, you know...But for a few months she wasn't herself. Maybe it was nothing." She bit her lip, the certainty that had been in her voice a moment ago slipping away. "She was pregnant at the time. Maybe it was hormones."

I recalled seeing some new poetry books on the shelves of the bookcase that I hadn't spotted before. I'd wondered who they belonged to—neither of us were poetry fans, or so I thought—but now it made sense. Niamh was right, though— for El to talk about resigning was completely out of character. She'd never mentioned anything like this to me.

"She'd taken up smoking," I said then. "Did you know anything about this?"

Niamh looked puzzled. "*Smoking?* Are you sure?"

Her reaction was identical to the other friends I'd asked: nobody knew a thing about a smoking habit. I would have been tempted to convince myself I'd been mistaken, but Max had confirmed it. Or maybe he'd repeated what I said. I told Niamh about the babycam footage, how we were all perplexed over the scene of El apparently talking to someone who shouldn't have been there or talking to thin air. At this, a shadow fell across Niamh's face.

"Are you sure?" she said.

I thought about it and said that no, I wasn't sure. I'm not sure of anything.

My mobile rings as I'm trying to put breakfast cereal out for Max, though Gerda is insisting on giving him croissants and Gouda. My sense of time is completely mixed up and I have to check the clock every five minutes to keep on top of things.

Finally, the screen of my phone reads "number withheld," and I know it's the call I've been waiting for. I called Welsh and told her about the conversation with Niamh, but they seemed unimpressed. El went to lots of groups—baby yoga, Toddler Tales, Spanish for Kids, etc. Nobody from her many groups has been particularly helpful, and I suspect that Welsh and Canavan are anxious not to waste any more police resources than they have to.

I answer on the first ring, and the caller speaks first.

"Lochlan?"

It's Sophie Ojukwu, the Family Liaison Officer. My heart stops.

"Who did they arrest?"

"The detectives would like to speak to you this morning," she says. "Can you be at the station at nine?"

"Of course."

The clock says eight twenty. My heart in my mouth, I throw on a clean shirt and grab my car keys.

"What do you know about Harriet Ayres?" Canavan asks.

I'm in his office at the police station with Welsh at one end of the table and Canavan at the other.

"Harriet Ayres?" I repeat, not sure I've heard correctly.

Canavan reaches for a file and pulls out an A4-sized color photograph of a tall man with white hair, an orange tan, and a full set of gleaming dentures, and a younger woman with caramel-blonde hair, twinkling eyes, and a red-lipped smile. I tell them that the man is Dean Wyatt, one of the partners at the firm where I work.

"Do you recognize the woman?" Canavan says.

I take a deep breath and inspect the image closely, my heart racing. "She's a colleague. Works in IT. I used to see her sometimes in the staffroom at lunchtime." I risk a glance up at Welsh. "What's she got to do with this?"

Welsh raises her eyebrows. "That's all you know about her?"

Sweat is gathering under my armpits and along my forehead. I look from Welsh to Canavan.

"OK," he says, setting the picture aside and leaning back in his chair. "Well, she seems to know a good deal more about you. She's been charged with stalking and offenses contrary to the Computer Misuse Act 1990 and an offense of Voyeurism contrary to Section 67 of the Sexual Offenses Act 2003."

An invisible wrecking ball hits me square in the chest.

193

"Wait, wait, wait. You're telling me that this woman . . . you're saying this is who took Eloïse?"

Welsh is quick to correct me. "We don't know that yet. She has confessed to hacking the baby cameras."

The room tilts beneath my chair. "This is who was spying on us," I manage to say. Canavan gives a faint nod.

"But you don't know if she took Eloïse?"

Canavan studies me coolly. "Did you and Harriet have something going on between you?"

"Don't be ridiculous." The words tumble out of my mouth before I can even think about what I'm saying.

"You sure about that?"

"I'm sure about that."

"She says otherwise," Welsh adds.

Inside my head, there's a storm. On the outside I am working as hard as I can to look appropriately shaken by the news that a woman I don't know has been spying on my family, at the same time as maintaining a dignified air of innocence in the face of suspicions that I was cheating on Eloïse. Beneath all of that, I am bleeding regret, anguish, terror.

What has Harriet done?

Canavan watches me carefully for a moment and then, when I fail to reengage my faculties of speech, proceeds to tell me what happens next. Harriet has been charged with this offense and will either be remanded in custody or released on bail, during which time the police and her defense will prepare their case. They currently have insufficient evidence that she had anything to do with El going missing. I nod and make noises that hopefully avert any suspicion that I am on the verge of bursting apart at the seams.

Harriet Ayres. I had expected anything but this. I had expected a terrorist plot, a conspiracy, aliens...Not this. Anything but this.

And yet, as the pieces slide awkwardly and painfully together in my head, I realize what Canavan is really saying. Harriet has killed Eloïse. The next stages of this investigation will simply tell us how and when.

I phone Sophie Ojukwu from my car and tell her about Harriet Ayres. I'm shaking with a fresh surge of adrenaline as I recount Welsh's line of questioning and Harriet's claims.

"Did DS Canavan provide any specifics?" Sophie asks. "Did he give you any detailed information about what this woman said?"

"No," I say, mopping my forehead. "But she seems to be implying that she hijacked our baby cameras because we had something going on."

A pause. "The detectives are obliged to ask you about it—it's nothing personal."

I bite down on the knuckles of my right hand. My whole body is rigid and the muscles in my neck and arms feel like lead weights.

"She's taken my wife, hasn't she? Anyone crazy enough to hack into someone's baby cameras is sick enough to do something like that, aren't they? That's why she was spying, isn't it? To work out when Eloïse would be alone."

I'm starting to lose it. Tears are rolling down my cheeks and I'm screaming into the phone. Everything is falling apart.

"Go home, get some rest," Sophie says soothingly, and her words pierce me because it's exactly what Eloïse would say if she were here now. I rub my face and take deep, quivering breaths.

She promises to call me once she's got more information. My phone goes crazy with yet more Facebook messages and texts, but now they're all about the newspaper article on Eloïse. I hesitate for a moment before calling my brother.

"Hello?"

I didn't expect him to answer and it catches me off guard. I make a fist, clear my throat, thrust the voice of my father into my head. *Toughen up, laddie.*

"It's me. You got a minute?"

"I've got several."

"I've found out who was bugging the baby cameras. Her name's Harriet Ayres. She's a…colleague. It's likely she's the one who took Eloïse. She says I had an affair with her."

He pauses. "And did you?"

I groan.

"For how long, Lochlan?"

"It wasn't an affair. It was just…"

"Either you had an affair or you didn't."

I have never breathed a word of this to anyone. Not to colleagues who probed, not to anyone.

"We never slept together," I blurt out. "It was all…a stupid infatuation. She came to the house when El was at her parents with Max and…"

"And what?"

"I couldn't go through with it."

He sniffs. "I see. Well, happens to us all at some point."

"No, not that!" I cover my eyes with my hand. I have never loathed myself more than at this moment. How stupid could I have been? Harriet and I seemed to bump into each other regularly, despite being from different departments. She'd always take her lunch at the same time as me, or she'd call into my section to check on the security software or Wi-Fi connection. She was young, fresh out of university, as yet unjaded by things like poor mortgage rates, childcare issues and the impact of an NHS on the brink of collapse. She was full of pep and aspiration. She talked sanguinely about her future plans, about her *life dreams*, about sailing weekends and evenings spent learning Chinese. She was saving to travel the world. I was mesmerized. *I remembered having free time like that, dreams like that.* The unmitigated zest that bled from her made me perceive that so many of the people I socialized with seemed to be trammeled by their own lives—and I was no exception. By comparison, Harriet was like oxygen.

We discovered a mutual love of Green Day and that we'd been to the same concert at Wembley Stadium in 2010, only she'd managed to get Billie Joe Armstrong to autograph her shoulder. She liked to one-up me, and it became a running joke: I'd seen a great white shark in Australia, she'd almost been eaten by one. University College London paid my undergrad fees, she won a full-ride scholarship at Cambridge University and came top in her year. I was an extra on an episode of *Casualty* in 1990, she had a speaking part in a Mel Gibson film at the age of eight.

I had no idea if any of this was true, but that was beside the point: our banter was energizing, and I felt a spark between us. And of course there was the fact that she was very easy on the eye—liquid gold hair to her shoulders, toned legs, flirtatious eyes. I started to look forward to going to work and replayed our conversations in my head on the way home.

In contrast, Eloïse seemed to be consistently irritable. Our interactions became rhapsodies of the inane: bills, disputes with neighbors, whether to get a vented tumble dryer or the condenser variety (we went with the latter). She sniped at me over stupid things, like not responding to a text or texting back with a full stop, which insinuated a "tone," apparently. Most nights, El slept in our bed with Max while I took to the spare room.

At a work party a few months after first meeting Harriet, I got very drunk. We were at a restaurant in Mayfair and Dean had plied the table with enough wine for a small country. One minute I was chatting with Rod Hammersmith about Grexit and the next I was in a corner snogging Harriet.

"Has she confessed to kidnapping Eloïse?" Wes asks.

"The police are working on it."

"You know where she lives?"

"Somewhere in King's Cross. I've checked Facebook, but she has blocked me. She's blocked my calls to her mobile, too."

What am I doing, discussing this with Wes? His methods are usually five fingered, knuckle dustered, and altogether unsavory, but they seem to be rather effective, and right now there is a fury in me that begs to be let loose. Crash the car, start a fight—my mind races through options of self-violence. If I could go back in time, I would go into my office the morning after our work party and I'd immediately apologize to Harriet. I would tell her I was drunk and, more importantly, married with a kid, and therefore any flirtation was a mistake. I would not follow up on our drunken exchange with more flirtation, more kissing, and an invitation to spend a weekend at my home.

I wouldn't do so many things.

When she arrived that night she looked stunning—her hair pinned up in fat curls, a black playsuit clinging to her slim figure, glossy pink lipstick on full lips. I'd felt nervous until that moment. She was so young, so naïve. Maybe I thought by being with her I was recapturing something lost, I don't know.

But when I saw her in the doorway I didn't hesitate to invite her in. She seemed nervous and excited, her eyes darting to the pictures of Eloïse and Max on the walls.

"This place is about three times the size of my flat," she said, and I told her about my first place in London, a loft apartment I shared with a friend from university. There was only one bedroom and we took turns sleeping on the sofa. I felt nostalgic telling her about it, suddenly wistful about being penniless and exploited and finding claw marks in the butter from our resident rats.

We had dinner and talked about work, about films we'd both seen, about her adventures in Vietnam last summer. Later, as we stumbled up the stairs, lips locked and her hands under my shirt, she happened to spot the babycam mounted on the wall of the landing.

"What is *that*?" she said, breaking away.

I buried my face in her neck. "Baby monitor. We've got them all over the house."

She pushed back from me farther and laughed. "That's a bit creepy. Won't your wife see what we're doing?"

I stopped for breath. "No. No, I made sure they were all turned off before you got here."

We continued to kiss, the bottle of champagne abandoned downstairs, Harriet's hair spilling around her shoulders. We made it all the way to the bedroom before the knowledge arrived in my gut like a bullet that I couldn't go through with it. It was like waking up to the knowledge that she was twenty-one, that I was married with a child. If we went any further, we would cross the point of no return.

Even with Harriet standing there between me and the bed, her eyes shining with anticipation, I had lost all ability to do what I knew, deep down, would signify the end of our family. I might lose Max. He had recently started to walk, staggering across the room into my arms with the most magnificent chuckle of self-satisfaction. How could I risk losing him?

In that moment, the desire I felt for Harriet alchemized into recognition of the unearthly love I had for my wee boy. Before, I'd acknowledged how cute he was, how lovely, that his existence involved singing nursery rhymes at three in the morning to get him to stop crying, enduring porridge and baked beans being thrown wildly around the room in the name of weaning, and dry retching while changing nappies filled with twice his body weight in poo. Presented with Harriet in a state of breathless near-undress and the promise of a long-awaited, hard-earned night of ecstasy, my ardor transformed to a conviction that I would fight dragons, go to hell and back, and most definitely walk away from Harriet Ayres for my son.

Poor Harriet. She watched me take a step back from her, the expression of excitement sliding off her face.

"What's wrong?" she said.

I shook my head, stung with embarrassment. "I'm so sorry, I—"

She stepped forward and tried to kiss me again, but I moved her hands and turned my face. "I can't do this. I'm sorry."

"Is it me?" she said, her face crumpling, a tremor in her voice. She started to pull her dress up over her shoulders, the hem down toward her knees.

"You didn't do anything wrong," I said, pacing. "I apologize. But I'd like you to leave."

Ah, hindsight. I can see now that I treated Harriet very badly. At the time, she looked ashen, even tearful, holding my gaze for a handful of seconds before storming past me out of the room, down the stairs, slamming the front door behind her. A screech of tires in the driveway announced her departure.

I fell on to the bed, head in my hands, utterly torn. Had I really told her to leave? Yes, and that was good. No, it wasn't. It was the stupidest thing I'd ever, ever done. There was no going back. I couldn't exactly send her a text message and make some excuse about a lapse of sanity. And I couldn't expect things to be the same between us at work. But that was a good thing—wasn't it?

I sent my apologies via e-mail and again by voice mail. To say I was sheepish doesn't quite do it justice—I knew I had been cowardly and schoolboyish, as though I'd run away from a fight. Worse, I was certain that Eloïse would find out. It would be hard to persuade her that it had all meant nothing. There had been feelings involved. In one particularly intense moment, Harriet had said that she was falling in love with me and I had said the same. It had been an emotional affair, not a sexual one. And perhaps that was every bit as bad.

Harriet and I crossed paths on the stairs the week after. She ignored me. After a while, I didn't see her at all. I'm certain she was avoiding me, and I took pains to check the attendance list of any company parties to ensure we didn't find ourselves in an awkward reunion. Last I heard, she was seeing someone from Accounts and I breathed a sigh of relief.

But as I turn the key in the ignition, I pause. Why would she spy on us, all this time later? Surely she wasn't so burned by that night that she wanted revenge? She was a sweet girl. She didn't strike me as the crazy sort, or at least, not crazy enough to spy, or abduct my wife.

But then, I didn't know her, did I?

Wes is talking on the other end of the line and I've missed half what he said.

"OK. So she worked at the same place as you. Are you still at Smyth and Wyatt? That place on the embankment?"

"Yes."

"Righto. Leave it with me."

"What are you going to do, Wes?"

"Well, you've let the police take care of things, haven't you? Now they've got the individual who likely had your wife disappeared. They'll charge her on some minor offense—but find Eloïse? Not likely."

Just then a woman crosses the road in front of me with a little boy in her arms who looks exactly like Max. His blond hair flaps in the wind and she plants a kiss on his cheek. I think of my wife, how much she must be craving that right now, wherever she is. I think of Max, how much he misses his mother.

"Take it easy, pal," Wes says down the line. "This is better news than you think. You've got a suspect. Now, we'll find Eloïse. You have my word."

March 27, 2015

Komméno Island, Greece

My new home is a cave on the south side of the island, close to the dock. Not ideal, but it's warm and dry and affords a magnificent view of the Aegean. Last night I lay out on a flat slab of rock that still held the sun's heat and watched the stars spilling out over the night like silver glitter. I saw shooting stars zip across the sky like rockets, and around midnight a scarf of vivid green light unrolled there, just for a minute. Despite everything that has happened, I was mesmerized.

This morning I woke to the sound of dolphins hooping through the water close by. When I clambered out to get a closer look, they circled back toward me and played for ages. It was remarkable—their slick bodies arcing through the waves, clean as bullets. I lay down on a rock and dangled my hands in the water, splashing at them, and they poked their heads up and clicked at me. I could have watched them all day.

After George's threat to shoot Sariah, I didn't dare go back to the farmhouse proper. I thought about camping in one of the outbuildings but they felt too close. George's bedroom window overlooks them and I knew I wouldn't be able to rest easy in the knowledge that he was watching me.

I explored the island, seeking somewhere safe to hide. The hotel was too eerie, the abandoned houses on the hill too dangerous. Many of the caves I found were too hard to reach, too damp or too dark, but this one is high enough to be away from the tide and on a slight slope so that sunlight can get inside and warm the rocks.

I spent the night there, too cold and shaken to sleep properly. I eventually drifted off when the sun came up and when I woke again it was high in the sky, beating down in hot waves. I was famished, and I reckoned that George would be off writing somewhere, so I tentatively made my way to the farmhouse.

Sariah was sitting in the front room by the unlit fire, holding an ice pack to her head. She didn't look good—still dressed in the clothes she'd been wearing the day before, her face weary and closed. I pulled up a chair and sat close by. When she saw me, she reached for my hand and squeezed it.

"How are you doing?" I said. I noticed a white dressing on the right side of her forehead close to the temple. Joe must have seen to her.

"I'm doing OK," she said. "More exhausted than anything. I need a good night's sleep to function properly."

"What about your head? How bad is it?"

"Joe looked at it. He said the cut was pretty small. I probably walked into one of the old farm tools in the dark."

I faltered at her tone. She'd been knocked unconscious the night before, but she didn't seem to hold George responsible. Was she protecting him? Or too scared to say?

"Did George say anything to you this morning?" I asked carefully.

She slid her eyes to the window. "He said things got a little out of hand last night."

I glanced behind me before telling her: "He threatened to kill you, Sariah."

She threw me a puzzled look.

"You saw him attack me?"

"Yes. No. He pointed the gun at you and threatened to shoot you."

I watched as she took this in.

"He was pretty drunk, wasn't he?" she said doubtfully, and I agreed that yes, he was, but his threat was also pretty damn serious. We had only gone to the barn because Sariah was worried about him. And why wasn't she reacting the way I expected? It was as though she was trying to downplay it. Whatever way you looked at it, the fact that George had threatened to *shoot* her was horrifying.

And then, a terrible thought occurred, and although it was the briefest of shadows across my mind, it made me feel sick, and I couldn't bat it away.

What if Sariah had staged her fall?

Hazel had told me that I wasn't going to leave. George told me the same. Joe somehow knew my name—not just my first name. My full name. I still had no clue how he knew that. What if there was something more sinister going on? What if

205

Sariah was complicit in some weird plot to get me to stay? What if they weren't visiting the island at all, but lived here, and now they wanted to keep me prisoner?

I told Sariah I was going to stay in the cave until Nikodemos came on Friday and, hesitantly, I suggested that she should get off the island, too.

"I'll be off this island soon enough," she said mildly, and I felt relief at the thought that my suspicions were wrong—they *were* visiting the island, after all. They had lives elsewhere. They would all have to leave in a couple of weeks, go back to their homes. George would have to contact Nikodemos sooner or later. Wouldn't he?

"Maybe you'll come and visit me," I said, still trying to gauge whether she was playing me or helping me. "When I figure out where I live."

She smiled. "Oh, I promise, I'll be there."

She took some leftovers from the fridge, some bread and bottled water, and put it all into a picnic basket. I felt very anxious at the thought of George coming back. But Sariah insisted I take a shower while she fetched me some clean clothes from Hazel's room.

"And then can we get out of here?" I said, glancing out the window.

"Of course. We can have a picnic at the cave." A wink. "You can show me around your new place."

I was worried that Sariah might not be up to the journey, but she insisted that she was fine. She wrapped a blue scarf across her shoulders and found a long wooden stick in a corner of the kitchen to help her walk.

I carried the picnic basket and a blanket and we took the long stroll down the hill, through the olive groves and all along the coastline to the cave. The wind was less fierce than the day before and the ocean a deep shade of jade, fanning out as far as the eye could see. Birds chirped happily in the trees. Sariah laid out the blanket on a slab of rock and we ate.

"Still no memories?" she said, pouring wine into two tumblers.

I shook my head. I was experiencing déjà vu and familiarity more often, and when I tried to think of where I lived or who I shared my life with, I could make out letters in my head, but still nothing concrete.

"Maybe when I get to see a doctor it'll get better. They must have medication for this kind of thing."

"The mind is a strange place," she said, looking out over the ocean. "Sometimes it reveals things to us to help us grow. Other times, it hides things from us to protect us."

"You think this *isn't* down to hitting my head?" I asked. "You think I can't remember because something happened that was too traumatic for me to deal with?"

She tilted her face to the sky and closed her eyes. "Remember what I told you about Pandora's box? About how, in the real story, Pandora knew exactly what was in that box and only hesitated because she wasn't sure whether or not she could face it?" She opened her eyes and stared at me. "Confronting dangerous or terrifying memories is complex. That's the real story. Not the box."

I nodded, because this was exactly what I had feared. I carried two different species of fear, now. The fear of what kind of person I might be—the sort of person who forgets their own child. And the fear that I was running from a past so terrible that my mind wouldn't yield it.

I woke when it was dark and Sariah was gone. I couldn't remember falling asleep. She'd left me the blanket, and so I curled up and went back to sleep in the depths of the cave.

My dreams have become wildly intense and vivid, a series of colliding and meaningless images so emotionally charged that I have been waking more exhausted than before I went to sleep.

I dreamed again of the cave with the beast at the end of it. This time I was at the mouth of the cave, about to step inside. Terror pierced me, and yet I knew that I *had* to go in. I had the cigarette lighter in one hand but no ball of wool. As I went to step forward I felt a hand on my shoulder. I turned and saw a man there. He had dark hair, late to mid thirties, a kind face, though he seemed worried. He handed me the ball of red wool and said, "Come home."

I know I wanted to say so much more to him. I had a great urge to *explain* something to him. But I woke up before I could, and no amount of brain-racking could prompt me to remember what it was I wanted to say.

I spent as much time as I could away from the farmhouse in the hope that some space would restore a better atmosphere between George and the others, though hunger was driving me insane. The island is teeming with lemon groves, and quite a few peach trees, but a diet of citrus fruit resulted in a severe case of the runs, leaving me dehydrated, shaky, and feeling pretty disgusting. I needed water, and a bath. So this afternoon I headed back up to the farmhouse, praying that the mood had changed and that Sariah would tell me they'd contacted Nikodemos.

But as I was walking up the bank, I looked up and found the farmhouse had been replaced by a pretty suburban semi-detached town house. It had a pitched roof and a white car in the driveway. I stopped and glanced around, shaken by the sudden change in my environment. Behind me was a garden gate, and behind that was a street. I turned back to the house and the farmhouse was there once more, the car and the house both gone. It must have been the effects of dehydration.

Shaken, I cautiously approached the back door of the farmhouse. No one was inside, so I staggered to the sink and drank cold water straight from the tap. It tasted bitterly metallic but I didn't care—I drank about a pint and then felt sick.

When I turned round, Joe and Hazel were standing behind me. I hadn't heard them come in and so I almost jumped out of my skin.

"I was getting a drink," I said.

Hazel watched me, unsmiling.

"Could I have my clothes back?" she said stiffly.

I was so thirsty that I continued drinking, refilling my glass with a trembling hand.

"They're over there," Hazel added, pointing at a bench. I could see my clothes there among a pile of bedsheets and towels. "I haven't had a chance to wash them. I figured you'd want to wash your own clothes, for a change."

Her sour tone made me want to turn and run out of there, back to the cave. Whatever I had done to upset the dynamics of the group couldn't be resolved. I looked to Joe but he glanced away, suddenly engrossed with opening and closing the cupboards. "I made some rosemary and sea salt bread the other day," he muttered. "Hazel, did you see it?"

I remembered the picnic I had with Sariah. We had had the most amazing bread and, now that Joe mentioned it, it did taste of rosemary and sea salt. I was about to tell him but stopped myself, though not before he caught the look on my face.

"Did *you* take it?" he asked.

I felt like a scolded child with her hand in the cookie jar. "I'm sorry, Joe. Sariah and I had a picnic."

He slammed a cupboard door and I jumped, suddenly scared. Where was Sariah? I needed her calming influence to sweep some peace back into the farmhouse, but she was nowhere to be seen.

As I glanced toward the door at the other side of the room, anxious for some sign of her, I noticed a small black thing on a shelf that seemed familiar. The satellite phone.

I moved toward it, picked it up, and extended the antennae. Both Joe and Hazel looked on in silence.

"Where's George?" I whispered at Hazel.

She walked across the room toward me, eyes like saucers, all her haughtiness forgotten.

"He's not here."

Joe had begun to fidget, visibly nervous. Hazel approached him and put an arm around his waist, both of them watching me in anticipation.

"Do either of you know Nikodemos's number?" I asked.

Neither answered. I studied the phone and found a button with an arrow looped backward. I pressed it, and the screen lit up with numbers. I held it to my ear and heard the faint buzz-buzz of a call connecting, my eyes glued to the back door in case George arrived. Each ring of the number made my heart beat in my throat.

At last a voice said, "*Embròs.*"

"Nikodemos?"

"Speaking."

My breath caught and I struggled to spill out my words in case the signal died. "Hi, Nikodemos. My name's Eloïse and I'm staying in your farmhouse on Komméno."

"Ah, yes—the stowaway," he said in a thick Greek accent. "So I have heard. You're wanting a ride to Chania?"

I nodded at the phone, and Joe and Hazel clapped their hands to their mouths. "Yes! Yes, please."

"OK. I will come for you at seven, that's good?"

"That's *perfect*. Thank you so much!"

Hazel and Joe were gesticulating and mouthing, *Tell him to bring food*, but then Nikodemos said, "And tell the others I am sorry for last week, but this week there will be a *mountain* of food. An Everest! They better make room in their bellies, no?"

"Yes, thank you. Thank you."

In a handful of seconds it felt as though the world had flipped the right way up. Everything would be solved once he came, I knew it. Nikodemos would help me contact the police, I would search for the people who were missing me, find answers...I was no longer terrified of what I might discover about myself, about what I had done. I would face it.

Nikodemos was laughing on the end of the line. "No problem. I'll see you later. At the dock by the hotel, OK?"

He hung up. I placed the phone carefully back on the shelf and dabbed my eyes with my sleeves. I told Hazel and Joe what Nikodemos had said about the food and they bounced up and down, making silent gestures of rejoicing. And right then Sariah came in—for one hideous moment I thought it was George, and my stomach lurched—and Hazel grabbed her and told her in excited hisses what had happened.

Sariah looked at me. "He's really coming?"

I nodded, and she set down her pile of washing and told me we'd better make tracks.

"I'll come with you to the dock," she said, pulling on a coat. "To make sure you're safe."

211

March 29, 2015

Potter's Lane, Twickenham

Lochlan: I told Magnus and Gerda about Harriet. I didn't plan to—it just came out in the heat of the moment. If I thought it was unbearable at home before, it has now become absolute torture to be there. I guess I have no one to blame but myself.

When I came home from the police station everyone was here—Magnus, Gerda, Max, and Cressida. Sophie had informed Gerda and Magnus that an arrest had been made in connection with the tampering of the baby cameras, and of course they were eager to know who it was and whether or not the individual had confessed to taking Eloïse.

I stood by the window, still reeling from the news. I told them it was a woman, Harriet Ayres, and that she was being questioned.

"But who is she?" Gerda spat, her eyes bulging. "Is she a friend of Eloïse?"

"She's someone I work with."

"She's someone *you* know?" Magnus said, lifting an eyebrow. "But not Eloïse?"

Gerda was pacing frantically, throwing her arms around. "You must know why she would do this, Lochlan," she shouted. "The police said it was a deliberate effort to spy on you all. Why would she do that? For what purpose?"

Magnus was studying me grimly. I remembered then that he'd had an affair many years ago. At least, that was what Eloïse had told me. She'd heard them arguing and he moved out for a couple of days. One of the housekeepers at their place in Geneva. Roughly twenty years ago. Still, there was a look on his face that spoke volumes to me. Perhaps that was what prized the truth out of me again.

I sank down into a chair, longing to curl up into a ball and wake up to find it was all a bad dream.

"We had a thing," I mumbled. "Harriet and I."

"What thing?" Gerda said, her voice rising in pitch. "When?"

I told them, in between loud, appalled interjections from Gerda, that flirtation had progressed to a deeper connection but not a full-blown affair. Gerda kept asking what I meant, pressing me until I almost screamed. In the end, Magnus said calmly, "I think he's saying that it never developed into sexual relations."

Of course, at this, Max ran in.

"Daddy, what's 'sexual relations'?"

"It's a type of coffee," I muttered, lifting him onto my knee.

"Did 'E' know?" Gerda snapped, folding her arms and speaking in code for Max's benefit.

213

I shook my head. As much as Gerda would have preferred to see me roasting on a spit just then, had she known how excoriated I felt inside I think she would have been satisfied. Still, she looked at me with burning hatred. The silence was filled with Max's questions about coffee and voices in my head telling me to kill myself and get it over with.

"Do *you* think she is responsible for what's happened?" Magnus asked, after I'd explained that Harriet was still being questioned about her possible involvement in El's disappearance.

"Of course she is," Gerda hissed. "It's far too coincidental. If we were in Geneva, she'd already be standing trial. Here, she'll probably say she was depressed and get off scot-free."

No one spoke after that. I could hear Gerda's agitated gripes through the ceiling as she vented to Magnus. I tried to distract myself by crawling beside Cressida as she lay on the jungle gym batting the mirrors and springs swinging above her. When I lay down beside her, she became absorbed by the pocket on my T-shirt. She turned over and reached out for it with both hands and I moved closer to her. Her little feet were bare, and I noticed for the first time since she was born how small her toes were, five smooth buds on each foot. She kicked her heels up and down against the mat, blowing bubbles with her lips.

It was such a simple thing, lying beside her and watching her explore, but it struck me that I hadn't taken any time at all to *enjoy* her. I guess that's what happens when you're frantically busy. When El was pregnant with Max those nine months were observed day by day, with regular app notifications announcing the scale of his development with meticulous precision. With Cressida, El's pregnancy seemed to whiz past and suddenly she was here, and I had very little of that new-baby awe that I'd experienced with Max. I was tired, I had deadlines, and I was glad she was healthy. But enjoy her? No, I really, really hadn't.

Wes phoned at eight on Sunday night. I was finishing up the tile job in the bathroom, finding a newly cracked tile for each and every one that I replaced. Penance, you see, for all the mistakes I made. I answered swiftly, glad for the chance to talk to someone about everything that had been going on, but he spoke first.

"I've found her."

"You've found Eloïse?"

"Harriet. She's here."

I reeled. "*Harriet?*"

"Aye, Harriet. The chick you didn't cheat with."

I stood up and walked toward the window, pricked by paranoia.

"Wes, what's going on?"

It sounded crowded in the background and I gathered he was in a pub.

"I'm at the Dog and Duck," he said.

"And she's there?"

"Yep. Right here. Not a bad-looking bird, I have to say."

I clapped a hand across my eyes. "Wes, how did you know she was going to be there? Unless you're going to tell me this is all a coincidence."

"No coincidence, pal. Facebook. This pub was listed under her go-to places and I figured she'd be thirsty after what she's been going through."

"But there's no way she can be there. She was charged. She was being held in police custody."

"They bailed her," he said. "She's due at the Magistrates' Court in three weeks' time. 'Til then, she's free to, you know, have a beer, socialize with people whose wives are missing…"

"How do you know this? Don't tell me Facebook told you that, too."

"Let's just say I was owed a few favors."

I didn't dare ask what Wes was owed for.

"What are you going to do?"

"Question is, what are *you* going to do, bruv? She's *here*. She's had a drink. I would have thought you'd like to ask her a few questions."

"I think that's probably illegal, Wes."

"Thought you'd want to know, that's all."

"Wait…"

"Yep?"

I squeezed my eyes shut. I would live to regret this entire conversation, I knew it.

"Text me the address."

"You don't know where the Dog and Duck is?" he asked, incredulous.

"I've got kids, Wes. If it was a soft play center, I'd be able to recite the postcode."

I tapped on Gerda and Magnus's bedroom door and told them I had to go out for milk. Then I threw on a jacket and a pair of shoes, got into my car, and drove to the Dog and Duck.

I texted Wes when I arrived and he met me a couple of minutes later.

"Is she still here?" I said, and he nodded. He turned and

walked back toward the pub, his eyes fixed on the crowd of people who had gathered on the narrow pavement.

"Inside," he said. "I bought her a few drinks and she's pretty drunk."

The thought of my brother getting Harriet drunk would have been a challenge for me to wrap my brain around any other day, but given the circumstances I figured anything was possible.

I followed him inside. The place was crammed and surprisingly dark, but Wes took me to a corner table where a woman was sitting, one leg crossed over the other, checking her phone. I hesitated before proceeding. She hadn't seen me yet. She hadn't changed much, either. I recognized the emerald green dress she was wearing and the flat ankle boots. I had complimented her on that dress, said it matched her eyes. I felt an echo of whatever emotion I'd felt for her before.

Wes gave me a nudge, and I went and sat down in front of her. She raised her head and gave me an unsteady, liquid stare. Then she stood up and edged away from the table. I followed her, pushing through the crowds until I found myself back out on the street. I didn't see Wes. I couldn't see Harriet either, because the crowd outside had thickened and groups of people were beginning to walk home, straggling across the road. I glanced around and jogged to the square. There, at the corner, I saw Harriet clinging to the railings, vomiting.

"Go away," she mumbled as I approached.

"Just tell me," I shouted. "Tell me what you did with her."

Her face crumpled and she started to cry. She was wearing vivid red lipstick that had smeared on her hands and chin, and her hair was pulled back from her face into a topknot.

"I told the police that I had *nothing* to do with your wife going missing," she shouted. "It has nothing to do with me, all right?"

I wanted to grab her and shake the truth out of her, as if Eloïse might spring out of her pocket, but there were too many people nearby.

"Harriet, you *have* to tell me the truth. There are children involved. Please."

We were so close that I could see her teeth, the slightly chipped front incisor, her breath clutching the fruitiness of beer. She looked up at me woozily and cupped a hand to my cheek.

"So stupid of me, I know. I only wanted to see...I wanted to see if you were breaking up with her. I thought...I was in love with you."

I grabbed her hand and squeezed, shocked by the current of anger I could feel driving its way through me. I wanted to hurt her, to beat the truth out of her. I let go of her hand, one finger at a time.

"Tell me what you did."

"Why didn't you want me?" she said, shaking her head. "I wouldn't have told her. I knew you were married. It's not my usual thing, married men. Honest. But I thought you and me...we had something."

She was right: we did have a connection. And I had hurt her terribly. This was the consequence. I took a step backward, torn between fury and remorse.

"Why were you watching us, Harriet?"

She gave a long sigh, then shook her head. "It was easy."

"Easy?"

A half-shrug. "I know that's no excuse. But once I was able to log on, I was hooked."

I stared at her. "And that's your reason?"

She looked away, ashamed. "I guess...I was...curious? I wanted to know what you had with her. What it looked like. And maybe I wanted to find out what she had that I didn't."

She leaned in and kissed me full on the lips. It caught me by surprise—I was deep in thought, trying to examine her words for anything that sounded like the truth—and recoiled sharply. She stumbled forward, falling on to her hands and knees. A few onlookers shouted over to check that everything was OK and I held up a hand.

"I've got this," I said, kneeling to help Harriet. I saw someone take out their mobile phone, and it occurred to me that now might not be the best time to be photographed and plastered all over Facebook.

Harriet turned and began to walk unevenly. I followed. "You really expect me to believe you were spying on us for over a year because you were *curious?*"

She didn't answer.

"You owe me an answer," I called after her, forcefully this time. "*What did you do with her?*"

At this, she spun around, her finger raised to my face.

"I'm going to court for my mistake, all right? I will likely do time because of what I've done and Dean will give me the sack. I'll have no way of paying rent, no way of getting another job in this industry with a criminal record. All because I pressed a button."

"Oh yeah? Well, I've lost *my wife...*"

She tilted her head back and gave a forceful laugh. "Your *wife?* Do you even know what a hypocrite you are?"

"Yes, my wife," I said, but my resolve had started to waver, and we both knew it. "I know you're involved..."

219

"I have *nothing* to do with it!"

"Stop lying to me!"

I grabbed her and she started to sob, her knees buckling beneath her. I had to hold her to stop her from falling and she wrapped her fingers around my coat, clinging on.

"I promise, I had nothing to do with this, Lochlan," she whispered in my ear. "I wasn't even here the day she went missing. I was in Cambridge. Ask anyone."

People were starting to approach us, worried about the scene. I helped Harriet regain her balance, studying her for any sign that she might be lying. My certainty was fading and I felt confused.

"When you were watching us," I said in a low voice. "When you were watching her on the babycams, did you see anything?"

Her eyes focused on me. "Of course I did."

"What did you see?"

She licked her lips, fixed her hair. "I saw a miserable, lonely woman. That's what I saw." A beat. "But you know what I didn't see?"

I waited, and she poked me in the chest.

"You. You were never there. And yet there was I, thinking you'd chosen her over me."

She shook her head slowly, and I looked down. I felt foolish and angry and I wanted to claw my skin off. She turned and walked away, her gait a little less woozy. I didn't stop her.

Wes appeared at my side a moment later.

"You OK?" he asked, but I stared ahead, too gut-kicked to answer. I knew Harriet had nothing to do with El going missing, but more sickening was the realization that I was so desperate to avoid the truth that I was prepared to waste time chasing down false leads. I was prepared to wound and hurt people, if only to distract myself from the cold fact of my own role in my wife's disappearance.

For reasons I still don't fully understand, my own selfishness was a factor in this situation more than anything else. It was an instinct that shouted loud and clear there in the street as I watched Harriet walk away.

The problem is, nothing my instinct says makes sense anymore.

March 29, 2015

Komméno Island, Greece

Sariah and I are waiting at the dock, the last rays of sunlight turning into gold tassels across the waves. Sariah is behind me on a hill, pacing with her arms folded and her face tight with worry. I know it's every bit as important to her as it is to me that Nikodemos comes—after all, she's got to eat. It is now ten past six.

She calls, "You see anything?"

I perch my hands above my eyes and squint against a bright bank of cloud ahead. I can see a white object bouncing over the waves. My heart leaps. It's a speedboat, as sure as I'm alive.

"Yes!" I shout. "It's him! It's Nikodemos!"

I can hardly believe it. There is no fear in me this time, no trepidation about getting into his boat and contacting the British Embassy. I will *force* myself to remember any detail that can connect me to where I am and who I have left behind.

"He's coming! He's coming!"

I bounce on my toes and wave my arms in the air, shouting "Nikodemos! Nikodemos!" Sariah runs up the pier toward me and joins me in the waving and jumping, the wood beneath our feet creaking so fiercely I think it might snap. Then suddenly she stops, squinting against the sunset.

"I can't see him," she says, breathless. "Where is he?"

The waves have swollen because of the boat, rolling toward the shore like green hills.

"He was right there. We'll see him in a moment."

But he doesn't appear. I keep waiting for him to rise up behind a wave, a hand in the air, the roar of the engine filling the air.

"I'm not seeing him." Sariah frowns.

"He was *there*! He was. I saw him!"

"Maybe he's changed direction." She stands on her tiptoes and peers into the distance. "He mentioned that the current out there gets pretty intense."

We decide to split up. Sariah says she'll walk east and I'll walk west, both of us keeping close to the shoreline.

I walk until I reach the north end of the island, where the path rises upward and the cliffs are so sheer that they look as though they've been sliced clean with a knife: smooth, glistening white. The sea here is calm, swaying like a peacock's tail.

I know I saw him. I saw a speedboat with that sharp, shark-like snout, bouncing over the waves, a white trail of disturbed water following behind. And yet there is no longer any sign of him. I worry that he has turned back, unable to make it through the currents, or perhaps the rocks.

When I meet up with Sariah again it is growing dark, the sky turning a deep purple and the sun an orange belt across the horizon. Sariah seems exhausted, her face damp with sweat.

"I ain't seen him," she pants, leaning her hands on her knees. My heart sinks. The thought crosses my mind that George has found out about the call, that he's contacted Nikodemos and rearranged my plans, but I bat it away.

"I went as far as I could," Sariah gasps. "I even climbed up on the roof of the hotel by the pier to get a better view. Are you sure you saw him?"

"Yes," I say, but as soon as the wind whips away the sound of my voice I am blanketed in a wrenching uncertainty. I have no doubt that it was him in the boat. But he couldn't have simply disappeared, could he? Maybe it was a mirage, like people see in the desert when they're about to die from thirst and starvation. My thirst is not for water, but for something—someone—I can't remember by name, sound, or even image, but by my emotions.

"Maybe he turned back," I say.

She nods and wipes her mouth on the back of her hand. "We'll have to call him again. He'll come back."

Sariah's right—as the night and its blanket of searing cold sets in we have no choice but to head back to the farmhouse. I am terrified of confronting George, but she assures me over and over that he'll be fine—after all, I did everyone a favor by arranging for Nikodemos to bring food. They're running dangerously low on supplies. Still, as we climb the steps to the kitchen door I can't stop dry retching with nerves.

Joe is sitting at the dining table, scribbling in his notebook.

Hazel is performing a solo waltz to Frank Sinatra on the radio. When she sees Sariah and me in the doorway, she stops dancing, leans over, and turns the volume down on the radio. Joe rises from his chair, his face full of confusion.

"What happened?" Hazel says, her voice sharp.

"Did you bring the food?" Joe says.

Sariah wilts into a chair and wipes her forehead with the back of her hand. "He must have turned around. Call him."

A loud crash makes me jump. I turn to see Joe standing in the center of the kitchen with both fists clenched, his long frame trembling, a shattered jug on the ground by his feet.

Hazel stomps toward the window and looks out.

"That'll be why he turned back—there's a storm settling in."

The rain is too heavy for me to consider returning to the cave. Thick bands of it, moving at an angle, the wind knocking at the window and lightning crackling across the sky. I venture silently to the attic and drag a wooden chest across the door in case George comes upstairs, but despite this I don't sleep very well.

In the morning, it is still raining. The sky is white with low clouds and the sea's gray and violent. My stomach growls but I daren't ask if there is enough food for me.

"Good morning," George says in a singsong voice when I enter the kitchen.

"Good morning," I murmur cautiously. I had hoped to tiptoe out the back door without being seen, but as soon as he speaks the others appear. Joe is surly and panda eyed, his black hair disheveled. He looks as though he slept in his clothes. Hazel declares her mood in a series of stomps across the floor, pursed lips, and slammed cupboard doors. She sniffs at me and glances down at my shoes—her tennis shoes, the ones she so freely gave to me when I arrived—before opening the door to the pantry and staring inside.

"Anyone fancy jarred pickles for breakfast?" Hazel says with a sigh.

Sariah sashays into the room in a long red dress with buttons all the way down and gold bangles at her wrists, humming. She catches sight of me and throws me a wide grin and a wink, and I immediately feel struck with guilt. I am putting her through so much.

Hazel sets about unscrewing a large jar, huffing and puffing with each turn of the lid. She pulls out a pickle and pops it in her mouth, pulling a face.

"Of all the things I've seen you put in that gob of yours," George says drily, "that's got to be the worst by a long stretch."

Suddenly Hazel lets out a shriek. She runs to the sink and spits out the contents of her mouth.

"Those aren't pickles!"

Joe picks up the jar and inspects the contents. He pulls out a long tentacle dotted with suckers. "It's pickled octopus." Sariah and George laugh, and Hazel squeals the house down.

"Hey, don't knock it," Joe says, deeply serious. "Might be delicious when it's cooked."

"If we can't get in touch with Nikodemos, we'll need to consider calling the police," Sariah says, surveying the skies through the window.

"The *police*?" Hazel says, gargling water. She spits into the sink and wipes her mouth on a towel. "What are they going to do, arrest Nikodemos?"

A look passes between Sariah and Joe that I've not seen before—a protectiveness on Sariah's part. "Well, folks," she says. "As much as I hate to say it, I think we may have to cut our retreat short this time. We can phone our families at home."

George finds this amusing. "Are you planning on calling them on an imaginary phone, Sariah?"

Sariah turns her face back to the window. "I was hoping you'd remember where you put it, George."

Hazel nods. "I know I didn't sign up to eat *pickled squid* or whatever that stuff is. I can phone my Tommy. He'll be out here for me in a jiffy."

"I doubt we'll get our money back from Nikodemos," says Joe.

George shakes his head. He pulls a cigarette from his pocket and lights it, taking a long drag with a thoughtful expression. "I think you're a pack of drama queens."

Hazel sneers at him. "Oh yeah? *You* eat the flipping squid then."

He flicks his cigarette ash into the sink. "All I'm saying is, we don't need to be worrying the folks at home unnecessarily. We've enough to last another fortnight, surely?"

Joe marches over to the pantry and flings open the doors. "What are all these jars?" He lifts one down and tries to interpret the label. "This one looks like rice wrapped in vine leaves," he surmises at last. "This one's some kind of tinned fish. Beans. Anchovies." He counts them up. "By my calculations, we've got about five days' worth of food in here."

"You're asking me to live on anchovies and pickled octopus, Joe?" Hazel says.

"It's better than nothing."

227

George inspects the cupboard. "Five days' worth, is there? For how many people?"

Joe lowers his eyes. "Well, four of us rented this place, so..."

George turns, very slowly, and looks at me. For a moment, I'm not sure whether he's going to suggest eating me or feeding me.

"And what about our visitor?"

A bewildered silence swells in the room. I feel at once relieved and pricked by guilt. "Look, I've gate-crashed your retreat," I say quietly. "I shouldn't be here. It's not fair on any of you."

Hazel shuffles to the kitchen table and noises agreement, but George raises his hand. "There's plenty of food out there. No one needs to starve. I'll see to it that we don't, all right?"

"George..." Joe says, but George shuts him up. "We'll be *fine*. What are you all worrying about? This place is Empyrean. We can stay here forever."

Sariah and I share a look.

"I gave you my word that I'll feed us, all right? ALL RIGHT?"

"All right," we chorus.

George grins, clapping his hands together. "That's better. Now quit whining and get back to writing."

Doubt has been niggling me since Joe smashed the water jug last night. Some of the glass shards had landed on the orange life vest that I'd been wearing when they found me. It was sitting on the ground, close to the window. It made me think of the moment I'd found the boat they said I'd traveled in, and I had wondered about the fact that I had been discovered wearing a life vest. Had I been traveling with someone? Had he or she fallen overboard and drowned? It was a larger boat than I'd imagined, too, and despite the damage on the side, I wondered whether it could be fixed. The sails, the red sails wrapped around the masts—I had never checked whether they were torn or still usable.

The sun thumps down brutal waves of heat. I make the mistake of journeying outdoors without eating or drinking, and after twenty minutes I consider turning back. But as I approach the cliff, a heavy wind kicks up and a light shower of rain sweeps over the hills and valleys, sending a cool wet breeze around my face and legs. After a few minutes I continue on toward Bone Beach.

Seawater tongues rhythmically at the boat, causing the long masts to scrape against rock. The sails have come loose and bedraggled. I can see no tears in the fabric, though they are badly tangled and the ropes are ragged.

I take off my shoes and climb inside to get a better look. It isn't a rowboat at all—from somewhere deep in the corridors of my mind springs the word "dinghy." It is a sailing dinghy, a small wooden boat about ten or twelve feet long. I open the stowage compartments to check for any belongings that might indicate whether someone traveled with me. I discover some food packets and rip open the foil without checking the contents or date, and it is only once I've filled my mouth with a white dusty substance that I realize they are dry porridge oats. I swallow and choke it down, but put the other three packets down my T-shirt for later.

There is a bottle of water which I drink, but surprisingly little else. A box of matches, a pack of red tubes that turn out to be distress flares, a few scraps of paper. There is an address on one of the scraps, however, that makes me stop and take notice.

Αγίου Τίτου 1, 71202
Χανιά (Chania)

It is a crumpled invoice, the tell-tale ledger lines and figures at the bottom revealing its purpose, even if the obscure language conceals what had been purchased. I can't make out a date, but it suggests that the boat originated in Chania.

Perhaps George's theory was right. Perhaps I did get drunk and fall into the boat at the harbor, which then drifted out to sea. There is no indication that I traveled with anyone, and the absence of supplies in the stowage compartments indicates that I hadn't planned to go sailing.

On the other hand, when George found me I was wearing a life jacket. If I'd been *that* drunk, I probably wouldn't have thought to put one on. Also, the invoice is crumpled but looks recent. Was it my invoice? Had I intended to sail? Where was I headed, and why?

As if through a fog, I see myself holding the tiller and using it to steer the boat. I am sitting on the edge of the boat, my life jacket on, looking out across mother-of-pearl skies and jade waves arcing toward the island. Komméno. And I remember heading there quite deliberately, excitement clasped by each of my breaths. There is no one on the boat but me. No child.

The memory renews my feeling of purpose—if I know how to sail, if I had managed to take on this kind of sailing adventure on my own, then maybe I could fix the boat.

When insistent waves begin to surge toward me, I try to shift the boat in order to access the damaged stern, but it is astonishingly heavy. As I'm struggling with it, a large wave rolls in with enough force to knock me into the water. I emerge gasping and drenched, seaweed wrapping itself slickly around my calves.

When at last I haul myself up, I see that the boat has moved enough for me to view the full extent of the damage. It's a long shot, but the smashed stern could possibly be restored with some planks of wood and tarp. I unroll the sails all the way out and survey the ropes, heartened to see that, for the most part, they are usable. The centerboard and rudder are a problem, however. I'll have to attempt to reconstruct these, and then there is the problem of launching. Even last night's storm has failed to shift the boat out to sea.

I climb back to the top of the cliff, intent on heading for the barn close to the farmhouse to see if there's any wood I can use, but when I reach the top I spot the derelict hotel in the distance. It has started to rain heavily and I am famished, having spent the whole day wrangling with the boat. My clothes are still damp from falling into the water and I am shivering from head to toe. But on the spur of the moment I fashion a makeshift rain cover from palm leaves and set off toward the hotel. The drum of the rain against the leaves is oddly soothing. I'm hopeful that, at the very least, the hotel might have a bed for me to sleep in.

The hotel is a four-story whitewashed building with sun-bleached wooden shutters and rusting balconies, much of its signage pulled off by high winds and perhaps vandals. *Minoan Palace* is written on an overturned sign. I was surprised when Sariah said the hotel only closed last year—it looks as though it's been vacant for decades. Maybe it's the ghostliness that surrounds it, like the aftermath of an apocalypse.

The rain has transformed the ground to clay, and my shoes are filled with it. I kick them off and sit beneath a plastic awning, rubbing my arms and thighs vigorously to keep warm. Mounds of fresh dung are visible around the entrance to the hotel—most likely wild goats—and I am nervous about going outside. The sun is low in the sky and the entrance is like the mouth to a dark cave. I close my eyes and take a few deep breaths before stepping inside.

My bare feet meet cold, dusty slate. The hotel bar is visible through a set of double doors to my right, and a small desk to my left is likely where the concierge would have greeted guests. I fumble around the bar—the large windows afford views of the sea and let in enough light for me to make out chairs and tables—but find nothing that I could use for the boat. I take the stairs to the first floor and head for the bedrooms.

The light is much dimmer here, and it takes a while for my eyes to adjust. A dark corridor stretches ahead of me. I try not to think what might lie behind each of the doors that lead off it, though a scuttling sound to my right suggests that rats have the run of the place. The carpet smells like sewage and feels damp underfoot.

I turn the brass doorknob to the first bedroom, a gold-plated number one nailed to the wood of the door. Inside, there's a metal bed frame stripped of its mattress and sheets. Purple curtains flap against a broken window, and the stench of damp and rot hang in the air. I stride across the floor, looking over the furniture. All metal, except for the chests of drawers, which are made of heavy wood. I yank out a drawer, sending a flurry of large spiders scuttling over the sides to the floor. I give a loud shriek and race out of the room, still carrying the drawer.

It takes a while to gather myself. I set the drawer against the wall and open the door to a room on my right. It has been trashed—the bed is tipped over and the mattress slashed, the wardrobe keening forward with its doors open toward me. It is creepy enough to make me turn around and walk quietly out the door.

I pick up the wooden drawer that I left leaning against the wall and make to leave, but then I hear something downstairs in the lobby.

Slow, echoing footsteps.

My heart beats in my mouth. The footsteps stop. I dare not breathe. I try to look down through the banister rails but I can't see anything. A low groan from the lobby. I hold my breath and freeze. Whoever is down there is taking the first stair, then the next.

It's George. George followed me here.

I look around for somewhere to hide or escape. The window ahead of me is broken, but a rapid scan of my memory tells me that there was no balcony there—only a sheer drop to the ground below. The staircase continues upward to two more floors, then a balcony on the roof. The footsteps continue slowly up the stairs. I could throw the drawer down at whoever is approaching, but if it is George I have no doubt he'll have his rifle.

Another sound from the lobby.

I take my chances and bolt up the stairs. The footsteps below escalate, clattering up the stairs toward me. I reach the top floor, my heart about to burst out of my chest, but the stairs don't continue up to the roof. No sign of a door. There is only the long shadowy corridor ahead of me with doors leading off to bedrooms.

Rats dart into the rooms as I hurry along the corridor. George has reached the second floor, his footsteps echoing off the tiled walls. I race toward the end of the corridor and see a staircase through the glass panels of the door there, but the door won't budge.

I shove and kick the door, pushing against it until I tumble through, falling painfully on my knees. I pull myself upright on the banister and climb up to the roof.

The rain is coming down in great sweeping chains and there

is nothing on the flat roof to offer protection. I stagger to the far edge and look down—a balcony juts out about fifteen feet below. I would have to climb down and hang on to the drain-pipe before dropping on to it. I swing my legs over the edge and look down, wiping the rain from my eyes with one hand. The balcony is tiled, and would no doubt be slippery after the rain. I would have to aim carefully.

I swivel to hold on to the edge of the roof while I lower my-self, but right then he is there in front of me, not four feet away.

A dark, shaggy coat. Orange eyes staring up at me beneath heavy lids. Alien, rectangular pupils. The horns startle me most, impossibly long and sharp, curled over the head and ridged like a spine. He is surprisingly big, more stag than goat. An ibex. He stares, sizing me up before giving a satisfied snort and turning to head back to where he'd come from, his hooves clopping on the tiles of the roof.

It's pitch-black, but I return to the farmhouse out of sheer necessity—I am so dehydrated and cold that I can barely walk for shaking. When I reach the back door I fall to my knees, unable to go any farther.

The door opens swiftly and Sariah reaches out to me, help-ing me to my feet. She brings me inside and sits me down at the table. It feels a lot like the night when they rescued me from the boat.

"Are you OK, sweetie?" I hear her say. "What happened? Are you hurt?"

I manage to ask for water, and she rushes to the sink and pours me a glass. As I drink it down, Joe and Hazel appear out of nowhere, both of them whispering and not coming too close.

"I saw a goat," I say.

"You saw a ghost?" Sariah says in a low voice.

It takes a lot of effort to shake my head. "A *goat.*"

"We need to get you out of those wet clothes."

I peel off my clothes and wrap myself in a blanket. Then I go upstairs to the attic, folding myself inside the moldy bed-covers and falling into a restless sleep.

At eight a.m., the sun is already high in the sky and the house strangely vacant. The others must have made their way to their writing spaces. Sariah is gone, too, which disappoints me—I had hoped to take her to see the boat and share with her my idea.

With much trepidation I head back to the hotel. The sun is bright and high in the sky, reducing the number of dark corners and making the whole place much less eerie. Still, I waste no time collecting the wooden drawer I'd left in the corridor, then locate the staffroom on the ground floor. By a stroke of luck, I find a toolbox with an old hammer and some nails. I drag the wooden drawer and toolbox all the way to the boat. I have no saw to trim the wood, but I manage to prize the drawer apart and fit a panel over the hole in the stern before getting to work on the centerboard.

I question myself all day long as I work on fixing the boat's centerboard, trying to wring some memories out of my mind. I figure that I can link my way back to memories by asking myself what I know. For instance, whilst collecting the drawer from the hotel, I recognized some Greek words. There was a sign hanging on the front door that read "*Kleisto.*" I know it means "closed." Nothing earth-shattering, but as I stop and contemplate *how* I might know this, I realize that I know other Greek phrases: *Tee kanis?* How are you? *Me lene Eloïse.*

My name is Eloïse. *Tha eethela na neekyaso meea varka.* I'd like to hire a boat.

It makes sense that I would know basic Greek, given that I was traveling across the Aegean. But I keep prompting myself, hoping that something else will occur out of the blue. And then it does, only it isn't Greek. I find a snorkel mask still in its plastic wrapper, ready to be sold, and as I try to decipher the Greek writing on the tag I notice the French writing there. I read it without hesitation. *Ne convient pas à un enfant de moins de 36 mois*—Not for children under thirty-six months. I glance around me and try to think of the French for everything I can see, everything I can think. *Il y a la mer. Il y a la plage. Quand vais-je quitter cette île? Qui suis je? Pourquoi je ne me souviens de rien? Pourquoi suis-je ici?*

I speak aloud in French for most of the day, mesmerized by this discovery, this treasure from an archaeological dig of my memory. I probably sound like a madwoman, ranting on in French. It feels good to voice my fears aloud, and in a different language, but it doesn't trigger any memories of my past.

I'm almost done fixing the boat. It was a complicated task, and I'm nervous about it, but I've secured the drawer panel with about twenty long nails hammered strategically into the wood, then a layer of tarpaulin pulled tight over the wood to keep it watertight. It probably could have done with having screws drilled into it, but that wasn't an option. It's not perfect, but the stern is high enough now to prevent water leaking in, and I've attached another panel to the centerboard. The last thing I need to do is fix the rudder and shift the boat for launching. It's going to take more than me to accomplish that. It's a small dinghy, hardly a cruise ship, but too solid and heavy for me to move by myself. I sit for a while and work out a way that I might do it. Without a tide, I'd have to rely on waves coming in from a cruise ship or heavy winds. The fastest way to launch the boat will be to ask the others to help me.

I sit until night begins to blot out the sun. It's not too cold, and I consider sleeping on the beach, but I'm famished and desperate for a drink of water. And, while I hate to admit it, I'm lonely. I miss Sariah and her words of comfort. My master plan to launch the boat and set sail is all well and good, but then what? Arrive in Crete with a handful of Greek phrases and expect someone to find me? The thought that I might not *want* to remember chills me to the bone. I need company.

I walk slowly across the rocky banks and through the tall reeds, trying not to jump at every sound. Night begins its transformation of the island, and the birds and creatures recommence their strange shouts and howls. Eventually I make out the lights of the farmhouse on the hill in the distance and hasten my pace.

But as I make it up the path to the back garden the sound of a gun going off makes me stop dead in my tracks. It is loud and echoing. All the animals fall silent, and a flock of birds rises up from the roof of the farmhouse. And then, a long, bloodcurdling scream.

Sariah.

George has shot her.

Without thinking, I break into a run.

Red Wool

November 14, 1988

Stockwell, South London

She was running harder than she'd ever run in her life. Usually she enjoyed dawdling on the walk home from school, but today she was sprinting home, calling *Mum! Mum!* under her breath, like a prayer. *Please don't let them be there yet! Please don't let them get there before I do!*

The problem was, Mrs. Kellogg was a perceptive teacher. Eloïse had been able to go to school before without disguising a black eye or a cut and nobody had asked questions. Plenty of kids turned up with signatures of violence. But Mrs. Kellogg didn't let it slip past her as easily. She'd asked Eloïse about the black eye. Eloïse had said she'd walked into a cupboard without realizing that everyone since the beginning of time had used that as an excuse to cover up physical abuse. When Eloïse missed school, which was often, Mrs. Kellogg wanted to know why. Eloïse felt flustered and had to be creative in her responses. She'd never been required to come up with reasons before. And then today, Mrs. Kellogg had asked her to stay behind after class.

It was Eloïse's fault for agreeing to it. She could have run out of there when the bell went; unless Mrs. Kellogg chased after her, there'd have been no way she could stop her. But she stayed, and Mrs. Kellogg closed the door after the other kids had gone and told—no, asked—Eloïse to pull up a seat close by her desk. Eloïse hadn't any visible bruises—the cigarette burn on her arm was hidden beneath her long-sleeved T-shirt—and she rarely got into trouble. Her schoolwork was top of the class, she made sure of that. She had long ago sussed out the correlation between kids who got poor marks and social worker visits.

"What's this about?" she'd asked Mrs. Kellogg after devouring the chocolate biscuit she'd been given.

Mrs. Kellogg was small, round, and wore glasses on a chain. She had a way of looking at you that made you feel as though you were made of glass. She reminded Eloïse of a very wise owl. She even had feathery hair to her shoulders in shades of gray, mouse brown, and white, round penetrating green eyes, and a flat face. Mrs. Kellogg passed the biscuit tin to Eloïse for another helping and said, "Last week at parents' evening I was very much looking forward to meeting with your parents and telling them how brilliant you are. I wanted to congratulate them on raising such a bright little girl. And I certainly wanted to share with them the news that you've been awarded the School Cup for Creative Writing."

Eloïse stared. "I have?"

Mrs. Kellogg smiled in that knowing way of hers and nodded. "But, unfortunately, no one showed up for the meeting. Now, I've checked with other teachers and, apparently, no one has ever met with either your mother or father." She leaned forward, which made Eloïse flinch, because the only time an adult ever moved close to her like this was to hurt her.

There was a long pause, and Eloïse realized a question was being posed.

"My mum..." she began. "My mum's ill a lot of the time."

"And what about your father?"

"Mum lives with her boyfriend," she said, before realizing that she needed to think carefully about what she divulged. "I mean, only some of the time. They don't always live together. He went to prison last year, so she's got a different boyfriend at the minute."

Mrs. Kellogg did her best not to reveal any surprise at this. She watched Eloïse take another biscuit before posing the next question.

"Sometimes I notice you have cuts on your arms, Eloïse. Are you self-harming?"

Two thoughts entered Eloïse's brain at this point. The first was that there was actually a name for what she did, and if there was a name, it meant that she wasn't the only person in the world who pressed a razor blade into her skin as a means of releasing some of the fire that swirled beneath it. The second thought was that she needed to get out of here, right now.

She stood up.

"Eloïse..." Mrs. Kellogg said.

"I'm sorry," Eloïse said, and turned to leave.

Mrs. Kellogg rose from her seat and followed her. Eloïse stopped before she reached the door, pricked by a sudden urge to turn and tell Mrs. Kellogg everything, even the things she didn't have a name for.

"Eloïse," Mrs. Kellogg said, and she sounded breathless and anxious. If Peter were here, he'd have said *She really cares about you.* But Peter was dead, and so were all the others. Every time she refused to do what Orhan wanted, he took something of hers. Somehow he always knew which of the toys she loved most.

"Eloïse, I'm concerned for your well-being. I want you to come home with me tonight, so we can discuss what steps to take. Will you do that?"

Eloïse shook her head and tried to say no, but it came out as a sob.

Mrs. Kellogg cupped Eloïse's face in her hands, and it was the strangest and most tender human encounter Eloïse could remember. She suddenly perceived herself from the outside, as though witnessing from a distance the scared, scrawny creature she had become, how her shoes and clothes had holes in them and her hair was so filthy that none of the other kids wanted to sit near her. If she had been older, she would have known that it wasn't so much the bruises that drew Mrs. Kellogg's attention as the tell-tale pricks of a needle on the back of her neck, where Orhan believed her hair would fall. Except, she'd cut her hair one night, and now the needle marks were visible.

Mrs. Kellogg looked deep into Eloïse's too-old eyes. "I've alerted social services," she whispered. "You don't have to go home. They're going to your home as we speak."

At that, Eloïse turned on her heel and ran. She thumped her feet on the squealing linoleum of the school corridor to drown out Mrs. Kellogg's shouts. She ran down the school steps and past the other kids at the bus stop, and she ran past tooting cars and through the queue at the post office. She ran until she reached the tower block where they lived, and then took the stairs to the fourth floor.

When she got inside she found her mother upstairs, throwing up into the toilet bowl. She was heartened by this: at least her mother was awake, and there didn't seem to be any sign of anyone having been in the flat.

"Are you OK?" she asked her mum, who continued being sick. Eloïse went to the kitchen and got a glass of water, brought it to her. Then the doorbell rang.

Through the slit in the curtains she could see two of them, both in beige trench coats and black high heels with clipboards and steely faces. She could spot them a mile away. Social workers. They all had one objective: to split her and her mother apart. To send her to another family.

She spent a couple of precious seconds righting the mess in the living room as best she could, glanced in the hallway mirror to check she looked OK. Then she opened the door and smiled brightly.

The one with glasses spoke first. "Eloïse, is it? Is your mummy home, darlin'?"

Eloïse broadened her smile, showing them a row of yellow teeth. "She's busy."

"Oh. Can we come in?"

"Will you be long?"

The women shared looks. "That depends."

She held the door open and they stepped inside.

"Can I make you a cup of tea?" Eloïse asked. She hoped that her pleasant manner would make it all OK, that they might tick whatever box they had to tick and be on their way.

But as she busied herself in the kitchen arranging chipped cups and stale biscuits on a copper tray, they were calculating her precociousness and frail, bruised limbs as hallmarks of a neglected child, the sort they saw regularly.

To her surprise, her mother appeared a few minutes later. She was dressed in jeans and a black T-shirt, with a bra underneath it, and her blonde hair was tied back with an elastic band. A slick of pink lipstick lit up her face. Jude was very attractive, and she'd pulled herself together enough to shake hands with the two women in trench coats and appear civil. Eloïse eyed up her mother, alert for the first time in weeks, and thanked whoever had heard her prayer.

The women explained that they wanted to "check in" on Eloïse, that they'd been passed on some information from the social workers in Brixton where Eloïse had last lived and wanted to get to know her. Jude nodded and smiled and explained the cause of the previous interventions by social services. She'd moved to London from Switzerland to be with Orhan, but things had gone sour. He'd been involved in an armed robbery and social services got involved. She was no longer with him, of course. New home, fresh start. She gave them one of her finest smiles, playing on the Swiss-German heritage that had gifted her with a long athletic frame and excellent bone structure, and an accent that sounded exotic and educated. Eloïse watched the women take notes, saw them visibly relax. Then they turned to her.

"And how are you finding Stockwell, Eloïse?"

"Fine," she said automatically. She paused. "Though I think I'd like to change schools. Would that be all right?"

"I don't see any problem with that," the woman with glasses answered. "But we will need a reason."

"I'm being bullied."

Her mother turned to her with such concern etched on her face that Eloïse thought something must have happened to her. All at once, Jude reached forward, wrapped her arms around her, and held Eloïse close. Utterly overwhelmed by this long yearned-for affection from her mother, Eloïse began to cry, terrible gulping sobs that she could barely control. Her reaction confirmed the truth of her account of bullying to the women in trench coats.

"There, there," Jude said, wrapping Eloïse in her smell of marijuana, vomit, and cheap perfume, suddenly shifting to German. "*Sagen Mama, die dich zu verletzen.*"

Tell Mummy who's been hurting you.

March 31, 2015

Potter's Lane, Twickenham

Lochlan: There's a Polaroid photograph on the wooden console table in the family room that El framed a while back. The console table was covered with junk until the police came and took it all away, and what was buried beneath was revealed like archaeological trophies: one of El's old sailing awards, Max's baby footprint and handprint captured in white clay blocks, a couple of framed family photographs, and this Polaroid. Unlike the other framed pictures, this one looks crumpled, blurry, and a bit random—I'm giving El a piggyback in the middle of the Champs-Élysées.

We are literally in the middle of the road with the Arc de Triomphe behind us and cars on either side. I'm wearing sunglasses, swimming trunks, and a wide, white grin. El is wearing a white strapless sundress and flip-flops, her legs straight in front of her, and her expression as though she's about to fall off, though she's laughing.

When I look at it, her laughter returns to my ears, an echo that makes my heartbeat race.

It was not long after we met. We'd gone to France for a few weeks with a couple of El's friends in her old clapped-out Ford Fiesta. A six-man tent in the boot, some cases of Budweiser. There was no pressure back then. No Monday mornings, no deadlines, no loft conversions and bin collections and decisions about childcare, and if someone had asked me what Calpol was I would've guessed it was something to do with the Californian police.

I've been thinking a lot about the places we visited in the early days, El and me. I've been thinking a lot about Chania. Close to where we got married. It keeps rising up in my mind. Not the wedding itself, but the island, Komméno. Eloïse looked different there, seemed different.

My focus shifts from the picture on the console table to Gerda, who sits in the rocking chair opposite, her face tight, her shoulders rolled forward. She clears her throat and waits for Magnus to sit down before telling me what she has to say. Magnus sits on a wooden chest containing wooden pieces of Max's elaborate village. He tugs his trousers up so as to not crease them and flicks a small, apologetic smile at me.

"What's all this about?" I say wearily.

"It's about the children, Lochlan," Gerda says sternly. "We want to take the children back with us to Ledbury. Magnus and I have thought about it and we feel that, given the circumstances, Max and Cressida would have a lot more stability and protection if they came back with us."

"I'm sorry—stability? Protection?"

She looks to Magnus, who keeps his expression mild and his eyes on a spot on the rug. "Well, it's chaos for them here. Their mother isn't here. It can hardly be easy for them, what with police turning up to search through the house."

"That happened once," I say irritably. "I can't imagine they'll be searching again."

"Well, Max is becoming very unsettled, and I don't think it's ideal for two innocent young children to be in the midst of all this."

"I don't think it's ideal either," I say quietly. She's punishing me for Harriet, I know it.

As if reading my mind, she says, "And this isn't about Harriet. Though when Eloïse comes back, I think you'll need to have a serious talk."

"Gerda..." Magnus says, and she lowers her tone.

"It's the last thing any of us needed to hear right now."

"This isn't what I wanted either," I say.

"Which is why I think you ought to let us take Max and Cressida back with us," Gerda says, returning to her original topic. "I mean, what about your work, Lochlan? Surely you're going to have to go back to work soon? How will you do that *and* look after the children?"

"I've no idea."

A short, satisfied smile. "There. See? The children have their own bedrooms in Ledbury. It's their home from home. I can register Max at the local Montessori and he'll settle straight in. He has some friends there already. Nice, well-mannered little boys."

My stomach tightens at the sound of this. "For how long?"

"Beg pardon?"

"How long do you intend to keep them? When will you bring them back?"

"Well, as long as is best, I'd imagine."

I let her words hang in the air, my eyes turning back to the photograph. Perhaps it is out of selfishness as much as love that I want my children to stay right here with me. But what would Eloïse want? What would she do?

"All right," I say at last, and Gerda claps her hands together and stands up, ready to take charge of the situation. She begins muttering about which clothes she'll pack for Cressida, about how they ought to leave as soon as possible to avoid rush-hour traffic. She urges Magnus to get up, but he shakes his head and folds his arms tightly against his chest.

"Magnus, what are you doing?" she says.

He looks away. "I'm staying here. You go."

Gerda looks appalled. "What?"

He raises his eyes to meet hers, softens his voice. "You take the children. I'm needed here." He turns to me and smiles. "Moral support, and all that."

Gerda is visibly perplexed by this shift in loyalty. She tries to gather her composure, but her eyes remain wide. She slips into German and mutters to Magnus, who shakes his head.

"I'll be able to pick up my prescription here," he says reasonably. "I'll call my doctor and tell her of this plan."

Gerda protests some more and tries to laugh, as though he's playing a prank, but Magnus raises his hands and makes a firm and conclusive statement in German. Gerda falls silent, though her cheeks flame and she stomps off upstairs.

Magnus turns to me, a smile on his face, then rises to his feet with a stretch.

"I think it's time for a stiff drink, don't you?"

March 31, 2015

Komméno Island, Greece

I race up to the farmhouse, shouting Sariah's name. The gun-shot reverberates across the sky, the scream's echo caught in my ears. Moonlight reveals four dark splats on the tiles of the doorstep. Blood.

Inside, George is holding his gun barrel down by his side, a bloody object slumped on the table, and Hazel is flapping her hands and freaking out. As I move closer, I see a large brown rabbit laid flat out on his back, its long ears flopped to one side, the legs splayed like upside-down wings. Sariah comes into the room and says incredulously, "You *ain't* just shot no rabbit."

George holds the rifle over one shoulder. His face is shining with sweat and pride, his naked gut hanging over his waist-band. His belly button is an egg-shaped indentation in stretch-marked skin.

"What I've done, Sariah darling, is brought you your dinner. Who's hungry?"

Hazel looks aghast. She looks from George to the carcass. One paw is white.

"You're not suggesting we eat that?"

"You got a better idea, Hazel?"

"But it's a cute little bunny!"

"He's a cute little bunny with a bullet in his head. And you'll be a cute little corpse if you don't eat him."

Her face falls. "My Tommy used to have one like that when he was a lad. We called him Billy. Billy the Bunny."

George rummages through a drawer and it takes me a moment to work out that he's searching for a carving knife. He finds one. Joe says, "You should sterilize it."

"What?"

"The knife. Make sure it's sterilized before cutting it up."

"Rubbish," George laughs. He turns and begins to cut into the rabbit. Hazel retches into her hand and turns away. I can't look either.

"You pack of pussies!" George bellows. "You lily-livered pansies! Haven't you ever had turkey for Christmas dinner? Or lamb chops? Where d'you think they came from, eh? At least this boy ain't got no hormones pumped into him. Free range, fresh as a daisy."

"No, no," Joe says, stepping in to prevent George cutting any further. This brings some relief, but then he says, "You need to skin it first. Make a slit there and you should be able to pull it off like a glove. Then you cut the head off."

"I'm not sticking around for this," Hazel says, and she stomps outside. Sariah folds her arms and watches sadly for a few moments before turning to follow Hazel. I hear Joe instruct George on how to remove the liver before I decide I can't handle it either.

Sariah is sitting on the wooden bench near the washing line, her legs apart, a breeze making her skirt sway. It's dark, but a steady stream of smoke from around the corner of the farmhouse tells me that Hazel's there, keeping out of the wind. Even so, it's a mild night. Sariah leans forward, her elbows resting on her knees as she looks out at the full moon casting a silver causeway of light across the ocean. I sit down next to her and glance around, hoping that Hazel isn't listening.

"Where've you been all day?" Sariah asks lightly.

I realize I haven't told her anything about the boat. I say, "I think I can get us out of here."

She looks at me. "What?"

"The boat," I say, leaning closer. "The sailing dinghy that got me here. I think I've fixed it."

"But you crashed that boat."

"I know. I had a go at repairing it and—" I take a breath. "I want you to come with me and sail back to Crete. We can get out of here. Tonight."

She glances around in case anyone is in earshot. Then, whispering, "I don't think this is a good idea, sweetie."

"Why not?"

"Well, last time you sailed a boat it didn't turn out so good…"

The old worry that Sariah might be deceiving me blooms in my mind, and I swipe it away.

"The satellite phone is gone, Sariah. We have no other option. You and me, we could go and get help for the others."

A deep sigh. "I don't know…"

"Why not?"

And then she fixes me with a stare that suggests a conversation entirely different from the one we have been having, a look that insinuates a complete shift in gear.

"There's something you need to know."

"Something I need to know?" I say, trying to keep my voice measured.

"About me."

My mind turns back to the night in the barn. George's rifle aimed at Sariah on the ground.

My suspicions that she staged it. But my suspicions are based on nothing. Sariah has been a friend to me, taking care of me when everyone else lost interest. I can't allow my fears to destroy our friendship.

"What do I need to know about you, Sariah?" I say.

She opens her mouth to answer, but as she does, Joe shouts from inside. "We're all done dissecting! You can come back in now."

"Lily-livered pansies…"

But the interruption has shaken Sariah's resolve, and she makes to go back inside.

"Please," I say, grabbing her hand. To my surprise she pulls away, leaving me grasping at air.

"Sariah…"

She doesn't move, doesn't look at me. I press her.

"What was it you wanted to tell me?"

She turns her face to mine. There is no anger there, no frustration. Only pity.

"The only way that you can get off this island is to remember."

"I'm trying to remember," I say, tripping over my words, because there is a warning in her words.

But before I can ask anything more she walks away, heading inside.

255

Joe and George are frying up the rabbit. Hazel pulls a face and stamps a foot in protest.

"I'm not eating that. I'm not. You can't make me."

George pulls a tablecloth from a drawer and flings it in the air, draping it over the table. Then he pulls out a chair and tosses me a broad grin.

"Why don't you come and sit at the head of the table?"

Joe, Hazel, and Sariah all turn to look at me. I glance across their faces nervously.

"Well, *go on*," Hazel snaps, and I jump. I move forward and sit down.

"There, now," George says, and he shifts back to the hob and forks a cooked leg of meat from the pan, tossing it on a plate. Then he sets the plate in front of me.

"Can I get you any sauce?" he asks. I shake my head, but he shouts over to Joe. "What goes with rabbit?"

"Meadows, friendly butterflies, Bambi..." Hazel mutters.

"We don't have any sauces left," Joe says, rubbing his chin. "I believe rabbit needs a good red wine, but we're flat out of booze."

Hazel raises her head. "We've run out of alcohol?"

Joe holds up a plastic tube. "We've got pepper, though."

Hazel begins to weep. Sariah lays a hand on her shoulder in comfort.

George clicks his fingers. He reaches over to the worktop and produces a pepper pot, sprinkling the meat with it.

"There we go."

He orders Hazel to sit down, then Sariah, and they do. He and Joe plate up the meat and take their seats, the mood strange and grim.

"Shall we say grace?" George says. Hazel sniffles and dabs

her eyes, her shoulders hunched, her curly orange hair all but covering her face. Sariah murmurs that yes, we should say grace, and Joe fumbles with his hands, not sure how to pray.

George claps his hands together. "Our Father, who Art in Heaven..." He pauses and turns to Joe. "What's the next bit?"

"That's not how you say grace," Joe says.

Sariah says, "Why don't you say it, Joe?"

Joe clears his throat and clasps his hands. "OK. Uh, Dear God. We are really grateful for this food that you have provided to us starving writers. Please can you let it taste nice and not poison us. And, uh, while you're at it, can you help me with my new poem, please, because I'm really struggling with it and I can't get the form to work..."

Hazel slaps his arm. "Joe."

"OK, sorry. Amen."

Hazel refuses to eat and although I am starving, I can't bring myself to, either. Sariah is poking at the contents of her plate, visibly trying to persuade herself to eat.

"It's not a sin to eat rabbit, you know," George announces.

"Try it," Joe urges me. "It's tasty."

Sariah cuts a small piece and puts it in her mouth, making a face that says it's OK. Encouraged, I do the same. Hazel raises her head and gives me a scowl of disgust. The meat is gamy, full flavored, but I'm so hungry I could eat the whole animal.

"Hazel, *eat* the damn thing," George says, pushing the plate toward her. "You need to keep your strength up. Brain food, and all that."

She pushes the plate back and covers her face with her hands. Then she begins to weep. Joe lifts the pepper pot and sprinkles some on her plate. "It *does* make it taste nice," he says sweetly.

"Oh, don't be such a baby," George says, and Hazel erupts, her eyes wild.

"Don't you *dare* call me a baby, George! I paid for this holiday, even though I'm flat broke!"

"Same here," Joe says, sadly.

"And now you say we're out of booze!" Hazel shrieks. "I want to go home!"

George's face darkens. He stays dangerously silent and still, though his mood is like a fine mist gathering in the room.

"We only have a couple weeks left, honey," Sariah says.

"I don't care!" Hazel shouts. "A couple of weeks might as well be an eternity if we have to *shoot rabbits* to survive!"

"Joe, might I trouble you for a glass of water?" Sariah says, holding her glass up and nodding at the water jug he placed on the table.

"Me as well," adds George.

"I'll fill it," Joe says, lifting the jug and heading for the sink. He turns the tap and we wait, but nothing happens. Only the squeaking sound of the ancient tap as Joe turns it, followed by a weird gargling noise.

"Hmm. This happened earlier today," Joe says, turning and turning the tap. "Should work in a moment or two."

"*What* happened earlier?" Sariah asks.

Silence.

"Joe?"

The sound of clanking fills the room, as though the pipes are grinding together. The tap chokes and splutters.

"Oh no," Joe says.

"What?" George says.

"Come on!" shouts Joe, thumping the worktop.

Hazel looks up. "It's the water," she says in a low voice.

"It came back on this morning," Joe says.

"It's gone, isn't it? It's all used up."

"What do you mean, 'used up'?" I say.

"The water comes from a cistern," Sariah says. "It collects rain and filters it."

George pushes back his seat, and says, "It *can't* be used up. It's been raining plenty lately. It'll be a blockage, that's all. Leave it to me." He gets up and walks out of the back door, slamming it behind him.

I push away my plate, unable to eat any more. Joe is banging the tap and shouting, but Sariah tells him to stop.

"What are we going to do?" Hazel says in a high voice. "No water, no food, no wine…"

"This is very serious," Sariah offers, and I nod.

"We *have* to find a way of contacting Nikodemos or someone on the mainland," Joe says. He seems calm until he reaches the table, and then I notice that he has turned deathly pale and is blinking furiously.

Hazel weeps.

We sit in silence for what seems like hours, lost in our thoughts. I want to ask Sariah about what she said earlier, about my needing to remember in order to get off the island. I don't want to ask in front of Hazel and Joe, and I don't want to leave her here. I need to wait until George fixes the water.

At last, there is the sound of cursing and stomping at the back door.

"There he is now," Sariah proclaims brightly, rising to open the back door. "He'll have fixed the cistern," she tells Hazel. "You'll see."

The door opens before Sariah reaches it, banging against the wall. George is stooped over at the top of the back steps, grunting and wiping his brow.

"Anyone want to give me a hand with this?"

We all look over.

"Give you a hand with what, George?" Sariah asks, watching as he stands his rifle upright against the inside wall. "You took your rifle to fix the cistern?"

"Never know...what you might...be up against...out there," George grunts, stooping to shunt something inside. We all rise from our seats, curious to see what he's doing.

"George, what are you—aaaargh!"

Sariah lets out a shout and staggers backward from the doorway, her hand clapped across her mouth.

Hazel looks from Sariah to George, panicked. "What? What is it?"

George walks backward through the door into the kitchen, both arms extended outwards as he hauls a heavy object over the doorstep. When he moves into the light, I see that he is dragging a creature with horns.

Silence falls like a guillotine. Sariah is whispering to herself, a ringed hand pressed against her chest to calm her nerves. Hazel is mesmerized, her terror replaced with curiosity. Joe moves to give George a hand shifting his kill.

Long, curling horns, ridged like the ones I saw on the roof of the hotel. Its gold eyes staring, seeing nothing. Dark, matted fur bloodied at the neck from a gunshot wound. Its cloven hooves motionless. I can't be sure, but it looks exactly like the one I'd encountered.

"Surprisingly big, this fella," George says proudly.

"So when you said you were going to fix the cistern," Joe

says in a dry voice, "what you really meant was you were off to shoot a goat."

"Ibex," George grunts. "The cistern's broken." He wipes his brow with the back of his hand. "Got a crack in it the size of my arm. Rats inside it. I'll go back tomorrow morning, when it's light, to see if I can plug it up—but we'll have to boil all our water. Don't want to catch the bubonic plague, do we?"

Hazel starts to hyperventilate. Sariah wraps an arm around her and murmurs soothing words.

George kneels down and tugs the horns. "Beautiful, isn't he? Ran into him when I was headed for the cistern. Reckon I'd get a pretty penny for the horns at the market."

"George, you're insane!" Hazel shrieks.

"This is enough," Sariah says firmly, having managed to calm her fright. "Tell me where the satellite phone is, George."

He throws her an inane grin.

"Please," Sariah begs. "We can't stay here without water. We need to phone *someone* who'll help get us off the island."

George rises, sobered. Suddenly he plucks the phone from his pocket and hands it to Sariah. "There you go."

She takes it, stunned, holding it in her hand as though she doesn't quite believe it's real. After a few glances at George, she extends the antennae. She begins to dial, then looks at the phone. She tries again.

"The battery's gone," she says.

"What's gone?" Joe says, glancing up.

"How do we charge it?" Sariah asks.

"Oh, it's fully charged," George says. "Found it this morning. It's dead. Kaput. Not. Working."

"Let me take a look," Joe says, rising to his feet and taking the phone from Sariah. He glances up at George. "The screen is lit up. Why's it not working?" He presses some buttons and glances up at the ceiling.

"No signal," he says.

"Yep," George grins. "You think I ain't already tried the phone outside?"

Hazel gives a huge wail and holds her head in her hands. "I knew this would happen," she shouts. "I knew it, I knew it!"

George drags the goat farther along the floor into the kitchen. With a groan he turns it all the way around so that its eyes are visible. At this Hazel slumps to the floor. Joe is fast to attend to her, catching her before her head cracks on the tiles. He kneels down to turn her on her side.

It is then, right as Joe is tapping Hazel's face and calling her name, right as George pulls out a measuring tape and begins to measure the length of the goat's horns, that I remember something. It so vivid, so bizarre and unexpected, that I gasp out loud.

"Don't tell me *you're* about to faint now," Joe says from the floor.

"You OK?" Sariah asks, glancing over at me.

My mouth is open but I don't speak. I'm lost in a clear, vivid memory of a man at a roadside. A car stopped in the middle of the road, both doors flung open. The smell of petrol in the air. The man walks toward me, grinning, saying, "Eloïse."

I have a sense it's a time from about four years ago, not more than five. I remember him telling me I had to do something, and the feeling of revulsion in my gut as I realized he was right.

The man I remember is George.

April 1, 2015

Potter's Lane, Twickenham

Lochlan: It's late. Gerda has taken the children away. I was fine, really I was, right up until they got strapped into their car seats and I had to close the door. Max hadn't seemed to realize that I wasn't coming, too, and so he spent a good length of time sorting out which toys he wanted to bring and getting excited about his *Gruffalo* Trunki. Then, right as I opened the front door, he turned to me.

"Aren't you coming, Daddy?"

I remained standing and ruffled his hair, determined to keep this all as light and easygoing as possible. "No, darling. Daddy has to stay here."

His brow wrinkled. "You have to stay here? But Cressida's coming. And Mamie."

"I know, Maxie, but Daddy's got some work to do." I realized as I said it that this was a phrase that I used so often it slipped easily off the tongue.

He started to wriggle out of his backpack and take off his coat.

"No, Maxie, what are you doing? Come on, keep your coat on. You've got to go."

I squatted to help him put his arms back inside his coat, but he resisted. A long moment where he held my face, working me out.

"Is this an April Fool's?"

I was puzzled until I worked out what day it is. "No, Maxie…"

"…because Mrs. Evans says today's April Fool's and that means you get to play jokes on people…"

"No, no. I'm sorry, Max. This is for real."

His face crumpled. "Where is Mummy, Daddy? Why are you not coming? I don't want you not to come."

He fell against me and wrapped his arms around my neck. Gerda was waiting in the driveway. I forced myself not to look at her, overcome with a sudden charge of hatred toward her for creating this situation. I had a vague memory of deciding that it was in my children's interests to go back to Ledbury. Why was that again? How was this benefiting them? A voice in my head said, *Eloïse would want them to go, she'd want them to be shielded from all of this* and I tried to pull myself together.

Gerda marched back into the hallway and set the car seat on the floor. Cressida was sleeping, her little face turned toward the T-shirt belonging to Eloïse that I'd tucked in with her to remind her of her smell.

"You have to go, Maxie," I said, blindly trying to pull his

arms away from my neck, but he was bawling now, insisting that he stay with me.

"You'll only be there for a little while," I promised, though I still have no idea how long this arrangement is in place for. A week? A month?

"Mamie's house is only a couple of hours away. I'll see you very soon."

"Daddy, Daddy! I don't want to go! No, Daddy! Please!"

I don't exactly recall how he ended up in the car. Maybe I was so worn out and upset that I missed the moment where Gerda lifted him and carried both him and the car seat to her car.

Magnus had materialized sometime during this, and it was his hand on my shoulder that suddenly made me buck up and wipe away my tears. Now that I think about it, I'd have been wrong to let the children go if Magnus had accompanied Gerda. His staying here indicates that he's chosen a side. Had he chosen Gerda's side, I'm inclined to think that she'd be getting that highbrow lawyer of theirs to file for guardianship.

I'm sitting in our closet surrounded by Eloïse's clothes. There's the red silk dress she bought in Sydney just before we came home from our honeymoon. She looked incredible in that dress. The black leather waistcoat she bought at the Grand Bazaar in Istanbul and never wore because she decided it wasn't "her." So many memories clinging to these clothes. I hold her denim shirt against my nose, breathing her in, and I am transported back to the holiday we took to Switzerland the summer we conceived Max. We always talked about that holiday in terms of how tired she was, how the smell of wine made her strangely nauseous, but then I remember the car accident.

We were driving through the Grimsel Pass with its labyrinth of winding roads through turquoise lakes and white-tipped mountains. It was dark, an enveloping and luscious blackness speared with moonlight. I thought I was taking the road carefully—braking hard before each hairpin bend, headlights on full beam, my eyes fixed on the road ahead.

I never saw what we hit until it was too late. A sickening thud against the bonnet and a screech of tires. For a handful of agonizing seconds, I thought we'd hit a person.

I pulled over hastily. Neither of us spoke until we'd raced back to the shape at the side of the road behind us, its heavy breaths rising like steam in the moonlight.

"What is it?" I asked, relieved when I saw hooves.

Eloïse got down on all fours and crouched by its head. "I think it's a mountain goat."

I pulled my keys from my pocket and found the torch I kept on a keychain. A halo of white torchlight revealed magnificent gold horns curled around the goat's head, each about a yard and a half long, and the blood that was oozing steadily from its side. The air around us thickened with brackish, bestial smells of earth, vomit, and a metallic odor of blood. The creature was twitching and grunting, clearly in a lot of pain.

Eloïse glanced up at me expectantly. "What do we do?"

"Nothing we *can* do, by the looks of it."

El ran her hand along a ridged horn, her other reaching out to hold the animal's head. She looked up at me, pained. "We can't leave him to suffer."

The goat lurched then, as though trying to get up. I stood up on alert.

"Please don't get so close," I told her. "Move away, El."

She knew I was acting protectively toward her on account of those long horns, but she ignored me.

"He's in so much pain," she said quietly, laying a hand on his side when he stopped trying to stand. The goat's cries became rhythmic, human sounds, his breaths slowing.

"Help him, Lochlan."

"I can't," I told her. "We're miles away from any kind of vet clinic."

I hadn't picked up that she meant a coup de grâce.

"For heaven's sake," she spat angrily. "Put him out of his misery!" Then: "Is that a rock behind you?"

I turned and shone my torch on a large stone on the ground behind me. I hefted it toward the goat. "Do you want me to do it?"

Her silence told me that she did. I felt it was the manly thing for me to be the one to kill the goat, but at the last minute the rock slipped out of my hands and landed on its head, injuring it but not killing it.

"Lochlan!"

The goat had started scrambling to get up again, its hooves kicking at the ground, its head thrashing and the horns swiping close to Eloïse. She picked up the rock and with both hands slugged it down hard on the animal's skull. Within seconds it stopped moving.

We stood over the body watching the steam and dust all around it settle quietly into stillness. Eloïse drew her hands to her mouth. I pulled her to me and gave her a hug.

"I've never killed anything," she sobbed.

I knew this wasn't completely true—she'd killed a few wasps and cockroaches in her time, and there was that snake she bludgeoned in Thailand—but I understood this was a different situation. It was a cold night, and so it wasn't long before we got back in the car and drove on through the night.

I strain to remember what happened after that, because it suddenly occurs to me that she wasn't right at all for a while after. We discovered she was pregnant almost as soon as we returned to London, and she was ecstatic, but frequently I'd be woken in the middle of the night by her yelling. I'd wake her and tell her it was OK, she was dreaming, but I'd never seen her so upset. Once, I got angry with her about it.

"It was a *goat*, El. An animal, not a human being. Get over it, will you?"

She was sitting upright, gleaming with sweat and trembling. She shook her head.

"It was my mother," she gasped. "I dreamt that we hit my mother on that road."

And that was how it continued.

Every other week or so she'd cry out in the middle of the night, and instead of murmuring about mountain goats or rocks she talked about hummingbirds and her mother not waking up. I'd ask her about it when we both woke up and she'd say she didn't want to discuss it. Somehow, though, I sense that the goat and El's mum were related in her mind. I don't know how.

She'd never had nightmares before the car accident. Did killing the goat trigger her? Even if it did, it would hardly cause her to walk out on our kids. Unless someone persuaded her with something else, something better than what she had with our family.

I can't stand all the cul-de-sacs in my brain. I get to my feet and trawl through her underwear drawer. Nothing's folded, it's all been stuffed in here any old how. It's a small detail and yet strange—she was always so meticulous, so neat. Everything was folded.

I pull out a mass of pink cotton with numerous straps that resembles a miniature parachute. A white tag that informs me it's a maternity bra. I press it to my face and pick up the faint, sweet scent of breast milk. I remember Eloïse buying this bra soon after Max was born. I remember her struggling to feed him. I remember running out to the shops at midnight to buy a breast pump. She had so much milk that she said her breasts were going to explode. Oversupply syndrome, the midwife said, and hinted that El should give up. But she expressed and fed him from a bottle for another four months.

I empty the drawer, tossing the contents on the ground. There are papers at the back. I feel sick that I didn't find these before, that the police didn't find them. They've scoured the house, taken away boxes of paperwork, shopping lists stuck to the fridge, and yet these have been overlooked. I fold them, a little relieved to see they're receipts from Sainsbury's and Tesco. Clothing for Cressida. A pair of shoes from Clarks. And a notebook.

Naturally, I flick it open. It's about A5 size with a pretty embroidered floral cover, Cath Kidston or Paperchase, maybe. Lined paper of a decent thickness. Eloïse has written her full name in the front: *Eloïse Beatrice Shelley.* I flick through it casually, assuming the notes and scribbles in Eloïse's handwriting to be related to her charity, and then I recall Niamh's mention of the writing group. The writing group! I never looked into that. But as I turn the page a series of questions written in bold black ink and caught in a thickly drawn circle makes me stop and read the page over and over.

Can you heal someone who's gone through hell?
  Can you ever be normal after abuse?

It looks like Eloïse's handwriting. I'm 99 percent certain that it is. But—abuse? What abuse?

I turn the pages more carefully, one at a time. They are filled with scribbles in a handwriting I don't recognize. Hasty, spiky writing all over the page, clusters of text at an angle, in the margins, running around the borders of the page.

It was her fault even Peter said so it was her fault she should have been nice and she could have stopped it at any time NO!!

The writing continues for many pages, barely any space left, and then it changes. A handful of pages contain a different handwriting altogether, still in black ink, but in lighter, looped writing that seems more feminine than the one before, the vowels like balloons. I see a title, *Sorrow Man*, of what appears to be a short story, but I don't read it, too intent on working out why other people would have written in Eloïse's notebook. Perhaps she lost it and then found it again, after it had been written in? Was it something to do with the writing group? Why would they write nonsense in her notebook? Nothing seems to make sense anymore.

And then another handful of pages in which the spiky handwriting reappears, and a poem that I can make out:

Union
I heard the creep of ice.
I heard the wolf-cry of the sea.

I heard the slowing dawn.
I heard the night drown in the trees.
I heard the return in the bend.
I heard the whisper of amends between darkness
and light.
I heard what the silence confessed.

It's signed "Joe." *Joe?* Who is Joe?

My heart racing, I sit back down on the floor among El's clothes, holding the notebook close to my eyes in case they're playing tricks on me. Maybe I'm tired. Maybe I need a second opinion. The handwriting keeps changing, and there are strange drawings, childlike sketches of scenes I don't understand. A man holding a child's hand, then the child curled up in a fetal position surrounded by black clouds. Over the page, El's handwriting returns, the familiar steady line of it, school-teacher neat.

Meditating twice a day for fifteen minutes. It's OK but I feel restless and it does nothing to help with flashbacks. In fact, I think it makes them more vivid. Tried smoking out of desperation. Unfortunately, it doesn't work, just makes me cough. My counselor talks a lot about objectivity, about trying to imagine myself as someone else, or the abuse happening to someone else. How would I feel then, she asks? I've explained that I feel like someone else too often, and that's the problem. My memories of the abuse are more painful than when I was going through it. I want to run from this.

No date. What flashbacks? *Memories of the abuse?*

The next page and the handful of pages after that are

271

scored out with heavy lines, leaving their imprint on the rest of the pages thereafter. It's as though someone else has got hold of the notebook and tried to censor what was written, though I can still make out some of the words: *my fault...Orhan...Peter said to run...stop STOP!*

None of this makes any sense.

I take the notebook with me and head downstairs to the kitchen, where Magnus is sitting, looking blankly out the kitchen window. It's a sight I've grown used to, as though he's lost in thought. He jerks when he sees me, clearing his throat and visibly striving to reenter the present.

"Lochlan, there you are. I was— What are you up to? What time is it?"

I slide onto the barstool next to him and set the notebook on the bench.

"I found this in Eloïse's closet."

"What is it? A diary?"

"Kind of."

He lifts it and holds it at a distance as he flicks through the pages, dispossessed of his reading glasses. "Can't see it. What's it say?"

I tell him it's a bunch of scribbles that Eloïse seems to have written, referring to things I know nothing about.

"I thought the police took all of Eloïse's belongings," he says.

"They must have missed this." A brief pause while I summon my words. "Did Eloïse ever smoke?"

"Smoke?" He shakes his head. "Not to my knowledge. Not that anything I know means much anymore."

I don't quite know how to ask about the other things. About abuse. Eloïse never said anything like this to me. I try to tell myself that perhaps she was writing about someone else, but when I flick to the page myself I see it there in black in white:

imagine myself as someone else, or the abuse happening to someone else

"I have to ask you," I say to Magnus. "Was Eloïse...was she ever abused?"

He is silent for such a long time that I search for an alternative word instead of "abused," but I can't think of one.

"I don't know," he says finally, his gray eyes on the window. "Her mother left us at a young age...she took Eloïse, she was only a toddler, Max's age...we never really knew what happened in between Eloïse moving with her mother to London and coming to live with us. Except, of course, that our daughter..."

His lips tremble, as if he's on the brink of tears, and I realize for the first time that Jude went missing, too. Magnus and Gerda experienced their daughter, their only child, running away and never speaking to them again. This must be doubly hard for them to face.

I put a hand on Magnus's shoulder. Instead of flinching he takes a deeper breath and pats my hand, grateful for the show of support.

"Our daughter died," he continues, a tremor in his voice. "We had never spoken to her once during that time. I still try to think of what I might have done to make her feel that she didn't want to speak to her own parents. Parenthood is so difficult. You think that, you know, if you do A plus B you'll get C, but sometimes that is simply not the case. You get XYZ instead." He laughs, grimly. "Anyway, you asked whether or not Eloïse was abused." He contemplates, biting his lip, searching his memory.

"There was a discussion," he says slowly. "Between Eloïse and Gerda. When we went to London we found Eloïse with a social worker. She was twelve, you understand, and very much in shock after the death of her mother. We were astonished, truly astonished, to learn that they'd been living in utter squalor. And unfortunately, Eloïse relayed certain things to Gerda and we were led to believe that she experienced some things that I wish, with all my heart, she had not. But we never talked about anything after that." He looks at me again carefully. "Do you think that has anything to do with her disappearance?"

I tell him I have no idea. It's illogical that it *would* have anything to do with her disappearance, because sense dictates that if something was bothering her she would have mentioned it. But then, as I flick through the diary, I notice a word written in the corner of a page in large, childish handwriting.

CHANIA.

April 24, 1990

Harlesden, London

She was so hungry that she felt she might pass out. There had been many times when she had gone to bed with that terrible gnawing pain of an empty belly, but this was so much worse. It had been weeks since they last had proper food. The cupboards were stripped bare. A couple of matchsticks, empty bottles of vodka, mice droppings. She had stopped going to school. No one knocked on the door this time, threatening her mother with jail. Their new flat was in the roughest part of the city. In fact, she had a suspicion that they were no longer in London. No one spoke to you on the streets around here, and no kids played outdoors. Police vans were regularly parked outside. There were always groups on street corners, always loud voices sounding panicked. Her mother's boyfriends stopped coming, too, though there was still one man who made a visit every week or so. Eloïse knew who he was. He wasn't her mother's boyfriend, though he spent the night every now and then. He was the one who delivered little packages that got burned up and injected into her mother's arm.

She stood at the window, looking out at the street. Surely she could go and ask someone for food? A slice of bread, even. Her mouth watered at the thought of it. No, she couldn't. It was too dangerous out there.

A bang on the door. Her heart leaped. She jumped down and ran to answer it.

She didn't recognize the man in the doorway. A stocky man with a tattoo of a spider on his neck, lots of pimples on his face even though he looked too old for acne.

"Big Gee wants his money," he said.

"What?"

"Money. Now." He held out his hand

She could see a car parked a little way behind him, the engine running. Two men watching her from the front.

"I don't have any money."

He grinned as if she'd said something funny. Then, when she didn't reply, he turned on his heel and walked to the car. She watched as he leaned over and spoke to the men inside, then turned and started walking back to her.

She was steeling herself to ask him if he had any food when he grabbed her and started pulling her out of the house. She screamed and kicked, but she was easy to lift and haul toward the car. A woman across the road stared. The man opened the boot of the car and threw Eloïse in, locking it.

They drove for about a half hour, then stopped and pulled her out. She was so scared she couldn't speak, couldn't scream, could barely see where they were taking her. Hands

276

clapped on to her arms and dragged her inside a house. The last thing she saw was a group of men and women in a living room and a well-formed cumulus hanging above them.

"Out you get."

A man's face looking down at her. She was groggy. Her legs felt like someone had filled them with concrete. A hand took her arm and hauled her roughly to her feet. The hard night wind slapped against her bare shins.

"Drink water, yeah?" the man said.

She nodded and gave him a wave, and he laughed to himself before getting in the car and driving off.

Her front door. She recognized the brass numbers and the cracked glass panel. She felt distanced from her body, as though she was slightly outside it. She had marks on her arm and blood running down her leg.

Inside was quiet. She took the stairs very slowly, thought to check on her mother. She found her sitting at the side of her bed, yawning and wiping her eyes. She looked up and gave Eloïse a weak smile.

"Where did you go last night?" she said.

"Nowhere."

Jude nodded. "Is there any food in the house?"

She shook her head.

"I think I've some money downstairs. I'll go out in a while, get some milk and cereal."

Eloïse tried to respond but found she couldn't. She was like a puppeteer trying to master the strings attached to her limbs. With an awkward spin she turned and made for the bathroom, ran the taps until the water turned hot, hot enough to burn the night off her flesh, before climbing in.

April 2, 2015

Potter's Lane, Twickenham

Lochlan: My phone buzzes after eight o'clock in the morning. I'm still in bed, surprised when I wake up. I was still awake at five but I must have drifted off. I thrash around for my phone, hoping it's a call from one of Magnus's contacts. We never located her Swiss passport, and somewhere along the course of the search, amidst the babycams and ex-girlfriends, this detail got lost. Magnus and I spent most of last night drafting yet another list of people to contact. Given that El's notebook contains the word "Chania," a city in northern Crete. We got married on her grandparents' island near Crete. It's a long shot, however. The island is completely deserted.

"RAMONA" appears on my screen. My secretary. I'd almost forgotten I had a job.

"Lochlan?"

It's so good to hear her voice. "Ramona. How have you been? How are things at the office? Am I sacked yet?"

"Not yet, but... look, I feel awful for calling you when all of this is going on, but... "

"What's wrong?"

She goes on to explain that the company had a cybersecurity breach last night, with data stolen during a merger-and-acquisition deal between a FTSE 350 company based in London and another in Tokyo. As she explains it, the gravity of the situation unfolds in my head—one and a half million customers' private information is likely being traded around the world as we speak. Bank account numbers, pensions, child trust funds—all compromised. And that's before we know how much money was leached from the M&A.

"Dean Wyatt will be sending out a press release in the next half hour," Ramona says. "But before that the security company wants all key holders to log on to the central system. Will that be possible for you?"

"Lockie boy!" a voice calls as soon as I walk out of the lift. A few yards down the corridor I see Paddy Smyth, sharply turned out in a new slate-gray suit, a perplexed expression on his face that reminds me, somewhat embarrassingly, that I probably look like I've emerged from a hole in the ground. Metaphorically, I have, and a glance in one of the glass partitions confirms it: I'm wearing a creased polo shirt with the collar flicked up, jeans with paint stains, I haven't shaved in two weeks, and my hair is wild and uncombed. I'm sure the dark circles under my eyes add a hint of madman to my appearance, too. I stride past Paddy and he skips to keep apace.

"How's your wife?" he says. "Have they found her yet?"

I can't bring myself to say no.

"The hell d'you do to your precious Merc, by the way?"

"I got drunk and crashed it into the garden gate."

"Oof. Didn't that thing set you back fifty grand?"

I fought with Eloïse over that car. I can hear myself saying, *For heaven's sake, El, I work in corporate finance! It's expected that I drive a good car!* She thought it was too expensive. It was a constant source of tension between us.

"She still driving OK?" Paddy asks.

"Good enough to get me here."

"Don't tell your insurers you were drunk. Unless you were breathalyzed. Were you breathalyzed?"

"No."

"Well, there you go. Get her fixed. Can't be roadworthy. Good of you to come in, though. I'll take you to meet with the tech security team."

He makes to take a left when my office is to the right. "I thought I had to log in."

"You do, but we also have to reset all the passcodes around the place and update all the software. Eye scanners, that kind of thing. You should see the conference room. The cyber-tech crew got all these new gadgets laid out. It's like *Star Trek*." He takes a step closer. "There was another thing I wanted to ask you about."

"Oh?"

He stuffs his hands in his pockets and gives a shake of his head as if he's thought better of it.

"What is it?" I say.

He looks briefly around to check that no one else can hear. "Look, I know this is a truly terrible time for you and your family. I shouldn't even mention it." He bites his lip. "It's only that... Well, you know that nobody here ever takes holidays. Not during the busy season. And right now, we're in the busy season. We're wondering if we need to replace you, or if you're thinking of coming back, you know?"

He holds me with a congenial smile and boyish blue eyes. It's the same face that he's worn in meetings with clients going bust, businesses he's taken over, with his ex-wives. I swallow back a torrent of expletives and desperate pleas for him not to let me go and say, "Yeah. Right."

"Glad you understand, Lockie. I know I can always count on you."

I follow him reluctantly to the conference room. The heavy double doors swing inward to reveal all the heads of the company sitting around the shining oval table, their jackets slung on the backs of their chairs, laptops open in front of them, a variety of gadgets strewn across the table. Paddy gestures toward a seat and I sit down.

"Is that everybody?" the guy at the top of the table asks.

A clink of wheels and cups announces the arrival of two catering ladies with silver trolleys. They shuffle to a table at the side of the room. I lean to the woman at my right—Jane Silverman, head of transaction services—and say, "How long is this meeting going to be?"

"I heard three hours," she whispers back, and I swallow hard.

"OK, everyone. I'm Bryan Maxwell from Fortress. Right now we all have a big emergency on our hands, so while the rest of my team attempt to get intel into who exactly has stolen all your data, I'm going to guide you through a reset of the company's malware and security passcodes, and we'll also have a training session on how to prevent future attacks, what to look for during future M&As, and so on. In a few moments, we're going to link up to your sister company in New York so they can go through the same process. Get yourselves comfortable."

I am too distracted to hear anything that's being said, and several times Jane leans over and taps something on my laptop that I'm meant to have done. A month ago I would have been alert, every bit as worried as Paddy looks. I would have been taking notes and joining in the banter. But I no longer care. The only reason I stay is so Paddy might consider keeping me on.

An hour passes, two. Suddenly through the glass partition I see a man striding up the corridor, flanked by two police officers. DS Canavan. I jump to my feet, and Ramona follows. I pull open the door to meet him, my knees suddenly weak. They must have found Eloïse, that's why they've come here. DS Canavan looks grim. They've found a body.

"What's happened?" Ramona says when I can't find my voice.

DS Canavan ignores her and addresses me.

"Mr. Shelley, I'd like you to come with us, please."

His tone is different: taut with anger. I hear myself say, "Have you found Eloïse?" but he glances away, and one of the uniforms steps forward, repeating the instruction.

Paddy appears at my elbow, horrified at the sight of police officers in his building.

"What's all this about?"

"We've been trying to reach Mr. Shelley by phone," Canavan says firmly. "We need to ask him a few questions. Can you come with me, please?"

Paddy pulls out his phone and asks for security.

"I'm afraid this is a police matter," Canavan tells him.

"Sir, I'm afraid I'm going to have to ask you not to interfere with police business," the uniform tells Paddy when he begins to argue, but from the far end of the corridor I can see two security guards approaching. Canavan eyes me darkly.

"Why won't you tell me what's going on?" I ask him, incredulous. "This is my wife we're talking about!" He doesn't answer. I look to Paddy, who stares back at me, bewildered.

"Come with us to the station," Canavan says sternly. "We can have our chat there."

April 2, 2015

Children of War Headquarters, Tufnell Park, North London

Gerda: I brought the children home with me yesterday afternoon, leaving Magnus in London. I was in high spirits the whole way back to Ledbury. I even stopped in Cheltenham and bought the children some new outfits and toys, a beautiful changing table and sleigh cot for Cressida, which will be delivered tomorrow. I arranged for Mrs. Sloan, our housekeeper, to put some balloons in the drawing room for us coming home and to fill the refrigerator. Max was excited when we got back and for the first time in weeks I was able to forget the terrible mystery that is my beloved granddaughter. I watched Max leap out of the car and tear into the house, and it was only when I managed to bring the car seat and all the bags in from the car that I realized why he was running through the rooms upstairs. He thought his mother was here. He thought that was the reason we had come to Ledbury. When I told him otherwise, he threw a huge tantrum and begged to go back to his father.

He eventually quieted down—Mrs. Sloan was on hand to help coax him to look at the ducks down at the bottom of the garden—but I felt so very low afterward. I felt like I'd done the wrong thing, bringing him and Cressida back with me. It had seemed right at the time. Or perhaps it had seemed that I needed to make a point to Lochlan. After all, he had cheated on Eloïse. He had spoken to her horribly in the past, and his decision to work half the week in Edinburgh appalls me. It's taken a lot to bite my tongue. What I want to tell him, what I would love to scream from the rooftops is this: Is it any wonder Eloïse has left, if indeed she has left voluntarily? She's been existing as a single parent. She put every last drop of her very soul into that charity and yet had to give it all up to support their little family. Who *wouldn't* have left? Who could blame her?

There was a stack of mail waiting for me at the house. A lot of sympathy cards from the ladies at the WI, the parish, and Magnus's golfing club. There was a card also from the team at Eloïse's charity, Children of War. I don't know why the idea came to me, but perhaps it started with the thought that I had never been to the office she set up in Tufnell Park. I had been to a few of her fund-raisers, of course, but never to her place of work. It was a part of her life that I realized had perhaps not been looked into very carefully. The police had overturned her home, scrutinized all her e-mails, paperwork, and finances, but once they'd established that Eloïse hadn't received any death threats at her workplace, they left it alone.

I didn't sleep very well last night, thinking about it. I tried everything to put it out of my head, but it wouldn't leave me alone. This morning I got Max and Cressida dressed and told them that we'd spend the day at London Zoo. I knew Max liked the animals there. He didn't mention his mother again, thankfully, and so we packed up and drove to London and spent a couple of hours looking at the animals. I didn't mention any of this to Magnus or Lochlan, but while we were there I rang the charity office again and told the man on the phone who I was.

"I'm Danny Holland," he said. "I took over when Eloïse went on maternity leave. We are all truly devastated to hear what's happened."

With a great lump in my throat I updated him as best I could: the *Crimewatch* appeal and newspaper reports. I stayed well clear of anything personal or family related for fear I'd break down and weep, though he sounded like a fine fellow. I asked him if the police had been in to search El's office and he said no, they hadn't.

"They accessed her e-mails, I believe," he told me. "But they've not searched the premises. We made sure none of the cleaners or other members of staff touched El's files. You're welcome to come and have a look, if you like."

And so, after we'd fed the lemurs, observed the otters, and squirmed at enormous spiders, I persuaded Max to leave, and we set off toward El's office.

I found the charity headquarters in Tufnell Park—the entrance was very obscure, a little door beside a restaurant down a narrow back alley—and quickly found myself with offers from the staff there to entertain Max and Cressida while I visited El's office. It was much different than I expected. I suppose I'd thought of it as a project, a kind of cottage industry that Eloïse set up with noble intentions, and instead I found myself in a kind of Tardis, a sophisticated hub spread across three levels that was buzzing with activity. A great number of the staff introduced themselves—there were eighteen of them there, and another ten located in Gaza, Syria, Afghanistan, Iraq, Rwanda, and other places around the world—though I couldn't quite grasp their names. I was very taken with a large display in the ground-floor reception area, where a digital map of the world marked all the places where the charity has made a difference. Max pushed some of the buttons, and instantly a film projection popped up of different boys and girls telling their stories. It was absolutely magical.

A young man came down the stairs and shook my hand. He was wearing a white shirt with the sleeves rolled up, chinos, and had a clean-cut, earnest look about him, a dark tan that suggested he'd recently been abroad. "Danny Holland," he said, and I remembered him from our telephone conversation as the CEO.

Danny took me upstairs to El's office while a woman named Shakina—the charity's finance director, I think—and a receptionist called Jade looked after the children. Danny took out a key and unlocked one of the doors.

"Like I said, I fully expected the police to come and search this place," he said, showing me inside. "But it remains as El left it."

The smell of her was instantly there. I can't quite describe what the smell is—it's not a perfume, although she was partial to Poême by Lancôme, it's a warm scent that I associate with her. The room was modest: a desk, computer, an Ikea chair, some bookcases, a rug, and pictures of Lochlan and Max framed on a shelf. Typical El. Danny directed me to her filing cabinet.

"I don't know if any of this will be of use," he said sadly. "We've all racked our brains in case there was anything we missed. She came in only a few weeks before this all happened, you know. To show us the baby."

"Cressida," I said, and he folded his arms and gave a nod. I could tell he was starting to become upset, thinking about it.

"She seemed to be doing well. Looked happy, you know? She talked about coming back to work in a year or so. We were all excited by that."

He glanced around with his hands in his pockets. I made for the filing cabinet and opened the first drawer. It was full of paperwork, all neatly filed, but I had no idea what I was looking for. Maybe I wanted to be close to something that was so important to her. More and more I felt weighed down by guilt at not taking more of an interest. I had made a terrible assumption that the charity was never anything that was going to take off and that, if I encouraged her, I would be building her up for a fall. I should have encouraged her.

Danny produced a cardboard box full of envelopes and set it on the desk. "There's her mail. She was due to come in for it in a week or so, but..." He bit his lip. I nodded and rolled up my sleeves in a bid to keep focused and not wallow in emotion.

"Thank you. I'll get cracking."

There was a lot of junk mail in there, some letters from organizations that seemed keen to partner with the charity. I made sure to pass those on to Danny in case he wanted to explore further opportunities.

I found a wad of tatty jotter paper inside an envelope postmarked from Uganda. Inside was a photograph of a little girl holding up a plant of some sort and grinning. She had black hair braided in two tight bunches at the side of her head and an adorable grin. Her name was Phiona and she had recently turned thirteen. The letter was made out to Eloïse, thanking her for Phiona's birthday gift, telling her what she'd been up to since she rescued her. It seemed that Phiona's parents had sold her for four cows into marriage with an old man who beat her up. I checked the girl's age again. Yes. She was thirteen.

I put the letter down. I had no idea, no idea at all of the kind of things El was doing here. She had never once asked Magnus and me for money to fund these children. I think Magnus made contributions, but we were capable of doing so much more. Why didn't I ask her about her work? Why didn't I listen?

I came across a letter at the bottom of the pile, however, which put everything else in the shade. It was postmarked from the South London and Maudsley NHS Trust. I opened the envelope carefully. A short letter, dated March 10 of this year, noting that Eloïse had missed her previous two appointments with Dr. Goff, and could she please contact the secretary to reschedule.

I read over the letter several times, trying to recall anything that Eloïse had said to me about a hospital appointment. Why would she go all the way to a hospital in South London when West Middlesex University Hospital was much closer?

I called Danny back in and asked if I could use El's computer. He set it up for me to go on the Internet, though I'm still a bit useless with googling things so I requested politely and casually that he look up the name and telephone number of the doctor in the letter: Dr. Tara Goff at South London and Maudsley Hospital.

"I've found her," he said after a few moments, and I squinted at the screen. "Are you sure this is the right person?"

I checked the details on the letter with the name and details on the screen. It was a perfect match.

"It says she's a clinical psychologist," Danny said.

"A clinical psychologist?"

"Says here she specializes in postnatal mental health, bipolarity, and severe personality disorders." He glanced up. "What's that got to do with Eloïse?"

Without asking Danny, I lifted the handset on the desk and dialed the number that appeared on the screen.

"Hello, yes. I'd like to speak to Dr. Tara Goff, please."

March 31, 2015

Komméno Island, Greece

I've spent all of today on Bone Beach trying to launch the boat, and I'm covered in cuts and bruises. I managed to dislodge the two big stones that were stopping it from being pulled out by the tide, but as I did so the boat swung around and caught me hard on the ankle with one of the masts. It was so painful that I thought I'd broken it. I'm pretty sure now that I haven't, but I'm still hobbling.

The sun seemed to go down in a tremendous rush. One minute it was a coin high in the sky, the next it was a bar of molten copper across the horizon. Time is slipping and jolting again.

I was so tempted to jump in and sail to Crete right there and then, but my life jacket is back at the farmhouse—and besides, I wanted to try and persuade Sariah to come with me.

Once I'd got the boat into position, I stripped off my clothes and lay flat on the dry sand in my knickers, looking up at the stars. I had no energy left to do anything else. I listed through a muddy kind of sleep, my thoughts distorted and swollen with images. I forced myself to recall the memory of George at the roadside. It was dark and we were outside, somewhere with a lot of mountains. It was a crisp night. We'd hit an animal. I heard George say, "You have to kill it." And so I did.

But it made no sense. I only met George the night I crashed my boat. That's what they all said.

As I pressed myself to think, I remembered more details about the other man I'd dreamed about. He was the same man I'd seen at the mouth of the cave, handing me the ball of red wool as I went into the labyrinth.

Who was this man? What was his name?

An image of a lock, and a key in my hand. Lock.

His name was Lochlan.

I drifted off to sleep, and what I dreamt must have been a mix of imagination and memory, the sensual quality rooted deep in my emotions. I dreamt I was in the labyrinth again, clutching my ball of red wool. Odd corridors of stalagmites leading to rooms in a messy house with empty vodka bottles on the floor and bags full of rubbish stacked up in the kitchen. The smell of stale milk and rotting food thick in my nostrils.

When I caught my reflection in a cracked mirror in the bathroom, I saw that I was a child, maybe seven or eight years old, holding a teddy to my chest. *Peter.* I had fine, white-blonde hair to my shoulders, pale, smooth skin that was marked with a purple bruise on my cheek. My lips were raw, cracked, my eyes haunted.

I heard shouting. A man's voice calling from one of the other rooms. *Eloïse! Eloïse, where are you?*

I was stricken by the sound. I knew I had to run and hide but I was in the bathroom and the window was shut. I climbed into the bathtub and tried to hide behind the curtain, but suddenly a hand plunged in and caught me by the hair. I gasped as he dragged me out of the bathroom and across the landing.

Somehow I managed to break free, and I ran into another room that led me back into the labyrinth.

And there, the small, light voice of a young child.

"Mummy? Mummy, are you there?"

I tiptoed into another corridor toward the voice, my heart racing.

"Mummy, where are you?"

A little boy. He sounded scared. It was so dark, and the ground beneath my feet was wet and slippery. The last of the red wool slipped out of my hands. As it ended, I came to the heart of the labyrinth.

Inside was a small chamber, with a single stone seat and a slit in the rock overhead where light bled through to reveal the occupant.

I guessed the boy to be three or four years old, his blond hair slightly curling at his soft jaw. His eyes were round and blue, filled with innocence. He was kneeling on the ground and playing with two toy trains on the seat, running them across it as though they were on tracks. He turned and said, "Hi, Mummy."

I knelt down beside him. I knew his face. I knew his name. I said, "Hello, Maxie. Are you OK?"

He turned back to his trains and looked sad. "I'm OK. When are you coming home, Mummy?"

I said, "I'm trying so hard, Maxie. I really am."

He set down his trains and thought about this. "Did you leave us because you weren't feeling very well?"

"I don't know."

"You need to get better," he said, deeply serious. "You need milk and a choccy biscuit. When I don't feel well, you give me milk and sometimes a choccy biscuit."

I laughed, though my eyes had filled with tears. "I don't want to hurt you, Max."

He brightened and gave me a deep look, his beautiful, gentle eyes holding mine. "Don't be silly, Mummy. Why do you think you hurt me?"

I tried to explain it in a way that he would understand.

"I think someone told me that, once. I think someone told me I would never be a good mother, and I felt I wasn't good enough for you."

He reached out and touched my arm. "You look after me. You look after all of us. Come home now, please."

I wiped the tears from my cheeks. "I will, darling. I need to remember where home is."

April 2, 2015

Smyth & Wyatt Building, Victoria Embankment, London

Lochlan: As I am being ushered out of the Smyth & Wyatt building all the most important figures in the company are looking on from the conference room overhead. The long windows at the end of the corridor overlook the car park where my mangled Mercedes sits, the right headlight shattered, the bumper hanging dangerously low to the ground, like a fat lip on a boxer's face, and the bonnet crunched in. In all likelihood, this is the last time I will see either my car or my workplace.

At the police car, Canavan tells me he is arresting me on suspicion of lying in a witness statement. I go to ask him what the hell that means—does he think I lied about Eloïse going missing?—but he ignores me.

"You do not have to say anything but it may harm your defense if you do not mention when questioned something which you later rely on in court. Anything you do say may be given in evidence."

I am too stunned to utter a word.

I'm informed that I won't be handcuffed, and we drive to the station in a swollen, braying silence: me, Canavan, and another male detective I faintly recognize. The quiet draws a circle around a new terror, possibly worse than Eloïse's disappearance. If they arrest me, what will happen to our children? Will I ever see them again?

At the station Canavan hands me over to a uniformed police sergeant who books me into custody. This involves being searched, purged of my belongings, and then stood numbly at a desk while the officer makes a record of my detention on the computers. He asks if I'll be needing legal advice and who I want to be informed of my arrest. I'm so dumbfounded that I tell them to call Magnus instead of my brother. Too late. I have no idea what Magnus is going to make of this.

After a while, another officer asks me to accompany him to the interview room, where I find DS Canavan sitting at a table with a digital tape recorder against the wall. I feel like I'm floating, not quite here. I look deeply into Canavan's face, his shrewd, silver eyes, and read the future there: They're going to charge me with Eloïse's murder. I'll never see my son or my daughter again.

"DS Cox and I want to ask you further questions about your involvement with Harriet Ayres," Canavan says in a tight voice.

In an instant, I realize that he knows everything about Harriet. I should have been up-front about it. I shouldn't have lied. How could I have been so stupid?

"Specifically," he continues, "we'd be interested to know what you were doing approaching Harriet Ayres at the Dog and Duck pub in Soho after she was released on bail in relation to computer misuse at your property."

There's a CCTV camera in the left-hand corner of the room. High-spec babycams, CCTVs, the thousand eyes of social media, yet no one has seen my wife. And the very thing I wanted no one to see has all come out in the wash.

"I'm sorry," I say, stumbling over my words. "I thought...I had to find out for myself if Harriet was involved."

The uniformed officer takes notes. As my own words appear on the page, I think of Eloïse's notebook. *Why was there more than one set of handwriting? It was a private notebook. She'd hardly share it, would she? If she wouldn't share such private information with her own husband, she's hardly going to share it with anyone else. Would she?*

"Mr. Shelley?"

"Yes?"

"I think you drifted off there for a second or so. I said, did you or did you not have an affair with the accused?"

A smart person would say "no comment."

"I did."

"Would you like to enlighten us as to why you lied about that the first time I asked you about the nature of your involvement with Miss Ayres?"

Say "no comment."

"I was afraid. I was afraid of anyone finding out about my involvement. And what that might mean for the future of my family."

Was El afraid? Was that why she didn't tell me about her past?

He glances up at the CCTV, turns an idea over in his mind. Whatever he's deciding is crucial to my fate, I know it.

"Well, I'm afraid that we don't look too kindly on deception, Mr. Shelley, and we certainly don't like witnesses being approached by interested parties while they're on bail."

Humble nod.

"I understand."

He gives a long sigh. "Well, what we're going to do now is take another witness statement from yourself containing full details of your involvement with Miss Ayres and your approach to her while she was on bail."

He lets that sink into my noggin. I give another deep nod and let all my body language shout out that I'm sorry, I know I'm stupid, please don't lock me up.

She would do anything to protect our children. Anything. Even if it meant leaving them behind.

Canavan leans back in his chair.

"Following that, providing all's in order, I'd like to give you some strong words of advice to ensure that we don't have to put you in the dock. Understood?"

"Fully understood. Thank you."

He asks me about my relationship with Harriet, and I don't hold back, though the CCTV in the corner of the room is beginning to burn a hole in the top of my head. I explain about the flirtation at work, about my increasing feelings of frustration at home and how much I began to enjoy Harriet's company. And it's only when I'm describing how she arrived at my home that evening, the picture of her at the door now vivid in my mind, that I realize how much Harriet reminds me of Eloïse. Not as she is now, but there *is* a resemblance, even beyond their physical likenesses. A resemblance in the nature of my relationship with Harriet, the energy that moved between us so freely and with such power—it is no excuse, I know that, but as I think back to my affair with Harriet, I am inclined to believe that I wasn't attracted to her. I barely knew her. I was attracted to the familiarity I felt with her, the resonance of a relationship I'd lost.

I don't explain any of this to Canavan. As my horror at being arrested begins to lessen into acceptance, I perceive with surprise that he's not hanging his suspicions on me quite yet. It is, however, understandable that he's mightily underwhelmed by my failure to disclose the full truth of the matter of Harriet. It hits me then that my brother—no stranger to the wrong side of the law—could face tougher consequences than I do as a result of my enforced reacquaintance with honesty.

"What—or indeed who—led you to discover Harriet's whereabouts?" Canavan asks.

"My brother." It hurts to say it.

"His name?"

I cover my eyes with my hands.

"Wesley Shelley."

"Address?"

I give it, pained by each syllable. I'm grassing on my own baby brother. How can I ever make this up to Wes? DS Canavan writes it down. I try to tell myself that informing me where Harriet was won't land my brother in jail, but then I know as much about the law as I do about lost tribes.

I tell Canavan about my argument with Harriet, recalling what she said, what I said, how I felt afterward. Hearing my own words out loud makes me realize how stupid I was to approach her like that, and how selfish. What did I think I was going to achieve? I've risked so much for so little.

Right as I think Canavan's about to renege on his decision to let me off with a warning and instead charge me with some major offense, a hard knock sounds at the door.

"Come," Canavan says brusquely, and the door opens. I turn to see DS Welsh.

"Sorry to interrupt, guv, but Gerda Bachmann's on the phone," she says. "Needs to speak to you. Sounds urgent."

April 1, 2015

Komméno Island, Greece

The sun is low in the sky. I am parched and woozy with hunger. My clothes have dried on the rocks, crisp and stiff, the boat moans beside me and the wind buries itself under the sails. I roll forward and will myself to wrap the sails around the masts in case they get torn. It takes tremendous effort, as though the sails are slabs of marble. When I put my clothes back on, my jeans slide down around my hips.

In the distance, a welcome visitor: the white rectangle of a cruise ship. It's about halfway between the island and Crete and seems to have dropped anchor, maybe for an hour, possibly for the night. I stand and stare out at it for a long time, trying to gauge how long it would take to sail to it.

There's no telling what the current is like out there, or how I might manage to sail, given that I'm so weak. On the spur of the moment I reach into one of the stowage compartments of the boat and pull out a flare, but as I do I find another life jacket, visibly unused, folded neatly behind the pack. Sariah's face flashes in my mind. I could bring her with me, if she's willing. I set the jacket down and fumble with the toggle on the flare until it fizzes high into the air with a huge bang and a burst of powdery red light.

What are you doing? I ask myself aloud. The cruise ship is hardly going to turn course and head toward the island because of one flare. In any case, the pier is designed only for small speedboats, and the rocks around the island make it much too dangerous for any large vessel to come close. My only option is to try and sail out to it before it lifts anchor and takes off.

The climb back up to the farmhouse is unimaginably hard, and to make matters worse it begins to rain, thick dollops of water bouncing off the ground. I tilt my head back and catch mouthfuls of it before turning to continue. Several times I fall over, slipping in the mud, and by the time I reach the top of the hill I am coated head to toe in mud. I stand for a moment, panting and arching my head back again and again to drink.

Bizarrely, as I reach the incline of the hill and face the spot where the farmhouse should be, it isn't there. Instead, a redbrick semidetached house sits a hundred yards away, surrounded by a tidy garden with rosebushes and a yellow hedge. I stop and wipe the rain from my face, squinting hard at the house.

This is my house, I know it is. *My* house. The white car in the driveway is mine.

The rain hammers down, forceful and angry. I have no answers for what I'm seeing.

In the next instant, the house is gone, replaced by the farmhouse. I think back to the boy I dreamt about. Max. My son.

302

I *know* he is my son, and like a steady trickle my feelings for him course through my body. The memory of carrying him. Giving birth to him. Holding him for the first time. The feeling of protectiveness toward him, of carrying him out of the hospital and being overwhelmed by how many dangers surrounded him. Unseen dangers, things I wasn't physically capable of defending him against.

Rivers of rainwater funnel down the hill, slippering my feet with mud and stones. I drop down on all fours, grabbing on to tree roots and bushes to haul myself up. My bare feet are gashed and bruised from the stony pathway, but as soon as I reach the farmhouse the pain dissipates—I'm buzzing with adrenaline, all my senses charged in case George appears. There's no smoke from the chimney. A good sign. Still, I wait a moment at the kitchen door, listening for voices. I'm dripping wet and shaking with cold by the time I gather the courage to push the door open and step inside.

The kitchen is in darkness. No one around, no notebooks anywhere. I see the life vest on the worktop and snatch it up, tucking it under my arm before jogging up the stairs to the bathroom.

Locking the bathroom door behind me, I pull off my wet clothes and turn the tap on to rinse off the mud.

No water comes out.

I find a towel and scrub vigorously—my face, shins, then my hair. The effort warms me up, but I'm filthy, smeared in dirt. I try the tap again, turning and turning, but to no avail. Just then, a clap of thunder shakes the room. A glance through the small window outside shows clouds the color of charcoal brewing over the ocean.

A storm is closing in.

April 2, 2015

Potter's Lane, Twickenham

Lochlan: We married on a Tuesday. We flew to Crete, paid a man to take us to the island that Magnus owned, and got married on a hill overlooking the Aegean. We had few guests: El's best friend Lucia and her partner Vincent as our witnesses, my brother Hamish as my best man, and the priest who married us.

El was wearing a yellow dress with daisies in her hair. I wore a white shirt and trousers. We were both barefoot. It was so simple and beautiful. Afterward, we went to the hotel close to the dock and had a beautiful lunch. We stayed a few days more on the island before returning to England to do it all over again, quite smug in the knowledge that we'd already had the real ceremony, exactly the way we wanted it.

I know it's easy to say now that I'm in this position, but I wish I'd done things differently. I wish I'd been a better husband. A better father. I wish I'd said "no" more often to my boss and "yes" much more often to my family.

How fierce love becomes when it is threatened.

I'd expected Canavan to throw me in the cells after our interview, but he jumped to attention when Welsh mentioned Gerda's phone call and I've been wary of asking what it's about.

After two hours' waiting, a woman walks briskly through the front entrance and introduces herself to the custody officer behind the desk. She's slim, mid-thirties. She's wearing navy Fly London sandals that mismatch her gray trousers and white shirt. No coat, strands of dark hair falling out of a hair grip. As though she's come here in haste.

"I'm Tara Goff," I hear her tell the officer behind the desk. "I'm here to see Detective Sergeant Canavan?"

A moment later Gerda walks through the door. I stand up and say her name, and she swings around, astonished to see me.

"Who told you?" she says, and I have no idea what she's talking about. "The letters," she adds as though to explain, but right then DS Welsh approaches. She shakes hands with Gerda, then the woman.

"If you'd like to follow me, please."

Gerda whispers to me as we walk along the corridor but I hardly hear a word she says. Canavan and Welsh are talking and glancing at me as we make for another interview room on the right. Inside we take our places around a table, and I'm relieved when Canavan doesn't join us.

"This is Dr. Tara Goff," Welsh says, gesturing toward the woman who came in before Gerda. "Dr. Goff, this is Eloïse's husband, Lochlan, and her grandmother, Gerda."

"How do you do," she says, reaching to shake our hands in

turn. Then, more soberly, "My sympathies to both of you at this incredibly difficult time."

Gerda explains in short, tense sentences that she went to Eloïse's offices in London and found letters that indicated contact between El and Dr. Goff. She was able to call Dr. Goff, who agreed to come and talk to us immediately. I'm still clueless as to what any of this means.

Welsh pours four cups of water from a jug brought in by a uniformed officer. I am rigid, analyzing every movement and gesture, weighing up the silence. There is nothing about this meeting that indicates Eloïse has been located. Dr. Goff's presence indicates a problem, and I feel sick.

"Is it all right if I record this conversation?" Welsh asks Dr. Goff, who nods and sips at her glass of water. Gerda and I share a nervous look. Welsh turns to a machine by the wall and hits a button.

"Now, then," she says, settling back into her chair. "First of all, thank you very much for coming to speak with us, Dr. Goff..."

"Tara," Dr. Goff interjects. "I ask all my patients to use my first name."

Welsh smiles. "Tara. Could you begin by telling us where you work, what it is you do, and so on."

Tara nods and sets down the cup of water, emptied. "I hold a senior position in clinical psychology at SLaM, which is the South London and Maudsley NHS Trust. I am also deputy director of the British Dissociative Identity Disorder Research Network and a member of the International Society for the Study of Trauma and Dissociation." A long pause, in which I try to work out how this relates to my wife. Tara glances across at Gerda and Welsh.

"I ought to say that normally patient confidentiality would not be breached unless you had already gained my client's permission to do so for her own (or others') protection. I'd like that to be minuted, please."

Welsh hesitates. "We'll keep a record of it."

Tara looks appeased. "Good. Because I've had to consult with my peers very quickly about whether or not I'm able to divulge anything at all about my patient in her absence." I'm still processing the words "my patient," when she continues, her voice lowered:

"Given that Eloïse has gone missing, and that there are young children involved, the situation is a little more...nuanced. So I'd like to ask Lochlan to formally give permission on Eloïse's behalf, given that he's listed as her next of kin."

Everyone turns to me.

"I...give permission," I say, and everyone's shoulders lower.

Welsh confirms that this is recorded. She glances at Gerda and says, "Mrs. Bachmann said that you had had consultations with Eloïse in relation to mental health issues?"

Tara nods, and I do a double take. I flick a glance at Gerda, who—oddly—seems compliant.

"Eloïse's records show that she was referred to our clinic by her GP in February 2005, which is ten years ago," Tara says, "and that she saw a consultant on and off for about six months after that. Now, I don't have any notes on a diagnosis, but what I do know is that she was prescribed a substantial dose of Flupentixol, which is an antipsychotic."

"El was prescribed antipsychotics?" I cut in.

"Ten years ago?" Gerda exclaims, our voices overlapping.

Tara continues carefully. "Eloïse stopped taking her medication due to side effects, and frankly I think she was scared by the insinuation that she was psychotic."

I ask Tara to repeat this, and when she does and the meaning of it still hasn't reached me, she shifts to a softer tone:

"Your wife was referred to my department again about four years ago, Mr. Shelley. After the birth of her first child."

"Max," I say, racking my brain for a memory of the referral. El was seeing a counselor, I knew that much. I had imagined a sympathetic midwife, not a clinical psychologist and antipsychotics.

"The notes indicated that she was doing well," Tara continues. "The sessions only lasted for a couple of weeks before she was discharged." A moment of relief. "But last August she made contact with our team again and was referred to me."

"Eloïse was pregnant last August," I say.

"Yes, I believe that's why she contacted us," Tara says. "Eloïse said that she didn't want to go on the drugs again. She had started to have very frightening flashbacks. And she felt anxious about having another baby."

"That's not true," Gerda says, though with less bite than usual. "Eloïse was joyous when she found out she was expecting again."

"Can you tell us about your sessions with Eloïse?" Welsh interrupts.

Tara shifts in her seat as though trying to recall their meetings, or perhaps trying to filter whatever seems most relevant.

"We spoke a great deal about her previous treatment. She had some difficulty talking about her childhood and I suggested she join a small writer's group set up by one of our clinicians who was exploring poetry therapy."

The writer's group! I start to babble about Niamh, how she mentioned a writer's group, and when Tara asks what Niamh said, I can only recall that she said El seemed different.

"Well, that's to be expected," she said.

"Can you elaborate on this writer's group?" Welsh asks.

"We had a small group of about four or five patients who were interested in using creative writing as a way to construct memories into narratives," Tara explains. "We've found it to be a useful way to enable patients to reengage with identity..."

"And did this affect Mrs. Shelley adversely?" Welsh asks.

Tara considers this. "I didn't see any signs of adverse effect. She began to tell me about the voices she'd been hearing over the years."

"Voices?" I say, aware that I sound apoplectic. But I don't care. They are describing someone else, not the woman I married.

"She said she was frightened when Max was born because the voices grew stronger, telling her she was a bad mother, telling her that she would harm him. That she posed a danger to him."

I just can't believe it. *She was hearing voices.* I think back to the babycam footage of El talking to thin air. Was that it? She was seeing things?

"Do you know why Eloïse was hearing voices?" Gerda asks quietly.

Tara hesitates. "I think the abuse played a significant part."

Welsh turns her eyes to mine, and my first reaction is to say I know nothing about any abuse. But then everything Magnus told me echoes in my mind.

"I didn't know," I say, surprised by how hurt I suddenly feel that El never told me. "I've only learned about it from El's grandfather."

"It's my understanding that Eloïse was taken by her mother from Geneva to live in London when she was four years old," Tara says.

"That's right," Gerda says faintly. "Jude was still a child herself when Eloïse was born. We never found out who the father was." She gives a long sigh, stares at her lap. "We thought about putting the baby up for adoption, but Jude said no. We brought her back to Geneva. She and Eloïse both lived with us. Magnus and I loved having another baby around, despite the circumstances. It feels like only yesterday. But then, everything changed."

"How did everything change?" Welsh asks gently.

Gerda looks like she's been backhanded. When she speaks, it's as though the words contain thorns. "Jude found a boyfriend, an older man. He persuaded them to leave Switzerland."

"Orhan," Tara says, and Gerda nods reluctantly.

Welsh glances at Tara. "Is that when the abuse occurred?"

Tara nods.

"Can you tell us what happened?" Welsh continues.

Tara takes a breath. "During the time that Eloïse lived with Jude, she was subjected to sustained and systematic sexual abuse. Her mother was a drug addict and there was nowhere for Eloïse to seek protection or guidance. She was kept out of school a fair amount. Jude kept moving around England, presumably to avoid being tracked down by social services. She had a steady stream of partners, many of whom subjected Eloïse to the same treatment as she'd received from Orhan."

Gerda begins to emit terrible sobs, her shoulders heaving

up and down. I have a sense that we're breaking through to another world I didn't know existed. I steel myself to keep listening, trying to process this horrifying new knowledge. *Sustained and systematic sexual abuse...* There are many questions shouting in my head right now. Why didn't she tell me?

"I think the thing to try to understand," Tara says, "is that a child as young as Eloïse was when these terrible things were happening to her simply doesn't have the emotional vocabulary to cope with it. It's also extremely common for the mind to respond by blocking out years of abuse. Even as an adult, it can take a long time to develop strategies by which to process it and attempt to live a normal life."

"But we *were* living a normal life," I say, though my conviction wanes the moment the words are out of my mouth. "At least, that's what I thought."

Tara is swift to answer. "Trauma can lie dormant for a very long time. Eloïse coped for a good while, and she was certainly very successful. Like I said, she sought me out when she was pregnant, and I think it was because her previous birth had acted as a trigger for some of these issues to rise to the surface of her memory."

Welsh produces a tissue and hands it to Gerda, who dabs her eyes, then hands one to me. But I'm too stunned to cry. The edges of reality seem like they're beginning to dissolve, the floor of the known world falling away from my feet.

"She was the age our son Max is now," I say, and Gerda lets out a loud sob. "She was so young. She was a child when this happened." It didn't sink in when Magnus told me, not really. A huge part of me tried to hide from the possibility of this happening to someone I love. But with every word that Dr. Goff speaks I feel something piecing together, only there is no relief or resolution. I'm standing at the precipice of a terrible truth.

Gerda looks as though her face has fallen in. Welsh is clearly itching to get answers, predictions, anything that will resolve the case. "Do you think there's a connection between Eloïse's mental health issues and her disappearance?" she asks.

Tara nods. "I would say it's very likely."

My stomach flips.

"Where do you think she would have gone?"

"I'm afraid I don't know," Tara replies.

"You think she's killed herself, don't you?" Gerda says quietly, her voice low. "That's what you're saying."

This time, Tara studies her hands in her lap, selecting her words, and my heart plummets. When she doesn't answer, Welsh presses her.

"You mentioned that you've been involved in cases of women with similar mental health issues who've gone missing." A long pause. Welsh lowers her voice. "In those cases, was suicide a common outcome?"

Tara lifts her eyes to mine.

"Yes."

April 1, 2015

Komméno Island, Greece

I'm wringing out my clothes in the bathroom when suddenly I hear George laughing, his deep voice booming rhythmically. I freeze, my hand reaching for the doorknob in case the lock fails. I'm naked. My clothes are too wet to put back on and there are no towels.

Holding the doorknob tightly I press my ear against the wood of the door to listen. I can only make out George's voice, but he must be talking to someone. I try to gauge his tone—is he addressing Hazel? When he begins to laugh, I open the door and tiptoe up to the attic, closing the door behind me as quietly as I can. He's still talking. Good. I'm flooded with relief at the sight of a pair of Hazel's tracksuit bottoms and a black jumper on the chair by the bed. I tug them on as fast as I can.

"Hello, Eloïse," a voice says behind me.

I yell in fright and spin round. George is standing in the doorway, a grin on his face.

"George," I say. "I...I was cold, so I came up here to get some clothes. That's all. I can go..."

A flash of lightning sets the room aglow, though his eyes appear dark, black holes in his face, his bulk blocking up the doorframe. Another clap of thunder rattles the roof. How did he get up here so fast? Where are the others?

"I'm beginning to wonder about you, Eloïse."

I hold up my hands. "George, please..."

He leans against the wall, his arms folded. "Every time you're around, things start to go wrong." His voice is low and unnervingly affable in tone. "Nikodemos, the cistern, the satellite phone..." Another bolt of lightning interrupts him. "And now a great big storm. Joe's wrong. You're not Eloïse."

I hold my hands up, trying to reason with him.

"I don't want to be here, George. I can go—"

"Where you going to go?" he says. His frame fills the whole doorway, so I've no chance of slipping past him. I'm trapped.

"You remember where you live yet? You remember who you are?"

"No, but—"

"Then you're staying here, right where I can see you. You're staying with me *forever*."

He takes a step back and slams the door. I hear the sound of a key turning in the lock, and as I pull on the door handle there is the sound of something heavy being dragged across wood. The door won't budge.

"George! Let me out of here!"

There is only the sound of the thunder rolling overhead and the rain pounding against the windowpane.

It must be about three o'clock in the afternoon. George locked me in here last night and I have no idea when he plans to let me out. I haven't eaten or drunk anything since yesterday morning.

My stomach has stopped hurting but I feel light-headed. My lips are cracked and my fingers are swollen. I can't get up from a crouching position on the floor. The sun has been beating down all day and the room has grown unbearably hot. I tried banging on the floor to get Sariah's attention, but I only lasted ten minutes or so before I felt nauseous. Through the skylight at the far end of the room I can see that the cruise ship has gone.

Perhaps it is the act of staying so still, or perhaps it is because I am dying, but my memory begins to awaken. That's the only way I can describe it—effortlessly, I recall great chunks of my past.

My little boy, Max. I remember planning a train-themed party for his fourth birthday. I had organized a cake to be made in the shape of *Thomas the Tank Engine*. He is the most beautiful child I could ever have imagined calling my son.

Suddenly I miss Max so badly that it almost turns me inside out. Knowing that he is somewhere else, somewhere I can't remember, is an unexpected torture. I can see his bedroom. I designed it so carefully. His gallery bookcase mounted on the wall opposite his bed, with all his favorite books positioned so he can choose for himself. His *Thomas the Tank Engine* bed-covers and shelves covered in *Peppa Pig* characters. His wall chart of dinosaurs. Is he still this young? Is he alive?

My beautiful boy. I wish so badly to hold you in my arms.

Memories continue to whirl in my head, unprompted and wild. I remember holding an infant, a little girl, and her name comes to me in a tremendous, heart-wrenching rush.

Cressida.

I remember trying to breastfeed her, a sharp, searing ache when she latched on. I remember the softness of her small, fuzzy head against the crook of my arm. She looked funny and almost ugly: milk spots dotting her face like pimples, her eyelashes not yet grown, her lurid pink skin turning to white scales along the creases of her wrists and ankles. I loved her with such intensity.

And yet you left her.

I remember laying her into a car seat as I stepped into a shower, then stepping out again in case she tipped herself out. I felt so stupid—she was strapped in, there was no way she could fall out—but the fear that she might be harmed hunted me like a wolf. Relentless. Day and night.

You could harm her without realizing it.

They said she's not gaining weight—your milk is not enough for her.

There are other ways that you pose a greater threat to her than anything else out there.

You could roll over on her in the night.

You could forget to tuck the blankets under the mattress of the Moses basket and she could pull one over her face.

You might leave her sleeping in a draft. She could die of hypothermia.

Slow, insistent ripples of recollection nudge the pieces of myself into new shapes. I remember my home, my job, Lochlan, my friends. I remember the voices I heard, the others. I remember feeling afraid that I could hurt Max and the new baby.

You left them.

What does that say about you?

April 2, 2015

Potter's Lane, Twickenham

Magnus: The infant is crying, endless, tormenting crying. I'm trying to make a bottle for her but I'm not marvelous at this sort of thing. The writing on the tin of milk powder is ridiculously small. How do they expect anyone to read this? It's microscopic.

I reach in and find a fiddly piece of plastic that looks like a doll's scoop, which I suppose I'm to use in order to get the powder into the bottle. It's only after I've shaken the mixture that I wonder whether I was meant to level off the powder. The milk seems too thick. I give it to Cressida anyway. Her screeching has my blood pressure off the charts.

And now my mobile phone is buzzing in my pocket. How anyone does this on a daily basis is beyond me. "All right, all right," I tell my phone, setting the baby on the sofa with a cushion propping up the bottle so I have the ability to answer the call. The bottle begins to roll away from her and I reach out to set it back, but then she manages to position her tiny little fists around it and feed it to herself. *Gut gemacht!* I tell her. *Well done!*

"Hello?"

"Hello? Magnus?"

"*Ja?*"

"Magnus, this is Nikodemos Mantzaris. From Chania. I have a message from my son to call you?"

"Ah, Nikodemos!" I say, and I'm so surprised by the call that I somehow manage to knock the tin of milk powder all over the floor. I swear loudly, and Nikodemos is on the end of the line, saying, "Hello? Hello?"

"I'm sorry," I tell him, beginning to babble in broken Greek about milk powder and my great-granddaughter, until it occurs to me that he won't understand any of this. I switch to English and get to the heart of the matter.

"Look, Nikodemos—thank you so much for returning my call. It's concerning my granddaughter Eloïse. You remember her?"

"Yes?"

"She's missing, Nikodemos."

Suddenly I can't speak, my throat is seized with sadness, and I stamp my feet on the ground to shake it loose. Now is not the time for silence and sorrow.

"Missing?"

"Yes, yes. You remember her, I'm sure."

"Of course I do. How old is she now?"

"She's in her thirties... married, two beautiful children. But we're very worried because she seems to have..." The tears come again, and my voice rises. I squeeze my eyes tightly and sing the words to the Bättruef in my mind to distract my feelings.

"You think she came to Chania?" Nikodemos asks.

And then, an idea occurs to me. "Have you been to the island lately?"

"Which island?"

"Komméno Island."

"Komméno? No, no. Ah, what a pity that the hotel closed down. No ferry means no tourists! The ferry companies are run by scoundrels..."

"But I wonder, Nikodemos—if you could ask around for me. Maybe your son, also? We are very worried about our granddaughter."

"I suppose I could go out there, if you think that would help?"

"*Ja*, that would be very good. Very good."

"...there is no ferry to Komméno, you see. If she were to go there, she would have to hire a boat, yes?"

"Yes."

He informs me that he will ask around and contact me if he discovers anything, but he doesn't sound hopeful. My wretched throat seizes up again and I stamp my feet, but this time the baby starts to cry. Better the baby than me. I tell Nikodemos that I'm grateful for his help and he ends the call. I don't expect I will hear from him again.

I hold the baby to my shoulder, rubbing her little back. It seems only five minutes ago that I did this with Eloïse.

I have called everyone under the sun about her whereabouts, even people who have never met her. Our friends in Switzerland went to our homes in Geneva and the chalet in

Sidelhorn several times to ensure she had not arrived. In my heart, I thought she might be there, and I was doubly saddened that she was not.

"You will have to be brave, little one," I tell Cressida, and she gives a hearty belch in response. "You're so tiny and you don't understand. Your mother must be missing you very much."

My phone rings again. I answer, expecting it to be Gerda informing me that she's arrived home in Ledbury safe and sound. But I'm surprised—it is Nikodemos again.

"My son called his friends at the harbor," he explains.

"Oh?"

"They haven't seen your granddaughter."

I give a long sigh. "Thank you all the same."

"But there is a name on one of the ledgers."

"Ledgers?"

"Yes, for boat rented. My son's friend seems to have rented a boat to Eloïse Bachmann. Is this your granddaughter, Magnus?"

April 2, 2015

Komméno Island, Greece

Motherhood ripped me into many different people. I see that now. I had to remake my identity. I had to re-become. "I" became "we."

I had clasped a second heartbeat in my womb for nine months, then another. When Max was born, my mind divided into multiple areas of worry for him: Is he breathing? Is he hungry? Is he too hot? I loved him beyond love. Every strong emotion I had ever felt was dismissed by this new tempest of feeling. Everywhere I went, he went too, and even when he was born there was nothing I did alone. "I" was "we." I could not speak of "me" or "I." I could not think of it.

I repressed so many emotions. A mother should not harbor hate, or anger, and I feared that these might harm him. I feared that *I* would harm him, that I would be a danger to him as my mother had been to me.

It comes to me in lurching images. Hiding in the bathroom from Orhan, clutching my teddy for comfort. The ugliness on his face is frightening. I called it his monster face, and sometimes I imagined him with long horns looping out of his head. He is so tall, towering over me like a colossus.

He drags me out of the bathtub by my hair, out of the bathroom and across the landing. Mum stands in the doorway of the bedroom, her pale hair messy and unwashed, her eyes empty pools. A red splodge shouts from the corner of her mouth and I know it is blood, not lipstick. I scream *Mum! Mum, help me!* But I can tell she is high again. She watches blankly as he punches me in the stomach and hurls me across my bedroom, slamming the door behind him.

Another memory of my mother sitting by the window in her underwear. No men in the house. Mum was so thin, but also very beautiful, even though she only ever seemed to be covered in scratches and bruises. She had a hummingbird in her hand.

What's that, Mummy?

It's a hummingbird, darling.

But where's its wings?

Sshh now. You'll wake him. He needs a little bit of blood. See?

Ouchie, Mummy.

This little hummingbird is a special kind. He has a silver beak and white wings folded against his body. We just slip his beak into my arm.

Doesn't it hurt?

She rolled her head back and closed her eyes. I watched, intrigued. I knew this was her bliss. She opened her eyes slowly and gave me a loose, watery smile.

No. It doesn't hurt. Life hurts, Eloïse. This is the nectar.

And then, the morning I found her. I had already left for school but got sent home again. This time it was because I had a black eye. The teacher sent me with a note for my mother, asking to speak to her.

I threw down my schoolbag in the corner of the kitchen and looked it over. It was tiny and crammed with rubbish. I had taken over the housework at the age of eight, but my mother and her boyfriends had an uncanny ability to trash whatever flat we got moved to.

Mum?

There was no answer. I glanced in the living room. Looked in the bedrooms, the bathroom. She rarely left the house. I checked her bedroom again and found her lying on the floor by the window.

Mum!

At first I thought she'd simply rolled out of bed. It wasn't uncommon for me to come home from school and find her still asleep. She said her body clock was all wrong: she preferred to stay up all night and sleep all day. I tried to help her back into bed, but she was floppy.

Mum, wake up, please!

She didn't respond. We'd learned first aid at school. I lifted her eyelids and saw her eyes were rolled back into her head. She didn't seem to be breathing. Her face was so white it seemed almost marble, saintly, her cheeks hollow. I felt for a heartbeat but there wasn't one. I gave her mouth to mouth. I had done this before. Many times I had rescued her from the depths of unconsciousness, and I searched for reassurance in that. But this time was different. She was too deep, too gone.

I slapped her face, then put one hand on top of the other and pushed down to waken her heart. Then I lay on the floor beside her and drew her limp gray arms around me, kissing the red puncture wounds there as though I could make them go away. I curled into her, crying. Despite how much she had neglected me, despite the terrible things she had allowed me to endure, she was tender sometimes. I had memories of her brushing out my hair and telling me how beautiful I was. Even as a young child, I had a sense of her as broken and that I had caused her to break. I had to heal her, put her back together again. She was my mother.

Maybe if I go to sleep too we can both wake up together.

When I woke it was dark. She was cold to the touch, her hands stiffened like a doll's. Her expression had changed, emptied of her. She wasn't my mother any longer. Her arms and legs had turned to stone. A noise sounded downstairs and I started, terrified in case it was Orhan. He had scythed in and out of our lives, in prison then out again, kicked out for good then back in her bed faster than I could blink. Mum would break up with whatever boyfriend she had at the time and Orhan would be back as though he'd merely been at work. He still had a set of keys. It could be him downstairs. He'd blame me for mum dying. He'd kill me for it. Or worse. There really were worse things than dying, I knew that. There were many worse things. Sometimes I told myself that the girl called Eloïse had died when she was four. That first time he locked the door.

I got up and hunted for the phone. We'd never had a land-line in any of the other places but for some reason Mum insisted we get one for this place. She kept a black book of phone numbers in her bedside drawer that she warned me not to touch. I pulled it out quickly and flicked past all the names of her boyfriends and dealers. I saw "Mum and Dad" written in the middle pages with a long number beneath. It looked like a foreign number, somewhere overseas. She'd talked about my grandparents some years ago, only once. Magnus and Gerda Bachmann, they were called.

I found the phone and dialed their number. I couldn't believe it when someone answered. A man. I told him who I was and his voice changed, like he was scared, or maybe very upset.

We'll come right away, Magnus said. *Stay right where you are.*

"Eloïse? Eloïse, are you in there?"

A hard banging sound wakes me up.

"Eloïse!"

It's Sariah. My mouth is so dry I can barely answer.

"I'm in here!" I shout, but it comes out as a croak. The handle judders as she turns and turns it. Eventually I pull myself up to my feet, and as I do the door bursts open. Sariah crashes to the floor on her side.

I move onto my hands and knees and edge toward her, but I'm too weak to be much use. She rolls up slowly onto her knees. As she does so I have another memory of kneeling just like she is now, leaning over my daughter. My little girl.

"I remember her," I tell Sariah. "My daughter's name is Cressida."

But Sariah doesn't waste time.

"George has gone out hunting," she says, rising to her feet. "We need to get out of here before he comes back. We need to get you on that boat and off this island right now."

April 2, 2015

Twickenham Police Station

Lochlan: I am released from custody. Welsh gives me back my phone, wallet, and keys and Canavan gives me a nod that suggests I'm to heed his caution and tread carefully from now on. It has no impact, brings no relief. How can it? I've pulled back the curtain on a world I didn't know existed, a world in which my wife was suffering from a severe mental illness and I was too distracted to know anything about it. In my head, I am screaming over and over.

Gerda and I confront each other, the tension between us dissolving in the light of what we've heard. It is likely that Eloïse has committed suicide. Nothing else matters. But something in me kicks against what Dr. Goff has said, against the possibility of my steady, hardworking, beautiful wife leaving the kids at home to go off and commit suicide somewhere. I can't process the fact that she was treated for psychosis, that she never told me any of it. I want to run to someone, to get answers. I want El so badly it crushes my lungs, my heart. I want to fall to my knees and howl in despair.

Gerda is stripped of her harshness, her face somber and streaked with tears. I can tell she's working very hard to dismiss everything that Dr. Goff has said. I can hear her thoughts. *She's a British psychologist. What do they know? Utterly inferior to Swiss psychologists. Of course my granddaughter hasn't taken her own life.*

For once, I want Gerda to be right.

"I took a taxi here," she explains, fumbling with her phone. "I guess I'll call the same company and have them drive us back to your house." She dials and gives the address of the police station to the operator.

"Where are Max and Cressida?" I ask in a choked voice, aching to see them, to hold them both. *How do I tell Max any of this? How do I begin to tell my son that his mother is dead?*

"They're with Magnus." Gerda's voice snaps me back into reality. She glances at her phone. "Oh, I've got a missed call from him." She dials his number and holds it to her ear. "No answer. Well, I suppose we'll be seeing him in a moment."

"Daddy! You're back!"

Max comes running up the hallway as soon as I open the front door. I catch him and lift him up into my arms. He's already telling me about the things Mamie bought him, and did I know that someone has discovered a new species of dinosaur that ate T-Rexes for breakfast, and did I bring home Kinder eggs? I nod and try to act normal but I can't speak. *What if we never recover her body?*

327

Cressida's in the family room, lying on her stomach beneath her play mobile. She's dressed in a clean Babygro emblazoned with "*I love Mummy*" and tries to lift herself up on her hands, tilting her head to me when I walk in, grinning.

Cressida will never know her mother.

Gerda is calling Magnus's name through the house. Eventually he comes downstairs, clearly flustered and pulling a jumper over his head.

"We have an issue," he says when he sees us.

"What is it, darling?" she says, and we follow him into the family room.

"Have you got your passport with you?" he asks Gerda.

She does a double take. "My *passport*?"

"I've got mine upstairs," I say. "Why?"

He tells us about a man who called him earlier from a town in Greece, the name of which I recognize. Eloïse rented a sailing boat from his company on the seventeenth of March.

I sink down into a chair as Magnus tells us about the man sailing to the island—Komméno, the island Magnus owns, the island where we got married—hoping to find Eloïse. He located the boat she'd rented, but it had crashed onto a beach on the west coast. No sign of Eloïse. He presumed she'd drowned.

"But it *can't* be her," Gerda says, turning to me. "You said she left her passports behind. She couldn't have traveled."

There is a pain in my chest that seems to swell and fill the room. Komméno Island. *It's likely that your wife committed suicide.*

"I never found her Swiss passport," I hear myself say.

Gerda's knees fold beneath her and she collapses, but somehow I reach out and grab her before she hits the ground. She is sobbing and shaking to the point that I am sure she's having a heart attack. Magnus kneels down and takes her by both hands, holding her close, his face blotched with grief.

"Ssssh," he says, rocking her, and she clings to him. Max runs up to me but is silent, stunned by the sight of us all in tears.

"I don't...I don't think I've come this far in my life to lose a daughter *and* a granddaughter," Magnus says in a wracked voice. "The island may be desolate, but there's a good chance Eloïse is all right. I stocked up the farmhouse very well. I left it ready for rent, remember? There's plenty of tinned food and water, and the solar panels should still be providing electricity. She might well be alive. And we can bring her home once more."

I realize then that Magnus doesn't know anything about what Dr. Goff has told us. He doesn't know what she's been hiding from him, from me, from all of us.

Gerda wipes her face and straightens to look at him. "*Du denkst?*" she whispers.

Magnus reaches for his coat from the coat stand. "Let's not waste time. I have arranged a private flight to Chania. We can get there tonight. Nikodemos will meet us at the airport and take us to the island on his boat."

April 2, 2015

Komméno Island, Greece

Follow me, Sariah says, and I stagger down the stairs after her. I stop midway and cling to the banister. Everything is hazy. The walls move inward and out, breathing. She turns to me.

Are you OK? What's wrong?

I'm sorry...Give me a second.

I am doing everything I can to keep my legs from giving out beneath me. After a few moments I give a nod to let her know I'm OK to keep going and we continue downstairs.

No sign of the others in the kitchen or front room. The farmhouse seems different, too. There is only a single chair at the table. Dust and clumps of dead grass carpet the stone floor, as though a herd of cattle clumped through the place overnight.

Where are Joe and Hazel? I say.

A sound outside makes her spin around. She reaches out and grabs my wrist, pulling me to the back door.

Come on, we have to hurry.

Outside, night is creeping in, and the rain is coming down like chain mail. Sariah holds on to me as she strides through the wet grass, pulling me along like a child. The bushes thrash painful welts across my legs.

I manage about a quarter of a mile before I fall to my knees on the wet ground.

I'm sorry, Sariah. I don't have the strength.

Behind us, a shout. I turn and see a figure on the brow of the hill. It is George, holding his gun.

Sariah! he hollers, his face twisted in an ugly snarl. I'm going to rip your legs off and shove them down your throat. Bring her back here!

My arms and legs are heavy. The rain pings my face, deliciously cold as it seeps between my lips. I fall back into the mud's clutches. Sariah grabs my arms and hauls me up into a sitting position.

Eloïse, you have to get up! You have to! Get up! Get up, please!

It takes so much effort to open my eyes.

If you ever find my children, please tell them I love them.

She hooks a strong arm across my shoulders and shakes me. Eloïse!

I try to stand. She pushes against my back and helps me up to a standing position.

We've got to move. He's coming.

I can hear George's feet thumping across the ground behind us. I know he's got the rifle. The boat is still so far away. The sea is heaving and angry, the wind in our faces. There is simply no way we can outrun him.

You go, I tell Sariah. You can make it.

I can't. I can't go. Not without you.

I nod. You can. It'll be OK.

No, I can't. I am you, Eloïse. Don't you get it? *I am you.*

Her words strike me like a gong.

I straighten and open my eyes. She wavers like a reflection in a puddle.

We're all you. All of us—me, Joe, George. Even Hazel. We're you, sweetie.

Her words clang in my ears. I force myself to focus on her but she continues to fade in and out like a mist.

What are you saying?

She's solid again and grabs my arms, her face close to mine.

I know, I know. I know it sounds crazy. But you have to listen to me, all right?

I nod.

I'm listening.

We are you, Eloïse. We are the parts of you that you couldn't bring yourself to remember. When you had Max and Cressida, you felt you had to be one hundred percent good, utterly perfect, no ugliness or meanness.

I can see my reflection in the dark mirrors of her eyes. Anger flashes through me and I start to cry.

Why are you saying this?

She shakes her head, dismissing my question.

You were so worried that the dark parts of your nature would cause the children harm that you tucked them away and refused to acknowledge them, but they haunted you. You worried that you'd fail Max and Cressida, and that worry enveloped you until it took over.

George is almost upon us. I can hear him running through

the tall reeds about thirty feet behind, huffing as his bulk thuds against the ground.

What about George, then?

George is the part of you that helped you survive. You're terrified of him because he is ruthless. But you need him. You'd never have made it without him. You had to come to a point where you would do anything to get off this island. You had to understand what was inside the box before you opened it.

What about the phone? The satellite phone? I spoke to Nikodemos. I know I did.

There was no phone, Eloïse. There was only you trying to figure out how to fix all the harm that Orhan and the others caused you.

George stands at the top of the hill directly above us, legs wide. He is naked to the waist, the rifle in his hands, his eyes fixed on me.

We can make it to the boat, Sariah says. We can make it. But you have to acknowledge that he is you. He won't go until you do.

I remember the goat at the side of the road.

I remember lifting a fork and stabbing it into the hand of one of my mother's boyfriends when he tried to touch me.

I remember leaving my mother's dead body in that cold, disgusting flat, and willing myself to leave who I was behind, still curled up in her cold arms.

George is below us now, at the bottom of the ravine, so close that he could easily lunge forward and grab me. I can see the rain on his face as he lifts the rifle as though to ram the stock into my face. He snarls at me.

I told you to stay here.

I am on all fours, trying to pull myself up the muddy bank toward the cliff edge that leads to the boat. I can hear Sariah panting above me, her hands pulling at me. But I know that I have to face him. There is no other way.

Slowly I turn, pull myself upright, and watch him as he approaches.

He lifts the rifle.

But right then Hazel and Joe appear, grabbing George from behind. There is a scream as Hazel is knocked to the ground, and as I lunge Joe manages to wrestle the rifle from George. Panting, he swipes the hair from his face as he aims it at George.

Enough of this, George! he shouts. Enough, or I'll shoot!

April 2, 2015

Potter's Lane, Twickenham

Lochlan: Komméno is derelict, a complete wilderness. When Eloïse and I got married there, it was a hidden paradise, thriving with a new hotel, shops, and regular ferries from Crete. They were building villas on the west bank and Magnus restored the old farmhouse that had sat at the very top of the island for centuries. It's where Eloïse and I spent our first night as man and wife.

But with the recession, the island's economy evaporated. The shops were the first to close, then the hotel and building contractors, and once the shops went the ferry operators shut down their scheduled routes. The farmhouse may still have clean water and some electricity from solar panels. Magnus tells me it was left ready to rent, that there would have been tins and jars of preserved food in the pantry, blankets and clothing in the bedrooms, enough wood around the place to feed the stove. But the transport links to the island have ceased and it is fiercely remote. Eloïse has been gone for two weeks. Even if she didn't go there to kill herself, there is every chance that she has drowned. I lurch between hope and harrowing certainty that she is dead.

Please be alive, El. Please be there. I'm coming.

Max runs in as I'm retrieving my wallet and an overnight bag from the closet.

"Daddy, where are you going?"

I kneel down in front of him, taking both his little hands in mine. He studies me with those beautiful, innocent eyes of his and I can barely speak.

"I'm...I'm going on a little journey, Maxie..."

"Are you going to pick up Mummy?"

And I won't ever leave you.

I pick through my words carefully. I have to hope. For his sake.

"We think we have found where Mummy might have gone. It's not definite, but—"

"Can I come, Daddy?"

I hang my head. I should have expected this. "No, absolutely not. It's best that you stay here..."

"I want to come! I want to come! I want Mummy!"

He bursts into tears, and I pull him toward me in a tight embrace. I want so badly to protect him. It's simply not fair that he should be caught up in all this. Before I know it, tears are sliding down my cheeks and wetting the collar of his T-shirt. *How can I tell him his mother is dead?*

Max doesn't let go, doesn't say anything, but allows me to wrap my arms around him and hold him tight.

When I let go, he pleads with me.

"*Please* can I come, Daddy? I promise I'll be good."

I wipe my eyes with a hand and reach out to stroke his cheek with the other. I can't say no to him, I can't. And besides, we don't have time to start organizing childcare.

"OK, Maxie. If you can get a change of clothes, you can come."

Even as a voice shouts in my head that I am reckless and downright mad for relenting, he darts into his bedroom and returns a minute later with a handful of briefs, a *Thomas the Tank Engine* backpack trailing behind him.

"I've brought clean pants. Have you got clean pants, Daddy?"

I stuff his underpants into the bag. Quickly he darts back into his room.

"Come on, Max. We've got to go."

He returns a moment later, his face crumpled in concern. "I want to bring Mummy my Rosie."

"We can't bring flowers on the plane, Max."

He grows upset. "No—Rosie...Mummy likes Rosie. I want to bring her Rosie so she'll very definitely come home."

My usual impulse would be to take his hand and pull him anyway, disregarding whatever he's trying to explain. But instead I resist the urge to rush him. I kneel on the ground before him, and seeing my own calmness he takes slower breaths and finds his words.

"Rosie the *train*, Daddy. Thomas is my favorite and Rosie is Mummy's."

"And you think if we bring Rosie to Mummy it'll make her want to come back with us?"

He nods and wipes his nose. I take his hand and walk into

his room, where we carefully pick through a box of toys until he discovers a small purple train with a female face. His face lights up.

"Found it! Found it, Daddy!"

"Good boy, Max."

He beams up at me. "Let's go get Mummy!"

April 2, 2015

Two Nautical Miles from Komméno

The day I left I heard something outside.

A wild thing calling.

A darkness, lulling me. As though the past rose up and gathered me in its claw.

It said, *How can someone as damaged as you be a good mother?*

I'm not sure whether it was the question or the answer that split me into a thousand pieces.

I left without a key, without a phone, without credit or debit cards. I was half-conscious of what I was doing, as though I had stirred in the middle of the night tangled in a dream. I was already an abstraction, no longer a person. Not a wife, not a mother. I didn't want anything tethering me to the children, anything with my name and face there. It would only tarnish them.

In the drawer of the hall table I found my Swiss passport and the envelope of money my grandfather had given me last time I saw him. Six hundred pounds. For the new baby, he said. I took the money and walked out the front door, closing it quietly behind me. I didn't want to wake the babies, Max and Cressida. They were both sleeping and so, so beautiful, like angels. I knew without any doubt whatsoever they would be so much better off without me there.

It was quiet outside. The click of the door sealed off everything that had gone before me—my life with Lochlan. Our children. My fears about being their mother, about damaging such precious, beautiful flowers. They were delicate as petals and I felt incapable of protecting them from what I might be capable of. It was what my mother had told me once.

You'll turn out exactly like me.

I believed her without question, as a child does. All the badness that had happened to both of us was my fault, my fault.

I walked up the street. It was so easy to do.

I felt like the world was stripping away from me. I was coming up to surface. I stopped in the middle of the park, suddenly hot, and pulled my scarf off. Then I took a taxi to the airport and got on a plane to Greece. I knew exactly where I wanted to go. I had been so many times that I could head there without thinking. I wanted to be where it all began. I wanted to be where Lochlan and I had started our marriage. I wanted to rewind time.

How could I have told him about the things that terrified me? I had tried to talk to him during the times that I felt strong. He was distracted, and I felt there was a wilderness in me that he could never understand or relate to. He would hate me for it. He wouldn't love me.

When I boarded the plane, I sat down next to an older man who asked me where I was going. I told him, but I could no longer tell him why. Lochlan's name rolled around my mind, shattering to a meaningless cluster of vowels.

By the time we landed I couldn't recall where I had come from. I hired a boat to sail to the island. I knew I would be safe there, that I would feel whole. I had felt whole there, once. I had felt like the best version of myself.

But there was a storm. Monstrous waves dived into the boat. I lost my coat, my rings and earrings. Somehow, I made it to the farmhouse where I met the others.

Except, I didn't. There was only me.

Sariah and Hazel half-dragged, half-carried me to the boat while Joe marched George along, rifle at his back. We clambered down the steep cliff to the beach, holding on to patches of dune grass when our footholds crumbled. The seabirds went berserk, wheeling around us and shrieking in case we wrecked their nests.

Below, the sea was already crashing in against the rocks, pawing the boat with white claws.

Keep your sails high, Sariah called from the shoreline, and I did. Hazel, Joe, and George lifted their arms and waved as I turned to raise the sails.

When I glanced back, all of them had gone.

Komméno is a shadow beyond the waves that crash against the sides of the boat. The wind lurches the boat to and fro, and I shift quickly from one side to the other, using my weight and the stars above to keep on course. It would have been so much easier if Sariah was with me.

I hear a noise in the distance, the low drone of a speedboat. With great effort I climb up the mast and look out to the north, and I spot it: a light in the distance. I fumble for the binoculars in the stowage compartment and adjust the lens. I see a speedboat bumping over the waves. A white-haired man at the wheel. There are others with him. A man with a child in his arms, a little boy. Another older, taller man. They are pointing and shouting, and I go to shout back. But then a wave crashes into the side of the boat, knocking the binoculars from my hands. The boat flips over to one side, the masts toppling into the ocean.

Time seems to slow down as I hit the water and slip below. A roar of bubbles against my cheeks, then nothing. I open my eyes. Blue light, stillness.

I am sinking.

My son, being born.

Such relief when he slid out of me, when they placed him in my arms, slippery as an eel. The cord, still attached. I had never imagined it as such as thick, blue rope, tying us together. I almost didn't want them to cut it. I didn't want us to be separated.

I held him to me, looking down into his little face, smeared with blood and so squished up from all that time in the birth canal. His beautiful arms, tight fists bunched against his chest. A miracle that he was mine.

It is tempting to stay under. I feel no pain or panic here, and it is lovely to be suspended in the coolness. I feel more sure of who I am, sure that the others never really existed. They were me. I was the strong one. I was the one capable of surviving.

My body jerks for air but I don't make any move to the surface. Above me, the light shifts. Shadows lean down to me. A distortion of vowels.

Eloïse! Mummy!

I drift upward.

A hand reaches down and grabs my hair, then the shoulder of my T-shirt, and I feel a great surge tugging me upward, plunging me into cold air with a gasp. And even as they haul me awkwardly into the speedboat and many hands are placed upon me, I'm returning to another surface, the cells and atoms in my body repurposing the new element of myself.

I spot my grandfather, ashen faced and shocked, and Lochlan kneeling over me. "I can't believe it! It's you!" he is saying. He has hauled me out of the water with what looks like a ball of red wool but is a long red rope, clipped on to the top of my life vest. He crushes himself against me and I find my arms—*my* arms—wrapping around his shoulders, every inch of my skin revived by recognition of his touch.

Max rushes at us, arms outstretched from a red life jacket.

"Mummy! You're all wet! Look, I brought you Rosie, Mummy. Don't you like Rosie? I thought you did so I brought her. I told you Mummy would be here, Daddy. I told you! Are you coming home now? Cressida misses you, Mummy. You smell funny. Is it really you, Mummy?"

I reach down to cup his face and, at last, find my voice.

"Yes, Maxie. It's me."

The Light That Moves Inward and Outward

April 3, 2015

Potter's Lane, Twickenham

I'm awake. I'm asleep. I'm not sure which. Somewhere in between. The haze turns into lace. A net curtain puffed out by wind. Slowly the space around me shifts into familiarity: the curtain is *my* curtain, swaying at the window of my bedroom.

The bed is full of arms and legs, the duvet crumpled over faces and fingers. Beside me the baby is laid on her back, arms raised at right angles by her head. Her small lips are pursed like a pink rose. Her eyelids flutter as she dreams. Such beautiful long eyelashes. On the other side of her I see the back of a head. Lochlan. My husband. The mountain of his shoulder, the faint rasp of his snoring. Someone else at my feet. I sit up slowly and look down. A head of blond curls and a blanket clasped tightly. Max.

A rustle of blankets as Lochlan stirs. He turns and looks at me. His black hair crumpled, his face unshaven. Dark circles under his eyes. He's lost weight, looks years older. He reaches out to touch me and for some reason I flinch. He withdraws his hand.

"How are you feeling?"

"OK," I say, but my voice sounds thin and he doesn't seem convinced. He rubs his face and yawns. The screen of his phone is visible on the nightstand. It reads 5:53.

"Can I get you anything?" he asks. "Are you hungry? Thirsty?"

I climb out of bed and make for the landing. Lochlan sits upright and calls after me in a worried voice, but I tell him to go back to sleep. More and more my memory returns; it's akin to the sensation of blood returning to the veins after your hand or leg has fallen asleep. A great overwhelming rush of familiarity. Our bedroom. My closet, with all my clothes. My husband. Our children.

I head on to the landing and down the stairs, looking over the photographs framed on the wall. I remember taking these photographs, posing for them. I know it was me who had them framed. And when I reach the hallway, I remember the moment I decided to walk out the front door. Max and Cressida were asleep upstairs. How could I have left them? Anything could have happened. They could have died.

"Eloïse?"

I can hear Lochlan in the hallway, his feet creating shadows at the slit at the bottom of the door. I'm inside the cupboard under the stairs, behind the coats that smell of old rain. I want to fold away inside myself.

It was different on the plane coming back to London. I

held Max so tightly and when he wore himself out from talking and fell asleep on my lap, I brushed the beautiful creamy curls off his forehead and kissed his soft cheeks. It was blissful to hold him again. There was none of the fear that drove me away from him, deep, unremitting love. When the plane landed we got in a taxi and drove back to Potter's Lane, everything inked out by night.

A light tap at the cupboard door.

"Eloïse, darling? Are you in there?"

I'm trying hard to control my breathing. I can't stop myself from taking great gulps of air. My heart is going wild in my chest and the only thing that stops me from feeling like I'm going to die is keeping my eyes shut and my hands in tight fists.

The door opens. I don't open my eyes but keep focused on my breathing. Steady, steady...I feel him moving on all fours, the coats batting the top of my head. After a few moments he settles beside me in an identical position, his knees drawn up to his chest. He doesn't say anything. I don't want him to say anything. I want the terror to leave me. Sometimes it lets go. I need the images in my head to stop. If I close my eyes, they might stop.

After an hour, I am able to crawl out of the cupboard. Lochlan follows me. Gold light rivers along the floor of our hallway. Sunrise. We live in a beautiful house. I can hear small, rapid footsteps upstairs, the sound of Max's voice calling for me anxiously. Lochlan faces me. He looks at me with tenderness. He hasn't looked at me like this for a long time. It's as though his eyes tell me so much more than words ever could.

He moves slowly, putting his arms around me and pulling me toward him. After a second or so, I realize he is crying.

May 3, 2015

Women's Residential Unit, Maudsley Hospital, London

The room comes slowly into focus. There's a woman with a kind face and glasses sitting opposite, a door with three glass panels far behind her. A coffee table with a vase of fat yellow tulips like hands cupped in prayer.

"Oh, hello, Eloïse," she says. "Are you back again?"

"Have I been somewhere?"

"You were Joe a moment ago, I think. Joe was telling us all about how he looks after you. How he knows the best way to heal you physically." She smiles. "How are you feeling right now?"

"A little woozy," I say, licking my lips. They're terribly dry, and I feel dizzy.

"Joe was telling me how he helped revive you after your journey to the island. He seems very resourceful."

"He is."

"And Hazel. I think I met Hazel yesterday. She's great fun."

"Is she?"

"Yes. A little quirky, too. She seems quite young." A long pause. "George, though. Do you think he doesn't like the others talking about him?"

Slowly, I nod.

"Why do you think that is?"

"I don't know."

"One of the things I'd like to do is invite each of your personality states to introduce themselves, and hopefully we'll be able to get them to communicate with each other, too."

"I think George is protective of Max."

"He is?"

"Yes. I think he doesn't want me to talk about it for Max's sake."

"He doesn't want you to talk about what happened to you as a child?"

"Yes. I think...if I don't talk about it, it hasn't happened. I can pretend it never happened. No one else knew."

"OK. So George wants to protect Max from knowing that?"

"From the reality of it. I feel like it was my fault. Part of me feels very strongly that I was to blame."

"You think the abuse was your fault."

"I know it sounds ridiculous, but it's how I feel. Maybe if I'd told someone, or been a better, more obedient child..."

"Eloïse?"

"Yes?"

"You went away for a few minutes. I think we had Sariah with us before."

"How do you know?"

"Your demeanor changes when Sariah visits. Your voice changes, too. Sariah told us that it's not your fault at all. She told us some of the things that happened to you when you were very young. She really wants to heal you, Eloïse. She wants you to know that you are a wonderful mother."

There's a hot ball in my throat.

"I love my children."

"And they love you..."

"I remember the day before I went to Komméno, I looked at Max when he was sleeping and he was so beautiful, so utterly perfect. And it struck me that I was probably his age when the abuse started. I would be lying in my own bed, the way Max does, when—"

I can't say the words. I can't describe what happened to me.

"It's OK," Tara says. She raises her arms and folds them across herself, a hand on the opposite shoulder, and I do the same. It helps me feel safe, and after a few minutes I continue speaking with my eyes closed.

"I think it overwhelmed me to think that I was a child like Max is, so completely innocent and vulnerable."

"You were not to blame. *None* of it was your fault."

The ball in my throat grows tighter, hotter. I squeeze my eyes shut.

"But how can I be a good mother to them? How can I possibly not damage them somehow? I mean, I left them. I walked out of the house, leaving them on their own. What if something had happened?"

"Eloïse, you experienced what is known as a fugue state, or dissociative fugue, which causes the usually integrated functions of consciousness and sentience to break down. I believe this was a result of the trauma you have been repressing for so long. Do you understand?"

"Yes."

"You were no more responsible for this result than you would be if you had fallen down the stairs and been knocked unconscious."

She speaks slowly and is careful with each word, as though each syllable is a sharp object.

"OK."

"Remember what we talked about yesterday," she says. "Trauma leaves a residual footprint in the body, specifically in the nervous system. You were so young that you had no way of processing the things that were happening to you. You dissociated from it, as though it was happening to someone other than you. You probably experienced hallucinations, and shorter episodes of amnesia throughout your life. As though the clock leaped forward."

"I remember one time I found over a hundred e-mails at work that I'd responded to but had absolutely no memory of writing any of them."

"E-mails for your charity?"

"Yes."

"It's likely that the role of one of your alters was to perform the duties expected of you as chief executive of the charity. I think you had guided meditation yesterday, where you saw yourself performing certain roles. Do you remember which of your alters went to work at the charity?"

A long pause.

"Sariah."

"What you have to remember is, Sariah is part of you. *You*

have that strength and that kindness. We will work to integrate her again with your identity."

"She kept telling me that she was looking after me. On the island."

"Do you believe that?"

"Yes."

"It's your mind's way of protecting you. Of enabling you to survive."

"But what if it happens again? What if I run away and leave them again? How could I live with myself?"

She smiles, which is strange to me.

"This is why *I'm* here," she says. "We're going to work this through. It's going to take time. But we'll get there. First, we need to get George to talk to the others. Shall we ask him again?"

June 25, 2015

Potter's Lane, Twickenham

Lochlan: "What story do you want tonight, Max?"

He looks at his bookcase, the one I've drilled to the wall, which allows all the books to face outward.

"I want *The Gruffalo*, please."

"All right. In you get."

He wriggles under his duvet. I've got Cressida on my knee and she's desperately trying to reach for something on the ground. I spot a teddy halfway under the bed and pick it up to give to her. She immediately chews on its ear.

"Read it, Daddy! Read it!" Max says, and so I read the story of the Gruffalo for the hundredth time. I've noticed that Max tends to match his stories to particular readers. When Gerda puts him to bed he makes her read *The Very Hungry Caterpillar*. Magnus occasionally puts him to bed, and his book seems to be *We're Going on a Bear Hunt.* They've rented a house a few blocks away to be close to us, though not too close. Eloïse's book of choice is *Guess How Much I Love You.* I think it's to do with our accents. Max loves it when I emphasize my Weegie accent for the Gruffalo beast, rolling my *r*'s. He laughs and tries to copy me. *The Grrrruffalo!*

Though as I read it this time, it occurs to me what this story is really about: a mouse defends itself against predators by making up a story about a terrifying monster that is supposedly the mouse's bestie. The predators decide not to eat the mouse in case the Gruffalo seeks retribution, until the mouse comes across a monster who is exactly like the one he made up: the Gruffalo, his deepest fear made manifest. By confronting and outwitting this fear, he becomes the hero of the story.

By the time I'm halfway through the book, Max is already asleep. Cressida is squirming on my lap, kicking her legs, and chewing Max's teddy bear to death. I hear Eloïse padding up the stairs and walking across the landing to the bedroom. From the brisk, quiet steps she takes, I know she's having a good day. I have learned to read her like this, become alert to the signals she sends through the rhythms of her body, speech, her line of questioning, just as she has been reading me all along, hiding the parts of her that she knew I couldn't understand.

The past can be so full of monsters that won't die.

Eloïse was hiding her fear, that's all. Such a small word for so complicated a thing. She is confronting it now, day by day. And I think that makes her a hero.

I never thought of her that way.

She got out of the inpatient unit yesterday. I brought her

home to a small gathering of the people who love her—Gerda, Magnus; her friends Niamh, Lucia, and Vinny; and of course Max and Cressida—and although I was afraid she might not be up to it, she seemed like her old self, keen to hear all about Lucia's baby news and delighting in Cressida's new thing of pulling funny faces. Max joined in, too, crossing his eyes and sticking out his tongue. I think it reassured her that nobody seemed strange with her after being in hospital. It took a lot to convince her to stay, but after discussing it with Dr. Goff I believed it was the best way forward.

We are still fitting the pieces of the puzzles together. I used to think that illness was illness, and you got a diagnosis, and a prognosis, and medicine, and that was that. Oh to be as naïve as I once was. Oh to be blissfully unaware of the many corners of the mind, and the shadows that live there. El's illness is complex, severe, and the journey is far from over. In fact, in some ways we've barely begun.

Gerda and I met with Dr. Goff—Tara—again two weeks ago, shortly after Eloïse was admitted to the inpatient unit. Tara had been meeting with her almost every day, and Gerda, Magnus, and I needed to know why Eloïse had left, and whether it would happen again. Niamh watched Cressida and Max while we went to her office at Maudsley Hospital.

Maybe it sounds weird, but it really felt like the three of us were searching for El all over again. Part of her had not returned. I imagined this part as captured, held hostage, in the past, the little girl she'd been, still trapped. Marooned. No one could rescue her. We could only try our utmost to help her find the way out.

The hospital was nice, as psychiatric hospitals go. No straitjackets, no electric-shock machines. So far so good. Tara was accommodating and personable. She took us to a room dedicated to "family dialogue" with windows overlooking gardens and a coffee table surrounded by plush armchairs. I knew the news wasn't going to be good.

"Now that I've had a chance to meet with Eloïse regularly," she told us, "I can see that she presents symptoms of derealization and depersonalization, whereby she sometimes perceives herself at a distance. She also presents extreme forgetfulness, even amnesia, and loses time. In the past she said she would receive responses to e-mails that she had absolutely no recollection of sending, or wake up in bed in the middle of the night without knowing what she'd done since that morning. I've not yet made an official diagnosis, but I can tell you that these symptoms are characteristic of dissociative identity disorder."

"You mean, multiple personality disorder?" Gerda said. We'd all been doing a huge amount of googling since El came home and we were bombarded with strange, foreign terms. *Dissociative fugue. Dissociation.* Words I'd never heard before.

"Multiple personality disorder is the old name for DID, yes," Tara told Gerda.

Magnus cut in, confused. "Forgive me, but what is dissociative identity disorder?"

"DID is when a person dissociates, or disconnects, from themselves, usually as a result of extreme trauma and attachment disorders," Tara said. "I have to say, though—I'm not a fan of the term 'disorder.'"

It was my turn to look confused. "Why's that?"

"It implies that the individual needs to be 'fixed,'" she says, making quotation marks with her fingers. "I see people as individuals, with very unique manifestations of mental ill health." She made to say more, but stopped short. "Anyway, I think that's a conversation for another time. Eloïse presents symptoms of what is classically referred to as DID. It is a form of mental illness whereby the individual forges another separate identity or personality state, and often numerous identities."

"Excuse me," Magnus said. "But I'm really not grasping this concept. What—exactly—do you mean?"

Tara explained that we all have different sides to our personality, but some people can experience a fragmentation of their personality into a range of different personalities or "alters."

"The reason that an individual creates these alters, or other personalities," she explained, "is part of the human mind's brilliantly sophisticated strategy for survival. In fact, this is the reason I hate the term 'disorder.' It's a psychological phenomenon." She shook her head and began to lower her voice. "As you are all aware, she suffered abuse as a very young child and had poor parental attachment during her formative years. A four-year-old child suffering unimaginable sexual abuse does not have the capability to deal with it."

Gerda raised a hand to her mouth. Hearing Tara say it aloud was like twisting the knife in my gut. It was unthinkable. My son's face rose up in my mind. To think of such a young child suffering like that...It broke my heart.

Tara continued, explaining it as gently as she could.

"I'm sorry," she said. "I know this is terribly difficult to process..."

"No, please," Gerda said, glancing at Magnus. "We need to understand. Please go on."

Tara took a breath. "If a child is abused by someone they trust, a family member, say, who is kind and loving to them in public and then does monstrous things to them in secret... The mind *has* to devise a coping mechanism. One of these mechanisms is the ability to create other identities who take over, take charge, and enable that child to carry on."

"How can you call developing a whole gallery of hallucinations *coping*?" Magnus said, looking from me to Gerda.

"It's what kept Eloïse alive," Tara said, deeply serious. "A lot of people who suffer abuse as children become drug addicts, have serious breakdowns, and can't function as normal adults. Eloïse's response was different. What we call dissociative identity disorder is precisely what kept her functioning. It's why a lot of people I see with DID claim to lose time. This is because their alters take over. The alters do the cooking, the cleaning, the day-to-day things that have become overwhelming for the individual," she said.

Magnus looked skeptical, but I'd read about this online, watched YouTube videos of people changing from one personality to the next. Now that I saw it, I knew I'd seen Eloïse do this a few times before. But I'd put it down to other things: hormones, a bad day, sleep deprivation. On the surface, she looked normal.

"These alters are so powerful and so distinct that they have their own names, their own likes and dislikes," Tara said. "They can have entirely different expressions and mannerisms, even different heart rates. Often their own handwriting differs from the alters'."

Handwriting. Of course, this struck a chord. "The notebook," I said, and Gerda and Magnus turned to me as if only now realizing I was there. "Right before we found El, I came across a notebook of hers," I explained. "It was strange...there were some poems and stories in different handwriting, some of them Eloïse's. I'd never seen them before. I attributed it to the writer's group that Niamh had mentioned. There were drawings, too."

Tara nodded as though this was entirely reasonable. "Alters," she said simply. "Did you notice any of their names?"

I thought back. "I think I saw 'Joe' in there."

"Yes, Eloïse mentioned Joe," she said. "He was the one who looked after Eloïse's physical injuries during the years she lived with her mother. Or in other words, she became very adept at caring for herself. She developed resources to deal with what was happening to her."

Tara allowed a long pause for this all to drop into our heads. Finally Gerda said, "We would have taken Eloïse earlier, had we known what was going on. Back then it was different. Grandparents in this country have very few rights, and certainly not enough to apply for a grandchild to be taken from her mother."

"Eloïse never blamed you or Magnus, Mrs. Bachmann," Tara said carefully. "I attempted to work through the complexity of emotional responses to her mother. I'm not sure we managed to succeed, but we tried."

"We tried to give her a good education," Gerda said. "Tried to put to right whatever damage had been done by Jude. We sent her money every month. If we'd known that she was using it to buy drugs..."

"Why now?" I said, because I sensed Gerda was about to steer the conversation toward Jude. I was sorry for Jude— actually, scratch that, I wasn't, because she contributed to

El's suffering—but I wanted to move on. "What sparked El's episode?" I asked. "What made her go to Komméno?"

Tara crossed a leg over the other and steepled her hands in thought.

"In my opinion, the fact that Max is the same age that Eloïse began to be abused is no coincidence," she said firmly. "She has mentioned it in our sessions. She was beginning to recognize herself in Max, to rethink how young and innocent she was...I believe that this new perspective jarred with the framework that she had assembled for her past. We are making a lot of headway in reconnecting to the child she had been, in deconstructing the things she had been made to believe."

"What sort of things?" Gerda asked.

"Eloïse had been taught to believe that she was to blame for the abuse. That she had somehow caused it. That if she'd been a better child, it wouldn't have happened."

Gerda started to sob. Magnus put his arm around her and I made myself useful by walking to the coffee machine in the corner and pouring everyone a drink. I took the opportunity to shake off the horror that was creeping into my skin at the thought of what my wife had suffered. And was still suffering.

When I returned, Tara continued, as gently as she could.

"It's important that you know that I see this very regularly in my work. Young children who are abused are often controlled by their abusers so that they don't tell an adult or attempt to fight back. The child becomes compliant because they believe they deserve it." She cleared her throat. "In terms of Eloïse's mental health issues and her disappearance, I think it's very possible that she left the family home because she feared she might harm the children."

"But she would *never* do that!" Gerda said, incredulous. "Eloïse is a wonderful mother."

"Yes," Tara said. "But in my opinion, Eloïse was finding it increasingly difficult to control her alters. She was physically and psychologically weak after the birth of the new baby, and Max turning four was a big thing in terms of her experiencing a child that was as young as she was when the abuse began. Her alters began to take over more frequently and forcefully, to the point where she experienced them as both personality states and hallucinations."

At this point, I dared to ask the question that had plagued me ever since Dr. Goff first entered our lives. It's a question I will probably never be able to ask my wife.

"Why did Eloïse never tell me?" I said. I held back from being specific, because I knew Dr. Goff would understand what I meant. *Why didn't she tell me about her childhood? Why didn't she tell me about the abuse, about her problems? Why didn't she talk to me instead of leaving?*

Dr. Goff gave me a look, then raised her eyes to the ceiling and took a long breath, formulating her answer. We both knew she could only guess—but at least it was an educated one.

"It is extremely difficult to describe the kinds of things that your wife experienced, Lochlan. If I'm to be honest, I think silence was part of the coping mechanism." A faint smile. "It has nothing to do with her feelings for you."

I gave her a nod to signal that I appreciated her attempt at answering the most unanswerable of questions, but I felt—and still feel—responsible for her withholding.

"So what happens now?" Magnus said. "Now that our granddaughter is in the psychiatric unit."

"Eloïse's therapy will involve three stages, broadly speaking," Tara replied. "The first is about stabilization, helping the patient feel safe to identify and label emotions. The second is trauma focused, enabling the patient to reprocess and discuss the past, reframe their beliefs and self-shame. The third stage is about reconnection, helping the individual move forward." She took a breath, checking how I was dealing with this information. "It's a much more delicate, nonlinear process than I've described, of course."

This delicate, nonlinear process involved a two-week stay at the inpatient unit. It took El a while to agree to this, but I begged her. I can't quite put it into words how desperate you have to be to plead with your wife to check into a psychiatric unit. I didn't even tell my father. I could already hear his words. *You're putting her in the nuthouse?* But I see things differently now. Everything has changed, and I don't think it'll ever be the same. How could it?

Tara took me aside when I checked Eloïse in the first day.

"I do want to warn you," she said. Gerda and Magnus weren't around, and I could tell that she wished to be straight with me now that she had a chance to speak with me one-to-one.

"This isn't a quick fix," she said, referring to the stay. *Quick?* I thought. El was going to be gone for two weeks. It had taken all kinds of bribes and coaxing for Max to be convinced that she was going to come home after everything that had happened previously.

"It's a positive step for Eloïse to stay at the inpatient unit for a fortnight, that's for sure," Tara added, "but she'll have to continue with her weekly sessions for a long time after that."

"How long?"

"Treatment can take three to five years, maybe more. It takes as long as it takes, is what I'm saying."

I shrugged. It wasn't as if I'd imagined this to be anything less than a severe illness. "OK."

She looked flustered, as if she wasn't getting through. "But what I really want to warn you about is the impact of this illness on families."

I recoiled. Why was she telling me this? She softened and lowered her voice. There was a path forward, she told me, but it was rocky. She had seen cases where a patient's alter hated the patient's partner. Where alters would swear and even hit the patient's partner or sleep around. Eloïse might well make a full recovery in a relatively short amount of time. Or she might relapse, develop a myriad of mental illnesses, and the woman I married might not ever return.

I gave her a flat stare and said, "In Glasgow we have a saying."

"Which is?"

"We could all be dead tomorrow."

"Dead?"

"It means, let's not waste time focusing on what bad stuff can happen. Let's focus on the now."

She gave a sympathetic smile. "Not a bad way to look at things, I guess. I do think you should get counseling, however, to prepare you for whatever lies ahead."

I held up my hands and pulled a face. "Counseling? Thanks, but I think I'll pass."

She didn't look convinced. "I want to make you aware of what it's going to take on your part. A lot of patience. A lot of time. A lot of love."

I went straight from the hospital and resigned from my job,

then sold my car. I might start looking for another job in a while, or even set up my own business. For now, I'll be serving as El's carer. Her illness is the real island. I won't leave her stranded again.

Cressida is asleep in my arms, the teddy clutched to her chest. I lean forward and kiss the top of her head before laying her down in her cot on the other side of the room. Max has claimed the wall above the cot as Cressida's art gallery, for which he has painstakingly created numerous crayon artworks on A4 sheets of paper. His latest creation has El, Cressie, Max, and me as stick figures holding hands underneath a rainbow. I have black spiky hair, Eloïse is drawn with long yellow hair and a big red smile. Max is holding her hand, and she seems to float slightly in the air. Max is the only one of us to have a red heart in the middle of his stick-figure chest.

Beneath he has written in purple capitals, "*family*."

Three Years Later, October 17, 2018

The Cressida Shelley Refuge Center for Victims of Gender Violence, Kampala, Uganda

I'll tell you what I never expected to see: Mamie allowing children to cornrow her hair. But there she is, sitting on a chair outside while Phiona and Blessed work their magic on her. They laugh and chatter, their voices swirling in the clear air as they tell my grandmother how much better she's going to look once they're done with her, and that her hair is like vanilla ice cream and would she like red beads or the blue weaved through it? I glance over and smile to show I'm proud of her for pushing herself to be more sociable and friendly, though mostly I'm interested in how she's going to look with those cornrows.

"Can you make me look like Bo Derek?" I hear her ask the girls.

They're nine and sixteen years old. I doubt they'll have the slightest idea who Bo Derek is, and they're much too busy with the task to hear her anyway.

It's ninety-five degrees today so I go back inside the center to help in the kitchen. It's almost lunchtime. We feed a hundred people here every day, sometimes more. It's amazing how much food draws people together. I had the construction team ensure that the extractor fan in the kitchen was big enough to pump the smells of food out as far as possible, and I think it's actually worked—you can smell it for miles around. And of course, word gets around fast. We've had visits from towns thirty miles away, and when people travel that distance, they stay for longer than one meal. And so we have educational classes straight after every meal on equality, the importance of education, running a business, self-defense, and contraception. Some of the girls traveling from other villages have revealed that they are about to enter an arranged marriage and I've been able to get them help. Little by little, we are making a difference.

"How do I look?" Mamie shouts at me.

"Just like Bo Derek!"

She pats her head and asks for a mirror. Blessed and Phiona race off to find her one, then return full of giggles. Mamie's face lights up when she sees the result. I approach and give it a closer inspection. They've only done a couple of rows at the side of Mamie's head but it's expertly done, their small fingers weaving the fine strands of her hair into delicate braids.

"I think I like it," she tells them, surprised. "Aren't you going to do the rest?"

Later, when her flounce of Aspen Oak–tinted hair has become flaxen chains across her scalp, she joins me in the dining hall and assists with serving food. She's been doing it now for two weeks, and we have two days left before returning to London. She's in her element here; I never expected that, either. She takes an interest in the women, despite how far removed their circumstances are from her own, and seems to thrive in an environment where she is needed. I think it also makes her proud to think that she paid for all of this. Every stone, tile, appliance, and ounce of grit came from her bank account.

There are risks, of course, in running the center. Some people say we're brainwashing the girls, challenging ancient traditions, and conjuring evil spirits. We've had to install security guards here, but even that poses a danger. The guards may have experience that makes them employable but I have no real way of knowing whether they'll give in to a bribe, or whether they share the views of our opponents. And working with girls who have experienced unimaginable abuse and violence does take a lot of resilience on my part, a lot of writing in my journal to help me keep track, keep centered. I am aware that I have certain triggers that may cause Sariah, Joe, Hazel, and George to take over, or even appear as hallucinations again. The hallucinations are a sign that I'm doing too much and need to rest. I haven't seen any of them for a long time, though Lochlan always tells me when I've switched and he's encountered one of them. So far, they all like him. Even so, Dr. Goff told me it would be a good idea to find an object that makes me feel safe. A totem that I carry at all times, perhaps a pebble, that reassures me and helps me stay in control.

Right now, I'm feeling tired after a late night of working with one of our newest guests. Patricia is eleven and came here severely injured. I've had her taken to hospital in the city, but the sight of her injuries and her distress lingers. I keep feeling the shiver that sometimes precedes a switch, a nagging from one of my alters to take over. I excuse myself from the kitchen and head outside to the garden, where the girls grow all the food that's used in the meals prepared here. There's a large Tugu tree that gives shade, and I sit there for a while to calm my nerves.

After a moment or so, I hear movement from the shrubs opposite, a swishing and crunching sound. I look up, expecting to see Blessed, or perhaps my grandmother, anxious to find out where I've gone. But it's a man. He's obscured by branches and sunlight, but I know it's George. He is lurking in the bushes, slightly stooped over, watching me.

My eyes lowered, I reach for my phone and hit "Skype." A moment later, Lochlan answers.

"Hi, darling. Is everything OK?"

I'm shaking from head to toe but concentrate on my breathing. "Yes. I'm OK. Just...wanted to hear your voice."

"Do you want to say hi to Mummy, Cressida? Look."

Cressida appears on screen, her dark hair in bunches at the side of her head. "Hi, Mummy. I did you a painting at nursery."

"Did you?"

She holds it up, a little too close to the screen. I still can't bring myself to look back at the spot where George appeared.

Lochlan's hand adjusts the position of the picture.

"Is that me and you at the park?" I ask Cressie.

"Yeah. And that's my pony."

"Your pony?"

"Yeah. The one you and Daddy are going to get me for my birthday."

I laugh. "Are we, now?"

"He's going to be called Rainbow Star. Rainbow Star Shelley."

A scramble of hands, and Lochlan is back on-screen. He looks worried.

"Seriously, El. Are you OK? Do you need me to help with anything?"

"George," I whisper.

"El, repeat after me: I am safe."

"I am safe."

"I find my center."

"I find my center."

"I am strong."

I inhale deeply and breathe out slowly. Lochlan's worried face moves closer to the screen.

"I know my name," he urges.

I pause. "I know my name," I repeat.

"I am Eloïse."

I bite my lip. I'm so scared in case the wrong name slips out.

"I am Eloïse."

"El, look at me?"

I open my eyes.

"I'm here, OK? I'm right here. Look around. Do you see George?"

I can't look. What if he's still there? What if he never leaves?

I keep my eyes closed and Lochlan tells me about Max's sports day this morning and promises to send me the video he took. I focus on Lochlan's voice, on the details of our life together, our home. I let my fingers find the totem in my pocket, a miniature Rosie train from *Thomas the Tank Engine*, and remember my mantra.

Light creeps in through the cracks caused by tumbling

through the hard spaces of life. But it's love that lets the light back out of us, moving inward and outward at the same time, dissolving the thresholds between past and present, between each other.

Invisible jaws are letting me slide from their grasp, the boundaries of reality and imagination hardening into their separate states. It is a feeling of coming home, reentering myself.

At last, I force myself to open my eyes and glance at the spot by the bushes. George is gone.

"I love you," I tell Lochlan. "I'll speak to you later."

He grins, visibly relieved that I sound more like myself.

"I love you too."

Acknowledgments

To Dr. Ian Jones, Dr. Helen Liebling, Carolyn Spring, and particularly Dr. Tracy Thorne for assisting with queries and research into dissociative identity disorder and puerperal psychosis.

To Stuart Gibbon for assisting with police matters.

To my agents, Alice Lutyens at Curtis Brown Literary Agency (UK) and Kristyn Keene at ICM Partners (US)—you guys are absolute powerhouses and I am so grateful to have you in my corner.

To Kim Young at HarperCollins (UK) and Wes Miller at Grand Central Publishing (USA) for wonderfully astute and dedicated editorial input.

To Claire Malcolm and all at New Writing North for their support over the last nine years.

To the Society of Authors' K. Blundell Trust Awards for facilitating a research trip to Crete in 2015.

To Nuala Ellwood, Kathryn Maris, Leanne Pearce, and C.L. Taylor for friendship and words of encouragement.

To Jared Jess-Cooke, for everything.

About the Author

C.J. Cooke is an acclaimed, award-winning poet, novelist, and academic with numerous other publications under the name of Carolyn Jess-Cooke. Born in Belfast, she has a PhD in Literature from Queen's University, Belfast, and is currently Lecturer in Creative Writing at the University of Glasgow, where she researches creative writing interventions for mental health. *I Know My Name* is C.J. Cooke's first psychological drama and was inspired by her creative work in mental health. It is being published in several other languages and a TV adaptation is in development. C.J. Cooke lives by the sea with her family.

Keep in touch with C.J.

carolynjesscooke.com
Instagram @carolyn_jess_cooke
Twitter @CJ_Cooke_Author
Facebook.com/cjcookeauthor